FROM THE SCOTTISH MOORS TO THE SHORES OF A NEW WORLD THEY FOUGHT FOR FREEDOM AND LOVE. . . .

SELENA MacPHERSON—A beautiful rebel, exiled from her native land, she swore to avenge her father's death at the hands of the British crown.

ROYCE CAMPBELL—A bold privateer, scion of a fabled Highland clan, he would stop at nothing to bring the hated monarchy to its knees.

From a New York prison to a sensual nightmare of sorcery and possession in Haiti . . . to the streets of Paris ablaze with the flames of revolution, they were destined to cheat death and share a dangerous passion. The unforgettable story that began with *Flames of Desire* continues for Selena and Royce, challenging them to overcome every obstacle, to seize justice, to embrace their future in . . .

FIRES OF DELIGHT

Books by Vanessa Royall:

**FLAMES OF DESIRE
COME FAITH, COME FIRE
FIREBRAND'S WOMAN
WILD WIND WESTWARD
SEIZE THE DAWN
THE PASSIONATE AND THE PROUD
FIRES OF DELIGHT**

QUANTITY SALES

Most Dell Books are available at special quantity discounts when purchased in bulk by corporations, organizations, and special-interest groups. Custom imprinting or excerpting can also be done to fit special needs. For details write: Dell Publishing Co., Inc., 1 Dag Hammarskjold Plaza, New York, NY 10017, Attn.: Special Sales Dept., or phone: (212) 605-3319.

INDIVIDUAL SALES

Are there any Dell Books you want but cannot find in your local stores? If so, you can order them directly from us. You can get any Dell book in print. Simply include the book's title, author, and ISBN number, if you have it, along with a check or money order (no cash can be accepted) for the full retail price plus 75¢ per copy to cover shipping and handling. Mail to: Dell Readers Service, Dept. FM, P.O. Box 1000, Pine Brook, NJ 07058.

FIRES OF DELIGHT

Vanessa Royall

A DELL BOOK

Published by
Dell Publishing Co., Inc.
1 Dag Hammarskjold Plaza
New York, New York 10017

Copyright © 1986 by M. T. Hinkemeyer

All rights reserved. No part of this book may be reproduced or transmitted in any form or by any means, electronic or mechanical, including photocopying, recording, or by any information storage and retrieval system, without the written permission of the Publisher, except where permitted by law.

Dell ® TM 681510, Dell Publishing Co., Inc.

ISBN: 0-440-12538-3

Printed in the United States of America
June 1986
10 9 8 7 6 5 4 3 2 1

WFH

Note

Certain of the historical events depicted or referred to in this story have been compressed in time for fictional purposes, in particular the years between the American and French revolutions. Those monumental uprisings of the human spirit, born of a common desire for liberty yet dissimilar in their specifics, provide the background for the ongoing story of Selena MacPherson, heroine of *Flames of Desire*. I want to thank the many readers who have written to me, requesting a sequel to that book. And I hope the long wait for *Fires of Delight* will prove to have been worthwhile.

V.R.

1 Escape Into Danger

Selena MacPherson's cell in the Battery fortress was eight feet wide, six feet deep, and just about six feet from damp stone floor to dripping stone ceiling. If she stood on tiptoe, the top of her head came within a few inches of the mortar-chinked rocks. Moisture seeped slowly through the walls too—the cell was below water level in New York harbor—coating the stones with a dewlike film. With a fingertip, she traced the American revolutionary motto, *Don't tread on me!* The brave words stood out clearly for a moment, but then the constantly seeping dampness oozed forth to blot them out.

Selena, cold, wet, and alone, was waiting to be interrogated by British Lieutenant Clay Oakley on suspicion that she had aided and abetted the cause of the revolution and the armies of George Washington in their war to throw off the colonial yoke.

Oakley's suspicion was well-founded.

"You are never defeated unless you believe it," said Selena aloud, steeling herself against the coming ordeal with the favorite expression of her beloved Royce Campbell. Oakley was sure to question her about Royce, who had won dashing reputation and a small fortune running guns and ammunition through the British naval blockade to Washington and his men. She and Royce were both exiles from their native Scotland, she a nobleman's daughter, he a scion of the fabled Highlands clan. In the eyes of the government of His Majesty, George III, they were less than outlaws. Selena had seen likenesses of herself on handbills affixed to the walls of New York. DEAD OR ALIVE, these notices proclaimed. ONE THOUSAND POUND STERLING REWARD!

Quite an honor, indeed, for a young woman who had fled Scotland years before, penniless and condemned, her father dead at the hands of a crown assassin, her ancestral home, Coldstream Castle, seized by the English monarch.

"My enemies make me strong," she murmured in self-encouragement. Because of the fate that had befallen her father and family, she had come to detest all hereditary monarchs with a pure, savage fire, a peerless, driving emotion which had drawn her instinctively toward the Colonial cause.

And which had landed her, now, in a British dungeon.

An iron door clanged open at the far end of the taper-lit corridor outside her cell, hurried footsteps sounded on the stones, and Lance Corporal Phineas Bonwit appeared outside Selena's iron-barred door. A grinning, towheaded Yorkshire lout, he brought her thrice-daily rations of black bread and barley porridge, and escorted her for an hour each afternoon to the walled-in cubicle known as the exercise yard, where he alternately leered and ogled as she trudged back and forth in her gray, sacklike prison garment.

"The lieutenant's a'ready t' go t' work on ye now, missy," Bonwit said, in the thick accents of his homeland. "Pray put on this blindfold, eh? I'll have t' be takin' ye to 'im."

He unlocked her cell door and handed her a stinking strip of coarse woolen cloth, which she reluctantly placed over her eyes and tied behind her head, cringing inwardly as she did so. She had been permitted only one visitor thus far, a charitable churchwoman given to calling upon the ill and imprisoned, and who had left Selena a small chunk of lye soap, a towel, and—wonder of wonders—a brush that the prisoner had used to groom her long, shining blond hair. Those locks were made for tiaras, not rags, but Selena had already known the best and the worst of life. She'd learned how to endure degradation without relinquishing a belief in a better life, a better time for which—she was sure—all humans yearned. Even Corporal Bonwit, who now grasped her elbow, propelling her forcefully into the darkness. *If there is a way to rescue me*, she thought, *Royce will find it. Had he not, in the past, fashioned a hundred ploys and ruses with which to outfox the clever British? Had he not, more than once, cheated death itself?*

Yet this hope brought small warmth and less succor. Even if Royce guessed that Oakley had brought her to the Battery fortress, he would have to cross water in order to reach her, scale stone walls, overpower dozens of English guards and—still more difficult—find her cell. She didn't even know exactly where in the vast stronghold she was being kept: the blindfold, always worn outside her cell, prevented any chance of her getting her bearings.

"Word t' the wise, missy," offered the corporal as he pushed her along, "best t' tell Lieutenant Oakley what he wants t' know right off. Save y'self the sufferin' an' the pain. Nobody can beat it anyway. They all talk in the end. I seen it happen time an' again with my very own eyes."

I shall tell him nothing, vowed Selena, with an attempt at bravery that was not totally reassuring. Because of her association with Royce and, through him, with revolutionary espionage in New York, she knew a great deal of information that Oakley would find valuable. The problem was that she did not know what *he* knew, or what had been happening in the outside world since her arrest.

It was incredible how suddenly the borders of her world had changed. Having received word through a friend, New York businessman Gilbertus Penrod, that Oakley's agents were on their trail, she and Royce had slipped out of the city and fled on horseback to Jamaica Bay on the south coast of Long Island. There Royce's great black ship, the *Selena,* rode at anchor, with its majestic, towering masts, its three tier of cannon that had as much firepower as any ship in the British navy, and, atop the mainmast, that cavalier swath of Campbell plaid, Royce's flag. But just as Selena and her betrothed had reached the water's edge, urging their mounts into the cold surf, they had been attacked, set upon and separated, by Oakley's dragoons. Selena had last glimpsed Royce clinging to the boarding ladder of his ship, one arm stretched out to her, in promise more than in farewell, his face a mask of horror and disbelief.

Until we meet again, she vowed, fighting back tears of loss behind the blindfold. She could not now permit herself to remember his long, hard body, nor how it had felt to hold him, to know his limitless stallion's power. And she would weaken, too, if she thought now of his touch upon her, or of her fingers on him, on his body or tangled at midnight in his black, wild hair. The magic of the emotions he evoked would forever be mysterious: how his dark, unyielding eyes so quickly softened when she gave herself to him, how tender were the kisses of his strong, almost arrogant mouth.

Selena could not let herself think of those wonders, so instead, despite the blindfold, she concentrated, counting her steps, remembering the sensations of this passage through darkness. Sudden perceptions of empty air beside her meant that she was being taken past other cells along the corridor. She counted eight of these before she and Bonwit reached the iron door. She knew that there were other prisoners in the fortress with her, but conversation was forbidden under pain of the lash. Then the corporal turned her toward the left. Twenty-four steps. Up a staircase, thirteen steps. Straight ahead for a hundred and ten paces, then up another flight of stairs. She smelled sea air and sensed natural light rather than the torches of the corridor. Bonwit hurried her along now, fifty paces, maybe a few more. He stopped her, swung open a door, and pushed her, not urgently, into a room.

"Here she be, Lieutenant," Bonwit said obsequiously, "just as ye ordered. Ye wish me t' remain?"

"No." The voice was deep and resonant, but cold as ice. "No, just remove her blindfold and withdraw."

Bonwit did as he was commanded. Selena blinked in the sudden light and stifled a gasp. She had heard much about Lieutenant Clay Oakley, chief of British military intelligence in America, had heard of his cunning and cruelty and fanatical devotion to his monarch. But the sight of the man was even more disconcerting, and she understood why he usually remained out of sight, acting through his network of agents. His head was abnormally large, an effect enhanced by total baldness, although he could not have been more than thirty years old. She wondered momentarily if he had been in a fire, because he had neither eyebrows nor lashes. Large, colorless, frightening eyes studied her as she stared at him, and his unusually small mouth twisted strangely beneath a bushy red mustache that appeared to be pasted onto his upper lip. She realized that he was smiling.

"You look startled, Selena," he said, addressing her in a parody of courteous familiarity, his voice at once limpid and quietly terrifying. "Don't be. I know you are partial to a man with a visage more appealing to the female eye, but I think you may find me worthy in other respects."

Oakley was seated at a small writing table on which Selena spied a stack of blank, cream-colored parchment, several quill pens laid in a neat row, and a small glass fountain of India-blue ink. Slowly, deliberately, as if he were enjoying himself, the lieutenant stood up so that she could take a closer look at him. He was not overly tall, perhaps six feet without the thick-heeled boots he wore, but his body was massive. His shoulders bulged beneath the fine fabric of his red-coated officer's uniform with its fringed epaulets and gold braid. His waist tapered to a wide, black shining leather belt. And the muscles of his powerful thighs bulged alarmingly in tight white breeches.

"You do not know the man who can best me," he said, again with that tiny, twisted smile.

The two of them stood there facing each other, the slim, fair young woman, whose wide, slightly slanted violet eyes could not hide a hint of defiance even under these circumstances, and the seemingly self-assured officer whose strength was as apparent as the brutal intelligence flickering in his immense eyes. Those eyes, and the mind behind them, would not miss much, if anything. Selena could not imagine a more intimidating interrogator.

She was puzzled, however. This room was no torture chamber. The only furnishings were Oakley's table and chair. A large, rectangular skylight admitted flooding warmth and shafts of sunlight that sparkled on the highly polished oaken floor. The walls were hung with—she counted quickly—about twenty fine, framed paintings and portraits, among which she recognized the small-eyed, heavily jowled visage of George III. The paintings, mainly English landscapes and hunting scenes, were reverently, beautifully done, soft-hued and evocative. Clearly the artist loved England as much as she herself appreciated the sere, stark moors of her homeland and the wild Highlands that rolled on to the north.

"I see that you have an eye for good art," Oakley said, not without respect. "I accept the compliment of your interest."

"You have chosen the work of good artists."

"Thank you once again," Oakley said. "I am the artist."

Astonished, Selena glanced once again at the massed paintings. This time she noted, too, the nature of the wall on which they hung, grainy and soft-looking. *Cork!* she realized. *How unusual!*

Then Oakley sagged into his chair and withdrew from his pocket a handkerchief of white silk, inhaling from it. Selena caught the strong scent of an astringent eau-de-cologne and she understood. This huge beast into whose clutches she had fallen had some sort of respiratory ailment. Cork was believed to filter the air; cologne was considered a specific in cases of asthma.

Indeed, the mere effort of standing for a moment seemed to have affected the officer. "Let us proceed," he said, wheezing slightly and dipping a quill point into the fountain of ink. Preparing to write, he fixed her with a merciless, baleful stare. "Today we shall have but a preliminary interrogation. I abjure you to answer my questions with the utmost truth. Your answers will be examined diligently for their veracity. If I find that you have lied or engaged in conscious obfuscation, we shall have a second appointment tomorrow morning in far less pleasant surroundings, the walls of which will be equipped not to enhance my comfort but to mute your screams."

Selena started. He meant every word of it. This strange man, who respected beauty but who was himself so ugly in feature, held his life in a balance of frigid intellect and private passion, characteristics of the most remorseless fanatic. Oakley combined the disparate aspects of beauty and beast.

"Your name?" he asked quietly.

Selena gave it and he wrote it down.

There followed a series of colorless questions as the lieutenant sought the basic facts of Selena's life. Even as she answered, she was trying to prepare herself for the dangerous questions that were sure to come. Once, while taking her to the exercise yard, Corporal Bonwit had said something about "heading home soon." Had he meant returning to England? And if so, did that mean the British were winning the war? Or losing it?

"Now," he said, lifting his eyes from the parchment and looking at her, "is it not true that your father, Lord Seamus MacPherson, was executed for treason against His Majesty?"

"No. He was assassinated. By an agent of military intelligence. Like you."

The memory of her father's death was burned into every fiber of Selena's being; she would carry it with her beyond the grave. The two of them, father and daughter, had fled Coldstream Castle one step ahead of Darius McGrover, special agent to the King. They had found refuge in a stone hut in far-off Kinlochbervie, a fishing village on the coast of northern Scotland by the tumbling seas of the North Minch. But McGrover pursued them there. And Selena had been forced to watch, bound and gagged, while her father's throat was cut.

"Ah!" replied Oakley, with his fey smile. "You are referring to my predecessor here in America. And wasn't his body recently found near the luxurious Battery Park home you shared until recently with your former husband, Lord Sean Bloodwell?"

Selena fought for control of her emotions. Oakley's question upset her in several ways. First, it was she who had killed McGrover, avenging her father's death by severing the assassin's windpipe in the cellar of her own home and watching the frothy black blood of his evil life bubble away. Although she called it vengeance, the law had other eyes. Second, mere mention of Sean's name was painful to her. She had married him years earlier, after hearing news that Royce Campbell was dead. And she had grown to love Sean too. But Royce's reappearance, alive and well in America, had changed everything. Sean had sensed it, saw it, and permitted her to go. He had always known of her depthless, awesome bond to the Highlands warrior, had understood with the grace of his clear mind and honest heart that fettered love led to nothing but unhappiness. Finally, Sean had been a Loyalist, devoted to king and crown, in reward for which he had been elevated to the peerage. Their lives had taken startlingly different paths, which Selena simultaneously accepted and regretted, because theirs had been a genuine affection.

"I am waiting for your answer, Selena," Oakley said, pressing the silk handkerchief to his shapeless fold of a nose.

"I don't know anything of McGrover's fate," she replied, "except that if he is truly dead I am not sorry."

Oakley laughed, a liquid, gurgling sound. "We shall, in time, learn what you know. Truth has a way of surfacing. Tell me, how does it feel to know your former husband possesses the legitimacy and honor you yourself so deeply covet?"

The man had an uncanny knack for sensing weakness! More than anything except Royce, Selena desired to reclaim Coldstream Castle, her rightful home. On countless nights she had dreamed of the as yet unimaginable day on which she would ride into the hills of her beloved Scotland, see great bonfires of greeting blazing on those hills, see Coldstream looming on the cliffs above the North Sea. And there were times beyond number when she had thrilled to think of herself riding through the castle's mighty gate, beneath the keystone in the arch that read *Anno Domini 1152*, with her people cheering all around. Someday, somehow, she and Royce would return to Scotland in triumph, but that time seemed far away, a glimmering wisp of hope to a prisoner in a fortress in America.

You are never defeated unless you believe it, she thought once again. "I am glad for Lord Bloodwell," she said. "He has won his heart's desire, and he deserves it."

"And what is *your* heart's desire, my fine young lady? A man? A castle? Is that all? You disappoint me. In time, the man will die. So will you. In time, the strongest bastion will crumble into dust. Even those paintings that I have created will some day fade and wither. No, a person like you must be driven by something more, by something timeless. Or am I overestimating you?"

"What I want you could not give."

"Tell me, and we shall see."

"Freedom," Selena said.

"For yourself? That is easy. Just answer certain questions of a military nature that I am about to put to you now, and in no time you will be walking the streets of the city, free as air, and dressed in garments more suited to your beauty than those rags you have on—"

"I do not mean freedom for myself," she interrupted, "but for this country, and for the people in every nation who struggle against tyrants!"

Selena spoke heatedly. She thought that Oakley would be angry. Instead, he simply shrugged and gave her a look that he probably meant to be understanding and indulgent. "You *are* very young. Your tyranny is my freedom and vice versa. I seek a world in which I am at liberty to honor my king and strengthen his empire. You and your bloody ilk would deny me such liberty. Thus I must crush your petty idea of freedom in the cause of a greater and more noble good."

"Who are you to say?"

He smiled. "Because I sit here backed by the greatest empire the world has ever known, and you stand before me in a filthy dress."

"Your men took away my clothes—"

"I'll rip that dress off your back too, if you're not careful. Enough of this." He took up the quill again and dipped it expertly into the inkwell. "Where is General Washington going to attack?" he asked suddenly. "New York or Yorktown?"

Too late, Selena understood that Oakley had been distracting her until now with questions and conversation of a vaguer nature. The dangerous part of this confrontation had come abruptly, and she was off-guard.

"I don't know what you mean," she replied, stalling for time as he gelid eyes bored into her.

"Lie to me like this tomorrow," he snapped, "and before you have time to take a breath I will scar you for life from temple to jaw!"

Disfigurement. Selena felt a wave of nausea pass through her, and realized how long she had been standing there. Her legs were beginning to ache; a hot flush of fear brought beads of nervous perspiration to naked skin beneath the clammy dress. Lieutenant Oakley knew exactly where and how to strike. Selena had imagined the prospect of pain, but not mutilation. . . .

"Naturally," said the interrogator soothingly, "a woman as lovely as you will want to protect her appearance. One never knows how a man like Campbell would feel about bedding a hideous wreck of flesh. . . ."

He let his voice trail off ominously. Selena suppressed a shudder.

"Let me make this a bit easier for you," Oakley said. "I know that the French Count Rochambeau and his army are in Newport. I know that Washington and his men are north of here, in White Plains, New York. They will shortly join forces, ten thousand men in all. With that number, they could dislodge us from New York. But that would be but a partial victory. Our main battle force, under General Cornwallis, is in Yorktown, Virginia, along the Chesapeake—"

Selena nodded. She knew all this. Royce had told her.

"—and defeating Cornwallis," Oakley continued, "would in effect bring an end to the war. But to attack Yorktown, Washington must cover a great distance. Besides which Cornwallis has a fleet in the Chesapeake Bay to support him. It would be stupid, even suicidal, for Washington to attack Yorktown without naval support of his own, and we have learned the hard way that the Virginian is neither stupid nor self destructive."

"At least you have learned something," replied Selena, managing a show of bravery.

"Why did your renegade lover journey to Haiti earlier this year?" Oakley pressed, leaning forward and glowering.

He's guessed! Selena realized frantically. Royce had gone to Haiti as a messenger from George Washington to the French Comte de Grasse, who had anchored his fleet there awaiting instructions. France, even though under the burden of a monarchy that was in many ways even more oppressive than that of Great Britain, was striking at the English by supporting the colonial upstarts. And at this very moment, Selena knew, de Grasse was sailing northward to aid Washington in what was hoped would be the final battle in the war for American independence.

At Yorktown!

"Royce Campbell is a sailor," said Selena. "That's all."

"Hah! He is a gunrunner, a smuggler, a complete opportunist—"

"He is not!" Selena cried.

Yet once—it was true—he had been. Selena admitted it to herself. The Royce Campbell she had first known would not have troubled himself for one second over the outcome of a political struggle, let alone an enterprise without the two elements he cherished most: high adventure and monetary gain, not necessarily in that order.

She believed that her dedication, her conviction, her own unyielding spirit had changed and gentled him.

She remembered the Christmas ball in Edinburgh at which they had first met, Selena just seventeen. He had stepped out of the shadows at the edges of the vast ballroom and asked to be her partner in the Highland fling, a tall, lean, broad-shouldered animal of a man whose black-velvet dress coat and diamond-pinned cravat seemed out of place beneath a rugged visage and peremptory eyes. The fling was wild, as always, and the ever-strange, haunting whine of the bagpipes underscored the pace of the dance. About them, dancers shouted and leaped, whirled and spun. Selena had never felt as free, nor danced as well. All around the ballroom, dancers flashed and twirled, and when it came time for her and Royce to take their places in the circle, they had already become strangely mesmerized by motion and music, caught up in a dark attraction that was more than dance, more even than the physical magnet of their opposite natures.

"Look at them," someone shouted, as she and Royce Campbell danced toward then away from each other in the leaping steps of the fling. Selena felt the blood pumping from her heart, her lungs aching for air, but it was glorious. Her golden hair was flying, her body too, and her very soul screamed for joy.

Royce had danced wonderfully too, with never a wasted motion, all economy and grace and style. And all about him, like an aura, was the glitter of the Campbell legend, of men who were more than mere men, of the timeless, moody penumbra of the Highlands. The Campbells were ready in the day, ready in the night, always ready for love or gold or glory. And if the wildest of them all had chosen her for this dance, what else might he have in mind?

The music pounded on and finally dancers began to drop out from exhaustion, but she and Royce kept on, the audience shouting encouragement, clapping time. Her lungs were shrieking now, and every muscle in her legs begged for mercy. But if he could go on, so could she. *That is it,* she had thought. *We are both thoroughbreds. We are the best.*

Afterwards, he had led her out onto a balcony overlooking the North Sea. There, with the *aurora borealis* blazing in the enchanted winter sky, they clung to each other in the cold wind, and he kissed her for the first time. It had been the beginning of everything, of a love—she was sure—that not even death would be powerful enough to end. . . .

And Selena believed that she had changed him, not by curbing or taming the seignorial impulses of his matchless nature, but by using her love to evoke the compassion that had lain dormant in his heart until they met.

Was she wrong?

Lieutenant Oakley certainly thought so. "How much do you really know about this lover of yours?" he asked sarcastically, smoothing the feathers of a quill pen. "Did he ever tell you that an agent of mine approached him to spy for us?"

"No, that's not true!"

"Yes, it is. It is true, my dear. And do you know how he responded? He said that we could not afford to pay him as much as the Colonials. That was, unfortunately, true. Lord North and His Majesty are men of economy."

Selena was about to reply that Royce accepted only expense money for his efforts—even General Washington was paid expense money by the Continental Congress—but then she saw the trap. Admitting such a thing would prove to Oakley that Royce *was* in the employ of the American revolutionaries. She bit her lip and said nothing.

"Why did Campbell go to Haiti?" her interrogator persisted. "Will Washington attack New York or along the Chesapeake?"

"I don't know."

Oakley let the silence linger. He pulled a chubby gold watch from his coat pocket and looked at it. "Time runs short," he said. "You know, Selena, I had intended to verify your answers by questioning other prisoners before I conversed with you again. I am not a man who enjoys inflicting pain, and until one has a feeling for the habits and intelligence of a witness, torture is inadvisable. The victim will say *anything* to mislead the interrogator and to avoid agony. That is not good, and the subsequent information is often unreliable. But I think that you are lying through your pretty teeth."

He fixed her with his awful stare. "Would you lie with no teeth at all?"

"I am not lying," replied Selena, her mouth dry. The muscles in her legs were screaming. She tried hard not to sway.

"Corporal Bonwit!" Oakley called loudly.

The door swung open and Bonwit appeared. "At y' suvvice, sir!"

"Take the prisoner to the Room of Doom. She has been particularly uncooperative, and events compel me to accelerate the procedure."

"No," gasped Selena, in spite of an effort to maintain her composure.

"Ah!" Oakley smiled. "You wish to answer my questions, do you?"

"I know nothing," Selena said, faltering.

"Selena, Selena. Is there not a bond between us? We both respond to beauty. Why can we not share a love of truth as well? You cannot elude me, you cannot evade me. I shall pursue you, as it were, down all the corridors of time. Once you feel the bite of the whip, our union shall be consummated. I had wished it to be a bond of understanding, not of pain. But—"

Oakley let his voice trail off. "So be it," he said, lifting a hand languidly and letting it fall. "Corporal, ready the prisoner for what she has chosen. I shall join you in a moment."

"Why couldn't y' 'ave told 'im what 'e wanted t' know?" whined the corporal, as he led Selena from the room. "I'll 'ave t' be there t' take down your answers, an' the wails an' the cries turn m' bowels all t' mush."

Afraid herself and preparing for the worst, Selena still retained the wit to notice that Bonwit was genuinely upset. He had even forgotten to force the blindfold upon her. They walked in the open air. She saw the low buildings of New York spread out along the harbor, and the great houses along the Battery, one of which had been her own such a short time ago. (Sean Bloodwell had risen quickly in America, had become a prosperous merchant before his elevation to the British nobility.) The sun was large in the sky, gloriously warm, but falling across the plains of New Jersey to the west. It would soon be evening.

"Y' know, I . . . I take a likin' to ye, Selena," Bonwit babbled. "If there be some way I could get ye out of this . . ."

Unlikely. Selena looked over the battlements of the fortress. She was about forty feet above the waters of New York Harbor, and it was at least fifty yards from the fortress to the piers along the shore. Quite a dive. Quite a swim. Broad daylight.

But she could attempt it.

"If you were to turn away for a moment—" she suggested.

The corporal shook his head. "No kin do, missy, no kin do. Or it'll be me a'screamin' in the Room of Doom. Why couldn't ye 'ave just told 'im what he wanted t' know?"

Loyalty, thought Selena. *Loyalty to a cause, and to the people who served that cause.* But loyalty is a double-edged sword, and she understood that Bonwit had his own neck to think about. Just before he guided her through a stone gateway, back into the gloomy interior of the fortress, she saw a small rowboat approaching the prison. It was filled with red-coated soldiers. They seemed excited, enjoying themselves, and she thought for a fleeting instant how wonderful it would be to be free again.

They passed down a long flight of flagstone steps and walked along a stony corridor, lit gloomily by waning torches in rusty sconces attached to the dripping walls. Selena's mind was racing. *I could tell Oakley that I don't know anything,* she thought, *and stick to it—if I can—until he tires of me. Or I can hold out as long as possible, and then confess that Washington plans to attack New*

York. . . . *Oh, God, Royce, where are you? Think of something, Selena. Think of something to distract your body when the pain begins. Yes, think of Royce, of holding him again.* . . .

Oakley's accusation that Royce was nothing but an opportunist niggled at the back of her mind. The lieutenant was deucedly clever. He knew how to attack the very foundation of personal assurance, which is faith. Strength may come from faith in a god, an idea, a nation, or a person. But when one is alone and endangered, thoughts for the safety of one's special being have a way of usurping noble causes one reveres in safer times.

Coldstream! The thought of her home came to her in a flash. *Yes, Coldstream Castle. Think of it, of its gardens and its magnificent courtyard, of its chapel and library and towers and mighty walls. The rightful heir to Coldstream shall not yield!* vowed Selena. *And even if I die my spirit will return there.*

But how much better to return alive!

Her spirit flagged, however, when, with a gulp, Corporal Bonwit reached up and twisted a sconce on the wall. Great stones slid soundlessly aside, revealing a door that opened into a chamber Selena could not have conjured in her darkest dreams. She exhaled in terror as he shoved her inside, and knew, as the stones slid back into place behind them, why this horrible cavern was called as it was.

The Room of Doom was half-cave, half-grotto. Chains and iron manacles were embedded in one wall. Clubs and whips, pincers and tongs of all sizes hung from pegs on another. Thick ropes dangled from the high, curved stone ceiling. A squat wooden chair and a long, odd wooden table, both equipped with strange pulleys, gears, and levers, caught Selena's eye. A coal fire burned in a grate at the far end of the chamber, the coals being stirred with a red-hot poker by a hooded figure who rose slowly and turned toward the two arrivals.

"Bonwit, ye dolt!" growled the hooded man, glaring at the corporal through eye slits in the ghastly shroud. "Ye forgot the bloody blindfold."

The corporal babbled apologies. "Lieutenant Oakley'll be jinin' us at any moment," he stammered.

The man seemed to nod—because of the hood it was difficult to tell—and stalked toward Selena. He thrust the fiery poker toward her face and she leaned away.

"What have ye done t' bring yuhself here?" he asked without rancor, without, indeed, any feeling except possibly a professional interest.

"Nothing. I—"

"Save yuh breath. Ye all say the same thing. I've heard it all before. Did Lieutenant Oakley say what he wants t' use on her?" he asked Bonwit.

"N-no . . ." managed the Yorkshireman.

The hooded man regarded Selena studiously through the slits in his hood, as if she were a piece of stone to be examined before sculpting.

"Pretty," he said. "Y' poor thing. Tell ye what. 'Tis out of me 'ands what Oakley chooses fer ye, but I'll hoist ye fer the lash, an' maybe he'll let us get away with it for a time. There's other things far worse. Ye're not made for pain, an' I'll try not t' hit ye too hard. But ye better confess whatever it is 'e wants t' know, or things'll be out of my control."

Before Selena could respond, or even consider the strange nature of what this hooded figure probably thought to be charity, he had dropped the poker, thrown a loop of rope around her wrists, tossed the other end of the rope over a wooden beam, and pulled her up so that her toes barely touched the floor. The muscles in her legs, strained from standing so long in front of Oakley's desk, began to ache even more. Very quickly, her stretched arms started to hurt as well.

"Please, just lower me a little bit."

"Best I kin do, lassie. An' don't say that when Oakley comes. 'E'll make me raise you in the air."

Gulping, Bonwit sought parchment and quill. The hooded torturer selected a whip as if he were examining and discarding apples. It took every ounce of Selena's strength to maintain even a shred of courage.

Then Lieutenant Oakley entered, walking heavily and breathing into his scented silk handkerchief. He looked disappointed when he saw her drawn up.

The hooded man swished the whip a time or two and bowed obsequiously. "All ready, sar," he said, "as ye kin see."

Oakley seemed to consider some of the other procedures he had mentioned in his office. "All right. Time is of the essence. Bonwit, write down everything I ask and everything she says."

"Yes, sir!" quavered the corporal.

Oakley stepped in front of Selena. Their eyes were at a level. "You have brought this on yourself," he said, as if pained. "Tell me, why did Royce Campbell journey all the way to Haiti?"

Royce. Coldstream. Royce. Coldstream.

"I don't know," Selena said.

She saw Oakley nod to the hooded man, who was standing behind her. She sensed a shiver in the air as the whip was drawn back, and braced herself for the blow. A governess had switched her once with a willow branch for purloining a specially baked holiday plum pie, complete with brandy, rum, and exotic bananas. She had eaten several pounds of the masterpiece all by herself and, in order to hide the evidence, had fed the rest to her favorite pets: a rat terrier named Spike, Boris the brood sow, and a tame skunk called Mitzi. After that, plum pudding reminded her of pain, but even so the switching hadn't hurt as much as the stomachache.

She knew this was going to be far, far worse.

"Wait," said Oakley, whose bald head seemed to glow in the light of the coals from the hearth. "Tear away her dress."

"No," Selena pleaded.

"Are you prepared to answer my questions then?"

"I don't know anything—"

She felt the rough hands of the hooded man at her collar.

Then the stone doorway slid open and a British soldier stepped into the room. He was excited, stumbling as he hastened toward Lieutenant Oakley who turned, somewhat irritably, toward the newcomer. "What is it?" Oakley demanded.

"Lieutenant, sir. Great news. We've just captured Erasmus Ward! The men are bringing him up from the water now."

Selena recalled the little rowboat she'd seen in the harbor. Erasmus Ward. No wonder the soldier seemed so pleased. Ward, a shy, scrawny little man, had forsaken his silversmith's trade to become the war's most illustrious spy since Nathan Hale. Religiously devout, uncommonly brave, and gifted with an encyclopedic memory, Ward had made use of his small stature and pale unobtrusiveness to cross battle lines disguised as a peddler, to enter British encampments posing as a beggar, to deliver urgent communiques between Washington and Lafayette. His gift was that, although people saw him come and go, they did not *notice* him. It was

Ward who had lit the lanterns in Boston's old North Church on the night of Paul Revere's ride. It was Ward who had actually signed on as a cook and camp helper in the baggage train of British General "Gentleman Johnny" Burgoyne, thus providing Benedict Arnold with information concerning Burgoyne's plans, ensuring a Colonial victory at Saratoga. Selena had caught a glimpse of Erasmus Ward just once, a legend out of the night, in the parlor of Gilbertus Penrod's New York mansion. Most people thought Penrod, a dealer in gems, furs, and fabrics, was loyal to the crown. They would have changed their minds quickly had they seen Erasmus Ward, Royce Campbell, Alexander Hamilton, and the Comte de Vergennes in the Penrod drawing room.

While Selena's heart plummeted at the news of Ward's capture, Lieutenant Clay Oakley could not conceal his delight. "Are you certain it is he?" Oakley demanded of the soldier. "So many times we've thought him ours, but always he gets away."

"No, sir. It's Ward all right, and we have him in chains up above."

Oakley thought things over for a moment, then looked at Selena. "I do not wish to be rude," he told her, "but a more deserving guest has arrived to take your place. We must postpone our conversation for the time being. Bonwit," he ordered the corporal, "cut Selena down and return her to her cell. You," he commanded the soldier, "bring Ward here immediately."

Selena felt the rope slacken. The muscles of her body began slowly to recover from the awful stretching. Her legs were numb. Needles and pins lanced through her arms as blood began to circulate again. Bonwit grabbed her shoulders and eased her toward the doorway.

"Do not forget, Selena," Oakley called after her, "I am not finished with you yet."

She did not turn to answer.

"Oh, Lord, oh, Lord," exclaimed the corporal, as he led her away from the Room of Doom, "'tis a lucky star ye been born beneath, I vow."

Selena was relieved for the moment, her immediate danger having receded, but she found no comfort in the situation. Because now another human being would suffer in her place, poor little Erasmus Ward, her confederate. And since Ward possessed so much information that Oakley needed, the ugly lieutenant would spare no effort, show no mercy.

"We got t' put on yuh blindfold," Phineas Bonwit remembered, digging it out of his pocket. Selena had no choice but to obey, but before the rag was in place she saw Erasmus Ward himself, being dragged past her by a squad of eager redcoats. Ward was barefoot, shirtless, with irons around his wrists and ankles. The soldiers hadn't bothered to blindfold him, so eager were they to get him to the interrogation chamber. Selena sent the little man a glance of recognition and sympathy as he was flung past her, and was startled to see not only that he seemed to know who she was, but also that his eyes were calm and clear. He seemed absolutely unafraid, as if he'd known all along that this dark day would finally come and that he was a match for it.

Around his neck, on a gold chain, was a small golden cross. Some pattern or design had been etched into the shining metal, but Selena could not see what it was.

Corporal Bonwit locked Selena into her damp, clammy cell, but lingered outside the iron-barred door. She sat down on her "bunk," two planks nailed together and suspended from the wall by a couple of rusty chains.

"Yes?" she asked, feeling his eyes on her.

"Ye know," he faltered, ducking his head absurdly, "if you was . . . if you was t' be a little bit nice t' me, might be I kin 'elp ye out. Not outta the prison, oh, no, but I kin get ye extra rations. . . ."

Selena had a very good idea what this clumsy dolt meant by being "a little bit nice." She didn't know whether to laugh at him or damn his soul. Before she did either, however, she realized that this gangly half-wit might somehow prove to be of use, if only she could devise a plan to flee the fortress.

"You're very kind, corporal," she told him, offering what she hoped was a convincing smile, "but I'm . . . I'm very, *very* tired and upset just now. Perhaps later—"

Even in the torchlit corridor, she could see him beaming from thick earlobe to thick earlobe in awestruck anticipation.

"I under*stand!*" he said. "An' I believe I kin sneak ye a cup o' tea right now. I'll go an' see."

After Bonwit had gone rattling off down the corridor, the point of his belted sword clanking on the stone walls, Selena lay down on the planks, thinking and trying to plan. *My entire life has led me to this moment,* she reflected, which was not exactly a sanguine thought. But she was somewhat cheered by the knowledge that she'd survived high peril and beaten long odds before: fleeing Scotland and Darius McGrover in the hold of a rat-infested freighter; surviving abduction by a cynical British procurer, Captain Jack, and escaping from the palace of the Indian maharajah Jack had sold her to; finding Royce Campbell again after believing him to be dead of the plague.

Fortune, don't turn on me now, Selena prayed. But then she thought, *No, it was not fortune entirely, it was myself as well, never giving up, remembering who I am and where I come from.* And Scotland, an ocean away, came to her when she summoned it, and she set it, like a beautiful jewel, between her violet eyes and the oozing wet stone. From the hard little village of Kinlochbervie, where her father lay buried in a hut of stone, to the dark, smoky lochs in the Highlands, to the honey-drenched moors, to fabled Edinburgh and its ancient aura, finally south to Coldstream, she saw it all, held it to herself for strength and hope, pure and fair and never to be tarnished.

Yes, she had always carried Scotland in her soul, when the days beat down her spirit, when the nights were dark.

And now another night was falling. Corporal Bonwit did not return with the tea he'd promised, nor even with the usual evening ration of bread and porridge. Eventually, in spite of a fearful, impotent agony over the fate of Erasmus Ward, a clutching emptiness in Selena's belly made her aware of the time. Bonwit was almost always punctual in his ministrations; something in the fortress was amiss. Even the prisoners in other cells along the corridor began to break the rule of silence, to wonder in quizzical hisses exactly what was happening. Selena was about to tell them that Ward had been captured, but held her tongue. The news was too demoralizing, especially for this already cheerless dungeon.

At last, the iron door at the far end of the corridor was flung open with a metallic clash. Selena heard Oakley's deep voice, with a breathless rasp, saying: "Throw the bloody traitor into the cell down at the end." He sounded angry. Selena hoped his choler meant that Erasmus Ward had borne up under interrogation.

Then she gasped in horror as two redcoats dragged the diminutive spy in front of her cell and stopped, one of them unlocking the iron-barred door to the empty cell across the corridor. They had been pulling him along by his heels, leaving a wide trailing streak of blood that glistened darkly on the torchlit stones of the prison floor. Erasmus Ward was quite unconscious, bleeding slowly from a slack mouth, bleeding from countless lacerations all over his body. Except for the little cross on the chain around his neck, the spy was naked.

The soldiers dragged him into the cell opposite Selena, and Clay Oakley appeared before her. He was breathing heavily. Broad, flushed face and shining pate gave his head the aspect of a monstrous tuber. He gestured toward the cell in which Ward had been deposited.

"Did you glimpse the handiwork, Selena?" he asked. "Unless you decide to talk, such will be your fate on the morrow."

She lifted her chin and glared at him, but said nothing. She was trying to think of a way to find out how much Oakley had learned from Erasmus Ward.

Inadvertently, he gave her a clue. "Pity the man had so little endurance," Oakley said. "With a fine, healthy young person like you, I expect things will be different."

Oakley wouldn't need to question me if Erasmus has already told him what he wants to know, she realized. The lieutenant, whose nature she was beginning to decipher, was, for all his menace, a creature of intelligence and strategy rather than random violence. For him, inflicting harm on his victims was only a tool, a means to a great end: the information he must have to serve his master well. But Oakley *was* utterly ruthless in that he would never shrink from the most terrible measures, to which the battered body of Erasmus Ward attested. Oakley was a perfectionist who would leave nothing undone, no task incomplete, no circle unclosed in the fine, cold whorls of his mind. In this, Selena realized, Oakley was more dangerous even than Darius McGrover, who had killed her father. McGrover's passionate nature, his hatred, his conceit: they had been weaknesses. Oakley seemed to have no such weaknesses: he was much more formidable. Selena understood that his very body, muscled by untold hours of struggle, was a triumph of will over the respiratory trouble that afflicted him.

"What are you going to do with Mr. Ward?" she asked the

lieutenant, as the two redcoats stepped out of the cell and locked the barred door.

Oakley shrugged. "If he lives, I shall question him again."

"If he lives—" said Selena in horror. "Won't you please get him a doctor? At least give him a blanket. Here," she added, turning and snatching her own threadbare covering from her bunk, "give him mine."

"As you wish." Oakley took the blanket and tossed it through the bars of Ward's cell, where it landed haphazardly upon the spy's brutalized body, which Selena glimpsed dimly. He was lying on the planks; at least they hadn't left him on the wet floor.

"I would prefer to chat further with you now, Selena," Oakley said in farewell, "but I have been called to headquarters for a conference. Sleep well."

With that, he and the two soldiers left. After they had departed, Selena called softly to Erasmus Ward, trying to rouse him. She did not succeed. Once or twice he seemed to stir, saying "no, no," but that was all. She said a silent prayer in his behalf; it was all she could do.

Presently, Phineas Bonwit appeared with the evening rations. He was accompanied, to Selena's surprise, by a priest. She had been raised as a Scots Presbyterian, but her own wild nature and her association with Royce Campbell, whose faith, if any, was ancient and pagan and wild, had not exactly enhanced religious impulses. *I'll have time for heaven later on,* she sometimes thought, putting the whole matter out of her mind. But now she recalled that Erasmus Ward was a passionately devout believer, and she was glad that someone had thought to provide for his soul in this hour of need.

But who? It certainly wouldn't have occurred to Oakley.

Corporal Bonwit, lugging a bucketful of water and a black kettle half-filled with lukewarm porridge, brought the cowled, cassocked servant of God to Ward's cell. Placing his burdens on the floor in front of Selena's door, Bonwit turned, fumbled with the keys at his belt, and unlocked the spy's cell.

"No . . ." Erasmus moaned.

The priest stood in the dark, grimy corridor, waiting for the corporal to wrench open the iron door. Selena, peering at him from behind her own bars, sensed something familiar in the set of his shoulders, the slightly stooped manner in which he carried himself. She shifted her position slightly, trying to get a look at his face in the shadow of the cowl, and he turned toward her.

It was no priest. It was Gilbertus Penrod, gem merchant and primary financial supporter of the Colonial cause. He was the man who had warned Royce and Selena that Oakley was after them. Selena's spirits leapt and soared. Was Penrod's appearance here part of a scheme to rescue Ward and her? The merchant's warning glance sobered Selena, however, and when Bonwit stepped aside, permitting Penrod entry into Ward's cell, her appearance was only that of a hungry prisoner awaiting her dollop of gruel.

"Sorry, Reverend, but I got t' lock ye in wi' 'im," Bonwit told Penrod.

"Good Lord, man! Do you think this poor wretch can escape?" Penrod shot back. "What have you done to him? He needs immediate medical attention."

Selena saw the horrified expression on the merchant's handsome, angular features.

"Sorry, Reverend, orders," replied Bonwit sheepishly, relocking the door. "Ye say wha'ever prayers ye want, an' I'll be back when I finish feedin' the prisoners."

Penrod bent over Erasmus Ward, taking his wrist and feeling for a pulse. Selena realized that even Phineas Bonwit might find such behavior unusual for a clergyman, and sought to distract him. "I thought you were going to bring me tea!" she said, feigning a pout and handing her bowl out through the bars of the cell.

He ladled a double helping of porridge into it and winked at her conspiratorially. "Sorry," he said. "Our whole detachment was prowlin' the streets of New York fer the past hours." He leaned close to her and whispered, "There's a fearsome spy loose an' we got t' catch 'im."

"Oh, my! How dangerous! You must be *so* brave. Who is it?"

"Ye musta heard o' 'im. Practically everybody has. Bloke named Campbell."

"No, I don't believe I have," Selena said.

"We're a'goin' lookin' fer him t'night as well. There's two thousand pounds sterling on his head."

Selena was annoyed—and amused at herself for being annoyed —that George III considered Royce to be twice as valuable as she.

"But I thought you were coming to see *me* tonight?" she teased, tilting her head and giving him the full effect of her violet eyes. She'd discovered their power early when, just turned thirteen, she decided she wanted to be kissed by Eric McCullough. Eric seemed nothing now, but then Royce was far in the future, his existence unimagined. And Eric McCullough was the most dashing man in Berwick and Roxburgh provinces combined, all of twenty years old and, moreover, betrothed to Jessica McEdgar. Selena had loathed Jessica McEdgar. The feeling was mutual because Jessica, an older woman of seventeen, scorned Selena as a "silly child" and a "failed flirt." But that was before Selena used her eyes and the tilt of her head and—if the truth be known—a tactical lifting of her blooming breasts to lure Eric McCullough into a public kiss at the Berwick harvest festival. Jessica was still furious about it four years later, even though she was Mrs. McCullough by then, and had cut Selena dead at the Edinburgh Christmas ball the night Selena met Royce Campbell.

And now Selena trapped Phineas Bonwit with her eyes.

"I reckon I don't need two thousand pounds sterling," he said huskily. "I'll try an' get t' ye later on."

A plan had begun to take shape in Selena's mind, and she hoped that Gilbertus Penrod's presence here, and Royce's rumored appearance in New York, meant that she would have a chance of escaping. Bonwit had gone down the corridor to ladle mush and fill water mugs, and Selena waited to have a word with Penrod. He had thrown back the cowl. He bent disconsolately over the savaged body of the war's master spy, and his friend.

"I'm afraid he's going," Penrod whispered to Selena. "Not even medicine can save him now."

"Are you sure? Isn't there something . . . ?"

Penrod shook his head. He tucked the blanket tightly around Ward's poor body. Then, as Selena looked on, he unfastened the gold chain and cross from the man's neck and tightened his hand around them.

"Guard!" he called loudly, stepping to the barred door. "Guard, I'm finished here. Let me out. Selena," he added in a whisper, "I must try to speak to you alone. Can you think of something?"

Bonwit was already shambling down the corridor, jangling his ring of keys.

"Please, corporal, I would like to talk to the priest," Selena said, as Bonwit permitted Penrod to leave Ward's cell.

"What about?" the lout asked suspiciously.

"I want to . . . I want to make my confession."

"Confession? Then let me go try an' fetch Lieutenant Oakley."

"Not that kind of confession." She gave him a telling look. "My sins," she said.

A light of understanding glowed in his dull eyes.

"Ah! I see. I don't know if it's allowed though."

"Come now, my man," interjected Penrod, who had replaced the cowl and did look quite like a monk. "The poor girl needs the comfort of the Lord in a place like this. Would you want to go to your reward without having the opportunity to put your soul in order?"

Bonwit mulled whatever moral transgressions he might have committed in life. They were sufficient to sway him. "All right," he said nervously, glancing anxiously up the corridor, making certain that this small lapse of discipline was not being observed. "I reckon I could give ye a moment wi' 'er. But no funny business, ye hear? I'll be just outside the cell."

"Bless you, my son," Penrod said, bowing.

The corporal unlocked Selena's door and Penrod entered. She wanted to embrace him, to feel friendly arms around her, but that was impossible. Bonwit, clutching the handle of his sword as if at any moment he might be attacked, took up a position beneath the torch at the opposite side of the corridor. Jittery about this breach of prison rules, he was not entirely out of earshot. Both Selena and Penrod realized that a true conversation was impossible.

"Please kneel, my child," Penrod said.

Selena felt the dampness of the stone floor invading her knees. There had to be a way to communicate with the merchant. But how? Even now, Corporal Bonwit leaned forward, prepared to catch an earful of her sins.

"Ask our Lord's forgiveness for your transgressions in this vale of tears," Penrod intoned, rather authoritatively under the circumstances. "Unburden your soul to me."

Selena shifted her weight from knee to knee and looked helplessly up at him. They were both trying to think of a way to talk without being overheard by Bonwit. Selena reached up and touched Penrod's hand, taking what comfort she could from his presence. He was holding the cross he'd taken from Ward's neck, and she looked at it. The design she'd seen on it earlier, when Ward had been dragged past her, was clear now: the letters of three words followed the shape of the cross itself.

```
            L
            I
            B
            E
            R
            T
FRATÉRNITÉ
            E
            G
            A
            L
            I
            T
            É
```

She knew a bit of French, of course. Those of her station usually did. But the words on the little cross meant nothing to her.

"I have sinned against God and my fellow man," she began.

"In what manner?" prodded Penrod dolefully.

At that moment, Selena shifted her weight again—the cold from the stones was creeping up her thighs—and steadied herself by bracing a hand against the oozing stone wall. Her handprint remained there for a moment, before the dewy dampness swallowed it up.

"I have committed sins of the heart—" she said, in a tone she hoped to sound penitent, meanwhile grasping Penrod's hand and pressing it against the wall where this print too became visible for a second.

"—and sins of the flesh—"

Bonwit was all ears now, but he could not see clearly, his view blocked as it was by Penrod's flowing cassock.

"—and sins of the spirit—"

Gilbertus Penrod watched his handprint disappear in the seeping moisture. His eyes widened as he understood.

"The Lord forgives you, my child," he said. "Now, recite with me the Creed."

" 'I believe in God the Father . . .' " they began, while Penrod, using a forefinger, traced a message on the stone, word by word.

Royce
Midnight
Pier

" '—forever and ever. Amen.' "

Royce Campbell would be waiting on the pier, across the water from this fortress, at midnight. There was no way that he could reach Selena; she would have to devise a strategy by which to get to him.

Penrod traced one final mark on the sweating stone as he helped Selena to her feet.

By this he meant: *Can you do it? Can you get out of here?*

She steeled her eyes and set her mouth and nodded.

"As God is my witness!" she vowed, not inappropriately.

"No, no . . ." moaned Erasmus Ward, across the way. It sounded like a warning. Selena shivered.

"God be with you, my child," said Penrod, pressing the cross into her hand, as if it were a talisman of safety and Godspeed.

"Ye be done now?" inquired Bonwit suspiciously, stepping forward.

"It is fortunate that I learned of Mr. Ward's arrest," Penrod told the guard as he edged out of the cell and watched the door close again on Selena. "A man's soul is his most prized possession. And a woman's too. Perhaps you will let me comfort the other prisoners?"

"No, sir! Reverend, I mean. I bent the rules fer ye too much already. Y' asked t' see Ward an' y' seen 'im. Be on yer way now."

"Pray, what is the time?" asked Selena, before the corporal escorted Penrod from the dungeon.

" 'Bout 'alf pa' ten," came the response. Bonwit thought she was telling him to make haste and return to her. That, in a way, was true, but he had no way of reading her real intentions.

A long, long hour went by. Selena counted the seconds, trying to keep track of time, growing increasingly apprehensive. If the British were searching for Royce, his presence on the pier, waiting for her, was tremendously risky. What if Bonwit did not return to her cell? What if Royce were to be seized? Then both of them would be prisoners.

At what she guessed must have been at least half past eleven, Erasmus Ward stirred suddenly on his bunk in the opposite cell. He lifted his arms jerkily into the air, flailing away at an unseen assailant. Franticly, as Selena flew to the bars of her own cell door, he beat the air, fighting, fighting. There was nothing Selena could do to quiet or comfort him, locked as he was in eerie struggle, but she understood that death had come for him. His terrible fit seemed to go on and on, although it could not have lasted more than a minute, and then he seemed to clutch at his own throat, as if trying to wrench free the talons of death that were choking his life away.

"*Sorbontay!*" he gasped, or something that sounded like "sorbontay," the bloody rasp of his cry sending a chill far colder than that of the stones through Selena's body. She felt a strange pall, like invisible fog, pass along the corridor then, and disappear among the wavering tapers and the smoky gloom.

Erasmus Ward was gone.

A tear came to her left eye. She brushed it away, fingering the little cross that she had put around her neck.

I shall remember you, she thought, or prayed really although not conscious of it. *I will wear this little cross always in your name. Someday, our cause will triumph.*

"And *I* will avenge your death!" she vowed aloud, picturing Clay Oakley's merciless eyes and grotesque, gleaming head.

Yet that goal, that satisfaction, lay a long way off in a trackless future. Everything now depended on the doltish concupiscence of one lance corporal. Selena felt the minutes melting away. She tried to imagine Royce now, perhaps slipping out of some hiding place, hurrying through narrow, darkened streets toward the harbor. For a lambent, shimmering instant, she thought her mind touched his, believed that she saw her own image in his heart as he hurried along. The sensation was so striking, so truly physical, that she was thrilled by it. Such communications, Selena understood, really did occur: even over vast distances, minds could meld, hearts could speak, if only they beat as one in the awful intensity of desire. She had learned that truth during her time in India from Davi the Dravidian, a dark, sorrowful, doomed little man. Alone in the court of the Maharajah of Jabalpur, Davi had befriended her, had taught her clarity of mind, pureness of heart, even as the maharajah violated her body in quest of the fierce pleasure she had learned to give.

"Things are never what they seem," he had told her, so often that she'd finally grasped the truth of it. *"In each circumstance, in every situation no matter how hopeless or profane, there exists its opposite, by which those blessed with purity of heart may be redeemed and freed."*

From his wisdom, she had taken the strength to avoid defilement.

But now, with his wisdom, could she escape this prison? Could she, in the depths of bondage, discover the key to freedom?

Perhaps the answer lay, more prosaically, in the big ring of keys on the belt of Phineas Bonwit, who managed to rattle the iron door only a little as he crept into the dungeon and hurried stealthily toward Selena's cell, holding his sword tightly against his leg so it would not glint and clatter on the stones. Selena imagined Bonwit growing up in some Yorkshire village, feeding the hogs, milking the cows, plowing the fields, not even dreaming that a larger world existed beyond the local churchyard, or beyond the graveyard fence where perhaps five-hundred years worth of Bonwits turned slowly into the English earth from which they had emerged. But great empires require cannon fodder, so Phineas had been plucked from roots and hearth, had been taken across the seas, where fate had brought him to Selena.

She hoped that she would not have to kill him.

"I managed t' beg off the search party," he whispered breathlessly. "I wouldna care i' Royce Campbell ne'er get caught. An' here, I brung ye a little bit o' somethin'."

He handed Selena a pewter mug through the iron bars, which she sniffed as he clumsily wrestled with the lock on the cell door. *Brandy? Yes. Well, good.* She needed it, and drained the mug in a gulp.

"Hey!" he said, grinning as he came into the cell. "Some o' that grog was supposed to be for me."

"Too much of it dulls the senses," she replied, filling her voice with coquettish promise.

Lurching forward, in a panic of arousal and want, the corporal wrapped his gangly arms around her, and Selena caught a very strong whiff of his breath.

"Why, I think you've had a goodly share already, haven't you?"

"Oh, no! I'm fine!" he promised.

To her disgust, he certainly seemed to be. He held her close to him and ground his body into hers. She felt his hardness against her belly and his thick sword against her leg. He was trying to kiss her; wirelike whiskers scraped her face.

"Wait! Wait," she chided. "What's the hurry?"

It must be almost midnight, she thought.

"Ah! I get ye," he chortled, easing his grip on her a little. "Ye're right. We got all night. An' it's more fun if ye don't rush right through with it, eh?"

"Yes, that's better," Selena said soothingly, slipping from his all-too-eager embrace. "And can't you take off that awful sword? It just terrifies me so!"

Bonwit grinned and began to unbuckle his swordbelt. "Don't ye be afeared, missy. This blade ain't meant fer ye."

Then he began to unbuckle his breeches. "But here's a blade tha' is—"

He'd let the sword fall to the stones and was dancing on one foot, trying to pull off the breeches. The big ring of keys slipped off his flopping belt and clanked down on the stones. Selena made her move.

She bent down and grabbed his breeches, which were now around his ankles, yanked as hard as she could and sent him crashing to the floor.

"Hey!" cried the corporal, stunned. "Ye don't 'ave t' be so eager—"

Then he saw her reaching for his sword and understood. A pained look of betrayal and disappointment crossed his face, to be replaced almost at once by an awareness of danger. If she escaped, he would be in great trouble with his superiors. . . .

He tried to scramble to his feet, but she had taken up the

sword. She swung it around, stepped forward, and held the point of the blade to his throat. He eased back down onto the floor, half-naked, bewildered, his arousal fading fast.

"Ye tricked me," Bonwit whined bleakly. "Why'd ye 'ave t' do that?"

Still, he lay between Selena and the cell door.

"I don't want to hurt you," she said quietly, trying to keep her mind off the trembling in her arms. She was poised at a pitch of tension, and the big sword was heavier than it looked. "Move aside. Slowly."

With the tip of the blade still at his Adam's apple, Bonwit scuttled crablike in the direction of the plank bunk. Selena wasn't quite sure what to do with him. Using his belt to tie him to bunk or bars occurred to her, but it was unlikely that he would hold still and allow that. Nor was she a match for him physically. The only thing to do was to slip out of the cell, lock it, and hope she got away before his yells brought aid.

"Hand me your breeches," she ordered.

"No, ma'am." He was offended at the suggestion.

She pressed down on the sword. "Ow!" cried the corporal. A tiny bead of blood appeared on the taut skin of his neck. He kicked off the breeches.

With a quick movement, Selena reached down, grabbed them, and thrust them between the bars of the cell and out into the corridor. So much for that.

"An' I thought ye was a lady," said Bonwit accusingly, covering his privates with gnarled farmer's hands.

Selena reached down to pick up the ring of keys. Just another moment now and—

She had to stretch in order to reach the keys. The blade of the sword moved slightly, giving Bonwit an inch. He took a mile, swatting the weapon aside, leaping to his feet. The sword flew from Selena's grip and spun in the air. She managed to catch it at the hilt, blade down, but he grabbed her around the shoulders, pinioning her arms. The sword was flat between their jammed-together bodies.

"Shoe's on t' other foot now, ain't it?" he growled in rough anger. "Now I aim t' get what I came for—"

Selena tried to move the blade, attacking him where it would do her the most good, but he anticipated her ploy—which angered him all the more—grabbed the handle with one hand and reached for the collar of her prison garment, ready to rip it from her body.

Then he saw the gold cross at her throat. He hesitated, staring at it for one precious second, wondering, *Hey, didn't the bloke in the other cell have this on before . . . ?*

Selena used the second, mustering all her strength to yank the weapon upward as hard as she could. It shot straight and true, catching Bonwit squarely in the chin. Bonwit collapsed onto the stones like a pole-axed bull, unconscious. Selena stood over him, shaking.

Thank God for that cross, she thought.

Then she gathered up the keys, left the cell—which Bonwit, in his passion, had neglected to lock—found the right key, secured the door, and fled up the corridor with the keys and the sword.

The big iron door opened easily. *Now the hard part.* Everything was dark. *Remember. Twenty-four paces to the left. Flight of stairs? Yes, here.* Up she went. A torch burned far above. *A hundred paces, had it been?* She found the second flight of stairs that Bonwit had used when taking her to Lieutenant Oakley. Now she smelled the sea air of the harbor, and paused at the top of the stairs. She was on the main level of the fortress. Torches flickered at regular intervals along its battlements. She stood in a stone gateway, peering around the corner. Two guards marched up and down, from one end of the prison to the other. They met briefly in the center, snappily saluted each other, reshouldered their muskets, about-faced, and marched in opposite directions once again.

Beyond the torch-lit battlements, Selena saw the flickering lights in buildings along the water. There was no moon, and she could not tell if there was any activity along the pier.

Then in the nether part of the prison, which she had just escaped, an excited voice cried: "Bonwit's been attacked. There's a prisoner missing. Everybody up above on the double!"

The two sentries were now at the far ends of their circuit. *Do it! You won't have another chance!*

Dropping the sword and the keys, Selena dashed across cobblestones, nerved herself, leaped atop the battlement, and without thinking at all, dived toward the black water below.

2 Turn of the Screw

Down she shot, through the cold crystal air of October and into the icy waters of New York harbor. Here—ages ago it seemed—she had disembarked upon American soil, having come from India with Sean Bloodwell, and all the world had seemed full of promise and light. Now there was only darkness and the prospect of disaster. The heavy woolen dress, instantly wet, grew heavier still, taking her down and down. Her lungs were bursting from the pressure, and the cold penetrated to the marrow of her bones. Thanking Bonwit for the brandy, she managed to wriggle out of the sodden, clinging garment, and claw her way back up to the surface.

Soldiers were yelling and waving torches atop the fortress walls.

"There she be! There she be!"

"Get into the boats!" somebody shouted.

Selena heard the creaking of rope ladders under the weight of scrambling men. Fighting panic, she set out toward the pier, trying to keep her strokes steady and even. The sounds of her pursuers faded a bit, or seemed to, and she tried not to think of the frigid waters. Her chest felt as if it were encased in ice, and she was trying to remember if sudden drops in bodily temperature could stop the human heart. There were lights on the fortress behind her and flickering lights ahead of her, and all of a sudden there was darkness.

Selena stopped, treading water. She was in the shadow of the pier. Weren't there footsteps on the thick wooden planks above? She could not stay in the water; she'd freeze for sure. But except for the cross, she was naked, her hair matted and sodden.

Gradually, her eyes adjusted to the gloom and she saw the massive tree-trunk-thick pilings upon which the pier was founded.

Coated with barnacles, slivered and gouged, they would tear her flesh apart should she try to climb one of them.

Selena knew that she was afraid, but slowly she became aware of another emotion as well. It took a little while to rise to the surface of her consciousness, but as she swam from piling to piling, the feeling got clearer and clearer: she felt outrage. To be hunted! To be quarry, like a pathetic rabbit or a terrified fox! There was nothing worse. Even in death one had at least the dignity of solitude. But this, *this*—

The anger fueled her for a few more crucial moments, and as if in reward for perseverance, her hand closed on the slippery rungs of a ladder leading to the top of the pier. She climbed out of the water and clung to it, crouching in darkness. The air felt even colder than the water had and her whole bare body felt numb. She did not hear the footsteps now, but the screech of oarlocks on the water told her that the boats were getting closer. Somewhere, in a tavern along the waterfront, people were drinking and laughing. No shelter there. She turned, appraising her surroundings, and saw the dark outline of a large ship anchored a little way out on the harbor. Probably a British man-o'-war protecting the harbor and the city. No shelter there, either. *Oh, God, where is Royce?*

She started to climb the ladder, stopping when her eyes were level with the wooden planks. Darkness here too, and no one seemed to be about. She saw the lights of the tavern now, across the street from the pier, and three men lounging in the doorway, mugs of grog in their hands. A redcoat on horseback came riding up the street, gaping at his comrades who were shouting as their boats drew near the pier.

My luck could not be worse, she thought.

Still, her only chance lay in flight. And she chose it, pulling herself up onto the dock, ready to run. There were textile warehouses and clothing shops in this part of town, and if she could reach one of them she'd at least find something to cover herself, even if she had to break a window or kick a door down in order to do it.

The horseman had paused about twenty yards away. His attention was directed toward the boats.

Selena ran.

"Duck in here quickly and don't make a sound."

A tall figure stepped out from the shadows of a waterside warehouse, intercepting her in mid-flight, and a strong arm gathered her in. She was whirled around and caught a glimpse of polished brass buttons, epaulets, and a tricornered British officer's hat. She clawed at the face hidden in the shadow of the hatbrim.

"My God, Selena," said Royce Campbell, "is this any way for a Scottish lady to carry on!"

Royce? It was. It was! Their predicament grew more threatening as the soldier looked toward them, raised himself in his stirrups, and shouted, "Halt! Who goes there?" But Selena felt a rush of safety and security course through her, like adrenalin or strong wine.

"Oh, darling!" she cried. "My God, I'm so glad. . . . Are you all right?"

She clung to him and he held her close. The brass buttons of his long, swallow-tailed officer's uniform pressed into her breasts, hurting her and imprinting images of the imperial British lion in her flesh. She didn't care.

"Am I all right?" he repeated, astounded. "The question is, are you?"

"I feel wonderful," she answered, wishing there were time to kiss him. Then she remembered her condition, her rat-wet straggly hair and lack of clothing. "Oh, I look just terrible—"

"On the contrary, my love. You have never looked better to me, but I think we'd better discuss it at a later time. You're freezing. Here," he said, slipping off the big coat, "put this on. Tie the tails around in front. It's the best we can do right now."

Selena complied.

"Now put your arms behind you as if you're bound," he said, rushing her along toward the horseman and shouting, "I've got her. I've got her. You. Soldier. Bring that horse over here right now."

The boats had reached the pier; soldiers in pursuit of Selena were climbing up onto the dock.

The horseman cantered over, reined his mount, and saluted, staring down at the officer and the half-naked woman with him.

"Devil be bound, sir. What on earth . . . ?"

Royce, with his arm around Selena, grabbed the horse's reins.

"Get down, man, and be quick about it. I've just seized the notorious spy, Selena MacPherson, and I must take her directly to

General Graves' headquarters on Wall Street. Get off. I need your horse."

The baffled yeoman, beginning to dismount, was partially cowed by rank, but also distracted by the shouting riflemen swarming onto the pier.

"Selena MacPherson?" he wondered. "Aye. And isn't there a price on 'er 'ead?"

"Yes, and I'll give you fifty percent of it," Royce snapped, dragging the man down from the saddle and pushing him aside.

"Ye seen a woman swim onto shore?" yelled one of the redcoats, racing toward them across the dock, the muzzle of his musket brandished like a guidon. "I say, ha'e ye seen . . . ?"

And he saw Royce lift Selena onto the prancing horse, swing up behind her, spur the beast, and gallop off into the night.

"'E forgot t' ask me m' name!" complained the now earthbound horseman sullenly. "'E promised t' share the reward money wi' me, but 'ow can 'e do tha' when he don't even know me name?"

"Oh, ye ninny and ye oaf!" decried the musketeer, as he realized that Selena had been snatched from under his very nose. "Ye'll be lucky not t' be 'anged, ye stupid lout."

With one arm around Selena, holding the reins with his free hand, Royce urged the fleet chestnut gelding along the waterfront. Selena saw the closed windows of shops flash by, and the darkened facades of houses shuttered against the night. She was freezing. The smooth leather of the saddle, as she rocked in rhythm to the horse's pace, felt sensuous, solid. But far more comforting was the presence of her beloved, better even than this strong horse or the refuge toward which it carried them. She began to feel warmer.

"They are looking for you," she told him, turning her head slightly. "I heard talk in the fortress."

She saw his strong teeth glinting. "It's nothing that hasn't happened before, now, is it?"

Then he laughed and so did Selena, and everything in the world was fine and good.

Perhaps half a mile from the point at which Selena had come ashore, Royce slowed the pounding horse and turned it into an alleyway. Here he reined the beast to a walk, picking their way slowly far back into a tiny canyon of darkness between two rows of brick houses. He was looking upward, searching for something. Selena could not imagine what.

"Home," he said then, halting the animal, "for the time being anyway."

He stood up on the beast's back as the animal shifted nervously, and pulled Selena up as well. Her bare feet slipped a little on the smooth saddle.

"All right," he whispered, "feel up along those bricks. You'll touch a ledge—"

She did.

"It's a window. Open, I hope. Pull yourself up and crawl inside. I'll be with you in a few minutes."

Don't leave me, she wanted to say, but did as she'd been told, clinging to the ledge for a moment, catching a toehold in the bricks. The ledge scraped against her belly and thighs, but then she was up and over and into a dark room. The outline of a table and chairs took shape in the gloom. Outside, in the alley, she heard the receding clip-clop of the horse, followed by a burst of excited shouting.

The redcoats! They had spied Royce!

The thought was too much to bear. For a moment, Selena debated whether to cry or not, but before she could decide, she felt the floor tremble ever so slightly, heard footsteps coming nearer, closing on her in the night.

A door opened.

"Selena? It's me. I'm safe. The British are chasing a horse."

Royce drew the curtains on the window through which Selena had entered, and then they held each other and lost themselves in a kiss that went on forever. She had grown to know the many nuances of his kiss, lazy or searching or tender, playful or powered by raw passion. But this kiss was one of gratitude and relief. He could hold her again, and she him, and it was as if a shroud of serenity descended out of the darkness to protect them.

When at length they drew apart, he lit a candle on the table. Selena saw a small, neat room, sparsely furnished. In addition to the table and chairs, there was a washstand with a cracked porcelain pitcher and bowl, a battered waist-high cupboard, and several rolled-up packets of bedding piled along the wall.

"Our agents use this place from time to time," Royce explained. "It's behind a false wall at the back of a harnessmaker's establishment. Erasmus Ward stayed here quite often, God rest his soul."

"You know?"

Royce nodded. "When we learned of his capture, we held a conference and decided to send Penrod over to the fortress in priestly disguise. I understand he suffered a great deal?"

"It was terrible. Oakley did not spare him. But I don't believe he revealed anything about the coming attack on Yorktown."

"Shh!" Royce cautioned. "One never knows where there are ears. We will even it with Oakley in due time. And you? Did he harm you?"

"He would have, had you not rescued me. Did you know I was in the fortress?"

"Not for certain. But I had a feeling. It was the strangest thing, as if you were speaking to my mind."

"I know." Selena smiled. What she had learned in the Orient regarding the mystical bonds between true lovers was indeed valid, and she was glad.

"Anyway, you saved yourself," Royce was saying. "I had precious little to do with it."

"Modesty sits strangely upon you, my dear," Selena teased. "What are we going to do now?"

"We'll remain here in hiding until late tomorrow night. Oakley will expect us to make a run for it immediately. Let us wait until he has lowered his guard a bit. I ordered the *Selena* to sail around Long Island to Newport. We'll ferry across to Connecticut and make our way up the coast. And then we're off to the Caribbean."

Selena, who had been rejoicing over the whole day they would spend together, and the fields of time that stretched out after that, was puzzled.

"The Caribbean?"

"Yes. It's rather a first stop. I have some plans."

He said no more, turning from her and walking to the cupboard. Opening it, he took out a bottle of wine, two glasses, a loaf of bread, and a large wedge of cheddar. Then from a compartment at the bottom, he also withdrew a fluffy towel.

The excitement of being with him again had momentarily put everything else out of Selena's mind, but the smell of bread, the sight of cheese, stirred the juices of appetite. She was famished. She was also bedraggled and suddenly aware of how she must look, standing there barelegged and draped in that purloined officer's uniform. Well, he would certainly tell her of his plans later. Curiosity could wait.

"Hand me the towel please, darling? Is there water and soap? Is there anything for me to wear?"

Royce set the wine and the food on the table. He smiled.

"I'm sorry. I didn't know exactly what you'd require. But Penrod will be coming by tomorrow. I'm sure we can ask him to get some clothes for you.

"It may be," he added, "that you won't need any until then."

"I hope not," replied Selena, meeting his eyes.

He uncorked the wine, sliced bread and cheese. Selena washed herself, feeling better every moment, and even succeeded in putting her hair back into a semblance of order, using Royce's own pearl-handled comb, into which—as into all of his personal effects—was set a small silver image of a wolf's head. That noble animal, so often misunderstood and reviled, was his symbol. More too. In a manner at once vague yet irrefutably clear, the wolf—which roams and hunts, which attacks only when provoked, which mates for life, and which will sacrifice itself for the safety of its own—was Royce Campbell's brother, mirror-image, empath. Once aboard his previous ship, the *Highlander*, he had held her in his arms in the hammock in his captain's quarters and told her what he had had to do to become a man in the eyes of the wild Highlands clan of which he was a part.

She had recently suffered the loss of her father, and the hidden meanings of life, if any, perplexed her, so first Royce had asked, "You even believe in God, don't you?"

"Sometimes."

"Well, that's all right," Royce said, giving her a lazy, indulgent kiss. "But I met him, and there are no longer any obligations attendant upon a vow in his name."

"What do you mean? You could not have met—"

"God," Royce said simply, and nodded. "It was my time, in the spring. The sun was falling that day, and I was readied in the usual manner. First I was stripped naked and my body was greased from crown to sole with bear oil, for symbolic strength and to protect me from the cold. We were in our hunting lodge near Loch Nan Clar, and the torches were lighted. I will remember forever the way my shadow loomed against the stone walls, and when I saw the shadow, the way the light had thrown my image upon the stone, I knew there would never be need of fear in my life. Selena, it was an exultation I cannot describe. I knew, at that very instant, that nothing could touch me. Not then, that night, nor ever.

"After the oiling, I was girded in the tanned hides of wolves, strong with the scent of the wolf, and dressed in boots and gloves and a hat of fur. I took up a dagger and sheathed it at my side, and I was given whiskey to take with me against the cold. Then I left the lodge and set out upon my quest."

"Were you afraid?" Selena had asked, pressing herself against his long body as they lay in the hammock.

"No. Excited. Overjoyed might be a better way to describe the feeling in my soul that night. Because, you see, my time had come. The time to be a man and to claim what was mine in the world. But first I had to succeed in the ritual. Midnight came and fled as I skirted the northern shore of the loch and began the climb toward the caves of Ben Kilbreck Mountain. I stopped for a time and had a bit of the whiskey, listening for the wolves."

"You were hunting wolves? How old were you?"

"Six," he answered casually, as Selena gasped. "You see, at that time of the year, the female whelps. She remains in the den with the cubs while the male brings prey for food. I found a cave, a den, and struck."

"You killed the father wolf?"

"No. Not then. I entered the den when the father was gone, dressed in the skins of a wolf, smelling like an animal. You see, my first task was to suckle from the she-wolf, then to kill her, then to skin her and remove the dugs, to take them home with me as proof of my suckling."

Hearing this, Selena had almost cried out. A boy with a dagger, crawling upon hands and knees into the recking stench of the den. That boy had become the man beside her, whom she loved as much as all the earth.

"You might have been killed!"

"No, I knew that I would not be. I knew it from the time I saw my giant shadow wavering against the stone wall of our hunting lodge. The she-wolf came at me, but I caught her beneath the throat with my dagger, and drank her bitter milk while the blood poured out. Her litter of pups squealed in panic, and in moments I could hear their father scrambling over the rocks outside the cave. But I was ready when I saw him, a dark, howling shape at the mouth of the cave, illuminated by a crescent of rising sun. The puppies, emboldened by his presence, were yapping and nipping at me now. I threw them off as the father charged. There is nothing to match the rage of an animal whose young are threatened, save perhaps the rage of women who want the same man, and I saw my death in the eyes of that attacking wolf."

"But why did they make you do that?"

"No one *made* me. I *wanted* to. It is the way things are, because we Campbells believe that the only thing one must fear is God—"

"And you said that you met—"

"—and that God exists only at the instant when man is poised upon the thin line between life and death—"

"—God, and he was—"

"—for me, that father wolf, charging, fangs bared, out of the dawn, with his whelps gnawing at me too. But I dropped him with a dagger to the heart. He died with his teeth at my throat. Then I cut his throat where the skin is soft. And on that dawn I drank the blood of God. . . ."

Selena had reached out hesitantly then to touch his skin, as if afraid that some alien force would be transmitted from his body to her own. But nothing seemed to happen; no charged current came from him to her. In truth, it could not. They were already the same. She did not yet know, had not yet learned, that they were both possessed by the power of pure impulse, that they shared heartbeats with a rare, feral universe.

"I killed the puppies too," he had told her casually, "except for one I brought back home. He was a symbol of the fact that I had sacrificed what I must, but also spared what I could. Wolves cannot be domesticated, but I cared for him until he was able to fend for himself, then set him free. I think of him sometimes, roaming those Highlands of mine, and I feel gladness for him and for me."

"And you chose his image as your own."

He had, and it suited him. Although, Selena had come to believe, there were differences. The man who seated her at the table now and wrapped more tightly around her the blanket in which she sought to warm herself, the man who brushed her forehead with his lips and poured her a glass of red wine, no, that was not a man who would roam wild ever again, nor set the selfish interests of lust and lucre above those of compassion and love.

Yes, she *had* gentled him and turned him from his willful ways.

"To us," he said, sitting down at the table with her and raising his glass.

They drank.

"To victory," she said, and they drank again.

Selena attacked the bread and cheese, even gulped the wine, as if she would never eat again. She'd had no idea how hungry she was. Royce sipped wine, smiling indulgently, but he cautioned her too.

"Don't overdo it, darling. You're not used to this fare."

Already, she felt the effect of the wine, a slow, soaring light-headedness, a voluptuous ease spreading through her body. "I never want to see barley porridge again, not for the rest of my days. I think I lost three or four stone in prison."

"Spirit is the thing you cannot afford to lose, and you haven't, as far as I can tell. Weight can always be regained."

"But not too much!" Selena cried, laughing and increasingly giddy from the wine. "Or would you love me fat?"

"Time will tell."

"No, I'll *never* get fat," she babbled, cutting an immense wedge of cheddar and putting it between two crusty slabs of bread. "When I was locked in the fortress, I thought—" She was about to tell him of how, lying half-famished on the plank bunk in her cell, she had sometimes recalled the great holiday feasts of her youth, of lamb roasted in spices and basted with sweet wine, of pheasant stuffed with honey and butter and baked, of bread, soft and white as clouds, of apples and pears and candies, of tangy sausages and cold, strong ale. She meant to tell Royce about those delicacies, but the wine intruded, and she remembered what he'd said earlier.

"Why are we sailing to the Caribbean?"

Was it the influence of the grape on her perception that made Selena think he looked startled by her question?

"I think it would be best if we absented ourselves from this part of America for a time. It is hardly safe for either of us, I'd say."

"But, darling, but, darling—" Now what the deuce had she been planning to say? Oh, yes, it came to her "—but, darling, if

48 Vanessa Royall

Washington succeeds against Cornwallis at Yorktown, the war will be over. Don't you want to be here for that? Don't you want to enjoy the victory for which we've all struggled so long?"

"Of course I do." He reached across the little table and took her hand. "Of course I do, but there are . . . but there are other things that require—Let's talk about it later," he concluded lightly. "I think you're well on your way to sailing three sheets to the wind."

"What? *What?* No, I'm not!" She started to stand, but suddenly the candlelight danced oddly, in leaping patterns of colors, like a bouquet of flowers, and—she was very, very sure—the room had begun to move like a slow carousel.

She sat down abruptly, giggling. "I'm purrfectly fine. . . ."

The blanket had fallen loose around her shoulders. Why was Royce looking at her so sternly? It was certainly not the way he'd ever looked at her before. Usually the merest glimpse of her bare breasts made him . . .

"Where did you get that?" he was asking. She heard his voice, as if from far away, through the surfeit of food, the delicious languor of wine.

"What? Where did I get . . . oh, this cross!" The fate of Erasmus Ward sobered her a little, only for a moment, but long enough to tell him that Penrod had given her the little object.

"Isn't it lovely?" she heard herself asking. "And do you know what he said, what Erasmus Ward said as he died? It was the strangest thing. 'Sorbontay.' What do you think of that?"

Royce Campbell's dark eyes widened suddenly, as if the word meant something to him.

"Do you know what it means?" she asked, reaching for the almost-empty wine bottle.

"No, no, I don't think I do," she heard him say.

Selena's hand missed its mark. The bottle tipped over onto the table. Red wine, like blood, pooled on the boards.

"Perhaps," Royce said, "it's time you had yourself a good sleep?"

"But I thought we could—"

"Later. First things first."

She sat at the table watching as, with dreamlike slowness, at a great distance, Royce spread a bedroll out upon the floor. He came toward her then, step by step, lifted her from the chair into his arms, carried her back to the bedroll, and laid her gently down upon it. Her arms were around his neck and she clung to him.

"Royce, let's. Please, darling. Now."

He unclasped her hands from behind his neck and kissed her briefly, as one would kiss a child at bedtime.

"Later," he said. "It will be much better when you're rested."

"Don't go away! You won't go away, will you?"

"Have no fear of that. I'll be right here. I have to plan a few things for tomorrow and afterwards, but I'm coming to bed in a little while."

"I'll be here," she murmured drowsily, feeling wine-dimmed and wonderful, her body already anticipating the pleasure to come.

He tucked blankets around her and kissed her on the mouth. "What will you do with the cross?" he asked, in a tone she could not just then decipher.

"I promised . . . I promised to wear it always . . . as a memory and keepsake."

"Yes. The little guy was probably the bravest man I ever knew. Sleep now."

"Ummmmmmm. . . ."

Selena drifted so gently into wakefulness that for a while she was not even aware of being awake, nor of her surroundings. For a moment, she thought that she was still in her cell and immediately regretted that sleep had abandoned her to its squalor. But these blankets were soft and warm, and there had been no candlelight in her fortress prison. Then she turned, saw Royce seated at the table, and remembered that she was safe. "I love you," she said.

He looked up, his face dark with concentration, and immediately blew out the flame, leaving the room in pale darkness. Selena had almost slept the night away. She could see, by the hint of light behind the drawn curtain, that it was almost dawn.

"Stay there," he said. His voice was quiet, but in its tone was something almost like an order. She could make out the outline of his big body as he undressed and draped his clothing over the back of a chair. Then he picked something up from the table and put it in the cupboard. Selena had just begun to wonder what it

50 Vanessa Royall

was, but he came toward her then across the creaking floor of this hideaway, and all thoughts of mundane things spun away.

They had made love the first time in his hammock aboard the *Highlander* years ago, made love the last time in a hazel thicket on Long Island just before Oakley and his men had captured her and separated them, made love countless times in between in every way there was.

And now it was going to happen again.

Selena felt a tremendous rush of expectant desire as he slipped beside her in the bedroll and put his arms around her. His kiss tasted of wine for an instant, but then it was just and only his kiss. It was enough. She closed her eyes, gasping hungrily as he caressed her breasts, ran his hand down along her taut belly, teased the warm insides of her thighs with his fingertips, and touched her finally where she wanted most to be touched. Her hands sought the staff of him, long and hard and throbbing along its great length, softer there, thick and sleek and rounded at the end. A pearly drop of moisture, bespeaking his desire, seeped from him, and with her finger Selena spread it out like balm over the need-swollen tip, rubbing it in slowly, massaging him with slow, delicious motions as he moaned.

"God, but I love you," he said. Her laugh of delight was husky, low. No man or woman on earth could possibly know the things they knew, or give pleasure so keen, or enjoy it so much. It was magic, all of it, when he came upon her, eased into her like coming home.

He was gentle at first, each approach, each questing stroke almost like an exploration. Their mouths were as ravenous for each other as their bodies were, and in the fire of their mutual need, the memory of pleasures they had shared in the past enhanced each sensation they felt now. Selena fitted herself beneath him, around him, until she became another part of Royce, moving with him, proudly feeling his urgency, a throb to the depths of her being. It seemed impossible that he could plunge so deep, but just when she thought she could not bear it anymore, he would begin to retreat. Then she held onto him as hard as she was able, crying out to have him deep again. His entire body trembled in her arms, and she drew her long, sweat-glistening legs up around him, locked her slim ankles behind his back—Royce riding higher, faster on her now—and her fading mind listened as she gasped and gasped again, felt her body, over which she had no control anymore, open and thrust, only to open and thrust and clutch and plunge again, maddened by pleasure and joy.

Selena felt the pressure building, but she no longer possessed enough of her conscious mind to hold onto reality. From far away, she felt her body moving, twisting, rearing faster and faster, and so too did the sweet body of her beloved by which she was mounted and ridden, by which she was melded by a magic greater than them both. He was moving into her now with strokes so powerful they made her cry out at each one, always wanting another and after that another, never wanting them to end.

In order to pleasure him more, she reached beneath him, teasing with swirling fingertips the heavy gourd of his nature. The feel of his leaping essence triggered her own release, and clinging to him, all of the world, all sensation, lived for an instant in an evanescent pinpoint of her body. He was her body then, and she his, in soul, in flesh.

Then, slowly, slowly in the afterglow of ecstasy, the pleasure spread throughout their bodies and into the very air, back into the wild universe from which it had come and for which it had been created.

Royce slept.

It was dawn.

Selena lay beside her beloved for a long time, watching him sleep, pressing her cheek against his warm chest, listening to his heart beating. Life was, indeed, passing strange. Every person on the wide earth, *every single person,* had heart that beat, lips that kissed, tongue for sweet words or sweeter flesh, arms that embraced. But the body of one's lover was ever a mystery, and even the best lovemaking no more than a feeble attempt to possess that body, to enter into it and know what it knew.

It must all be part of some vast plan, Selena mused, kissing Royce's neck where the big vein beat, *and we make love over and over, trying to know that which is unknowable.*

A very good plan, she decided.

At length she arose, pulled a sheet around her, and walked to the window. Cautiously, she drew an edge of the curtain aside and peered out. This room was at the end of an alley, as she had surmised on the previous evening, but she was surprised to see how close the harbor was. She saw the Battery fortress, squat, ugly and ominous, and the Union Jack atop it, whipping in the breeze. If Washington were to be successful, God grant, in the forthcoming campaign against Cornwallis in Virginia, the Stars and Stripes would fly above that fortress soon. The moment had been a long time coming too. It was October of 1781; the war was over five years old.

Selena noted as well the many ships lying at anchor in the harbor, the freighters and the little gunboats and three monstrous British men-o'-war. She saw another ship too, which, by its position in the harbor, she knew to be the one she'd seen while clinging to the pier ladder last night. Neither warship nor freighter, it was low and sleek. A row of cannon gleamed along its main deck. She saw no flag atop its mast, but the one word *Liberté*, stood out along its gleaming hull.

French? That was impossible. It would have been the height of lunacy for a French captain to bring his vessel into New York harbor, which the British Navy dominated so thoroughly.

Maybe it was a captured French ship.

Still, the name of the vessel struck a chord, and she fingered the golden cross at her throat.

Then she washed, ate a piece of bread left over from the night before, and drank some water from the pitcher, wondering how soon Gilbertus Penrod would arrive. She would have to ask him to try and get a dress, a coat, and a good pair of shoes. Royce's clothes—the British officer's uniform—sagged across the back of a chair, his boots on the floor beneath the table. A good disguise for him if they meant to get out of New York unaccosted. She would need rather fine garments as a woman travelling with such a man. One thing you had to say for the British: They knew how to outfit an army in style.

Too bad for them that they did not know how to win wars.

Royce stirred, rolled over, sighed luxuriously, but went on sleeping. Selena smiled. What a glorious day this was!

Growing restless, however, she got up and walked around the room. It was small, but after her tiny cell, it seemed like the great hall of a palace. She traipsed about quietly, exulting in freedom. Then as she passed the little cupboard, she remembered that Royce had gone to it just before he'd joined her in the bedroll. Glancing over at him, she stooped and opened it. Another bottle of wine, some apples, and a rather woebegone blanket. She took an apple and bit into it greedily, noticing as she did so a small, dark bundle half-concealed by the blanket.

She reached in and took it out.

A pouch made of leather with a rawhide drawstring. Its contents were lumpy and hard.

Taking the apple and the pouch, she went back to the table, sat down, and undid the drawstring.

An observer, had there been one present, would have seen her eyes widen in astonishment, even alarm, would have noted how she seemed to gulp and stop chewing the bit of apple in her mouth.

Selena looked into the pouch and saw a cache of gold sovereigns along with emeralds, rubies, sapphires, and several diamonds of various sizes.

There was a fortune in the pouch!

More startling, the gems were cut and polished. It appeared that they had been deliberately and expertly removed from their settings in brooches or rings, bracelets or necklaces or earrings.

Why did Royce have these jewels?

Looking over at him now as he slept on, she could not help but remember what he'd been like when she'd first met him, and how he had cherished adventure on the high seas, enriching himself with the bounty of plundered ships.

But he was no longer like that at all.

Was he?

Mystified, distracted, and a little worried, she tightened the drawstring and returned the pouch to its hiding place.

"I'll ask him about the gems when he awakens," she said to herself.

No, she decided a moment later. *He must have a good reason for being in possession of those things, and he must have had a good reason for placing them out of sight.*

Who wouldn't hide a fortune?

Besides which, the pouch was none of her business. Trust must exist between lovers, or their relationship is surely founded upon quicksand, or worse. He *must* have a good reason, she reassured herself. He'll tell me about the pouch if it is something that concerns me.

Still, she was a little perturbed, and when Royce awoke a short time later, he asked her why she seemed so pensive.

"Just feeling lonely," she fabricated, going to him, and when he took her again she forgot all about the bag of gold and jewels. Indeed, Royce gave her another fortune in gems, which danced in colored lights behind her closed eyelids, as with his body, strong from sleep, he sorcerered her dazzled flesh once again. Selena, still luxuriating in the ebb of previous pleasure, felt every sensation more keenly this time. With her fingers clinging to his shoulders, his back, with her head, her wild hair, whipping from side to side, she thought she could not bear it, and writhed as if trying to cast him off. But the thrashing, turning, twisting only increased the power and the splendor of delight, and when the glowing rush did come for both of them, when she squeezed him with her body as tightly as she could, he had to muffle her sobbing cries with a gentle hand.

"If Lieutenant Oakley has ears to hear"—Royce smiled after they had collapsed in glorified exhaustion next to each other—"he could hear you all the way to the fortress."

"Oakley!" she pronounced, her loathing for the man reborn, and while Royce dressed she told him of the lieutenant's strange nature, the balance between savage fanatacism and professed love of truth and beauty that existed within him. Royce was surprised to hear of the paintings, but suggested that talent often coexisted with mania.

"In Oakley's case," he said, "it may be that the dark side has the upper edge, perhaps due to his unfortunate visage. A person serene of soul looks out upon a world of color and light, and the world reflects back those same qualities. But if it is otherwise, the world may seem very black indeed."

"All I know is that I am afraid the lieutenant will pursue me to the ends of the earth. He as much as said so. Something about beauty, beauty and truth, and there being a bond between us."

"Then we shall break that bond," vowed Royce, going to the window. "I wish Penrod would hurry, but it may be difficult to slip through the British."

"If I'm captured," said Selena in jest, recalling Royce's words with the horseman on the pier, "you'll doubtless have to share the reward money."

"Not bloody likely," he shot back, matching her tone, "you know I'd want it all for myself."

His words brought back to mind the pouch of sovereigns and gems, and Selena fell suddenly silent.

Gilbertus Penrod, dressed in his fine business clothes of handmade linen, wearing a silk shirt and carrying a pearl-knobbed walking stick, entered the room worriedly just before noon. He also had with him a traveling bag of supple, expensive leather, and after greeting Royce and kissing Selena, he set the bag on the table.

"This will have to do, I'm afraid," he said. "There are redcoats on the streets of lower Manhattan today. I won't be able to make the trip again without arousing unnecessary suspicion."

Penrod opened the bag and began to remove a set of clothing. "Royce," he continued, "I knew you had an officer's uniform, so I decided it would be best to outfit Selena as your manservant." He set upon the table a pair of knee-length breeches, black stockings, buckled shoes, white shirt, gray woolen jacket, and a black hat with a small crown and flat, circular brim.

Selena gazed doubtfully at the clothing—drab was rather the word for it—but Royce was pleased.

"Wise choice, Gil," he said. "All officers have boys to serve as valets and wait on their personal needs. I don't know if Selena will take kindly to being a boy, however."

"I'll do the best I can," she promised, as the two men laughed.

"I also brought," said Penrod, reaching into the bag again, "sustenance!"

He showed them a bottle of wine, a smaller container of brandy, a long, thick stick of hard salami, a metal can full of hardtack, and a jar of strawberry jam. "Best I could do," he said.

"Splendid," said Royce.

"What are your plans?" the other man asked.

"We'll hole up here until dark, slip out, make our way to the west side, and hire a boat to take us up the Hudson. We'll cross Westchester into Connecticut and then proceed to the *Selena* in Newport."

"How does it feel to have a ship named for you?" Penrod asked Selena.

She pressed herself against Royce, smiling. "It depends on who's done the naming. In this case I'll accept the honor."

He put his arm around her. "Gil, I'm a little low on funds. . . ."

This statement surprised Selena as she knew about the sack of gems. She was almost certain now that something was going on about which she did not know and which she wasn't at all sure she'd like.

"I understand," Penrod said. He pulled a thick, alligator-hide wallet from his waistcoat pocket, and counted out a number of bills. "Here're both British notes and Continental Congress paper. You'll be ready for either eventuality.

"Well, I guess that's it," he added, facing them. "I'd best slip out now. Godspeed."

The two men shook hands warmly, the hearty grip of comradeship, which is also male affection. Penrod leaned over and bussed Selena lightly on the lips.

"Don't let go of him this time," he advised tenderly.

"Never again," said Selena.

Penrod crossed to the door, then turned. "Oh, Selena, I almost forgot. I gave you that cross in prison yesterday because I was afraid the British would take it. . . ."

"Yes?" said Selena, who thought he meant that he hadn't wanted the English to have Erasmus Ward's last possession. She pulled the sheet she wore a little way down from her neck. "Here it is. I'm wearing it in honor and memory of him."

It happened very quickly, but Selena was sure she saw Penrod and Royce exchange a veiled glance.

"It's all right, Gil," Royce said. "The cross is in good hands. Or should I say around a fine neck?"

"Absolutely," agreed the businessman, nodding. It was as if the two men were discussing something, something quite important too, beyond Selena's ken.

Penrod left then, and Selena set about preparing a breakfast of brandy, hardtack, and strawberry preserves.

"Is there some significance to this cross?" she asked, keeping her voice even, as if she were not at all interested.

"Of course not," replied Royce, with a similar—and equally feigned—insouciance. "Why on earth would you think a thing like that?"

Selena almost—almost—brought the issue to a head then and there, the issue of the cross and the gems. Later she would wish that she had, but she didn't. They had a gay breakfast during which Royce allowed that sometime in the future they would be sailing to Europe. But such a trip seemed so far away, the brandy was heady and sweet, and he was hers.

When he slipped the sheet from her shoulders and breasts, she shuddered. And when he drew it down over the swell of her hips and let it fall to the floor—dropping to his knees as he did so—she closed her eyes, threw back her head, and made a strange involuntary sound of wonder, almost a snarl.

"Don't move," he ordered hoarsely. "Feel everything. I want you to enjoy every bit of sensation."

She obeyed until nearly the end, as he worshipped her with his lips and mouth and tongue, sending quicksilver flashes of startling raw pleasure throughout her body. She obeyed, and did not move at all until nearly the end when he lifted her, light as air, to her toes, lifted her with ecstatic kiss alone, and she gave out a stifled wail of joy, both for what he was giving her and for what now had to end.

Then he rose and Selena fell to her own knees before him, slowly, so slowly undoing the drawstring of his breeches, bringing forth as she had so many times before the mysterious pulsing staff that could so easily rouse her to spasms of delicious frenzy. He cradled her head between his hands as, with her lips, she explored the length of him, and with her fingertips the taut vessel in which nestled the twin orbs that made him a masterpiece. Pleased with the pleasure she gave, rejoicing at her ability to make him jump and sob, Selena exulted when she felt the leaping currents of his essence, all down the long length of him and into her.

For most of the day, they held each other, sleeping, resting, now and then rising to eat or drink. Later on, in waning twilight, they hurried to dress. They split the bills that Penrod had given them, and as Selena struggled to pull on the buckled shoes—Gilbertus had erred complimentarily in his estimate of her size—Selena saw Royce furtively slipping the pouch of gems into the leather bag.

"I'm afraid you'll have to carry this," he told her, handing over the bag. "Servants work, you know."

"Yes, milord," she replied, dipping slightly in a parody of a curtsy.

Then they opened the window and dropped from the ledge

down into the darkened alley, Royce going first and Selena following.

They left the alley and turned into the street just as Jean Beaumain, captain of the *Liberté,* left his ship, accompanied by five of his comrades, for an evening of cards and drinks and carousing.

3 A Change of Plans

Before she had walked more than a couple of hundred paces, walking rather slowly so as not to arouse suspicion, Selena's shoes attacked. Their frontal assault was made upon the joint at which the small toe meets the foot. A simultaneous, dastardly charge from the rear occurred where the hard leather of the low shoes dug into the tender flesh atop Selena's heels. The stockings were no help at all, thin and old. If anything, they betrayed her as well, showing off her well-shaped calves. Few men had legs like that. To make matters worse, her hair, which she had tied up and jammed beneath the silly little hat, was beginning to loosen. The hat swayed, side to side, to and fro, upon her head like a lily pad on a windy pond.

"Darling, stop, I've got to take off these damn shoes!" Selena declared, bracing a hand against his epauleted shoulder and reaching down to remove the instruments of torture.

"It won't look right," he said, scanning the street ahead of them even as two British soldiers, marching in lockstep and carrying muskets, turned a corner and approached.

"I'll be bleeding shortly," complained Selena.

"We'll both be bleeding anyway if we don't get out of New York fast."

Regretfully, recognizing the truth of his words and sobered by the oncoming troopers, Selena stood up and moved ahead.

The two men wore, respectively, the uniforms of a corporal and a sergeant. Royce was disguised as a major. Under normal circumstances, subordinates would not have dreamed of addressing their superior unless ordered or invited to do so, but sentries on guard, under specific orders to challenge everyone, would have been derelict in their duty had they failed to hail King George himself.

"Major, sir, please state your business," the sergeant said, as he and his partner stopped in front of Royce and Selena.

"Good work, sergeant," replied Royce smoothly. "I'm glad to see you're alert. I am Major Shaddy, attached to General Graves' headquarters."

The guard was unimpressed. There were many officers working for General Graves, and an enlisted man savors the moment when he is permitted to deal with a ranking officer on an equal footing.

"Aren't you off in the wrong direction a bit? You ought to have turned two streets down."

"What? Is that right? My mistake. Thank you. You see, I only arrived from England last week. My man here"—he gestured toward Selena, who sensed trouble in this encounter—"and I have just come from a fitting at my tailor's."

"Is that correct?" demanded the sergeant of Selena, peering at her in the gathering darkness.

"Yes, sir!" she said crisply, thanking the good Lord or whomever for her naturally husky speaking voice, which she had lowered an octave on this occasion.

"I don't believe a ship arrived here last week," the corporal piped up.

"What is this, an inquisition?" Royce snapped, making a show of anger that one as cooperative as he would be subject to prolonged scrutiny. "I arrived in the Chesapeake aboard the *Princess Rose* and proceeded here by carriage. Would you like to accompany me to headquarters for verification?"

Any trooper worth his salt knows that headquarters is a place to avoid at all costs. Being there means running the risk of being spotted and assigned to any extra duty that might have occurred to some officer coming out of his afternoon nap. Royce had won.

"No, sir," the sergeant decided. "Your word is good enough for us. Pleasant evening."

"Let us walk up in this direction a bit farther," Royce said to Selena in a voice loud enough for the departing sentries to hear. "I want to see this part of town."

"Whew!" he added a bit later. "They are certainly on the prowl tonight."

Selena agreed. She could not, however, bear the pinching shoes a moment longer, so she took them off and slipped them into the bag, noticing as she did so that Royce was watching her carefully. The sovereigns and gems were on his mind.

"Now that's better," she exclaimed in relief, walking along in her stockinged feet. "How much farther . . . ?"

She didn't finish. A splendid hansom, drawn by two sleek grays, was wheeling toward them up the street.

"Just keep walking," Royce said.

The hansom flashed past. Out of the corner of her eye, Selena saw the fine horses, the glittering spokes of the wheels, the flickering lanterns mounted on the sides of the cab, and the bald, gleaming head of Lieutenant Clay Oakley in the cab, upon whom the lanterns shone. He had been looking their way.

"Oakley!" she blurted.

"Are you sure?" asked Royce, turning instinctively. "Oh, no, what evil luck—"

Selena turned too, and saw that the hansom had begun to swing back around toward them. She could see the booted and liveried driver sawing at the reins and snapping his long whip.

She and Royce looked at each other.

They ran.

"How did he know?" she panted, the coarse gravel of the roadway biting into her feet.

"He couldn't have," muttered Royce. "Everyone is being challenged."

"No. He did know. Know it was me. The man is uncanny. There is something about him—"

Hoofbeats clattered on the road, gaining on the fugitives. "Halt! Halt!" Oakley was shouting. Royce and Selena heard the sharp bark of a pistol, heard the hot ball of lead hiss by. The driver, standing on his seat behind the horses, was holding the reins with one hand and firing with the other.

"We've got to split up," said Royce, as they came to an alley so narrow not even a single horseman could have entered it. "You go that way. I'll run on ahead. Cut left after a time. I'll meet you along the river."

"No!"

The pistol spoke again. A chunk of brick, dislodged from the side of the building in whose shadow they stood, fell at Selena's feet. The hansom was closing fast.

"Please get moving," implored Royce. And Selena obeyed then, racing up the dark, dingy alley—no more than a pathway really—between two bleak, unending rows of shuttered hovels. Dogs barked. Something that must have been a rat skittered beneath her feet, and she was glad for a second not to be wearing a skirt.

Far up the alley, thinking that she was at least out of sight, Selena turned. The hansom had stopped at the alley's end. In the light of its little lanterns, she saw Clay Oakley climb out. Disbelieving, she saw him start to come after her, heavily, ponderously, implacably. The hansom rolled on again, its driver hunting for Royce.

"No, God!" she prayed.

Oakley was coming. She could not yet hear his footsteps, but the swift currents of air at work in this narrow space already bore the scent of his cologne, mingled with the stenches of ordure and garbage dumped in the alley, as was customary, by the residents of these hovels for the rain to wash away.

Selena began to run again, more breathlessly perhaps even than Oakley. It was then that she realized the leather bag was still in her hand.

With the pouch of jewels inside it.

She also realized that the bag, which was quite bulky even though almost empty, hindered her flight. Without thinking twice, she opened it, took out the pouch and slipped it into her jacket pocket, and flung the bag into the shadows next to someone's back stoop. She hoped whoever lived here had use for a piece of fine luggage and also possessed small feet.

Running on, no longer smelling the cologne, Selena saw a light burning at the side of a building up ahead. She slowed down and approached. The illumination came from a whale-oil lantern affixed to the doorjamb of an establishment called the Nest of Feathers. Those, at any rate, were the fading words painted over the door. From within, she heard the sounds of rough laughter and rougher talk.

It was surely no place for a lady to be, not at this time of night or any other, but there were living, breathing people inside, and her disguise might serve her at least for a little while. The Nest of Feathers seemed more desirable than standing in a cold alley, alone, waiting for Clay Oakley to imprison her again.

A whiff of cologne urged her over the brink of decision. She opened the tavern door and went inside.

To her relief, it was ill-lighted. She was particularly concerned about someone noticing her feminine features, her incongruous disguise, and her stockinged feet. A small, squat bar stood at one side of the tavern, covered with dusty bottles, dirty glasses, and numerous puddles of liquor or water that had not been wiped. A whale-oil lamp burned on the bar, behind which a sultry, buxom barmaid lifted her head to stare expectantly at Selena. Candles burned on each of three tables, at one of which five men were drinking and playing cards. There were no other customers. The Nest of Feathers, on this night anyway, was not enjoying an impressive or numerous clientele.

A couple of the men glanced Selena's way as she entered, but turned immediately back to their cards.

"What'll it be, mate?" asked the barmaid.

Selena knew she did not have much time before Oakley would stumble in, making inquiries. She had to think of some way in which to ensure her safety. Posing as a toper seemed a likely first step. She had not had much experience in taverns of this sort, however, save one in Liverpool years ago. There she had bewitched and inveigled a seaman named Slyde into smuggling her aboard his vessel in order to escape Darius McGrover, who had killed her father and wanted to do the same to her.

"Give me whatever those blokes are drinking," ordered Selena, stepping over to the dim bar.

The barmaid, whose rather pretty features were marred by the ravages of smallpox, seemed impressed.

"A cannonball, eh? You look a mite young, lad, for such poison, but it's your funeral."

She took a large mug and filled it halfway with beer. Then she added a good slug of rum, some brandy, and a bit of dry gin to top it off.

Selena gulped. She seldom drank anything stronger than brandy, and most of the time just wine.

"What's that accent?" inquired the barmaid in a not unfriendly way as she slid the mug across toward Selena. "Scots, eh? Don't hear a whole lot of that in these parts."

Selena had worked on her speech for a long time, and thought she'd been quite successful in achieving the diction and modulations of upper-crust English. Apparently, her roots were still evident to the common ear.

"Just askin'," said the barmaid in apology, reading offense in Selena's mildly startled expression. "Don't mean nothin' by it, lad."

Now she was starting to take a closer look at her new customer.

Selena lifted the mug, lowered her head, and letting the inadequate hatbrim partially conceal her face, sipped.

It was all she could do to keep from coughing as the strong, fiery concoction burned its way down her throat. The cannonball was not misnamed, at least not as to its effect.

Then Selena noted, on the wall next to the bar, a jumble of flyblown bills which had been posted there. A recent addition had been fastened above the others with a tack, and on it was her own likeness, or a close approximation thereof. The sketch artist had erred by depicting her oval-shaped face as rather square, but he had done well with her small, straight nose and strong, slightly rounded chin. Her high cheekbones and large, exotic eyes were done to perfection, however. It was Selena MacPherson all right, as the notice stated, and the price on her head had been raised to twenty-five hundred pounds sterling.

She wondered if Royce would be pleased, even as she realized that, for anyone present in the Nest of Feathers, twenty-five hundred pounds would constitute an unimaginable fortune.

"Damn fine drink, my girl," Selena said in the lowest voice she could manage.

"Aye! And much as I appreciate the compliment, I value cash as well."

"Oh. Oh, yes." Selena fumbled in her pocket for the notes Royce had given her. "British or American?"

"American, if it's all the same to you. We don't cater much to the English, a place like this."

That was good to hear. She could picture Lieutenant Oakley lumbering up the alley, his heavy body brushing against the bricks on either side.

She slid a bill across the bar.

"Hey!" exclaimed one of the men at the table. "You've got money, lad? Then come over here and join in a friendly little game of Black Pete."

Black Pete was a high-stakes game that Royce had taught her, although he'd beaten her every time. Still, being seated with a group of toughs would make her less vulnerable than standing alone at the bar. Moreover, the man who had hailed her, although roughly dressed in a collarless shirt with wide, horizontal red-and-white stripes and canvas jacket, did not seem unduly threatening. He had a broad, open face. His long, shoulder-length blond hair was partially held in place by a soiled, once-white headband.

"Come on over, lad," he invited again, his white teeth shining in the lamplight, "and bring your drink along. You won't regret it."

Selena must have appeared a little doubtful, because as the barmaid gave back change from the bill, she said, "It's all right if you don't bet too much. That's Jean Beaumain, a sailor. As long as you're not a woman, he'll pretty much leave you alone. But if you were a woman," she added with a sly wink, "I'm here as proof you wouldn't want him to."

"Sure, come on over and join the game," exclaimed another of the men heartily. They were all coarsely dressed, but not at all common. Their teeth were good, and they exuded a confident, vaguely reckless air.

Selena went over and sat down in the chair that Jean Beaumain had pulled out for her.

"Put your money on the table, boy," he said expansively. "What's your business? How'd you manage to find a dive like this?"

He gave her a close look then, and she noticed that the other men were staring too. She ducked her head, hiding behind the hatbrim again, and thinking of the jewels in one pocket, took some paper money out of the other, setting it on the table amidst the cards and mugs.

A big hand reached out suddenly and seized her wrist.

"What have we here?" he said slowly, in a playful, wondering voice. "A lady's hand? I do declare—" Then he looked her full in the face for a moment—she saw the undeniable glint of interest in his eyes—and yanked off her silly little hat.

All her golden hair spilled down.

Behind the bar, the tavernkeeper let out a gasp of astonishment. The men at the table were more appreciative.

"You've found yourself one for tonight, Cap'n," said a blackhaired young man with quick, intelligent eyes.

"You might just be right, Rafael. Now, young lady," Beaumain asked, with a proprietary hand on her shoulder, "how on earth did you have the good luck to know I was here?"

He was grinning, and with the way he looked her up and down, Selena was glad for the jacket that concealed her breasts. The barmaid had been right. Jean Beaumain's interest in women was genuine and most direct. Yet it was not mean or tawdry, however blatant his approach, and she noted, with considerable relief, that his eyes were friendly. She thought she saw, only for a moment, something in or behind his eyes that could not be interpreted, but the measure of his gaze bespoke primarily a man who had known many women, liked almost all of them, and who had been oft rewarded with reciprocal affection.

Selena almost felt that she could trust him.

In the next moment, she knew that she had to, because the barmaid helpfully yanked the poster down from the wall, brought it over, and threw it onto the table.

"Twenty-five hundred wonderful pounds!" she cried. "Now, there's six of us, so if we split evenly that means—"

"Pipe down, Liz," ordered Beaumain. "I'll see you get what you deserve." He turned toward Selena.

"It is really you, isn't it?"

She nodded.

"Tell me, how'd you get out of the fortress last night?"

"You know about that?"

"It's all over lower New York. Everybody's heard. You're a heroine. Why, I bet there's old women and little kids on their knees right now, praying that you'll escape."

There was no time left. Selena thought she heard heavy footfalls closing on the door.

"I'm asking for your help," she said quickly, glancing at the rest of them and settling her gaze on Beaumain. "Any moment now, Lieutenant Oakley of British Intelligence will come through that door to arrest me. He was following me up from the harbor roadway."

"Oakley!" said Beaumain. He spat on the floor. "We've been looking to put a little tar in his wings, haven't we, mates?"

The other men murmured in eager assent.

"Rafael, give me your pea jacket there. Louis, your hat. Hand it over. Quick." He gave the barmaid the little hat Selena had been wearing. "Liz, ditch this, will you?

"Now," he added, turning toward Selena and slipping the big coat over her shoulders, "there's just one thing. I never do something for nothing. What can you offer me in return for the aid I'm giving?"

Selena was hurriedly pushing her long hair up beneath Louis's high-domed headpiece.

"Money?" she asked.

"Ha, *hu!* I've got plenty of that. How about you spend the night aboard ship with me?"

The tavern door crashed open and Clay Oakley appeared, his powerful body outlined against the night.

"All right," Selena told Jean Beaumain, thinking: *I'll worry about that later.*

"Deal!" exulted the sailor, and when Oakley entered, he saw six men bent to their cards and the barmaid busy washing mugs.

"On your feet!" Oakley commanded those at the table. He was wheezing heavily; his face seemed scarlet in the light of the lamps and candles. "On your feet, by order of His Majesty George Third."

Nobody moved. Selena did not know what would happen. Slowly, Jean Beaumain stood up and walked over to the lieutenant. Selena kept her eyes averted, but peripherally she could see the sailor as he stood, hands on his hips, before the sputtering Englishman.

"I am French, as you know," he told Oakley. "Your sniveling monarch means nothing to me. What is the meaning of your intrusion?"

"I am looking for a spy. A woman. Selena MacPherson. Have you seen her?"

"I wouldn't tell you if I had, but go look around if you want to make a fool of yourself."

Oakley hesitated, and Selena guessed why. The lieutenant was alone, and he was far too astute to provoke a brawl, which in spite of his strength he could never hope to win.

"Is there a back room to this pit?" he demanded of the barmaid —a transparent ploy to salvage some small tatter of honor. "I'll look there."

Officiously, he disappeared momentarily into a curtained doorway behind the bar.

"You ought to clean up in there," he admonished Liz upon

reappearing. "It's a nest for rats, not feathers. Now all of you, at the table, I want to see your papers."

"No," said Beaumain, standing in his way. "We're not your subjects. We'll show you nothing."

Oakley moved forward. Jean Beaumain pushed him back. Livid, the lieutenant drew back one of his mighty arms. Beaumain closed fast, grabbing the other's solid torso. They scuffled. Something fell to the floor. Selena's glance informed her that it was Oakley's mustache. The lieutenant's one piece of hair was false, affixed to his upper lip by glue.

With a cry quite like anguish, the humiliated Englishman pulled back from Beaumain, retrieved his dinky prop, and backed hastily toward the door.

"Beaumain," he ordered, "if your ship does not leave the harbor at dawn, I will confiscate it."

"You haven't the right. I'm a private merchant. I—"

"Hah! We all know what you are. Nothing but a privateer. We've left you alone so far because, as far as we can tell, you haven't shipped contraband. But I can bring up charges and hold your ship here until you go broke!"

"That would take a long time. Longer, I'm afraid, than you British are going to *be* here. But no matter. I was planning to sail tomorrow anyway."

Oakley departed without closing the door. Beaumain kicked it shut. "Good evening!" he said.

His men applauded when their captain sat back down at the table.

"Thank you," Selena said, in admiration as well as gratitude.

"No, darling, you will do that later," he grinned. "Whose deal was it anyway?"

It was after midnight when they left the Nest of Feathers. Selena, whose mind had been occupied primarily with how to elude Beaumain, had played badly, losing all of the money that Royce had given her. She also suffered a mounting concern about him. Where was he now? What would he think, do, now that she was separated from him once again? Even worse, what if he had been captured?

"Do you think the barmaid will inform the British that she's seen me?" Selena asked Jean Beaumain, as she walked with him and the sailors down the narrow alley toward the harbor.

"No. I gave her my winnings tonight and I promised to spend a lot of time with her on my next trip to America. Liz is a good woman."

The way he said "good" made the sailors laugh.

They walked in a dark column down the darkened alley. Selena saw that there was no hope of slipping away. A cold wind had sprung up, coming down on them from the north, out of the wide Hudson valley. It struck with particular force when they left the alley and came out onto the Battery. Selena shivered, and Beaumain put his arm around her, patting her shoulder possessively through Rafael's heavy coat.

"Not long now, my love," he said.

They took a dinghy from dock to ship, and Selena climbed a rope ladder, boarding the *Liberté*.

Great, ocean-going ships had carried Selena in her time, and dismal freighters, river barges, three-masters, even rowboats on the Teviot River in Scotland long ago. But never had she been aboard a vessel like the *Liberté*. Every touch was just right. From the solid-oak decks to the teak railings, from the tall, imperial masts to the sleek, exquisite sweep of her hull, she was superb. Royce's *Selena* was larger, and possessed of more cannon, but the *Liberté* was built for poetry of flow upon the sea, for speed.

It was also built for comfort; Jean Beaumain was obviously a man who loved his pleasures and could afford them.

Selena's initial impression of him as being a forthright, good-natured merchant of the oceans was dispelled when he led her belowdecks—their companions had discreetly disappeared—through wide, glossily paneled gangways. Captain Jean Beaumain was—or appeared to be—a very wealthy man, and a highly unusual one. Most freighters were designed to provide their greatest space for cargo. Officers' quarters were generally small and Spartan. Crewmen, quite often mean, illiterate, and pugnacious, slept in hammocks or high-sided wooden boxes in spaces so grim and grimy they would have driven most animals mad. But aboard the *Liberté*, it seemed each officer, each crewman, had a cabin of his own. Selena judged that there could be very little hold space for cargo, given the lines of the ship. And however Beaumain presented himself to harbor officials at his ports of call, he was obviously no mere trafficker in common merchandise. His vessel gave no stench of transported slaves, nor the heavy reek of rum or molasses, nor the scents of hides or textiles, indigo or rice or hemp.

But even had Selena the impulse then to comment on these observations, she would have been forestalled. Because Beaumain, holding on to her hand, led her up a steep, short stretch of stairs, threw open a door, and ushered her into his quarters.

Privately, Selena admitted to a slight feeling of competitive dismay. The *Liberté*'s captain enjoyed a cabin more elegant than did Royce on the *Selena*. If the two ships clashed at sea, of course, there would be no contest. The *Selena* was more heavily armed by far. But in luxury, Selena had to admit that Beaumain's quarters were superior.

The cabin was situated below the ship's aft deck, above the rudder, and the view through three adjoining sections of small-paned windows gave one a great sense of height over the water. Writing desk and captain's chair stood near the windows, desk, chair, and all other furnishings of the finest mahogany. Next to the desk was a map table, on which was spread a projection of the entire earth. A globe rested on the table, and Selena noted that there were small red flags in similar locations on both map and globe. There was a small dining table as well, a sideboard, and a hammock hanging between two mighty timbers looked wide enough to sleep three. The hammock contained blankets of fur. There were rugs of bearskin, leopardskin and sealskin on the floor.

"Welcome, Selena," Beaumain said grandly. "I shall do my best to make your visit enjoyable."

That's what I'm afraid of, she thought, removing Rafael's coat and Louis's hat. Beaumain, swaggering a bit when he noticed Selena admiring his quarters, hung the garments on a peg on one of the beams, and rang a little bell that he lifted from his desk. Within seconds, a uniformed steward knocked on the door and entered.

"Yes, sir?" he asked, paying Selena no heed whatsoever. Female visitors aboard the *Liberté* did not, apparently, create much of a stir.

"We'll dine, shall we, Selena?" pronounced Beaumain. "Drinking always whets my appetites." She did not miss the plural. "Steward, bring us some beef stew, if you please. And champagne. We must have champagne."

"Right away, sir."

Beaumain sat down in his captain's chair, selected a long, black cigar from a humidor on the desk, and lit it lovingly, savoring the taste, sending her a disarming grin. She felt her guard lowering in spite of herself. Dammit, the man was immensely likable, and also very attractive. Moreover, he seemed in no hurry whatsoever to collect his due . . . which she had decided he was not going to get anyway.

"I heard about Erasmus Ward," he said. "I'm sorry."

"We are going to miss him. Do you support the revolution?"

He laughed in reply, blowing a thick, perfect ring of blue smoke, which rose to the curved ceiling of the cabin and melted into the dark timbers.

"No. I admire the Americans for their combative spirit, as much as I loathe the British for their contemptuous arrogance. But I am a man without politics. Selena, I'm forgetting my manners. You oughtn't to be standing. Here, take my chair. Or take a seat on the hammock."

He half-rose, but she waved him down. "I'm fine. I'll just"—she wandered over to the map table—"walk around. . . ."

The last thing she wanted to do was get trapped in that hammock!

"How can a person be without politics in times like these?" she asked. "Have you declared a plague on both their houses? You're French, aren't you? How do you feel about your own country?"

"France? She means nothing to me. She is simply the place where I was born."

"But . . . but your country has given us so much . . . General Lafayette, for example, who came to us in our hour of darkest need. And Comte de Grasse, who is sailing now from Haiti to aid Washington at Yorktown."

"Ah, Haiti!" Beaumain said lovingly.

"You are familiar with it?"

"That is where I make my home. Off the coast, that is. I own an island. St. Crique."

"You *own* an island?"

He laughed. "I took it for myself and so far no one has managed to get me off. But as for your Lafayette and de Grasse and the others, I spit on them!" He seemed genuinely angry. Selena was surprised. He did not appear to be a man easy to anger. "I despise them," he continued, puffing his cigar furiously now. "They are of the nobility that is destroying France."

Selena thought of this luxurious ship, and looked about the well-appointed cabin. "I would think," she observed, "that you are no stranger to the finer life yourself."

Jean Beaumain laughed again, but bitterly this time. "Not quite," he said. "I was born the son of a fisherman on the coast of the province of Côtes du Nord, hard by the English Channel. In our part of the country, everyone obeyed a certain *vicomte*, whose name is Chamorro"—the intensity with which he spoke this name sent shivers through Selena—"and woe betide him who did not. One had to pay him fifty percent of whatever one earned. You could not hold a job, not even the lowest, stinking sort of job, without his approval. A man could not even *marry* without his permission because, you see, the nobility in France are in league with the clergy. They have you nailed down and shut up tight from the moment of your birth until you are laid in the ground. It is a common practice, or did you know, for the clergy not to bury the dead until a grave tax has been paid."

"My God!" exclaimed Selena. Even when Scotland suffered under the British yoke, things had not been *that* horrendous. "But you are here, free—" she began.

They were interrupted by the steward, who entered with a steaming kettle of succulent beef stew and a bucket containing a jeroboam of champagne. He set it on the small dining table, also laying out glasses of cut crystal, fine bone china, heavy silver.

"Let us partake, Selena," Beaumain said, seating her.

Be careful, Selena warned herself. *Perhaps he is simply putting you off your guard with his talk*—interesting though it was to her. Or maybe there was a drug in the food or the wine.

No, hardly the wine. Before her eyes, the steward uncorked the wine with a resounding pop, poured some into both glasses, and withdrew.

Beaumain himself ladled stew onto Selena's plate, then onto his own, and began to eat with relish.

So did she. From the first mouthful, all other considerations were subjugated to an overwhelming, resurgent hunger. The bread, hardtack, and cheese that she'd shared with Royce, good as they had been in comparison to prison fare, could not come close to this stew. The chunks of beef were juicy, butter-soft. Potatoes, onions, carrots, and peas complemented the meat, and the champagne teased her palate.

Go slow, go slow. . . .

Yet she had to eat, to drink—the cannonball she'd wisely left mostly untouched at the Nest of Feathers—and it had always been thus. Sometimes to her chagrin—the plum pie for example— but more often to her satisfaction, Selena indulged her appetites. She saw the wisdom in the ancient country air: ". . . there be no drinkin' in the grave."

Nor anything else.

"So what will you do with me," she heard herself asking, filled to satiety and bold with the wine, "after you've taken your debt?"

Beaumain wiped his mouth with a napkin and looked at her with amused appraisal.

"You're certainly welcome to remain aboard. We sail for the Caribbean in the morning."

Haiti. Of course. And Royce was planning to sail to the Caribbean soon as well.

But he would now—she reasoned—be making his way to the *Selena* in Newport. He would probably expect her, if she could, to join him there.

"I had really planned to go to Newport," she said lightly. "Perhaps you could take me there?"

"You don't know how you'll feel about that at dawn, now, do you?"

He had the male look in his eyes now, powerfully.

"Tell me more about this Chamorro whom you mentioned earlier," she said, buying time.

Once again, the man's mere name stirred Beaumain. Selena saw clearly in his eyes what she'd sensed at the tavern: something vulnerable, haunted, and ruined. It was startlingly out of character, given his bearing and charm. But it was there.

"Yes . . ." he said slowly, his concupiscence for the moment ebbing. "Well, Vicomte Chamorro was, in every way, our lord and master. But I was something of a renegade from the time I was a boy. By young manhood, no risk was too great. I set fire to the priest's house when he refused to bury my penniless grandmother.

I stole freely from the gardens and orchards of Chamorro's château. I lied about the size of my fishing catch, saved the money, and began to make plans of my own.

"And I was never caught. *I* was never caught. But once, in my absence, Chamorro and his men came to our house. They accused my father—who knew nothing about what I'd done—of falsifying the catch. He denied it and begged for mercy, but they cut off his ears and his nose, and came hunting for me.

"But, learning of this, I gathered friends of mine from Côtes du Nord who felt as I did, and commandeered one of Chamorro's sloops. He has a great fleet of ships; he is a merchant prince. Using this small ship, we surprised one of his merchantmen just as it was entering the channel, took the ship, then took and sold everything aboard. It was the foundation of my fortune."

Selena felt pleased at the way he had ended his story, but Jean Beaumain seemed gloomy. Perhaps the maiming of his father—she recalled the impunity with which Oakley had threatened to slit her face—was a wound that could never be erased. *That burden would explain,* she thought then, *his haunted look in repose.*

"I can never return to France," he said. "Not that I care. Chamorro is alive and powerful, and my father is dead. I will settle with Chamorro in due course . . . but for now I am sometimes a privateer, sometimes an outright pirate, and occasionally—as on this trip to America—I am a legitimate shipper of ivory and spices and furs."

He still seemed downcast. Selena arose from the table and walked about the cabin, wandering over to the map table.

"What are all these red flags for?" she asked.

He looked up. "Those are the locations at which Chamorro has been sighted."

Selena looked at the flags again. Morocco. Zanzibar. Cape Hatteras. Cape Horn. New Zealand. Nippon. And she began to realize that the big, usually good-humored Beaumain, the French peasant lad become a millionaire, was driven by some tremendous desire to track his nemesis to the edges of the world.

She did not understand then, not completely, just why this should be true. Nor could she, with his origins and apparent unconcern for his homeland's political fate, be sure he could conceive of her own desire to return to Coldstream Castle.

"Now," said Jean Beaumain, arising from the table and casting aside his lugubrious reverie, "the night still holds pleasures for us."

He came quickly across the floor and took her in his arms. "Give us a kiss."

He slipped his big arms around her, began to wrestle playfully, seeking her lips. She was still wearing the boy's jacket that Penrod had given her, and was afraid that Beaumain would feel the bag of jewels and sovereigns in her pocket. Best to take it off. Yet the thin shirt she wore beneath the jacket afforded scant concealment, and Jean was unlikely to be gentled by the outline of her breasts and nipples beneath the fabric.

Still, it would give her a moment to think. He said he didn't want money; he wanted *her*.

But would one of the jewels buy him off?

Considering that, she said, "Let me hang up my coat at least?"

His answer was a grin of delight. He let her go.

"Of course. Hang everything up, if you like."

She slipped out of her jacket and, to her mild surprise, he reached up and extinguished the big glass-chimneyed lantern by which the cabin was illuminated. She heard him undressing as she found a peg for her coat. She stood there, unmoving.

"Selena?"

"Mr. Beaumain," she replied formally, "I know I owe you a debt of gratitude—"

"You surely do, madame."

"And I wonder if there isn't some way . . . some *other* way . . . that I can repay—"

"Hey! A deal's a deal," he chortled, tracking her by the sound of her voice and embracing her again. He was naked and ready. And strong.

"What?" he asked, lifting her into the air and swinging her up and onto the hammock. "You've still got your clothes on. We can't have that. . . ."

Seeking her lips with his own, he tore open the filmy shirt and started to tug at her breeches, laughing happily as he did so. Obviously, he was one of those men who thoroughly enjoy sex in the sporting sense. It wasn't serious at all for him, or darkly passionate, or possessed of great meaning. For him it was fun, as a toy might be to a boy.

Just as obviously, given his forthright nature, he felt that her protests were mere coyness, adding to the fun.

"Please, Selena," he said, "I can't wait."

It was like dealing with a big, happy, overgrown child eager to arrive early at a county fair.

He had one hand inside her breeches now and he'd found her mouth. She resisted, and kept on resisting, but to her amazement Selena found herself liking the kiss. Probably because it was almost impossible not to like him, even under these circumstances, she had trouble finding words to dissuade him. During the struggle she continued to offer, her hand closed around him. He gasped, relaxed, and loosened his grip on her.

"Oh, Selena, that's—"

Good. She stroked and caressed him, lightly, quickly, up and down, now and then pausing at the end to bestow a special squeeze.

"Oh, Selena, stop—"

But she didn't, and very soon his great excitement and need gathered force, sending vast pulsing showers into the air.

"Give me a moment, Selena," he said lazily, snuggling next to her, "and then we'll—"

"But this is all I can do."

"What?"

"Just now," she said. "At this time."

"Oh, I *understand!*" he said, after a pause. "Why didn't you tell me?"

This was as good a time as any, Selena thought, to try another ploy. He was temporarily—all too temporarily, she feared—sated by her expert ministrations, and sympathetic as well.

"I have to tell you that I'm . . . betrothed," she said. "I've promised myself to another."

Jean didn't like that, and there was even a bit of jealousy in his voice when he asked, "Who?"

"Royce Campbell," she told him.

Long pause. "Royce Campbell, the gunrunner?"

Royce is much more than that, she wanted to tell him. But she held her tongue. Jean was the kind of man who believed all women should put him first in line, as if it were simply the nature of things.

"Royce and I were trying to slip out of the city when we were separated tonight. Now I must find a way to go and meet him in Newport."

Beaumain was silent, miffed at this turn of events.

"You love him?" he asked finally.

"Oh, yes, more than anything."

"I've heard a great deal about him. The man would do *anything* to turn a dollar."

"That's not true. The aid he's given the revolutionaries cannot be measured in money."

"I'll bet," Beaumain replied scornfully. "But, look, I will tell you one thing. Jean Beaumain does not need a woman who favors another. There are all too many who favor him!"

"I know there are. You're a very desirable man, and a gentle one too."

He leaned up on an elbow and looked at her in the waning darkness. It was close to dawn now, and outside the *Liberté*, first faint rays of day were lancing upward into the eastern sky. "Is that what you really think?" he asked.

"Yes," said Selena truthfully, but aware too that things were beginning to work to her advantage. "If I weren't in love with Royce, it would be difficult not to be smitten by you."

Those words pleased him. "Is that right?" he asked. "Is that right? Well, how do you plan to get to Newport, then?"

Selena decided that it wouldn't hurt to try. "I was hoping I could persuade you to take me there."

He laughed. "You're a woman filled with hope. But I must return to St. Crique."

"It won't take long. Only a few days' sail."

"If the wind is good."

"I'll pay you well."

"Hah! What will you pay me with, pray tell?"

Selena slipped out of the hammock, went to her jacket, found the pouch and withdrew one of the jewels. She held it in the dim light coming through the windows. A sapphire, blue and exotic at dawn.

"This," she declared, walking back to the hammock and handing it to him.

He examined it carefully while Selena fastened the few shirt buttons he hadn't torn off, and slipped back into her jacket. When she looked at Jean again, he was still in the hammock, studying the gem, and she saw, around his waist and along the back of his shoulders, shadowy markings on his skin. Possibly these were tattoos, but she could not see clearly, and when he noticed her looking at him, he immediately pulled a fur covering over him.

She thought it odd, because otherwise there didn't seem to be an ounce of inhibition in his more than two hundred pounds.

"Where did you get this?"

"Royce gave it to me."

Beaumain drew the wrong conclusion. "You mean to tell me you'd try to buy me with the gift of your betrothed. Do you think I would take such a thing?

"Shame!" he added, for good measure. "I am not a man like that. I shall take you to Newport, Selena, for nothing, simply because I like you. Now what do you say to that?"

Before she could reply—actually she had a strong impulse to kiss him—there was a peremptory pounding on the door.

"Cap'n! Cap'n!"

"Yes, what is it?"

"There's a boat rowing over toward us from the fortress. It's filled with redcoats. I think they're plannin' on boarding us, maybe for a search."

"God *damn!*" cried Jean Beaumain, leaping from the hammock. Selena noticed that he kept his torso and shoulders covered as he slipped into his breeches, and put his jacket on in such a manner that she had no further glimpse of what she thought she'd seen on his skin.

"Wake all the men and have them come on deck," Beaumain ordered the messenger. "Selena," he said, looking directly into her eyes, "this might be a routine episode of harassment. It happens with the British. But they might also be looking for you."

"Isn't there someplace I can hide?"

"I'm trying to think. . . . This is not a large ship; we haven't that much hold space. . . . Wait, there is one chance. Are you afraid of heights?"

"No . . . I don't think—"

Without a word, he hustled her up on deck, took her to the mainmast, and told her to climb. Before the British drew close, Selena was curled like a cat in the tiny basket at the top of the mast that was called a crow's nest. Atop this perch, sentries scanned the horizon for storms or sails, friendly flags or quarry.

Fires of Delight 79

The climb hadn't bothered her; she was too intent on hiding from the British. But now, looking down, the deck of the *Liberté* appeared as small as a toy dropped from a cloud, and each gentle ripple of water that washed the ship's hull seemed to sway the crow's nest wildly from side to side.

From her precarious aerie, Selena saw the British longboat draw closer and closer, soldiers sweating at the oars, Lieutenant Clay Oakley standing magisterially at the bow. Beaumain's men were lined up at the *Liberté*'s rail. She saw that they carried arms, as did Oakley and the soldiers.

"Stand aside. We are coming aboard!" declared Oakley, his deep, chilling voice booming out over the stillness of the dawn harbor. His tension showed, however; he was holding his scented handkerchief, occasionally breathing into it.

"State your business," Beaumain demanded coolly.

"I have reason to believe that the escaped spy, Selena MacPherson, is aboard your ship."

The boat had drawn up next to the hull of the *Liberté;* the redcoats had brought along ropes and grappling hooks. They were in no mood to be dissuaded.

"I'm sorry, but Selena is not here," said Jean, mocking Oakley with his laugh. "Whyever did you think it?"

"Don't lie to me, Beaumain. I returned last night to the Nest of Feathers after you had departed, and had a long chat with the barmaid, one Liz Randall. She knows you well, I was informed. A strategic, and I regret to admit, painful application of thumbscrews elicited the information that you and the MacPherson woman left the tavern together."

"You loathsome bastard!" cried Jean. "Is Liz all right?"

"She won't be using her hands much for a time, but it could have been worse. Now, about Selena?"

"She's not here," answered Jean. "She gave me the slip, I'm afraid."

"I don't believe you."

Jean's voice dripped with sarcasm. "If she could escape from your prison, it might just be possible for her to get out of other binds as well."

The lieutenant, who was again sporting his fake mustache, laughed heavily, mirthlessly. "Even so, we are coming aboard."

"Suit yourself."

Selena cowered in the crow's nest while Oakley and the British searched Jean's sleek ship from bow to stern, once and twice and then again. Not once did any of Beaumain's men so much as glance up toward her perch, and she thought with gratitude how fine was their mettle and how praiseworthy their loyalty to him. There was a sense of fraternity aboard this vessel that impressed her, and she wondered if the ship's name had anything to do with the cross she wore around her neck.

She would ask him about it.

Finally, reluctantly, the lieutenant gave up in humiliation, a chagrin that deepened in the laughter with which the French sailors bid him farewell.

"In due time," called Oakley, as the boat drew away from the *Liberté*. "In due time we shall meet again, Beaumain, my friend."

"I'm looking forward to the pleasure," a cocky Jean shouted back.

Then he gave the order to set out. The anchor was weighed, sails were unfurled, and the rudder swung into position. Everywhere beneath Selena, great white flapping wings of sail reached out and caught the morning breeze. The *Liberté* began to move slowly out upon the harbor, then down through the Narrows into the thunderous Atlantic and the wild sea lanes of the western world. She stood up in the crow's nest, and waved to Jean Beaumain who was watching her from the deck. But she did not want to come down just yet, beset as she was by a mingling of sadness and exhilaration. She would soon be leaving America, perhaps forever, and a part of her soul would always be here. But there were journeys ahead, and as the wind stung her face, as ropes creaked and sails rippled, she felt almost drunk with the promise of the future.

Then the *Liberté* slashed out upon the high sea, all sight of land gone now, flying effortlessly before the wind with the preternatural speed for which she was fashioned, taking Selena to Royce.

4 Obsession

"Here, let me give you back your love-stone," said Jean Beaumain, handing Selena the sapphire. It was late afternoon. They stood together on the *Liberté*'s plunging bow. The wind had been steady and strong all day; soon they would cut past the eastern tip of Long Island and turn northward toward Newport. It had occurred to Selena that she might well arrive there before Royce. Wouldn't he be surprised to see her though!

"The gem is yours if you want it," she told him.

But he shook his head and pressed it into her hand.

"It is a gift from someone else to you," he said soberly. "I cannot accept it."

So serious was he that she regretted misleading him.

"Royce Campbell must have done exceedingly well as a revolutionary," Jean observed, with a slight edge to his voice. "Much better than most, I'd estimate."

The comment troubled Selena a little. Jean was referring to one small stone. Royce had somehow acquired an entire cache.

"How much money does Campbell have?"

"I really do not know."

"I bet I have more."

"That may well be. Does it matter?"

"It might. But that is really not my point. I'm very attracted to you, Selena, as you must know. And, let me be bold, I care about you. I may not have learned as much as I ought to have in my time, but I haven't missed everything. And one of the things I've observed is that people really do not change greatly. Oh, they can acquire skill in presenting various facades, and seem to be what they are not—"

"Do you mean anything specific?"

Jean paused, looked out at the ocean for a moment, then turned back to her. "Selena, Royce Campbell once had a savage reputation throughout the world. On every ocean, he was known as a ruthless plunderer. I confess that I have never met the man, but the oft-repeated weight of testimony holds that he was once a reckless adventurer, even a charlatan—"

"That he was," she admitted, "once."

"So. And what I am saying is that he may still *be!* What I am saying is that perhaps you ought to examine things more carefully before you pledge yourself irredeemably—"

"You are making me angry!" she snapped, a little surprised at the sudden fire that brought those words forth. She *knew* Royce was not as Jean claimed him, possibly, to be. So why ought she ruffle her feathers?

Beaumain retreated. "Well, perhaps you will introduce me to the man when we reach Newport?"

Selena was about to reply, crisply, that, yes, she would, she would indeed, and then he could judge for himself and see how ridiculous his insinuations were, but high above them the sentry in the crow's nest let out a great shout. At first Selena did not understand, but he called it again.

"Chaaaamooorrro!"

In a flash, Beaumain was gone from her side, scrambling up the mainmast to have a look himself. She watched him climbing, saw in his taut body and tense, excited features the hint of a person she did not know. It was as if one man lived inside another, waiting to be awakened and called forth by one word: *Chamorro.* That the *vicomte* had treated Jean's father with unspeakable cruelty could not be denied, but there was in the sailor's desire for revenge an element of surpassing and unnatural dedication, quite like the quest for an unholy grail.

Watching from the deck, it looked to Selena as if Jean were pushing the sentry out of the tiny perch. He grabbed the spyglass from the man, who slipped from the crow's nest and clung to the mast, and scanned the eastern horizon.

"It is he!" Beaumain cried in savage delight. "All hands to the sails!"

Almost all of the men were already on deck, having been alerted by the sentry's call, and Selena caught sight of Rafael, gazing upward at his leader with an expression that could not conceal a measure of anguish. She went over to the man. There seemed to be no actual rank aboard the *Liberté,* one man was as worthy as the next, but the lean, dark, taciturn Rafael appeared to serve as Beaumain's alter ego and aide-de-camp.

"What is happening?" she asked him. "I thought we were sailing to Newport?"

"Forget Newport," he said quietly, shaking his head and looking at her with sympathy. "It is out of the question now, because we pursue Chamorro."

"Raise the flag!" Jean ordered then. Selena had thought it odd that, up until now, Beaumain had not flown a banner. But she was far more bewildered by the sight of the ensign itself, a huge, blood-red piece of silk upon which, diagonally from top left to bottom right, were the shapes of three creatures in white: a camel, an elephant, and a serpent coiled, ready to spring.

"What does the banner signify?" she asked Rafael.

He lifted his shoulders, a small shrug. "Of all God's lower creations," he said, "those three remember forever people who have done them ill, and they will wait for the right time to take retribution. The camel is mean by nature. We all know about the elephant. And in certain parts of the world, the snake is even used to accomplish the revenge of one human being upon another. An article of clothing is stolen from the victim, and placed inside a cage or wire basket with the snake. Then the basket is placed over a low fire. The snake remembers the pain of the fire and the smell of the clothing—it might be a scarf, or a glove, or just a cravat—and then he is set free in the quarters of the victim. It is deadly, and quick. There is no escape."

Selena shuddered. Jean Beaumain, for all his good humor and frank directness, was being consumed from within by satanic passion.

Yet she had to admit, retribution was something that she had also sought, and on occasion she had obtained it. Few things in her life had given as much satisfaction as slitting Darius McGrover's throat.

"Some of us also need revenge," Rafael continued, as if reading her thoughts. "It may be that we are among God's lower creatures too."

Quickly, Selena analyzed her predicament. There appeared to be no way that she could rejoin Royce now—already the *Liberté* was slashing full sail eastward into the Atlantic—and there were mundane matters that demanded attention.

"Rafael," she said, "these are the only clothes I have." She gestured toward the togs Penrod had given her. "Is there something else, perhaps more suitable, on board?"

He inspected her inadequate costume. "There are some bolts of fabric in the hold, I think. Do you sew?"

"I am neither designer nor couturier, but I have done most everything in my time. I could at least try."

"All right," he agreed, "I will bring you what you need. But for the time being, come with me."

To Selena's surprise, he took her back into Jean Beaumain's cabin, opened a door which she had not previously noticed, and led her into a surprisingly spacious wardrobe. Jean's clothing hung there on wooden hangers, and next to his belongings were dozens of dresses and expensive gowns.

"Whose are these?" Selena asked.

"I do not wish to say, but take several. They will be of use while you prepare your own."

"But Jean will notice that I am wearing them. Maybe it would be better not to."

Rafael shook his head sadly. "As long as we are in pursuit of Chamorro, my friend will notice nothing."

With a vague feeling of guilt, and something else that she soon recognized as jealousy—for she had, against her wishes, developed a certain proprietary regard toward Jean—she inspected the garments. They belonged to a rather tall woman apparently, but what seemed unusual was that they were of two vastly different types. Half were expensive, elegant, slinky and deliberately provocative, with long slits running up the skirts, bodices plunging toward the navel. The others were well-made, but modest of design, garments of subdued color and pattern. She chose two of the latter, one of pale-blue linen with a floral print, another of solid burgundy cotton, well-made and eminently serviceable. She also selected the least provocative of the other type, a white silk, flowing garment, high in the throat and tight at the waist, that exuded the scent of some rare and disquieting fragrance.

"Best return these when you have no further use for them," Rafael suggested. "Now, there is an empty cabin amidship on the port side, where you can live and work."

"Fine. Thank you so much."

"I am doing it for you, but also for my friend. I do not know how long you will be with us, but I think that you will be good for him."

Selena appreciated the compliment, and said so.

Rafael took her to the cabin, which was small but cool, and later brought a bolt of navy-blue silk, scissors, needles, thread, and thimble.

Outside, on deck, the chase was going on, through the afternoon and into the gentle evening. All hands were in the sails, milking every morsel of speed from the taut, aching white sheets of canvas. Selena lay for a while on the small hammock in her new quarters, thinking of Royce, trying to send her thoughts to him through the invisible air. Somehow, these thoughts must reach him; he must come to her. But try as she might, concentrating, listening with an intensity so fervent she thought her heart might break, no hint of a message came from him to her.

Finally she arose, and before settling down to the unfamiliar and painstaking task of making a dress for herself, she tried on the other three.

The two conservative garments fit her a bit loosely, but were exceedingly comfortable and—she thought—handsome. The white gown, however, was quite different. While it fit her perfectly, it gave her the unsettling feeling of being encased in ice, or a shroud, a most disquieting, alien, yet strangely compelling sensation. The longer she wore it, the more she felt that way, less discomfited than bewildered.

So she took it off and set to work.

She had decided to make a blue dress based on the pattern of the burgundy-colored one that she had selected, but the task proved even more tedious than she had imagined, and by twilight she had scarcely begun. Fatigued and suddenly very hungry, she debated for a moment, decided that she needed something dramatic to lift her spirits, slipped back into the white dress, and went up on deck.

The mysterious, compelling, uninterpretable sensation returned directly she had put on the dress.

Jean was no longer in the crow's nest, but standing on the bow of the *Liberté* as it knifed silently, remorselessly, at incredible speed through the water. He did not appear to recognize her.

"Here, Landa," he said, or something that sounded like

"Landa"—she guessed it was some obscure form of address from the Côtes du Nord—"have a look through the spyglass."

He handed her the instrument through which he had been peering, so excited that he almost dropped it. Selena held it in both hands, found the quarry on the far horizon, and adjusted the powerful magnification.

She saw a large three-master of white or whitish-gray—the multihued twilight made it difficult to tell for certain—perhaps five miles ahead of the *Liberté*. All of her sails were out, and she too was travelling at great speed, but it was clear to Selena that Jean Beaumain was gaining.

"I have him this time!" he exulted, in that strange world of his obsession. "It is a Beaumain wind for sure. By dawn he will be under my guns."

"What will happen then?" she asked hesitantly.

"Why, when Chamorro sees that he cannot outrun me, he will swing about to fight. But I have more cannon and better cannoneers. Then if, God willing, he lives through the shelling, I will board his ship and take my trophies."

"What trophies?"

"Oh, Landa, you know, you *know!* Don't trouble me now, all right?

"Beaumain wind," he repeated, talking to himself, "please, God, Beaumain wind . . ."

He was in another world. Selena gave back the spyglass and stepped away from him in fascinated dread.

"Is he all right?" she asked Rafael, who had been watching the two of them.

"As well as can be expected. It is like a fever."

Selena hoped it was a fever she never caught; it was too primordial, too all-consuming.

Rafael had ordered the ship's cook to bring food from the galley and up on deck, so that the sailors might remain close to their work. There was a long night ahead. He settled down next to Selena, seated against the railing. They ate peppery swordfish chowder, black bread and butter, and each drank a mug of rum-spiked tea.

"If there is a battle," she asked somewhat anxiously, "what do you think the outcome will be?"

"All I know is that it will be a fight to the finish."

"Are you eager for it?"

"Not for myself, but for Jean. We have all made a vow to him. The depravities of Chamorro must be ended, and Jean's soul put at peace."

That sounded reasonable enough to Selena, from what she'd learned about Chamorro, but there was also something called the peace of the grave. It did not sound at all satisfying to her.

Finishing her meal, drinking another mug of rum and tea, she began to feel as she had when she'd first donned the dress, enclosed, different, somehow disembodied and exalted at the same time. A certain languor crept through her body as well, which she at first attributed to the rum, exceedingly pleasant and . . . strikingly familiar. With a start, against all reason, Selena realized that she was becoming physically aroused. Realization fueled the condition, and in another moment the fire of need burned in her loins.

What is this? she wondered, her mind working even as her body wavered.

It was dark now, and she glanced to see if Rafael had noticed anything.

She could see his eyes from the flickering light of the deck lanterns, and was stunned to observe the expression in them. His eyes were hard on hers, inviting, suggestive, alive with the brew of evil and night.

Before she could speak or move, his arms were around her. His mouth hunted for her lips, up her throat, across her burning cheek, and she felt his hands at her breasts.

Yet even as she experienced these things, and savored the sensations attendant upon them, she saw the two of them as if from above, as if she were standing outside herself, looking down and laughing.

"Rafael!" she gritted, as with all her strength she twisted away from him and leaped to her feet.

He stared up at her for a moment. "What happened, Selena?" he asked then, embarrassed. "My God, I didn't mean . . . I'm sorry."

"I don't know what happened either," she answered truthfully. They separated in considerable puzzlement. Selena went back to her cabin.

Yet the feeling of passion, the need for satisfaction, not only lingered but increased. Selena lit a lamp, paced from door to porthole and back again, fighting an overwhelming need to put her hands upon herself. Presently, a demon, a beguiling satyr, the image of Royce Campbell slipped naked into her mind. It was as if her hands were upon him, he inside her, the pressure building. In a torment of heat and need, she pulled off the white dress.

And instantly began to regain her equilibrium.

Selena was not a woman who had ever felt uncomfortable with passion. She had, ever since coming to know physical love, savored it, sought it, invented ways to heighten its delight.

But this time the sensations had been wildly different, more than simple abandonment, bordering on the corrupt and depraved.

The dress.

She had thrown it carelessly onto her hammock, and there it lay now, white and deadly, appearing almost to move, almost to be alive in the flickering light of the lamp.

It had to be the dress.

Yet what was the garment but pieces of silk sewn together in order to enhance the female form? A dress, discounting particulars of fabric, workmanship, and expense, was only a dress.

Wasn't it?

Gingerly, she picked it up, and although her fingers touched only silk, the garment transmitted to her the aura of some sleek, living thing. It was like stroking a lazy cat and feeling the crackle of static electricity on one's fingertips.

Experimentally, Selena ran her hands over the fabric of the two other dresses.

Nothing.

Then she again picked up the white gown and began to examine it thoroughly, even turning it inside out. Running her hands along the stitching, she found, at the hem, a small, curious piece of embroidery.

A dot and a circle within an elongated oval. Selena did not know what to think. The embroidery, moreover, was amateurishly done, not remotely comparable to the worksmanship of the dress itself.

Upon inspection, neither of the other dresses possessed this symbol.

Yet how could a few stitches of thread explain the powerful but inappropriate physical sensations she'd experienced while wearing the gown?

Selena knew, intellectually, that they couldn't. Yet they had. The lessons of Davi the Dravidian returned to her again: *"There are mysteries in this world far deeper than mind can ever plumb."*

She did not want the dress in her presence any longer, so slipping into the burgundy garment, Selena left her cabin, proceeded to Jean's quarters, and returned the white gown to its hanger in the wardrobe.

As she left the chamber, swinging the door shut, she was certain that she heard—subliminally, as if in another dimension—a sound of laughter. The laughter had a musical quality to it, outwardly pleasant, unthreatening, as if a good joke had just been played on Selena. Yet beneath this ostensible amiability, there was also an inexplicable, fathomless malice, a mocking, triumphant spite.

Awakening on the following morning, Selena knew at once that Jean Beaumain's wind—or his god—had failed him. As she lay there in the hammock, covered by blankets, the cabin tilted first to port, then to starboard, in addition to the pitching, plunging motion of the *Liberté* herself. Glancing out the porthole, she saw roiling, gray-black clouds, heard the cold, angry howl of a storm wind.

On deck, Rafael handed her a raincape, apologized again for what had happened on the previous evening, and bade her keep her hands either on the railing or on the ropes that, for safety's sake, had been strung from stem to stern. The seas were quite heavy, but the ship was in no danger, at least not yet. Clouds and mist, however, had diminished visibility to less than half a mile. Selena smelled rain.

"Chamorro weather," commented Rafael resignedly. "The man has the very devil's luck."

Jean Beaumain's nemesis had disappeared into the mountainous folds of driving waves, the valleys of spume-flashing mist.

"Where is Jean?" she asked.

"At the bow, as he has been all night. He won't move. He is drenched and shivering; the men and I fear he will become ill."

"Would you see to it," Selena asked, "that hot tea and food are brought to his cabin? I'll see if I can convince him to go below."

Rafael gladly agreed. Holding on to the ship's railing, Selena made her way slowly to the bow of the ship. All except two small sails had been furled, and these were merely to give the vessel a bit of stability and maneuverability in the rising wind. All hope of pursuit was over, yet this fact had not seemed to dawn on Jean.

"Landa?" he said doubtfully, glancing briefly at Selena as she stepped up beside him.

He seemed to have aged ten years in the space of a night, and Selena was instantly alarmed. She had to persuade him to take shelter. Spray from the waves, which even as she stood there washed up over the prow and soaked her feet, had drenched him to the bone. His blond hair was matted, pressed to his head like a skullcap. His clothing, even the raincape, stuck to his flesh. And his fatigued breathing came in labored snorts, sending white clouds of vapor into the air.

Still, he held the spyglass and peered off toward the horizon, where he had last seen Chamorro's ship.

"Give it up for now," Selena said gently, slipping close to him and putting an arm around his waist.

"But he's there! He's out there! Here—" He handed her the spyglass. "Look!"

She accepted the glass but lowered it to her side. "No, he's not there, not now, and neither of us can see him anymore."

"Yes, he is!" Jean maintained, trying to grab the spyglass. She held it out of reach and used her body to force him away from the bow railing and back along the deck. He took one step, then another.

"I must remain here and watch him," Jean protested vaguely. "He is a master of ruse and deceit. I cannot let him out of my sight, now he is so close to me."

Rafael and Louis and several other sailors were watching silently near the base of the mainmast, mutely applauding her efforts.

Fires of Delight **91**

"Chamorro can't go anywhere in this storm," she explained patiently. "When the weather clears, he'll be right there on the horizon as before. No ship is as fast as yours. We'll overtake him."

She knew, of course, that a storm can blow ships helter-skelter. There was no way whatever of predicting where the *Liberté* or Chamorro might end up. But Jean's vengeful fever underlay his need to believe.

"Yes, he'll be right there when the clouds roll away, won't he?" There was a light of renewed hope in his eyes.

"Yes, he will," Selena affirmed.

She walked him as far as the main gangway, where Rafael came to her aid. Together they managed to get Jean belowdecks and to his cabin. He looked around his quarters as if he had never seen them before, as if map table, compass, sextant, charts, all of these things were artifacts of some ancient, long-dead civilization. It was while trying to help him wrestle free of the sodden raincape that Selena realized Jean was burning with fever.

"Get me towels and blankets right away," Selena told Rafael. "And compresses to put on his forehead. Bring some rum as well; it can't hurt."

"Landa, Landa . . ." muttered Jean, as Selena slipped off his rain-soaked shirt . . . and cried out in horror.

Branded into his flesh, across the width of his broad shoulders, was the name

CHAMORRO

And around his waist was an angry scarlet strip, four inches high, where his skin had been torn away. The wound was like a livid, perpetual scab, more evil-looking than the branded letters. This was the reason Jean had, while dressing yesterday, shielded himself from her. He bore the marks of a shame that he felt must be concealed.

He was too delirious now, however, to notice or care that she saw him. Selena managed to get him to the hammock, and when he lay down in it, she yanked off his boots and peeled away the sopping breeches, aware even as she labored of his powerful body and splendid manhood.

Rafael came in with towels and blankets. Together they rubbed him down thoroughly and covered him with blankets and furs. Only after Selena had placed a cold compress on Jean's burning forehead did she ask, "However did he come by those terrible wounds?"

"We do not speak of it," the man replied. "He will tell you if he chooses."

If he gets well, Selena hoped. To the disorienting influence of his quest for revenge, Jean Beaumain had now added an acute, debilitating affliction of the body.

"I'll stay and watch over him," Selena decided, taking off her raincape and hanging it on a peg. "I'm sure you and the men will have enough work contending with the storm."

Gratefully, Rafael agreed.

The storm continued to build in ferocity throughout that day, and Jean's fever raged on as well. Rafael had turned the ship into the wind, every sail furled now, and the *Liberté* was nothing more than a chip of kindling on the mighty deep. It was all but impossible to remain standing in the tossing cabin, so Selena crawled into the swaying hammock with Jean, occasionally rising to replace his sweat-soaked bedding or to fetch a cool, fresh compress. He passed alternately through spells of troubled sleep or vocal delirium, most of it meaningless to her.

"The flowers are lovely, Marguerite," he said once, "they add so much." And later, "Landa, Landa, give it to me now, that way, as before, that's right, that way, don't stop and never stop. . . ."

Selena, no stranger to the way men carried on during high flights of passion, began to suspect the existence of a woman named Marguerite, whom Jean apparently also referred to as "Landa."

Once again, as had happened when she'd seen all those dresses in Jean's wardrobe, Selena felt a twinge of jealousy. She could not help but feel attracted to this bold man, and touched by his passionate quest. But after all, here she was, caring for him during a time of danger and need, and he was raving on about *someone else!*

Don't be silly, she chided herself. *You've only just met him. You know almost nothing about him at all. And Royce will always be the only one for you.*

Somehow, though, the thought of another woman still rankled. She recalled her early infatuation with Royce Campbell. After they'd met at the Edinburgh Christmas ball, she hadn't seen him again for a whole year, and for a whole year she dreamed of their kiss on the windy balcony above the North Sea. He'd sailed off to sea somewhere, and she'd gone back to Coldstream and school and all the rounds and rituals of daily life. But she was certain that he held her as vividly in his mind as she held him, and to say that she was looking forward to the next Christmas ball would have been only one-tenth of one percent of the truth.

When the holiday season came, she and her family journeyed to Edinburgh by coach and took up quarters in the palace. She learned that Royce had also arrived; she bribed a chambermaid to discover the location of his suite and proceeded thereto.

Her hand was on the door handle and she heard the click of the mechanism as she depressed it; she felt the door move as she pushed it inward. Her eyes adjusted to an odd dimness in the room. *Sir Royce, it's Selena. I was so happy to learn of your arrival and I wanted to renew our acquaintance. . . .* But the room was dim because the heavy draperies had been drawn in mid-morning, but why? *Sir Royce, I wanted to renew—*

"Yes? Who is it?" he snapped.

Selena started, her eyes still adjusting to the gloom. There, in a canopied bed next to the fireplace, was Royce Campbell. He was sitting upright and looking at her. The bedclothes had slipped away, and above the powerful chest and shoulders was his dark, chiseled face, in which his eyes were blazing like slow coals. Then the eyes softened, almost with amusement, as he recognized her.

And there, in that bedroom, on that long-ago holiday morning, he had laughed.

And Selena had stood there, incapable of movement, not looking at Royce now but at the woman in bed with him. She lay on her side next to Royce, black hair fanned out on the satin pillow cover, her soft white shoulder and upper arm exposed. But beneath the bedclothes she was obviously caressing Royce.

"Really, Selena," Royce had said, still laughing, "I'm quite glad to see you again, but don't you think we might meet a bit later?"

The black-haired woman had been Royce's mistress at the time, Veronica Blakemore, and her laughter as Selena fled in humiliation had been much like the glee Selena had sensed in Jean's wardrobe last evening.

Oh, yes, Royce had learned in good time that Veronica was manipulative and evil—Selena, of course, had helped make him see that—but ever afterwards she had kept her eyes open for rivals.

It was ridiculous in this situation, though, wasn't it? She had no claim on Jean, nor he on her. This shadowy "Marguerite" or "Landa" or whoever meant absolutely nothing.

Having put things in perspective again, Selena replaced Jean's compress and settled down beside him, thinking of Royce. Surely he would find her. Or, when she arrived in Beaumain's home on St. Crique, she would send a message back to Newport. Or she would take the next ship from Haiti, seeking him.

Yes, that was the way it would be!

Just before nightfall, Jean fell into a deep, peaceful sleep, and his skin was measurably cooler to the touch.

"I think the worst is over," she told Rafael, who came to the cabin bearing brandy, a pot of steaming broth, and bread. "The fever has broken."

"Shall we try to get some of this broth down him?" Rafael asked.

"Not just now. Leave it, though. What about the storm?"

"Good news on that front too. It should be clear weather by morning. The ship has not been damaged. I was worried about the masts for a while, however. I've seen them snap like twigs in winds like these."

"It shows never to give up hope."

"That it does." When Selena had been a little girl, her father had used an expression that had remained with her ever since: *"Selena, the sky begins here."* By that he'd meant every day was new and filled with promise. Life belonged not to those who dwelt upon the past, which could not be recaptured let alone relived, but on the golden morrow when dawn would rise again.

Tomorrow, she thought, *where the sky begins.*

Rafael withdrew. Selena had herself some brandy, bread, and broth. The ship began to quiet a little, then more, and even the ceaseless howling of the wind diminished. She was studying the great map, having located St. Crique off the north coast of Haiti, when Jean Beaumain stirred, murmured something indistinguishable, and tried to sit up.

"Easy, now," she said, going over to him. "You just rest. Feel hungry?"

"God, yes! What hour is it? What happened? Where is Cha—?"

"Shh. None of that now. We can talk about it if you like, after I've gotten some nourishment in you."

He obeyed, settling back down in the hammock, and when she saw his boyish grin and the way he'd decided to comply with her nursely wishes, Selena knew he was his usual self again.

First she gave him some broth, which he gulped avariciously. Brandy lifted his spirits, but bread did not suffice to sate his appetite, so she called to the galley, from which ripe, fall New York apples were delivered. Presently, Jean had had enough, and lay back again with a contented sigh.

"How mad was I?" he asked, a little sheepishly.

"Quite mad, I would say."

They both laughed, then Selena turned serious.

"Who did those things to you?"

"Of course, you've seen. Well, it was Chamorro."

His eyes darkened, hardened, and for a moment she was afraid that he would drift away again into the perfervid world of his mania.

"Sometimes it helps to talk about things," she suggested quietly. "It can't undo what has been done, but sometimes it does truly help."

"You're right." He sighed. "And after what I've put you through, you do deserve an explanation. How strong is your stomach?"

"As strong as it has to be."

"Good. Well, I have already told you how I revenged myself upon Chamorro for what he did to my father, and how, with his ship, I founded my fortune. But he is not a man to let things lie. I knew he was pursuing me, but I paid little attention. I grew arrogant, careless. One night in Tenerife, in the Canary Islands, I went ashore to celebrate. My men and I had seized a Portuguese freighter that day, bound from Brazil and fairly brimming with gold. I drank too much, wandered out into the streets, and Chamorro's men seized me.

"They took me to his ship, which unbeknownst to me had been lying off the coast, and chained me in the hold. The next morning Chamorro himself came below. He is a man of consummate cruelty and evil, and he promised that I would die slowly. I spit in his face. There seemed no reason not to, and I am still glad that I did. I knew I could expect no mercy from him, and I was right.

"He set sail for I knew not where, and once every day he would come below to brand me with a letter of his name. Most often, I would become unconscious at the touch of the hot steel, but when I awoke there would be the pain. I cannot describe to you how awful it was—I cannot describe it to anyone—and every day, with every brand, it would grow worse.

"After he had completed the letters of his name, I was still alive. Chamorro required new amusement, so he decided, to flay me alive, slowly. He had me hung from the yardarm so all his men could see and laugh, and he began daily to peel away from my abdomen a thin strip of skin. He meant, as day passed into day, slowly to strip my bones. That went on for God knows how long. I usually became unconscious as he was ripping away the skin with a pincers, and next morning I would find myself once again chained in the hold.

"Selena, I would have killed myself many times over, had I the resources. But no such felicitous opportunity presented itself. All I could do was suffer. The fiend made certain that I had enough bread and water to keep me alive, you see. He wanted his sport.

"But as time went on, and the torture became more routine, as I weakened, he grew careless. Or rather, his men grew careless. There came a night in which I awoke unchained in the hold. I could barely crawl, but I managed to make my way up onto the deck. We were off the coast of one island or another—later I learned it was the Azores—and I dived off and drifted from the ship to the shore. But not before I had set fire to his ship with a deck lantern. The salt water in my wounds hurt horrendously, but served as a disinfectant. Indeed, the ocean is probably the reason that I am alive today."

"And Chamorro?" asked Selena tremulously, overcome by the horror of what Jean had borne.

Beaumain shrugged, accepting fate. "He had gone ashore that night. Twenty of his sailors perished and his ship was lost to fire, but he himself was safe. Some peasants hid me until I healed—

they held no love for Chamorro, who had raided their coastal villages before—and eventually I was able to send a message to my men.

"Since that time I have been in pursuit of the vulture. Someday I will find him, and I will bring back as trophies his head, his ears, his nose, and his private parts. I will bring them back as trophies in a box."

"But what if he finds *you* first?"

"That will not happen. He is afraid of me now, truly afraid. With the *Liberté,* he knows I can outrun any ship that sails upon the seven seas. He *knows,* and is afraid."

Selena, seeing the look in Jean's eyes, could tell that Chamorro had good reason to fear. His eyes, at that moment, made *her* afraid.

Thinking to quiet and gentle him, she slipped an arm beneath his shoulders and pressed her cheek next to his.

That was how it began, innocently and unplanned.

In response to her gesture, Jean turned toward Selena, saw that her eyes were wet with the tale of his agony, and sought to comfort her with a gentle kiss. Their lips met, held, and the kiss became something that neither of them had intended, but that kept them in its thrall nonetheless. It was a combination of sympathy and affection on Selena's part, of gratitude and smoldering physical desire on his. They went down and down into the kiss, until somehow his hands were beneath her dress—it was the burgundy one—setting her breasts and thighs afire.

Selena thought to stop it, but only for a moment. Then it was too late to do anything but ride along on vaulting waves of passion.

Royce, she thought guiltily, somewhere far back in her mind. But that region was in an area of consciousness soon blotted out by incessant assaults of sensation, which, when set alive, like a hunger, required more and more ecstasy. Or doom.

She closed her eyes so as not to see, so as to shut herself entirely in this wonderful vortex. The destiny of flesh did the rest. His lips upon her nipples caused her to cry out, and she was stroking him with the instinctive skill of a woman who knew love and knew how to give it. The force of his desire as he moved upon her, into her, sent ripples of burgeoning passion from the dewy, need-filled petals of her flesh to the very center of her being, and Selena gave as he gave, her body pushing upward toward his strokes, falling away and thrusting again and again to savor the immense shape of him, the very measure of a good man. And when she felt the rushing flood of his enchantment, knowing that she had pleased him utterly, Selena cried out as much for his pleasure as for her own.

But afterwards, lying beside him, there came an attack of doubt and troubled spirits. He was murmuring words of gratitude, words of endearment, but she heard them indistinctly, as from a great distance.

"Selena, what's the matter?" he asked finally.

She looked at him with sad eyes and shook her head.

"You're thinking of that Royce Campbell, aren't you?"

Her silence was an affirmation.

"We both lost control," he went on. "I didn't mean for this to happen any more than you. But I'm glad it did, and I shall always be."

He kissed her lovingly, high on her cheekbone, and tasted the salt of a fleeting tear.

"Selena, love," he said then, looking deeply into her eyes, "why would I think less of you just for being human like me?"

Nevertheless, she could tell that he was falling more deeply in love with her, even though their intimacy was not repeated, as the *Liberté* changed course and made its way toward Haiti and St. Crique. The knowledge both troubled and pleased her. Jean Beaumain was a man whose attentions would flatter any woman, yet only Royce could ever stir her to her soul. Jean was more like a friend, whose needs she understood, whose spirits roused her as much as his anguish touched her. She did not want to lose his friendship, but when she saw his eyes upon her, saw the scarcely hidden hope in his gaze, she knew that mere comradeship was not what he wanted from her at all.

He wanted the kind of raw, sudden love they had shared in the hammock, wanted it again and again.

So Selena spent much time in her cabin—she had sewn herself three dresses by the time they neared St. Crique—or went on deck and looked out at the ocean through the spyglass, always imagining that she would see, far out on the horizon, the great white sails, the implacable black hull of the ship that bore her name, streaking toward her out of the north.

But she did not, and one afternoon in late October, the sentry in the crow's nest hollered "Land ho! It's St. Crique, dead ahead!"

Everyone came up on deck. Jean Beaumain slipped his arm around Selena as they stood together at the bow, and nuzzled her hair.

"I hope you like it," he said. "Next to love, *home* is the best word in the world."

5 Voodoo

St. Crique Isle, a lush, low-lying atoll, a startling green jewel of a cay twenty miles off the north coast of Haiti, immediately entranced Selena with its untamed, indolent beauty. The eerily blue waters of the Caribbean rolled gently upon its white sand beaches, beaches that rose slowly toward a rain forest of exotic, dazzling flowers, ferns, palms, primordial vines thick as tree branches, and trees laden with exotic, multihued berries and fruit. Above the whole island, under the sun, shimmered a still, hot haze.

"It's gorgeous," said Selena, "but where is your home?"

She could not see a hint of settlement or domicile.

"I call it 'Hidden Harbor,'" Jean replied, even as the *Liberté* rounded a narrow peninsula and sailed straight for shore. There, to Selena's amazement, was an opening in the thick foliage, through which the ship slipped—Jean's men were bringing down the sails now—into a lagoon of clear, placid water, sparkling and diamond pure. At the far end of the lagoon, ivory-white on a rising sweep of jade-green grass, stood a splendid, sprawling house shaded by palm and rubber trees.

"There it is," exclaimed Jean Beaumain quietly, proudly, as the *Liberté* drifted to a halt just offshore. "Home."

And even as Selena marveled at this luxurious architectural masterpiece in the midst of nowhere, she thought how different it was from Coldstream, or from any place that Royce would have chosen. Hidden Harbor reflected Jean's deepest nature. It was neither monument nor statement nor challenge to the world, but rather a place of respite and peace. Flowering gardens, symmetrical in their arrangement and tended to perfection, ran down from the veranda at the front of the house to the water itself. A pier thrust out into the deep water, to which the ship drifted. And upon the pier, waiting, stood two women.

Jean waved at them and they waved back.

Fires of Delight **101**

Selena saw a handsome, brown-haired woman of middle age, shapely, tall and serene. Her companion was of the same height, about Selena's age, perhaps in her early twenties. Her skin was the color of old honey or gold, set off by gleaming jet-black hair. Selena's competitive instincts were immediately aroused. She had seen great beauties in her time—she herself had often been deemed one—but this creature, even from the distance of high deck to low pier, was surpassingly gorgeous.

"The older lady," said Jean, noticing Selena's interest, "is Martha Marguerite. She is the wife of the man who designed Hidden Harbor. He died last year of tropical fever, tragically, and she stayed on to manage my household affairs. But she is a Parisian noblewoman and really yearns to go back home."

"And the other one?" asked Selena, trying to manage a matter-of-fact tone.

Jean permitted himself the hint of a smile. He saw the manner in which Selena was regarding "the other one." "That is Yolanda Fee," he said. "She's Haitian. An octaroon. That is, she's of mixed blood."

"And what does she do here?"

"She's my mistress."

"I see. She's very beautiful."

"But so are you," said Jean.

While the *Liberté* was roped to the pier, Selena looked at the two women and they stared at her. In India, Davi the Dravidian had, among other insights and advice, once said this: *"Selena, it is sometimes difficult to know a friend, but enmity stands out like a black panther on a field of snow."*

Selena smiled pleasantly at the two women, feeling waves of hatred coming up at her.

She did not know from which of them the hatred proceeded.

Maybe both.

Martha Marguerite wore a scarlet gown, high-necked, long-sleeved, and flowing. Yolanda was dressed in a peach-colored, frilly little garment which exposed her breasts almost to the nipples, and which, with its tight waist, accentuated the voluptuous curves of her body, a body made to drive men mad.

Now Selena understood to whom the two types of dresses in Jean's shipboard wardrobe belonged.

She herself was wearing one of the blue satin dresses she had made during the trip, conscious of its makeshift quality in comparison to those of Martha and Yolanda. She was still wearing Ward's cross, of course—Jean had noticed it without much interest, saying only that the words upon it "were being used by some revolutionary hotheads in France." She gathered up the other two dresses she had fashioned, along with the bag of sovereigns and jewels—about which Jean did not know—and went down the gangplank onto the pier. Jean Beaumain made the introductions. Martha Marguerite could not have been more pleasant as she smiled and offered her hand.

"Welcome to Hidden Harbor, Selena. I shall do everything in my power to ensure that you enjoy your stay here."

The manner in which she said this, however, seemed to indicate that she hoped such a stay would not be long. And on the third finger of her right hand, she wore a ring of gold, onyx and diamond; a dot, a circle and an oval, the shape of an eye.

"You have suffered much," observed Yolanda Fee, gazing at Selena with her hot, black eyes as Jean told what had happened in New York. Her eyes were depthless, full of feeling, but Selena sensed no malice. The only unusual part of the encounter was the way in which Yolanda stared at the cross and gold chain around Selena's neck.

"We have heard news," Martha Marguerite said, "that the Americans were victorious at a place called Yorktown. The war is over. America is free."

Jean threw his hat down onto the deck in exultation, and Selena shivered in what might well have been called an ecstasy of triumph. If only Royce were here with her now to share this news! Rafael, Louis, and the other sailors, who had secured the *Liberté* and were now clambering down the gangplank and onto the dock, shouted and cheered in joyous unison.

"It is a great time, a great time," Jean pronounced, "particularly for Selena." He told the two women of her background, her struggle, her deeds. "We must have a huge feast tonight in her honor," he declared.

"I shall see to it right away," said Martha Marguerite, not quite as excited as Jean was.

Yolanda Fee just smiled and said nothing, reappraising this newcomer in the light of the adventures her lover had related.

Martha Marguerite, friendly in a cool, detached manner, led Selena up the pier toward the great house.

"I'll get you settled, my dear, and see that you have suitable garments"—her opinion of Selena's handiwork was not wildly flattering—"and we can talk more later when we dine this evening."

As she was shown into the house, high-ceilinged to preserve the cool, teak-floored, with vast white walls, Selena turned for a moment and noted Jean and Yolanda. They were walking up toward the house too. His arm was around her slim waist, and her lips were pressed close to his ear. Jean was smiling, and Selena knew that the sloe-eyed Haitian beauty was promising things she would do to him in just another minute, when they were alone.

Martha Marguerite read Selena's thoughts.

"If you have dreams of him, give them up," she said, not without sympathy. "No matter what may have happened on board ship—and I'm certain that something did because I know Jean like a son—forget about it. Because Yolanda Fee is a temptress and a witch. Nothing stands in the way of what she wants."

"Thank you, but I'm afraid you have the wrong impression. I am betrothed to another, and he will come for me or I will go to him as soon as possible."

"But meantime you are here," Martha Marguerite observed pointedly, "and I saw the way Jean was looking at you."

She clapped her hands. Three white-garbed servants appeared.

"Show the young lady to the rose bedroom. She will wish to bathe, I'm sure. Call for the seamstress. Prepare a plate of fruit. Fetch wine."

The servants bowed and scurried away. Martha Marguerite was very much in command of Hidden Harbor.

Before Selena was taken to her quarters, Martha Marguerite leaned close to offer a warning terse and strange. "Do not cross Yolanda in any way," the woman hissed. "She knows the secret of black magic. I have seen it."

Black magic? wondered Selena a while later, as she soaked in the scented waters of the bathing pool, alternately savoring sections of an orange and sipping port. *There is no such thing as black magic.* Oh, in Scotland during her girlhood she had heard tales of peasant women who mixed strange concoctions which, when consumed, were said to guarantee winning a lover or curing the ague. But magic was superstition, a leftover myth from Europe's Dark Ages. These were modern times. No one believed in that sort of thing anymore.

Languidly, she stepped from the pool, dried herself with a fragrant towel, and slipped into a thin, lemon-colored robe she had been given. The rose room, named for the primary color of its walls and furnishings, was a marvel such as Coldstream Castle did not possess. Clear water from a hidden source emerged mysteriously into a spacious tub of rose-tinted marble, flowed about, and sank away. The effect was luxurious, soporific.

Selena lay down on the wide, soft bed, drifting against her will toward sleep. She wanted to dress, go out, and have a look around.

Black magic . . .

At the same time, somewhere in the indeterminate distance, there were sounds that held slumber at bay, low, intermittent keening moans, oddly familiar and . . . exciting.

The sounds of passion.

These persisted, and presently Selena arose. The rose room, wide and spacious, gave out onto a tropical garden in which a flagstone path seemed to disappear into tropical undergrowth. She opened the French doors and stepped out into the garden. The sounds, the gasps and cries, were clearer now, and she was sure they were coming from the undergrowth itself.

Looking around, guessing that she was unobserved, Selena sped down the flagstone path and tentatively pushed aside the leaves and vines. To her surprise, they parted easily, like a curtain, and revealed a continuation of the path itself. She stepped through the veil of greenery and once again looked about. At the end of the path, she saw a small, domed structure like a miniature temple. The keening cries were more audible now, and they were coming from the temple.

Curious as always, and already thrilled physically by the moans of ecstasy, she tiptoed stealthily along the flagstones, approaching the temple. An insinuating fragrance came to her then, and she recognized it as the perfume she had smelled on the vexing white dress aboard the *Liberté*.

Then Selena crept up next to the temple itself, pressed close to it, and peered into one of the airy, vaguely oriental slits with which the structure was perforated.

She did not know why her gasp of wonder was not overheard.

Jean Beaumain, his body glistening with sweat and oils, was in the center of a great circle of burning black candles. He was naked. His eyes were closed and his head was thrown back in the transports of ecstasy.

He appeared to be suspended in midair, levitating, unsupported by anything that Selena could see.

Kneeling outside the circle of candles, naked and oiled herself, her eyes closed and her hands pressed together as if in prayer, was Yolanda Fee. Her lips moved from time to time, and when they did Selena noted that Jean would rise in delight, that his maleness throbbed as if he were being teased and stroked.

Yolanda was making love to him as if with her mind alone, the two of them lost utterly in some strange trance beyond Selena's ken. Jean's delight went on and on—possibly, if conscious, he could not have borne the bliss—and Yolanda began to writhe in ecstasy herself.

Transfixed and astounded, Selena could not tear herself away from the preternaturally gorgeous woman and the man upon whom she worked in a way so unfathomable, from the wonder of her sorcery.

Finally, Yolanda cried out, and Jean Beaumain cried out, and from his body erupted tide after tide after tide, which, as he settled to the blanketed earth, Yolanda Fee crept forward to consume.

Selena fled.

Yolanda was waiting for her inside the rose bedroom.

She was loosely clothed in a wrap of green silk. Her hair hung limp and wet around her triumphant face. She smelled strongly of strange perfume, and of Jean.

"I was just . . . outside . . ." Selena faltered, wondering what secret passage Yolanda could have taken to come so quickly here from the temple of delights.

"I know where you were," the other said. "But it does not matter. What did you see?"

Selena sought words.

Yolanda smiled. "You saw only what you wished to see, what you wished to see in your own imagination."

"But out there—"

"Out here?" asked Yolanda, stepping toward the French doors and leading Selena once again into the garden and down the flagstone path. "Out here? What?"

They came to the part of the path where the veil of vines and leaves seemed to hide the temple beyond. Yolanda moved the leaves aside . . . to reveal nothing but more leaves, more vines, and impenetrable undergrowth that ran on into the jungle of St. Crique Isle.

"You must be very careful of what you allow into your mind," advised Yolanda helpfully, as she took Selena back inside the rose room. Selena sank down upon the bed, her senses spinning disorientedly, her usually clear mind in a turmoil of wonder.

"I want you to know," said Yolanda, not at all threateningly, "that Jean is mine."

"I love someone else . . ." Selena began. "I do not desire—"

"Ah. But he desires *you.*" With that, she knelt down beside the bed and took Selena's hands in her own. "Listen," she said fervently, as if she were Selena's sister, "we must be friends. We must fight together."

"Fight? Against whom?"

"Why, Martha Marguerite of course. She is insanely jealous of Jean. She will destroy both of us, if she can. Did you see that ring she wears?"

Selena managed a nod.

"It is the source of her powers. Somehow she must be divested of that ring. Will you help me?"

Selena remembered how Martha Marguerite had warned her against Yolanda's black magic. "If I can," she temporized. "But I don't see *how* I can."

"Leave it to me," replied the other woman, with a sloe-eyed grimace that might have been a smile. "You help me when I ask it of you, and I shall do all in my power to speed you to your lover."

"But I intend to go to him anyway, as soon as possible."

"Yes, but do you know that Jean will seek to keep you here?"

"No, of course he won't—"

Yolanda nodded soberly, knowingly. "Believe me. You must. Jean will attempt to keep you here, and Martha Marguerite, outraged at his attentions to you, will seek to destroy you. I have seen it—"

"You've *seen* it? Like a vision?"

"My power is not so great as Martha's—because she possesses the ring—but I have managed to learn a few things. Trust me and be my friend, and all will be well with you."

Yolanda stood up, moved to the door, and turned.

"Why do you wear that talisman around your neck?" she asked.

"This cross? It was given to me. I treasure it."

Yolanda seemed doubtful. "You mean it is not a source of power?"

"What? No. Just a remembrance."

Yolanda remained dubious. "But just trust me," she said, going out.

And leaving Selena uncertain about whether she could trust anyone at all.

A musky whiff of savage scent, and the spilled smell of Jean Beaumain, hung in the air.

The initial flurry of hospitality extended to Selena at Hidden Harbor fairly overwhelmed her. A seamstress appeared to take her measurements—aboard the *Liberté* she'd regained the weight lost in prison—and to give her a gown to wear to dinner. A houseboy, dark, shy and soft-spoken, knocked on the door to ask, in French, if her quarters were adequate. Did she need more towels, pillows, linen? She did not; the rose room was equipped to meet the needs of the most demanding queen. And a servant appeared with tea, brandy, and a tray of biscuits and sweets.

Yet, while Selena appreciated the attention, she realized that the constant flow of servants posed a problem: how ought she to conceal the pouch of jewels?

Temporarily, she had hidden her inexplicable cache beneath the mattress, but that would not suffice for long. Who knew how many times a day they changed the beds in this white palace?

She looked around the rose room, thinking it over, calculating. The walls were solid plaster; the wardrobe was stark and empty; there were no bureaus or drawers. At length, she buried the pouch among the roots of a potted rubber plant, surreptitiously discarding the excess soil in the garden.

As darkness began to fall and the time to dine drew near, she took another long bath, groomed herself, and put on the dress that the seamstress had brought her. It was satin, sleek and shiny, and had about it the voluptuous feel of a living thing. It was black, which displeased her. The color of mourning. But when she saw in the mirror how it set off her golden hair and the deep tan she'd acquired at sea, Selena felt better.

At least until, again, she began to experience the nervous, burning, needful sensations of physical arousal.

Pulling off the garment, looking, she found again inside the hem that mysterious, embroidered eye.

And thought immediately of Martha Marguerite's ring.

Perhaps Yolanda, for all her strange ways, was right about the power possessed by the older woman.

She'd just decided to wear one of her own makeshift creations, damn it all, when there was a subdued rapping at her door.

Martha Marguerite entered, with a slippery white silk gown draped over her arm.

"Wear this to dinner," the woman said, handing Selena the gown. "And don't be alarmed. It is much in fashion at Versailles."

Court of the French king, Louis XVI. Selena was impressed.

Martha Marguerite withdrew. Selena instantly inspected the hem, found neither mark nor symbol, and slipped on the dress.

And knew why Martha had expected her to be alarmed.

A tight-fitting, floor-length garment, it exposed a bit of her hips, all of her back, her left shoulder and left breast. She blushed even as she looked at herself in the mirror, reddening in face, throat, and all the way down to her bare breast, where her nipple stood at attention.

I can't wear this! she was thinking, when Jean Beaumain knocked and entered simultaneously.

"Jean!" she cried, covering herself with her hands.

He smiled. "When in Rome, Selena. Come, let's go to dinner. And let us humor Martha. She wants tonight to seem as if we were among the nobles of Paris. Her one dream is to be among them again, as she was when she was young."

Selena continued to balk.

"Come now," he persisted. "She herself will be in a dress similar to yours."

"When in Rome . . ." Selena repeated, steeling her nerve and following him out of the rose room. At least this dress did not elicit those dastardly sensations of arousal.

Also, to her surprise, she began to feel almost comfortable in the garment, and proud of her body.

Moments later, entering the dining room, she felt something else entirely. Already seated at the banquet table was Yolanda Fee. Her dress was identical to Selena's!

The two women stared at one another in considerable hostility.

Also at the table, seated between Louis and Rafael, was Martha Marguerite, who had on a demure lavender creation, which covered her from throat to wrist, from clavicle to ankle.

The woman is toying with Yolanda and me, Selena realized.

Veiling her discomfiture, acutely conscious of male eyes, she took her seat at the table on Jean's right. Yolanda sat opposite him, brooding and remote. Only her great black eyes were alive.

"The light and the dark," exuded Martha Marguerite, with a theatrical gesture toward the two young ladies. "Aren't they beautiful?"

None of the men disagreed.

A servant came forward to pour champagne, and as Selena accepted the toast that Jean made in her behalf—"to a brave girl whose visit here we honor tonight"—she noted that her hand was a bit unsteady from tension. So was Yolanda's, however, and Selena was secretly pleased, even though her opinion of Martha Marguerite had declined. It seemed the older woman was deliberately provoking some sort of confrontation.

Yet nothing like that happened.

The dinner proceeded from lobster bisque to roast peacock to turtle steak and tubers, from champagne to white wine to red, and a vastly pleasant, eminently civilized air filled the candlelit dining chamber. Rafael was somewhat taciturn by nature, but Louis possessed a quick, if somewhat bluff, sense of humor, and regaled them with tales of his boyhood in Brittany. He'd been the youngest of thirteen living children—eight others had died at birth or shortly thereafter—and it had been the dream of his parents to have at least one of their offspring enter the religious life.

"I protested," he related, "but in the end they shipped me off to the local monastery. I was ten years old, but big for my age, and I had heard a great many stories from my older brothers. I decided the only way to escape my fate was to seem unworthy of it, so I sought out my confessor. 'I have committed sins of the flesh,' I said. He was somewhat alarmed, given my years, and inquired about what these sins had been. Very penitently, I related everything my brothers had ever told me! I was expelled that very afternoon."

"Ah, home!" sighed Martha Marguerite, after the laughter had subsided. "What I would not give to return!"

It was a feeling that Selena could understand.

"Why don't you go back?" she asked, thinking there might be some dangerous or complicated reason that prevented such a trip.

"I shall, when Jean is ready to take me there. You did promise, didn't you, Jean?"

Beaumain ducked his head and admitted that he had.

"But," he said to Selena, "I don't want to return myself until I settle with Chamorro and bring my trophies to throw upon the gates of the King's palace. I want his majesty to regard well how an honest peasant deals with the savage cruelties of the rich and titled."

"From what I have heard," offered Rafael, "his majesty may soon learn precisely that from many quarters. France is becoming, more and more, a revolutionary tinderbox that will make the American war seem but an afternoon's promenade."

"Come, come," said Martha soothingly, tolerantly, twirling a goblet of red wine in her long fingers. "The great majority of the people love their king. I realize that they do not much revere his queen, the Austrian, Marie Antoinette, but it is the stability of the upper order that has kept our beloved France ascendant for hundreds of years—"

"It is the nobility which is tearing France apart," said Rafael. "The nobility and the clergy. Privilege, *pffffttt!*" he declared. "I tell you, the people will not bear it much longer."

"Ah, but if you had had the life I enjoyed," Martha went on as if she hadn't even heard him, as if his opinions—the sincerity of which Selena could not doubt—did not matter, "you would think differently. Gracious, I see it as if it were before my very eyes, that great house of my father's on the right bank of the Seine. It was five stories high with dormers beneath the steep, slanting slate roof. How I loved to go up there as a child and look out over Paris, and see the boats on the river, and Notre Dame! There is no sight like it in all the world. Summers we spent at our château in Côte d'Or."

"Does your family still own these homes?" Selena inquired.

"Of course, my dear. And that is why I want Jean to take me back. If my dear husband Hugo had not died while building Hidden Harbor, I expect I would be in France right now."

"You had better return soon then and see to your property," commented Rafael. "When the tornado of revolution touches down on French soil, I suspect many nobles will be quickly relieved of such properties."

"Never," maintained Martha Marguerite, with a bit less assurance than she'd shown thus far. "But all the more reason for Jean to take me back soon. Jean?"

Beaumain smiled noncommittally.

Selena glanced at him, then looked past him toward Yolanda, who had said nothing whatever during the course of the meal. She held her tongue now as well, but Selena had noted that whenever Martha spoke of going back to France with Jean, the Haitian beauty showed a combination of anger and distress. Her large eyes widened in moody alarm; her dusky breast swelled with great, anxious inhalations.

Something else too: At every reference, no matter how casual, to Jean's putative departure, the candles on the table seemed to blaze more brightly.

Testing a theory that was taking shape in her mind, Selena said: "Jean, I think it would be sweet of you to take Martha back to her home."

Yolanda widened her eyes, scowling.

Again, the candlelight leapt.

It was as if Yolanda's emotions were sent forth from her body into the very air with the power to touch and alter the state of surrounding objects.

"My own problem," she said hastily, changing the subject, "is to find my friend, Royce Campbell. I hope I shall be able to do that soon."

Jean had apparently resigned himself to the fact that Selena's love was too great to breach, let alone break. A discussion followed, introduced by Jean, which led to the decision that Rafael would depart in a few days for Port-au-Prince, Haiti, there to make inquiries regarding Campbell and also to determine when the next ship would set sail for America.

"You'll be safe there now, Selena," Jean said. "Oakley and his men will be gone, having lost the war."

"Oakley!" said Selena in disgust.

"Who's that?" Yolanda wanted to know.

Selena told her, describing the lieutenant's great bald head, hairless face, flabby fold of nose. She also added the information that, incongruously, the man was a gifted artist, able to paint with subtle, spectacular effect.

Yolanda listened, saying nothing, taking it all in.

"You speak of him as if the force of his hatred is with you still," commented Martha, her odd ring glittering.

"I'm afraid it is. He is the kind who does not forget. I picture him pursuing me like a hound of hell. 'We have a bond, Selena,' he said. And he *believed* it."

She shuddered. Yolanda's eyes widened, and the candles flared. As the beauty lifted her hand to brush back a tendril of raven-black hair, Selena saw, in the palm of her left hand, a tiny five-pointed star, like a tattoo.

Another symbol, she thought. *But signifying what?*

Perhaps nothing. Perhaps the star was only a kind of beauty mark, a graphic residue of Yolanda's superstitious, dream-haunted homeland.

After dessert, a rum-flavored banana puree spiced with nutmeg and cinnamon, the dinner ended. Jean, rising from the table, said that musicians were waiting to play for them on the veranda. But Selena demurred. She felt very tired suddenly, a languor born of many things, not the least of which was the uninterpretable tension between Yolanda and Martha Marguerite.

"I'm afraid you'll have to excuse me," she said. "I think I'll retire for the night."

The two women, along with Rafael and Louis, rose as Jean helped her up from her chair. The men seemed disappointed that she would not be joining them, and the women pretended to be.

"Come on, Selena," urged Jean, as he walked her toward the rose room, "change your mind. I find pleasure in your company."

"I'd like to listen to the music, truly. But I'm so tired. . . ."

They paused outside her door. "Let me come inside for just a little," he said huskily, slipping an arm around her waist and cupping her bare breast in his hand.

"Jean—"

"Please. Just for a little while. You don't know how much I desire you."

Yes, she did. She could feel, through his breeches and her gown, exactly how much, and it was quite a lot. Moreover, his expert attention to her breast was having an effect. His lips were just above her own, and she very much wanted to kiss him.

"That time on board your ship—" she began.

"I'm thinking of the time on board my ship, and how you felt."

"It shouldn't have happened. I thought we'd agreed—"

"I don't recall agreeing to anything." He smiled.

"But what about Yolanda? Think how badly she'll feel if she finds out."

"Selena, she is merely my mistress. I'm in *love* with *you.*"

"But you said you'd send Rafael to Port-au-Prince to help me go back to America."

"Yes. And in the meantime, you're here. Just give me that time to love you, Selena. I want to make you feel what I felt with you. If I can. You may be surprised to find that you will love me too."

He was rubbing his thumb lightly over her taut nipple, back and forth. Maddeningly, sensations flashed down through her body to where she felt his hard strength pressed against her.

"Oh, Jean, I just can't," she said, in genuine distress.

At that moment, she was all too ready to make love, and if it had not been for the image of Royce, she'd have pulled Jean inside her room, stripped in a flash, lain him down, opened herself to take him, to ride until there was no more.

"If I try very hard, I can pretend to myself that I was not totally responsible for the time on your ship. But if I give myself again, I'll have to live with the knowledge that I've been deliberately unfaithful to Royce. You can understand that, can't you?"

"Sure I can." He grinned, kissing her neck and running his hand along the sweet curves of her body. "Sure I can, but it makes no difference to me."

He was jesting now and Selena realized—with just a faint, fading disappointment—that he had decided not to force the issue. Not then anyway.

"Good night, my love," he said lightly, kissing her—too briefly, it seemed—on the mouth, and leaving the touch of a final caress on her bare breast. "I hope you dream of me."

"I probably will," she murmured to herself, entering the rose room and closing the door. There were few physical sensations in the world worse than to be completely ready for love, but not to be able to do anything about it! The trouble was that, even though one's mind and body recalled the precise shape of a man, memory could never hope to approximate, let alone experience, the actual feel of him deep down.

Deciding against another bath, Selena undressed, hung up the shameless wisp of cloth she'd been maneuvered into wearing by Martha, and slipped naked between the satin sheets of the voluptuous bed. Warm climates had their advantages. In cold Scotland, a person would invite the grippe or worse without flannels and stockings and a nightcap. Unless, of course, one could find an agreeable partner.

Gradually, attenuated desire sank away until the next time it should be evoked, and Selena drifted toward sleep. The moon had risen, soft and majestic in a star-riven sky, filling the bedroom with a lambent, rose-tinted haze. Selena watched the way in which the color changed as the moon eased across the sky, saw through veiled eyes the shadows of the rubber plant on the floor.

And saw Lieutenant Clay Oakley standing beside the rubber plant!

She sat bolt upright, incapable of crying out, and clutched a sheet to her bosom.

It was Oakley all right, in all his leering, muscular malevolence, and he advanced toward her with heavy, implacable tread. There was something unusual in his gait, jerky and uncoordinated, as if he were a dead man called from the grave by strange powers to attack Selena in the night.

"What do you want?" she managed, her voice barely a whisper.

He said nothing, just stared at her out of his enormous, icy eyes. She saw in his right hand something slim and long like a stiletto, but as he approached her bed and loomed over her to strike, she saw that he held not a weapon at all but . . .

An artist's paint brush!

Then he melted away, disappeared instantly, utterly, into the rose-colored air.

And Selena was alone.

My God! she thought, getting out of bed, feeling the cool floor beneath her feet. "What on earth—?"

Her mind was whirling, her heart pumped crazily, but she forced herself to be calm and tried to think.

Oakley had been there, true to life in every detail. But why the paint brush?

After several minutes of tumultuous consideration, Selena thought she had the answer. At the dinner table, she had vividly described Oakley for the benefit of the others. And she had added the information that the peculiar lieutenant was a painter. Thus, someone present at the table, in order to terrify Selena, had projected the image of Oakley into this very room! The paint brush was an incongruous error, either of perception or projection, but there was no denying the vast, eerie power of . . .

Who?

Yolanda, with her brooding aura and barely hidden animosities?

Or the apparently serene Martha Marguerite, with her singular ring?

Or someone else—one of the silent, scurrying servants perhaps —who had an unknown reason to harass the new guest?

Selena did not know.

Agitated, unsettled, she pulled on a robe and began to pace about the room. Should she go and tell Jean Beaumain what had happened? He would be on the veranda with the others. She could hear the sounds of violins in the distance, a song half-forgotten, melancholy, inexpressibly heartbreaking, conveying the sadness of someone who had already been dead for centuries.

No, she decided. *I don't know what is happening, or why. I won't make a fool of myself. I'll bide my time.*

Continuing to pace, she wandered over toward the rubber plant and felt, beneath her bare feet, the grit of dirt spilled on the floor. *What?* she thought. *I cleaned very thoroughly when I hid the pouch. . . .*

Unless—!

Her premonition proved to be correct.

The soil in the pot, around the roots of the rubber plant, had been disturbed.

The pouch of jewels was gone.

6 Eye of the Beholder

Rafael journeyed to Port-au-Prince and returned a week later, the bearer of much news, most of it disquieting. He sat with Jean and Selena on the veranda in late afternoon, the three of them sipping tea and sherry.

"First of all," he said, "Lieutenant Clay Oakley and a number of his men are in Haiti now. I saw him myself in the barroom of the Black Prince Hotel, a most disagreeable-looking man, if I do say so. And, Selena, he is looking for you."

"I *knew* it," she murmured.

"The British defeat in America seems to have stung him badly. There is much talk of recoupment and revenge. He is showing, to whomever will pay him heed, a handbill with your likeness on it."

"Oh, Lord," Selena said.

"Very curious. He carries with him at all times a scented handkerchief and breathes through it constantly."

"It seems to be his one weakness," she explained. "It is as if there is not enough air in the world for him."

She did not understand how that weakness could do her much good, unless it were to lead to premature demise.

"Also," continued Rafael, "there is news that Royce Campbell was sighted aboard his ship near Trinidad—"

"Yes?" she exclaimed excitedly, as Jean tried to veil a frown.

"—and he is looking for you as well."

"Oakley is much closer," Selena said. "Are any ships due out for America or Trinidad?"

"There are always some. But suppose you went to Trinidad? Royce might already be gone."

"Eventually, he might come here," she said hopefully.

Jean Beaumain took a swallow of the sweet sherry and set down his glass. "Selena," he said, having made a decision, "it would be too risky for you to appear in Haiti just now, for any purpose. I will tell you what I shall do: When next we learn of Royce Campbell's whereabouts—and I will make sure we are kept informed—I myself will take you to him aboard the *Liberté.*"

"Would you do *that?*" she cried, delighted.

He was surprised, but not at all displeased, when Selena bestowed an affectionate kiss upon his lips.

But that decision, so readily made and received with such joyous acquiescence, proved to be dependent upon the future convergence of disparate and unpredictable people and events. News of Royce would have to reach Haiti and St. Crique. It could not be old information; Royce would have to be within reasonable sailing distance. And Jean Beaumain would be the one to make the decision about when to weigh anchor.

He held all the cards so to speak. Selena was in his power, as well as indebted to him.

Fall turned to winter on St. Crique Isle, but it hardly seemed to matter. The days were warm, as were the nights. The skies were peerlessly blue, and out on the ocean the mighty Gulf Stream moved in its mysterious current. Time itself seemed to slow down as week melted into week, and an odd, uncharacteristic lethargy settled over Selena. Always so vibrant, she was puzzled by it, and finally thought that she recognized the cause of her state: she had begun to accept the apparent powerlessness of her situation here. Instead of instigating a search for her missing treasure, she had settled in to wait for some hint or clue about who had stolen it. Instead of actively pursuing relationships with Yolanda or Martha Marguerite—relationships which might at least have provided the clues she needed—she had kept her distance from the two woman, a distance with which they seemed quite comfortable, thank you. Martha continued to coddle and fuss over Jean as if he were her son, and to chatter about Paris. Yolanda disappeared with Jean for great parts of the day, and always for the night, to gift him with sensual delights that Selena could all too readily envision.

Selena was in the library when she decided that she'd had enough of waiting, of leisure, of debilitating inactivity.

"I am going to act!" she declared aloud, to the sudden, startled carping of a couple of caged mynah birds. "I am finished with laying about!"

In truth, what roused her to this pronouncement was not completely her own impulse. A piece of news in a British paper, which Rafael had brought back from another of his gloomy forays to Port-au-Prince, caught her eye and quickened her blood.

LORD BLOODWELL APPOINTED
TO HIS MAJESTY'S SERVICE

Lord Sean Bloodwell, by order of His Majesty George III, has been appointed to the diplomatic corps. He will serve as Deputy Minister for Anglo-French affairs, a most crucial area at this time due to the turbulent winds of revolutionary havoc stirring the Continent.

Lord Bloodwell, a Scots commoner who rose to mercantile fortune in the American colonies and who was elevated to the peerage for his unswerving loyalty to His Majesty, has stated: "War is a horror that must be avoided unless there is no honorable alternative. But revolution is a terror that rips nations and families apart. . . ."

Ah, did Selena not know it! This man, whose life she had once shared, had been all but heartbroken when he'd learned that her loyalties were with the Colonists, with the revolutionaries, with the enemies of his monarch. Yes, they had been different people, but had that fact diminished the pain of their foredoomed separation. No, it had not.

Yet Sean had gone on, forgiving her, permitting her to go her way, yes, but proceeding along the path he had planned for himself. He was *doing* something!

While she was sitting here in the library of Hidden Harbor, waiting and brooding and . . . going stale. And the very sight of his name on the printed page of newspaper could not but evoke a spell of poignant reverie. After they had helped each other escape from the Maharajah of Jabalpur, after Selena had been certain that Royce was dead, she'd accepted Sean's offer of marriage. It had seemed so right, even necessary. They'd brought with them a tiny little orphan girl named Davina in honor of Davi, the Dravidian wizard, a blond, blue-eyed creature of English blood whose fate in the Orient would have been disastrous. Selena and Sean were, in effect, the child's mother and father even before they took their vows on the deck of the SS *Blue Foray,* bound for America. The sky had been brilliant, cloudless, swept clean by the trade winds, royal blue to the north, shimmering where the sun was.

Selena had had no wedding gown. The white, billowing sails were her wedding gown. Innocence and truth were in her heart, as they had been when she was but a little girl. She and Sean had stood before the ship's captain—Flanders his name was—remembering their pasts, the brave but evanescent dreams that had brought them to this day. Wind surged, filling the sails, lifting the ship, and they moved forward into the future, locked together for a moment by a destiny greater than—and unknown to—both of them.

Over the rail of the *Blue Foray,* Selena saw the ocean rolling on forever. The same ocean that had robbed her of Royce Campbell, adrift into death on his plague-ridden *Highlander,* had also led her to India and to Sean Bloodwell: love given and love taken away.

"I do!" she had cried, in answer to the captain's query. "I do!" As if to God and the sky, and to all those she had loved who dwelt now in far regions. She wanted them to hear, to know, and in the absence of chronicles and chisels, the very walls of Coldstream Castle must be imprinted with this faraway call of her young and beating heart.

And there aboard ship, taking her vows, which by the first law of love only Royce Campbell could transcend, she had recalled returning to Coldstream on journeys with her father, and how his subjects lit great bonfires of greeting on the highest hills, fires of delight to welcome them home.

Were those fires gone, never to blaze again?

After the wedding ceremony, a huge black thunderhead of a cloud had appeared in the northern sky, assuming for one fleeting moment the shape of a wolf.

Only Selena had seen it.

One final item in the newspaper story brought a tear: "Lord Bloodwell lives with his adopted daughter, Davina, at his home in St. John's Wood."

It had been right of course for the little girl to go with Sean. What kind of life could Selena have offered, running, hiding, rushing hither and thither in the revolutionary maelstrom of New

York? But the child should have a mother, and how Selena yearned to hold her now.

"Brace up," she ordered herself. "Selena, the sky begins here."

Resolving to seize control of her own fate once again, Selena sought out Martha Marguerite. The older woman was in her study, brooding over a map of France. She seemed edgy and distracted.

"I must talk to you," began Selena forthrightly, "about certain perceptions I have had since my arrival."

Curiously, the expression on Martha's face seemed almost to be one of relief.

"Please be seated," she said, offering Selena a chair. "I had begun to fear that you would never come to me. Indeed, I had begun to fear that you would go to *her.*"

"Yolanda Fee?"

"Who else, my dear? But now that there are two of us united, we may be strong enough to best her. God willing," she added.

Selena saw the strange ring on Martha's finger. It was as good a place as any to begin.

"It may seem bizarre of me to ask this," she began, "but does your ring, or the symbol of the eye upon it, confer any special benefits?"

The other woman smiled. "And how do you come to ask such a thing?"

Continuing to gamble on her hunch that Martha was friend rather than foe, or at least more friend than foe, Selena pressed on. "I am missing some things of value that I brought here with me. Frankly, I'm sure they were stolen."

"And you suspect Yolanda?"

"Yes. If it is possible to be in two places at the same time."

She described how the items in question—she did not say that these were jewels, nor did Martha ask—had disappeared while she and Yolanda were both at dinner.

The older woman shook her head. "So she is capable of *that* as well."

"I beg your pardon?"

"My dear, Haiti is a strange land. The rules of the physical universe seem sometimes to be suspended or altered there, for those who are trained in its secrets. And I fear Yolanda was so trained. She wears a certain scent that is said to be powerful enough to rouse passion—"

Now Selena understood. She herself had been affected by that very scent on Yolanda's clothing.

"—and it is also rumored that those possessed of the witchcraft can be in two places at once. They are also able to mix potions that will change the shapes of their enemies, or even kill them. On the other hand, has Yolanda made any threatening gestures against you?"

"No, not directly," Selena admitted.

"Someone else might have taken your things. It is possible. Who is your houseboy?"

"That shy, dark little fellow. I think he's called Campanale."

"Have you spoken to him about this?"

"No, you're the first person I've told. Besides, he seems quite harmless."

"Always beware of appearances, my dear. I assume, since you've come to me, that you have a plan in mind?"

"I do. But I need your help. I would like to get into Yolanda's quarters and have a look about."

Martha Marguerite's eyes widened. "Are you sure?"

"Yes. What's the matter?"

"Well, insofar as I know—and that encompasses the nearly three years since Hidden Harbor's completion and Yolanda's presence here—no one but she has ever been inside. Not even Jean. She goes to his bedchamber when they—"

Martha Marguerite hesitated, thinking it over.

"All right," she agreed, "I'll help you. But mind, be extremely careful."

It was decided that Martha, two days hence, would feign a small physical indisposition and send for Yolanda's help. Whatever her mysterious powers, the beauty was known to possess healing skills as well, which she delighted to use. "She likes to show off," Martha said. "And while she is with me, you take the opportunity to inspect her chamber. But you must promise to look carefully at *everything* you see, and to tell me *exactly* what you noticed."

Selena said that she would. It did not, under the circumstances, seem to be an unreasonable request.

The day before Selena was to embark upon her stealthy foray, however, news arrived that promised to make an inspection of Yolanda's rooms unnecessary. Campanale, her diminutive houseboy, and several of the other servants had taken a sloop to Port-de-Paix in order to acquire supplies for Hidden Harbor's kitchens. Port-de-Paix, on the north coast of Haiti, was a tiny village, much nearer to Hidden Harbor than Port-au-Prince. It was rumored to be a smuggling base for all manner of contraband, and it might well have been—Jean admitted as much—but it was primarily a dusty market town. Jean and his men had taken the *Liberté* on a short jaunt over to Cuba in quest of bullion that was believed to be available there, and when Selena heard Campanale and the others babbling to Martha Marguerite she feared that something terrible might have happened to Beaumain.

Selena heard the agitated chatter, a mixture of Spanish, French, and deep-woods Haitian dialect out on the veranda, and hurried to see what the trouble was. The houseboy was waving his arms, talking to Martha Marguerite, but when he saw Selena coming to join them, he pointed at her vigorously. "Selena! Selena!" he cried excitedly.

"Yes?" Selena asked apprehensively.

Martha turned toward her. "My dear," she said, with a faintly bewildered expression, "our little Campanale here says that, in the harbor of Port-de-Paix, there lies a great black ship with your name emblazoned upon its hull."

"*Royce!*" cried Selena, or rather she choked on his name a little, since her heart was in her throat just then.

He had come!

And Port-de-Paix was no more than twenty sea miles from St. Crique Isle.

"I must go immediately," she declared. "The men must take me on the sloop, since Jean is away."

Martha, who knew about Royce—and approved of his existence, since it meant that Selena had no permanent interest in her beloved Jean—gave the necessary orders. Forgetting about the missing sovereigns and jewels—what could they matter now?— Selena boarded the sloop. As it began to move, she saw both Yolanda and Martha Marguerite waving to her from the veranda in farewell. Neither of them seemed at all distressed to see her leaving.

The wind was good and the journey quick, but as the sloop

drew near the Haitian coast, as Selena scanned the horizon, she saw in the little harbor of Port-de-Paix not the massive *Selena* with its masts and cannon and proud swath of Campbell plaid, but rather two British men-o'-war lying at anchor.

Little Campanale, manning the rudder, was puzzled.

"Those not be here before," he said, gesturing toward the British ships and looking to her for instructions.

Oh, damn it all! thought Selena. Royce had been almost close enough to touch, but now . . .

"Put into shore west of the village," she ordered disconsolately, "I'll see if I can learn what is going on."

She was all too well aware of the probability that one of the ships might carry Lieutenant Clay Oakley.

Campanale and his fellow servants did as they were told. Selena waded from the sloop to the shore and began trudging down the dusty road toward Port-de-Paix. She was wearing a dress made for her by the seamstress at Hidden Harbor, a decorative, fluffy little pink thing, and the few peasants she met along the roadway stared at her in fearful wonder. Who was this lovely, tall, blond creature appearing out of the Haitian foliage? They used their hands to make pushaway gestures toward her as if she carried a curse or worse, and one little boy, riding in the back of an ox cart, made a furtive sign of the cross.

On the outskirts of Port-de-Paix, which was comprised of perhaps twenty low, ramshackle buildings, all whitewashed to reflect the heat, Selena ducked behind a mango tree at the side of the road and looked.

A number of British soldiers, four of them carrying a stretcher, were walking toward the village dock. There a rowboat waited, and in the rowboat, his smooth ivory pate gleaming in the sun, was Oakley himself. The mere sight of the man sent shivers through Selena.

Carefully, the stretcher-bearers lowered their burden into the dinghy—Selena saw a soldier lying motionless upon it—and presently the little craft moved out toward the warships. Selena guessed, from the lack of attention being given to the man on the stretcher, that he was dead.

Royce?

She waited until the rowboat was far from shore, until the rest of the soldiers were also out on the water in a second dinghy, and then made her way into the village in which awful, keening shrieks of grief had begun to rise. The reason for these soul-shattering ululations was immediately apparent. Three Haitians—two men and a woman—lay dead on the pale white dust of the village square. They were naked and trussed with rope. The hands and feet of one man had been lopped off. These lay in the bloody dust with the gouged eyeballs of the second man and the breasts of the woman.

Friends and relatives of the victims were kneeling around the bodies, wailing in grief, rocking back and forth, side to side, the universal motions of impotent despair. They were too preoccupied even to notice Selena. Glancing around the village, she saw in the shadowed doorway of the largest building a wiry, leathery man in European clothes. He stared at her for a moment, then ducked out of sight.

She walked over to the building, which was a market or store of some kind, and entered. There were shelves filled with casks of rum and wine, bins stuffed with vegetables, and freshly slaughtered hogs and chickens hanging from hooks. Myriad flies buzzed around the carcasses. The man she'd seen was standing nervously in a corner next to a reeking side of butchered beef, as if trying to conceal himself.

"Yes?" he asked, coming forward a little when he saw that he couldn't hide. "What do you want?"

"What's happened here?"

He was mean-looking, but his eyes showed intelligence. "What business is it of yours?"

She decided to come right out with it. "I'm here looking for Royce Campbell. I had news that his ship was here a little while ago."

His grin of surprise was also sarcastic. "Well, you missed him, lady. And so did those British. I guess he is too fast for you."

The man, who had first spoken in French, was now addressing her in colloquial, if accented, English.

"Who are you?" she demanded. "Do you know Royce?"

"That's for me to know and you to find out," he shot back, moving past her toward the door. "As for me, I'm leaving."

"Wait. Please wait just a minute. I have to know about Royce."

He hesitated in the doorway. "Lady," he said, "there are three dead Haitians outside, and a whole group of very live, very angry ones. We are the only two Europeans here, and I think we are going to be dead very soon. Do you understand?"

Selena did. Foreigners had just killed three natives, and their kin would not hesitate to take retribution. But Royce came first. She had to know about him.

"Mr. Campbell *was* here, though?" she persisted.

"Yes, he was. I handed over to him a cache of valuables that I had been entrusted to hold for him—"

Selena thought, wonderingly, of her own purloined pouch of jewels and sovereigns.

"—and he left one step ahead of those British barbarians. Also, I am afraid he unwittingly left you and me holding the proverbial bag. Oh, Lord, here they come!"

He stepped back from the doorway and Selena saw the enraged Haitian villagers advancing upon the building.

"They're going to kill me!" he cried, slamming and barring the door. "They've already killed a British soldier."

"Why?"

"Because I was in league with Campbell, you fool! And Campbell—whom they do not know—brought the British in his wake, and now three of their people are dead. That bald British officer tortured them to find out where Campbell had sailed to. Of course, the victims did not know."

Angry howls, increasing in intensity, rose outside the store.

"Why didn't the British torture *you?*" Selena asked.

"Because I *hid,*" he snapped. "And I doubt that those crazed people outside are going to give me much credit for it. They blame me for what's happened."

Selena's thoughts turned to her own safety, but not before she had registered the troubling information that, yet again, Royce had been involved in the kind of dangerous, sinister transaction which had been his forte in the old days, and which had colored his name in the ports of the seven seas.

She and the man heard a dull *thunk* on the thatched roof of the store. Then they heard a slow, crackling hiss.

"They've set us afire!" He pulled a small derringer from his boot. "If they get us," he said, "fire will seem preferable to their ways of pain. I prefer a bullet." He gestured toward Selena with the pistol. "You?"

The grass roof had flared fully now. Already heat and smoke

were filling the store. The sounds of the people outside were inhuman. Perhaps the man was right, but . . .

"No," she said.

"Suit yourself." He put the barrel of the pistol into his mouth and pulled the trigger.

The shot from such a weapon was not sufficiently powerful to blow a man's head off, but it was deadly enough. The man's head jerked forward, then back, and he slumped to the dirt floor as if he'd been struck a knockout blow in a prizefight. A bit of blood appeared at the corner of his mouth and his eyes blinked spasmodically.

Selena bent over him. Flames were licking at the walls of the store now, and she knew that she had to get out before the fiery thatch collapsed upon her. The derringer had fallen on the floor next to the man. She picked it up. Useless for anything now! It was a one-shot weapon.

"Ahh!" he said, looking at her. His features were contorted and his eyes were fading. There was surprisingly little devastation, only that thin trickle at the corner of the man's mouth, a bit more blood pooling in his left ear.

"Why did you have to do that?" she asked helplessly, bending over him and cradling his head in her hands. As she did so, Erasmus Ward's cross came out from beneath the top of her dress and hung down.

With his last flicker of life and knowledge, the man's eyes widened.

"Sorbontay!" he gasped.

And died.

Selena had no time to contemplate either the word or his death, because a section of burning roof collapsed. She leaped away from the flames and headed toward the door. Throwing aside the bar with which it had been secured, she dashed outside to be seized immediately by three enraged Haitian men. They howled in triumph as they grabbed her, an exultation that was only slightly lessened when they determined that the man in the store was dead.

"Wait!" cried Selena. "Please!" But they dragged her to the center of the square where their kinfolk lay dead, and one of the men produced a long, curved, evil-looking blade.

I'm going to die, thought Selena. *I'm really going to die. . . .*

At a time like this, it was said that a person's past life flashed before her eyes. All that Selena could remember, though, was her sixth or seventh birthday, when she'd received two kittens, one black and the other white, from her mother. She'd named them Yin and Yang.

The blade flashed, slicing Selena's dress from throat to hem and leaving a bloody slash no wider than the mark of a pencil from her Adam's apple to her abdomen.

The crowd howled in glee.

Then little Campanale and the men from the sloop raced into the square, waving and shouting. The man with the knife hesitated. Selena pulled her dress closed, feeling the burning wound of the blade.

Campanale began to speak excitedly, angrily, in the dialect of the region. Several times he mentioned Jean Beaumain.

The man with the knife stepped away from Selena with an embarrassed expression on his swarthy face. The rest of the crowd moved back as well. Campanale walked over and inspected the damage done to Selena.

"It is fortunate," he quavered, in his falsetto tones, "that Jean Beaumain's name is respected by these people." He took her hand. "Come, let us go."

Yolanda and Martha Marguerite were not especially pleased to witness Selena's return to Hidden Harbor, but the older woman was solicitous about the knife wound. She provided an ointment and maternal advice as Selena applied the stinging white salve.

"Rub it thoroughly but carefully into the cut," she said. "It should help heal the wound in a matter of days. How fortunate you were not more seriously hurt."

"I would have been, I assure you. At least now I know that I can trust Campanale anyway."

Martha did not respond to that assumption.

Selena told of the European man who had been in the village.

"Yes, that is—was—LaValle. He had a most unsavory reputation. It was said that he operated a smuggling business out of Port-de-Paix. The natives tolerated him because, in addition to his clandestine affairs, he brought trade to the village and its inhabitants.

This time it was Selena who did not respond. She was thinking that if Royce had had dealings with LaValle, he too must be involved in business that was less than upright. The thought saddened her greatly, because now she could no longer try to deny the possibility that her betrothed had never really changed his stripes at all. Was Royce, at his core, still the unprincipled adventurer and opportunist of old?

No, I won't believe it! she declared to herself.

And yet . . .

"Does the word 'sorbontay' mean anything to you?" she asked Martha Marguerite.

"Why, no, I don't believe so, my dear. Should it?"

"I guess not," Selena replied. "It doesn't mean anything to me, either."

Yet two men, two very different men, Ward and LaValle, were dead. And both of them had spoken the same dying word.

"Well, the way things have turned out, I must proceed with my plan to investigate Yolanda's quarters."

Martha Marguerite once again promised her cooperation, and on the appointed day she withdrew hastily from table—Jean had not returned from Cuba and the three women were lunching by themselves—complaining of internal distress. A short time later, as Yolanda speculated with Selena about the nature of Martha's malady, a servant brought news that the older woman was calling for the Haitian girl's aid.

Yolanda excused herself with a smile of satisfaction, and went to minister to Martha Marguerite.

Tension mounted within Selena, but she forced herself to appear calm, finished the crab-and-lobster casserole she'd been eating, and even called for a small bunch of grapes and some Madeira. Finally, she motioned the servants to clear the table, got up, and started toward the rose room. When she was certain that no one observed her, she doubled back, slipped out the front door, and walked along the veranda to the west wing of the sprawling, gracious house. Whether by accident or plan, Selena and Yolanda lived at opposite ends of Hidden Harbor.

Yolanda's quarters opened onto a small garden similar to the one that Selena enjoyed. Glancing about, Selena swung over the veranda's railing and dropped into the grassy garden. While her own was well-tended, however, the bushes and flowers here had been allowed to grow wild, creating the effect of a miniature wilderness. The air was hot and still beneath great, wet, hanging leaves, and Selena began to perspire immediately.

One second later she was as cold as a North Sea stone.

Something was sliding toward her through the grass.

Selena had assumed that the Haitian beauty would take some precautions to protect her rooms from trespass—she had equipped herself to deal with locks, if necessary—but a serpent was something else entirely. Lifting her skirts, she dashed toward the flagstones outside Yolanda's French doors, pressing herself against the glass and wood.

She could not see the snake itself—the grass was too high—but she did see the blades of grass ripple and shiver as the serpent changed directions and came toward the French doors.

Oh, Lord, now what? Selena thought. The damn things had poor eyesight. But they hunted unerringly by scent alone.

And now she remembered Rafael telling her about snakes being used in plots of vengeance, the scent of a piece of clothing . . .

Had Yolanda done something like that? Had she taken an article of Selena's apparel and trained a serpent to strike?

Then Selena saw the snake's hooded head rear up over the top of the grass, swiveling this way and that in eerie menace, looking for her, seeking the scent.

Just get inside! she told herself, as the serpent, goldish-black and ugly, lewd in its peculiarly glistening thickness, slithered up onto the flagstones.

Prepared to break a pane of glass if need be, Selena tried the handle on the French doors. It moved. The door swung open. Selena slid inside. The snake, coiling and uncoiling, edged sideways over the flagstones and struck at the glass with its jagged yellow fangs.

The glass did not break, but the serpent was there, as if on guard.

Selena, just on the verge of abandoning this entire mission and getting out of there while she was still able, turned away from the French doors. What she saw in the room struck her motionless. This was not a bedchamber at all, but rather some form of depraved, savage chapel. Two of the walls were black, two red, and thick red draperies obliterated most of the forest-heavy daylight. A low, black table, much like an altar, stood on the floor in the center of the room. Seven black candles burned thereon, illuminating what appeared to be a glittering black pillar made of terra-cotta, or something similar. Facets of the pillar gleamed and wavered as the candles burned and, peering more closely, Selena realized that the artifact was larger at its top than its base, an unmistakable, contoured shape of the male phallus.

Then Selena became aware, too, of Yolanda's singular scent throughout the room. Musky, insinuating and perverse, the fragrance seemed to close around her. It was as if a living thing, shapeless and insubstantial but undeniably *there*, were tempting her flesh toward unspeakable sins. Selena felt a glowing rush in her loins, and there was a sudden, vacant place where her heart had been. Writhing images of Royce, of Jean Beaumain, of Sean Bloodwell and all the men she had ever known swarmed in her mind, and she realized that she was panting as if in the high throes of stark, unholy lust.

Only the bizarre, disgustingly familiar lumps on the altar, spaced evenly at the base of the black pillar, kept Selena from throwing herself down on one of the many low couches in the room, there to stroke and flail at the burning root of need.

Curiosity, horrible as its object proved to be, impelled her to reject desire. She stepped forward, farther away from the serpent whose forked tongue hissed on the glass, and knelt before the altar for a closer look.

Thirty eyes stared back at her. Thirty dull zombie eyes in fifteen shrunken heads.

One of them had belonged, a short time ago, to LaValle of Port-de-Paix.

Choking down her gorge, trembling, Selena glanced at the others. Jean Beaumain had been gone now for several weeks, and . . .

But his face was not among these men and women who had come, by God knew what misfortune, into the devilishly skilled hands of Yolanda Fee. Their skin was uniformly wrinkled like the outsides of dried, brown apples, and their hair was as lustreless as their eyes. Yet it was possible, even by candlelight, to see that most of the men had been attractive in life, and that the women had been beautiful. They may, indeed, have been Yolanda's lovers and rivals. For a dark, fleeting moment, Selena imagined her own little head resting upon this evil altar.

Abruptly, she got to her feet, forcing herself to think. Yes, she was here all right, but what of use had she learned?

That Yolanda was a witch?

Selena had already been told.

That she commanded access to unspeakable secrets?

Selena saw no reason to doubt.

That she was, at last, consummately dangerous?

Selena believed.

You're here to find that pouch of wealth, she reminded herself. So, forcing back the loathing evoked by the altar, and the concupiscence elicited by the mocking scent, Selena began a search. The couches revealed nothing except the fact that given their unusual shapes, each had been designed to facilitate a different position in the physiological symphony of love. The altar she had already inspected. Even the walls and floors appeared to conceal nothing, although Selena was afraid that her tap-tap-tapping could be heard throughout the house. She ran her hands over every inch of drapery fabric, again with no result.

Then in the gloom at the room's innermost wall, Selena found what at first appeared to be another curtain, but which, when pushed aside, revealed a drawing room of conventional design, the furniture somewhat heavy but well-made, the furnishings and paintings unremarkable, common. There was a bedroom adjoining this chamber, with everything neat and predictable, including a big brass four-poster with an embroidered silk canopy atop. Either Yolanda Fee sheltered two very different people in her one devil's bait of a body, or she was very adept at showing whichever nature she chose to whom she chose.

Selena began to wonder how much Jean Beaumain himself really knew about his mistress. The short walk from the primitive chapel to these spacious, European-style rooms would have taken a civilization twenty thousand years to traverse.

And then Selena entered the combined wardrobe and dressing room.

The scent again, with its beckoning lure to lust and degradation, all but overpowered her, but Selena fought it off. She looked everywhere, going over each of the hundreds of garments here, but found not a trace of sovereigns or jewels.

What she did discover, to her initial bewilderment, was the symbol of an eye sewn somewhere upon every article of clothing.

Also, in new thread, in hurried, irregular stitching, there was a small embroidered cross.

Selena stood there in the dressing room, staring at her image in Yolanda's gigantic mirror, wondering.

The mirror—not the mirror itself but its power of reflection—catapulted Selena to the conclusion that came to her there.

Yolanda, born, raised, and trained in a world where magic was as elemental as breathing, obviously feared both Martha Marguerite's ring and Selena's cross. Thus she had sought, by stitching those symbols into the fabric of her garments, to ward off their presumed powers, to guard herself from anticipated assaults.

The shrunken heads, the phallic tower, the candles: these meant nothing. Yolanda was a girl who lived in terrible fear.

Selena believed that her cross represented no threat to anyone. But if Yolanda was afraid of the eye-shaped ring, she might have good reason.

And that would mean Martha Marguerite was the truly dangerous person here at Hidden Harbor!

If so, Selena had approached and consorted with an apparently cultured, obviously intelligent woman who might be far more threatening than the simple, superstitious Yolanda Fee could ever hope to be.

Selena held this theory for three full days, until she found a time to steal into Martha's suite and discover, in every garment the woman owned, a tiny, embroidered, five-pointed star.

Checkmate. She still had no idea whom to trust, if anyone.

But she did not find the jewels in Martha Marguerite's rooms either.

"I've been waiting for the chance to ask you this," whispered the older woman one afternoon on the veranda, where she and Selena were having tea and hoping to catch sight of the *Liberté* on the horizon. "How went your expedition?"

"There are more things on heaven and earth," Selena replied, "than I dreamt of in my suspicions."

Martha gave her young guest an odd look, but said nothing.

7 Strange Nectar

A month went by, and then another, yet Jean Beaumain did not return. Winter arrived, blessing St. Crique Isle with splendid warm weather by day and with cool, gorgeous nights for sleep. Yolanda, growing fretful at her master's absence, traveled to Haiti for a fortnight, but returned to Hidden Harbor sullen and unapproachable. Martha Marguerite received, via Port-au-Prince, a long letter from her family's Parisian attorney advising her that a certain Uncle Pierre, who had been in charge of familial affairs, had died of pneumonia. Decisions had to be made, he said, especially in the light of a rising revolutionary *animus* against the titled nobility. Martha ought to come to Paris, he pleaded, at first opportunity. The woman fretted over the matter at breakfast, luncheon, tea, and dinner. Selena's usually generous supply of sympathy waned; she began to take many of her meals alone.

She, too, had decisions to make, a pressure that increased with each day that Jean remained away. So, early in April, she had Campanale and several other servants take her to Port-au-Prince aboard the sloop. Once there, she learned that a Spanish freighter was due to arrive any day from Venezuela, en route to New York. Selena no longer had the slightest idea if Royce was in New York —or even if he was alive, for that matter—but at least she had friends there who might know of his whereabouts and who would give her comfort and shelter.

The main problem was that she hadn't a cent to her name. Damn the soul of whoever had taken those jewels! Damn the jewels anyway! And damn Jean too for being away so long!

But in truth, she'd begun to fear for his life.

Campanale suggested that she attempt to sell or pawn her gold cross, but Selena would not hear of it, besides which the amount it might bring would not suffice to take her to America. Just when she'd decided to inquire after a loan of money, word came that the Spanish vessel had been destroyed in a hurricane off the Tortugas. There would not be another ship to New York for two months.

Thus, it was back to Hidden Harbor for Selena, but not before reading a story in an English newspaper—six months old—that reported Lórd Sean Bloodwell's arrival in Paris to take up his duties in the diplomatic corps. He had been received by the French monarch, Louis XVI.

As the little one-sailed sloop glided slowly out of Port-au-Prince, it passed on the port side an inbound British frigate, the HMS *Prince William,* named for one of the royal sons. Its sails were ripped through and there were more great, jagged holes in its hull. Obviously there'd been a battle at sea. Since the *Prince William* was British, Selena wished the damn thing had been sent to the bottom.

But when they arrived back at Hidden Harbor, Selena's spirits, heretofore bleak, soared immediately.

The sleek *Liberté,* intact and unscathed, lay at anchor, and Jean Beaumain himself was waving from the veranda. He embraced her when she joined him up at the house with sufficient enthusiasm to flare the ever-present fires of animosity in Yolanda's sultry eyes, to put a quick look of concern on Martha Marguerite's face. He had been telling them of his adventures and now over brandy he regaled Selena as well.

"When we reached Cuba," he said, "I did some trading in Havana that turned a small profit, but I also learned of a prospective deal in silver that was abrew down in Caracas. So of course we set sail for Venezuela immediately. . . ."

He looks wonderful, thought Selena, watching Jean as he lounged cavalierly in the veranda chair. He was deeply tanned, and the sun had turned his blond hair almost to a white-silver hue. His eyes were sparklingly blue, and every inch of him was lean, honed.

". . . Once in Caracas, I was informed that a lode of silver had been discovered and was being mined somewhere in the Amazonian basin. We proceeded to Brazil where I managed to buy, at a very good price, some of the best ore. I brought it back to Caracas, made a deal, and ladies, I must tell you that it was one of the best! I could retire now for the rest of my life.

"If I chose to do so," he added, grinning.

Martha betrayed nothing by her expression, but Yolanda Fee looked discomfited, almost hurt. Clearly, she *wanted* Jean to cease his wandering and remain at Hidden Harbor with her.

Selena, for her part, said only that she was happy to see him safe and home. She wanted to get him alone for a long talk, but decided to wait for a time that would not further arouse the hostility of the other women.

When Jean had finished relating his adventures, Martha chimed in with her news from France, adding the urgent plea that he take her there as soon as possible.

"I will think it over," he allowed. "I myself will not set foot on French soil until I have done with Chamorro, but if you must go back, you must."

This satisfied Martha Marguerite, although it caused Yolanda to leave the veranda in a sloe-eyed huff.

Jean paid no attention. "Now I am going to bathe for a long, long time," he announced, rising, "and then we shall dine."

"And how did you fare in Port-au-Prince, my dear?" inquired Martha, when Jean had gone inside to his ablutions.

"Not so well," Selena admitted. "Not so well."

Martha got up and left too, leaving Selena with Rafael, who came from the ship looking fit and happy.

"You've had a successful trip?"

"One of the best, Selena." He sat down with her, helped himself to a mug of brandy, and lowered his voice. "I saw your Royce Campbell in Caracas," he said.

Selena's heart skipped several beats. "You *saw* him?"

"In truth, I spoke to him. I told him you were here. But Jean does not know about this. He is in love with you, as you know, and I did not wish to upset him."

"What did Royce say?"

"That he would sail here for you. In fact, I was somewhat surprised to see you. Campbell left Venezuela a week before we did. He ought to have arrived here by now."

"You're sure you told him how to reach Hidden Harbor?"

"Yes. Precisely. I drew him a map. He was very happy when he learned that you were safe. But, Selena—"

"Yes?"

"Are you . . . are you *really sure* about that man?"

"Of course I am! Why would you ask such a question?"

"I get the feeling, Selena, that he is involved in something very complicated and very dangerous. At every port, things seem to be going on just beneath the surface. It is nothing that one can put a finger on, but the feeling is there, and Campbell seems to be a part of whatever is happening."

This was information Selena did not wish to treat. She would discuss it with Royce when they were together again.

But she did mention the hapless LaValle from Port-de-Paix.

"I cannot say I am surprised." Rafael nodded. "Now that man was something of a scoundrel—"

And Royce dealt with him! Selena brooded.

"—and in the end scoundrels always meet such fates. Well, I suppose it is better than dying in one's bed. Now *that* is ignominy for you!"

They both laughed. "Ending up as a shrunken head on a pagan altar is not exactly noble, either," said Selena.

Rafael was mystified. "What do you mean?"

She told him about Yolanda's primitive chamber.

"You're jesting," he exclaimed. "You've been listening to too many stories about Haitian black magic."

"No!" she said, getting up and taking his hand. "Come along and I'll show you."

She pulled him along to the end of the veranda, gesturing toward the garden outside Yolanda's quarters. "Have a look at that!" she challenged.

"So?" he asked, puzzled.

Couldn't he *see?* She turned toward the garden.

It was immaculately manicured, just like the one outside her own rose-tinted chamber. The grass was clipped level and short. Plants and flowers stood placidly in their perfectly tended beds.

This must be how people feel when they begin to lose their minds, Selena thought. "Well, come and see something else," she ordered, pulling Rafael along with her over the veranda railing. So eager was she to prove the validity of what she'd seen, she didn't even care if anyone saw them crossing the lawn and approaching Yolanda's French doors.

"What am I supposed to say?" Rafael asked in bewilderment as she bade him look through the glass into Yolanda's strange room.

"What? Isn't it obvious?"

Selena herself peered inside.

And saw only a room like her own, except painted in a light shade of becoming blue. Yolanda was sitting on her bed, pouring a glass of rum. She saw them and came over, opening the doors.

"Yes?"

"I was . . . we were just . . . admiring your garden," Selena faltered.

The Haitian permitted herself a slow smile. "Come in and join me in a drink?"

"No. No, thank you."

"Selena, are you sure you're all right?" Rafael inquired solicitously when they were back on the veranda.

"I don't know," replied Selena. "I guess I just don't know."

Oh, Royce! Get here soon!

Darkness had fallen. Dinner time drew near, and Selena was seated before the mirror in her room, brushing her hair. Slowly, methodically, she brushed and brushed. The very mindlessness of this grooming ritual had a calming effect, of which she was badly in need, and the thin silk chemise she wore felt cool and luxurious on her skin. Across the back of her chair lay the gown she would wear, a sea-green velvet dress with dark-green piping. It covered both breasts, but not too completely. She hoped Jean would like it.

On the inside of the hem, minutes earlier, she had stitched an eye, a cross, and a small five-pointed star.

"When in Rome . . ." she murmured. "What is happening to me? Here I am, a modern woman, bereft of superstitions, apparently beginning to believe in dark forces. And yet I *know* what I saw in Yolanda's room!"

The black image of that terra-cotta phallus with its many-faceted glitter stood out as clearly in her mind as Coldstream Castle. She vividly recalled the shrunken heads. And Yolanda's evocative scent was as real here at Hidden Harbor as it had been aboard the *Liberté*.

"I am *not* dreaming!" she said aloud. "I am *not* going mad!"

"I certainly hope not," said Jean Beaumain, slipping into her room.

Embarrassed, she started to get to her feet, but he crossed the room quickly, grinning, and took her into his arms. He wore a loose-fitting white shirt and scarlet breeches, and smelled of brandy and soap.

"Jean . . ." she said, but his kiss cut off a half-formed, complicated thought, which combined her pleasure at seeing him again, a concern that he still wanted her as much as before, and a need to tell him what had transpired since his departure.

Moreover, it felt good—God, did it ever feel good—to be kissed and held again. She decided to let herself go with the kiss a little, to enjoy it fully, but that decision, once made, weakened her resolve when it came time to decide to stop. So she didn't decide. And then he was kissing her harder, pressing against her, bursting with strength and hard need. She was not even aware that he had pulled the flimsy chemise down over her shoulders until she felt his hands on her breasts, gentle and sure. Need rose in her like a pillar of fire, and she clung to him, her eyes closed, still kissing him, as he lifted her and carried her to the bed. He did not remove the shirt covering his scars, but somehow his breeches were off, her chemise was on the floor, and he was inside her as far as could be. The love was like a sudden summer storm raging out of a clear sky. Selena felt the first ripples of approaching ecstasy like warning droplets of rain, and before she could move or take shelter, the storm broke savagely all around, tremendous in its fury, spent itself in violent jolts of power, leaving both of them drenched and shuddering in the afterglow.

"Selena . . ." Jean gasped, lying beside her and putting his lips to her flushed breasts. "Selena, that was so good."

She could not answer for a moment. Jean was right. She felt shaken and limp and . . .

Guilty. "You shouldn't have done that," she murmured.

He was silent for a moment, then laughed softly.

"I didn't think that I was the only one involved," he said.

She had to smile. "I guess you're right," she admitted, patting down his hair, curled and damp from passion. "It's just—"

"Still thinking of Royce Campbell, are you?" he guessed, without anger. "Forget him. If he'd desired to find you, he'd have done so by now—"

Selena could not tell him of Rafael's conversation with Royce.

"—but he hasn't, so you're mine. I am so rich now that the world can be ours. Let's belong to each other. Let's start right now."

He reached down to pleasure her. She was trying, unsuccessfully, to writhe away when a soft rap sounded at the door.

Jean may not have heard it. At any rate, he did not bother to move. Selena hurriedly drew a sheet over them. Hidden Harbor was a place filled with servants and it was not at all unusual—indeed, it was accepted—for the staff to move about freely in household duties. Before Selena could call out, asking who had knocked, the door opened and the little houseboy, Campanale, stood there with a silver tray balanced on the flat of one hand. On the tray were a pitcher and two tall glasses.

"I'm so sorry . . ." he said, nonplussed, as he saw the two of them in bed.

"It's all right," Jean reassured him, smiling the lazy smile of a man who has just been well-satisfied and looks forward to being satisfied again. "What have you there? Bring it in and set it on the table."

"Rum punch," replied the boy, averting his eyes as he skirted the bed and put the tray on the table.

"What have you brought?" asked Selena.

"Why, it's the refreshment you ordered, ma'am."

Martha Marguerite had instructed him that women of the British Isles were addressed in that manner.

"I didn't send for anything," she said.

"Well, I'll have some," Jean decided. "Pour me a glass. Pour yourself one too, in honor of my safe return. We'll drink together."

Selena was a bit chagrined. She understood that Jean wanted the houseboy to bruit it about that she was Beaumain's woman now. He was forthright and direct, but he had his wiles too.

Campanale filled the two glasses, handed one to Jean, and lifted the other to his lips.

"Here's to your return, sir," he said, and drank.

Selena shifted slightly in the bed just then, arranging the sheet more adequately about herself, and her sudden movement caused Beaumain to hesitate. He did not sip the drink.

Thank God for him.

Little Campanale smiled, had several swallows of the punch, and grinned at them.

Then he was jerked to his toes as if by a rope, and his entire body began to tremble. "Ahhhhh . . ." he said, but that was all, because right there before the eyes of Selena and Jean, his skin seemed to shrink upon his body, his face became a death's-head, and his slick, glossy Haitian hair turned as white as the sand on St. Crique Isle.

He turned from an adolescent into a withered little old man before their eyes.

And as a little old man he died, gasping and quivering, on the floor beside the bed.

"It was the drink," cried Jean, hurling his glass away and leaping up, naked, to sniff the pitcher of rum punch. "You didn't send for it?"

Selena bent helplessly over the houseboy. "My God, no. It is poison. It is more than poison. It is—"

"—a potion of some kind," finished Jean Beaumain. "Who would have—?"

He slipped into his breeches, heading toward the door. "I'm going to get to the bottom of this right now. . . ."

Selena continued to kneel over Campanale. The rum punch, she knew, had been meant for her and Jean. Someone had intended to kill them and, for good measure, turn their youthful bodies into withered husks.

Shrunken bodies. Shrunken heads.

Yolanda?

Or Martha Marguerite, skillfully concealing her acts behind methods that would cause suspicion to fall upon the Haitian girl?

"Wait, Jean!" she cried, as he reached the door. She was afraid that he had misread a situation that, apparently simple in its sheer deadliness, might nonetheless have proceeded from a devilishly complex and scheming mind.

The feel of Jean outlined her insides, she was awash with his essence, he was a part of her, so she cried out and stopped him at the door.

"Don't go just yet . . ." she began.

Her concern saved both their lives.

8 A Cross in the Sand

A shriek of alarm sounded in the hall outside the rose room, followed by a deep-throated command, *"Halt!"* and the explosion of a blunderbuss. A jagged, splintered hole appeared in the door, inches from Jean's head, and a ball of lead shot whined through the bedroom, shattering a pane of glass in the French doors as it exited. Footsteps came down the hall at a run, servants were yelling, and there was a second explosion and a cry of agony.

"What? We've been invaded?" wondered Jean.

In the hallway, Selena heard the low, icy voice of Lieutenant Clay Oakley. "Search everywhere," he ordered with limpid malice. "I know she's here and I want her alive."

Yolanda or whoever may have had the power to evoke a visual projection of Oakley? But the voice outside was real, and so was he.

"It's the British," said Selena. "They've come for me, not you. Let me give myself up before they destroy your home."

"Nobody's giving anything up," vowed Jean, thinking fast. "They couldn't have sailed into Hidden Harbor, so they must have come as a landing party from the beach. Here, put on your dress," he said, tossing it to her. She did, and they left via the French doors. Out in the darkened garden, he outlined his plan.

"I'm going to slip into the weapons room and arm myself. You run down to the dock and summon my men from the *Liberté*. Shout as loud as you have to. Some will be asleep. Get them up to the house as soon as you can. Now go."

Scarcely thinking, Selena did as she was told, racing down to the pier and hailing the ship, on which Jean's men were quartered. Rafael and Louis came immediately up on deck, and she told them that Hidden Harbor was under attack. Within minutes, armed with swords, knives, and guns, they were running with her up toward the house, inside which another explosion of gunfire sounded. Selena hovered outside the front door. The sailors, heedless of their safety, poured into the house, enraged and determined. For a while there were shouts, sounds of running and scuffling, then silence. Selena slipped into the foyer, armed herself with the bronze statuette of a sea nymph, and advanced into the drawing room.

There she saw why things had quieted down so abruptly. Five fearful redcoats were forced up against a wall, disarmed and vulnerable. Jean's men, twenty in all, pressed them there with swords. Terrified servants watched from doorways as Jean and Lieutenant Oakley faced one another in the center of the room.

Oakley held Martha Marguerite between him and Jean. He had a thin stiletto at her throat. Martha's eyes flashed every which way, but she seemed in control of her emotions by sheer effort of will.

"Ah, Selena!" said Oakley, catching sight of her. "I knew we would meet again. Come away with me, and let us complete our business."

"Drop the knife or you're a dead man," Jean told him.

"Then so is this lady I hold," Oakley replied.

"Why have you invaded my house?"

"To arrest Selena, of course. She is a spy against my monarch."

"The war is over," Jean said, stepping close to Oakley. He held a great-snouted pistol, and was trying to get into position for a shot at the lieutenant.

Oakley pressed the tip of the stiletto more closely against Martha's throat. She winced.

"The war may be over," Oakley admitted, "but Selena is still an enemy of the British Empire, which I serve. Moreover, she and I share a regard for beauty, for the perfect symmetry of existence, if you will. Our circle must be closed. Isn't that right, Selena?"

"You're mad, you know that?" said Selena.

Oakley just grimaced. One side of his mustache threatened to become unstuck.

Selena dropped the statuette she was holding and stepped forward. "Take me then, but release Martha. She has done you no harm."

The lieutenant loosened his grasp on Martha Marguerite, a sly look of triumph on his bleak, misshapen face.

"No, Selena!" cried the older woman. "He will kill both of us if he can."

At that moment, Selena knew that Martha Marguerite was not her enemy. She realized at the same time that Yolanda Fee was nowhere in sight.

"How did you come to know I was here?" she asked Oakley.

He shrugged. "I have my ways. I know many things. You may wish to die anyway when I tell you what I also know."

Something eerily dry and slithery, like Yolanda's magic snake, curled beneath Selena's breastbone.

"Stop talking to him, Selena," said Jean. "We can overpower him and his men. He's just buying time by pretending to information he doesn't—".

Oakley actually laughed. "I know that Royce Campbell is dead, Selena," he said. In truth, he fairly crowed this news, as an insane cock might have addressed a triumphant dawn.

"You're lying!" Selena managed.

The lieutenant shook his head in prideful satisfaction. "No, it's very true. I myself was aboard the *Prince William* when that worthy frigate, along with the men-o'-war *Cliveden* and *Duke of York,* cornered Campbell west of Haiti. He all but wrecked the *Prince William* and left the warships dead in the water, but through a spyglass I saw him dead and bleeding on the *Selena*'s deck before she limped away toward La Tortue."

This was a sizable island perhaps fifty miles from St. Crique.

"You're lying," Selena said again, in a faint, dry, wispy voice.

"No," declared the lieutenant.

Jean, who had listened to this tale without comment, turned to Rafael. "Kill the redcoats," he snapped.

Oakley's eyes widened. "Don't," he cried. "They're good men. They're only following orders."

In spite of her concern about Royce, Selena realized that Oakley possessed yet another facet which might be considered honorable. A good officer, he was mindful of his subordinates' safety.

"We'll let the men go if you release Martha," she said.

"Selena, don't—" said Jean exasperated.

"What about me?" Oakley inquired.

"You can go too."

"*Selena—!*"

But to Selena, it seemed the only way to avoid bloodshed in this house, to which she was conscious of having brought sufficient trouble already.

Jean stood there, glaring at Oakley and calculating the costs of various courses of action. All of the costs were high.

"All right," he agreed reluctantly. "Life for life. But I will kill you if you ever set foot upon my isle again. I will kill you if I *see* you again."

Oakley released Martha Marguerite, who stepped away from him quickly, gasping for breath and massaging her throat.

"Fair enough," Oakley said, keeping his stiletto at the ready. He glanced menacingly at Selena. "There is much time in this world," he muttered enigmatically.

The sailors were disappointed at the outcome of this confrontation—after all, a servant had been wounded—but yielded to Jean's authority.

"*Au revoir,* Selena," called Oakley, as he panted breathlessly after his men, who had set out for the St. Crique beach.

"Rafael," said Jean, "ready the *Liberté* for sailing. Oakley must have a ship off the coast. We are going to pursue her until I'm satisfied that the threat to us is over, and that Oakley is bound for the high seas."

"Let me come with you?" Selena asked plaintively.

Jean's glance was quizzical.

"Perhaps we might . . . pass near the island of La Tortue?"

Where the *Selena* had last been heading.

Jean's face darkened. Royce. But he nodded. He understood.

By mid-morning of the following day, it was clear that the HMS *Prince William,* with Lieutenant Clay Oakley aboard her, had set a northeasterly course, perhaps toward England itself.

"Good riddance," said Jean Beaumain, standing on the bridge with Selena. Then he gave the order to come about and begin the search for Royce.

Hours before they drew within sight of La Tortue, which Jean Beaumain intended to circumnavigate, Selena was up in the swaying crow's nest, scanning the endlessly rolling blue-green ocean, seeking a glimpse of the ship that bore her name. She knew that it hurt Jean to see her there, he who had done so much for her and treated her so well, with her heart set upon finding another man.

Years afterward, Selena would still remember, with heartaching clarity, the unvoiced tension of emotions she bore then, knowing that Jean was helping her to find Royce but hoping that she would not; knowing that, if she did find Royce, he might, as Oakley had reported, be gone from life.

Oh, please God, if the Selena *went down,* she prayed—she prayed but little, yet this was a genuine prayer—*let her have gone down in shallow water, so that I will at least be able to gaze upon the place in which she lies. Don't let her be gone forever in the trackless deep.*

So sure was she that the ship was lost—especially when no trace of wreckage appeared—that Selena even began morbidly to imagine divers, centuries hence, coming upon the great, black, decaying relic of hull, to find within only washed, white bones and crumbling timbers. One of them might swim with languid curiosity through the space that had been Royce's cabin, neither knowing nor caring that once, three or four or five hundred years earlier, the best of Highlands warriors had made love there to Selena MacPherson, a Scottish girl lost to time. They could no more touch her, or know the reality of her years, than she could know theirs.

There was only one span of time for each living soul, and to lose whom you most loved during your time was the most terrible thing that could befall.

Oh, yes, did Selena not know it!

Finally, when they had sailed almost all the way around La Tortue, Selena came down from the crow's nest. She had not given up, but she was immensely sad and disspirited. Jean Beaumain was standing at the ship's railing, scanning the coast line through his spyglass.

"We might as well go back to Hidden Harbor," she said.

"Perhaps not just yet," he answered, handing her the glass. "Don't jump to conclusions, but I've seen something that might warrant investigation."

She looked toward shore. At first she saw nothing but the beach sweeping up to a palm-fringed thicket, with a small village in the distance. Then a flutter of colored cloth caught her eyes, many pieces of cloth attached to wooden stakes that stuck out of the earth. No, they were not merely stakes: they were makeshift crosses.

And the rags affixed to them were scraps of plaid.

Campbell plaid?

"Oh, no—"

"Do you want to go ashore and have a look?" Jean asked.

"I . . . yes. That is, I don't—"

She didn't know if she could face it.

Jean understood. "You ought to know for sure," he said. "I'll go for you."

Jean anchored the *Liberté* and rowed the dinghy a few hundred yards to the beach. She saw him inspecting the eerie little graveyard beneath the palm trees, and then he was out of sight for a time among the trees. When he reappeared, he waved to her, then rowed back to the ship.

She watched his approach from the railing, and when she saw the half-worried, half-sympathetic expression on his face, she guessed that her worst fears had been realized.

"Selena," he said, still in the dinghy, looking up at her, "perhaps for your . . . for your peace of mind in the future, you should come ashore."

Stifling her sobs, already too numb to feel the full flood of grief, she clambered down the rope ladder and got into the little boat. Jean said nothing as he bent to the oars, taking her on a journey so short that it seemed to last forever.

Nine crosses stood in the sand, each bearing a tiny flutter of Campbell plaid, each bearing the initials of the man who lay beneath. The men who had died during the *Selena*'s battle with the *Prince William* lay here. And on one of the crosses, scratched deeply into the wood, was the word "Campbell."

This is how it ends, Selena thought, kneeling down upon the sand before the cross. *This is how it . . .*

Then she noticed an old woman watching her from the shadows of the surrounding foliage. Cronelike and withered, she regarded Selena with a mixture of curiosity and suspicion.

Jean Beaumain brought the woman over to Royce's grave. "This is Lodie," he said, "who comes from the nearby village. I went there to find out what had happened. She speaks only dialect, but you may ask her anything. I'll translate."

At first, Selena could think of nothing to say, so stupefied was she by the overwhelming fact of death. Finally, the necessary questions came, and Jean conveyed in a low, tender voice the responses given by old Lodie.

A black ship with snow-white sails had appeared offshore. The sails were tattered and the ship had great jagged rents in her hull. (Here Lodie gesticulated energetically with her wrinkled hands, describing the awful proportions of the holes.) Several small boats came ashore from the ship, and sailors carried the bodies of nine dead men up beneath the trees. Graves were dug. (At this point old Lodie jerked and groaned as if she were shoveling earth.) The bodies were placed inside the graves, crosses made, names and initials scratched into the soft wood. Lastly a flag from the ship was torn apart, a piece of the flag affixed to each cross. That was all. The men went back to the ship and it sailed away.

"Ask her," said Selena, "if she saw the bodies clearly."

Lodie appeared somewhat miffed when Jean conveyed this question, as if her word were not believed.

"She says that she saw it all," he told Selena. "She says she was right here, as close to the bodies as she is to you."

"Then tell her what Royce looked like," she went on, biting her lip before giving her own description. When she gave his great height, which Jean translated into dialect, Lodie reached her hand up over her head and nodded. When Selena spoke of Royce's broad, powerful shoulders and deep chest, Lodie nodded and slapped herself vigorously, swiveling her shoulders to show that she had seen the mighty man to whom Selena referred. Hair? Lodie touched Jean's blond locks and shook her head, then pointed to her own black eyebrows.

Selena tried to think of more questions to ask, questions that Lodie could not answer, any question that might give her the hope of Royce's continued existence.

But there were no such questions, and no such answers.

"Face it, Selena," said Jean, coming over to her and putting his arm around her waist. "I'm sorry."

Then the full knowledge, the complete force of death came down around her, and she fell prostrate on the sand in which the flag-marked cross was standing. She could not help herself, nor stop herself, howling her grief to the cross and the sand, the wind and the sun and the sea. Never before, not even when she'd seen her father killed, had Selena felt so devastated, so helpless. So alone. Wailing, shouting unintelligible syllables, now defiant, now despairing, she alternately cursed God and mourned herself. It was not *right* that this cross should stand here; it was not *right* that Royce Campbell, wild Highlands pagan, should lie beneath this sand. And she began to claw at the very sand itself, throwing great fistfuls of sand into the air, where it came down into her hair and upon her body. To Lodie, it seemed that the crazy golden-haired woman was trying to defile grave and torment spirit of the dead. She fled. And Selena, in her grief, was all alone. . . .

Not so.

Presently, she felt Jean Beaumain's arms around her. With difficulty, he stilled her flailing hands and drew her to her feet.

"It can't be . . ." she was shrieking.

"Selena," he said, holding her closely and crooning. "Selena. There, there. If Royce could see you now, what do you think he would do? Eh? What do you think he would say?"

Jean's question brought the image of Royce to Selena. What would Royce do, say, if he saw her carrying on like this?

He would doubtless draw back from her a bit, and give her an ironic look. There would be a trace of amusement flickering at the corners of his mouth. And after a moment, perhaps after permitting himself a faintly mocking censurious scowl, he would say as he had when catching her, fighting and naked, on the New York docks: *"Is this any way for a Scottish lady to carry on?"*

And he would tell her now: *"You are never defeated unless you believe it."*

"I guess I almost believed it this time," Selena murmured, trying to stop her sobs and dry her tears.

"What?" asked Jean Beaumain, who hadn't caught her words.

"Nothing. I'm sorry you had to see me like this."

"Let's go back to the ship," he said, "or do you want to say a prayer?"

Selena shook her head. "I'm not sure he'd want that. The way in which I remember him will be more important."

That night, sailing back toward Hidden Harbor, Selena went up on deck in the black, moonless, star-blasted night, and there in memory she blessed and worshiped Royce Campbell, whom she had loved as no other. *I will choose one memory,* she thought. *I will take, from among all the times we shared, one soaring moment, and it shall be my prayer and my memorial.*

The time they had made love aboard the *Highlander*, made love as Selena had vaguely heard, uncertainly imagined it could be made, and which was called forbidden on all the fearful pulpits of Europe. It was a sweet, lingering speech of flesh itself, in which Royce had given her long, aching instruction. It was more than mere treasure, it was transcendence, transport to a strange new world. Ripples of indescribable softness washed again and again and forever upon the walls of her soul, until blood as well as flesh found tongue. Tender waves spread behind the horizons of her lidded eyes, driven gently by her cry, and proudly rocked the easy boats that lay embanked in touchless time.

The salt taste of him had been as welcome as the world.

The taste of herself on his lips had been communion.

"I'll always love you," she said softly to the black sky, in which the stars seemed embedded like jewels in stone.

9 Showdown

The *Liberté* reached Hidden Harbor shortly after dawn. Jean Beaumain and the others were surprised—and a little apprehensive—when they saw how quickly Selena left the ship and stormed up the dock toward the house. Jean, concerned for her, had first watched from the shadows as she'd stood on deck gazing into the sky. He'd been fearful, after witnessing her spectacular outburst of graveside grief, that she might again give way. And twice he had looked briefly into her cabin during the night. Once she'd been sewing a piece of fabric over that little gold cross she always wore. The next time he'd checked, Selena seemed to be jabbing at her hand with a quill. Very strange.

So Jean was worried, and he trotted up the dock after her. "Selena, hold up. What's your hurry—?"

She neither turned to answer him nor slackened her pace. In moments, she was on the veranda, then across it, pushing open the door.

Selena heard him call, and she heard his footsteps on the dock as he hurried to catch up with her. But just now, she had neither the time nor the inclination to explain anything to anybody. Because, at last, she understood everything, and she must strike before it was too late.

Dimly aware that Jean Beaumain, Rafael, Louis, and some of the other men were behind her, Selena charged through the central part of the house, and turned down the wide corridor that led to Yolanda Fee's quarters. If she proved to be right in her divinations—she was acting on the basis of intuition, not logic—then all would be well.

But if she were wrong . . .

"I'm not wrong!" she said, reaching Yolanda's door and grabbing the metal, European-style handle.

It scorched her skin. She cried out and jerked her hand away.

Fires of Delight   151

But undaunted and without hesitation, she seized the handle with her other hand, her left hand, on which she had, in ink, marked herself with a tiny, five-pointed star.

This time all went well. Her theory regarding Yolanda's powers appeared to be correct. The doorhandle was cool to her touch. The door opened, offering Jean and the sailors, who hurried toward Selena, a side of Yolanda that they had not seen before.

She was on her knees, naked, crouching in front of the little altar, dipping something over and over into a miniature cauldron, in which a dark liquid frothed and sputtered. On the altar stood the glittering pillar of phallus, the circle of shrunken heads, seven candles burning low, and a wire cage in which a blackish-gold serpent writhed and roiled. So intent was Yolanda on her work that she had not noticed how close the snake was to the candle flames. The room was as it had been when Selena had first entered it, with black and red walls and the suggestively shaped couches scattered about. On three of these lay men, some of the Haitian manservants, in various stages of unconsciousness and undress, rendered thus by Yolanda's sensuality or potions, or both. She had spent an energetic evening.

"My God!" breathed Jean.

Yolanda turned, offering in the process a view of Campanale's head, which she was in the process of treating. It was only half-shrunken as yet; the open eyes and mouth seemed to implore help in a battle that was already lost.

Before Yolanda, lean and splendid in her high-breasted beauty, could intervene, Selena crossed swiftly to the French doors, throwing them open, and also moving the heavy draperies away from the windows. On the afternoon of her previous visit there, the room had been obscured in gloom, but now the full light of dawn flooded in. Yolanda's room was like the set in an horrific stage play. Thin, lugubrious curtains hung floor to ceiling from the walls. By removing these, along with the couches and the altar, she could readily restore her chamber to its ordinary appearance.

But it was too late to do so now.

"Yolanda!" cried Jean Beaumain. "What is the meaning of this?"

"You trusting fool," the Haitian beauty sneered, getting to her feet. "Did you think, merely to have you, that I would give up the ways of my ancestors? And do you think, now, that I will permit this interloper"—she pointed a long-nailed finger in Selena's direction—"to steal you from me? I would have *you* dead first!"

Having said that, she sprang at Selena who, unready for the assault, fell to the floor beneath the other woman. The two of them grappled fiercely there, and before the men could even move to pull them apart, Yolanda's razor-sharp talons closed around Selena's throat.

"You are going to die!" Yolanda gritted threateningly, "for I have negated the mark of your power!"

Her eyes sought the cross around Selena's neck, and widened in alarm when she saw that it was concealed by a cloth. Then Selena moved her star-marked hand. Yolanda saw it, jerked as if slapped, and involuntarily loosened her grip. Gathering all her strength, Selena fought, writhing, twisting, and threw the other woman away. Yolanda rolled across the floor, striking and upsetting the altar. Candles fell, flaming, and the wire cage confining the serpent snapped open. The creature, maddened by incarceration and proximity to fire, caught a whiff of Yolanda's unmistakable scent and struck toward it with the force of a hurled javelin, burying its yellow fangs in her proud left breast.

She was dead before Selena could get to her feet, before Jean and his men could extinguish the burning candles.

Yolanda's Haitian lovers dozed on, oblivious.

The toppled phallus glittered in the light of dawn.

10   Bound for Glory

From St. Crique to Bermuda, from Bermuda to the Azores, and now from the Azores toward the Canary Islands. The *Liberté* and her passengers were on their way to France.

Much had happened since the awful morning on which Yolanda Fee had met her doom, and most of those things had been good. Jean had thought it strange that Selena should ask to have —"as a trophy," she'd claimed—Yolanda's terra-cotta pillar. But he knew the lure of trophies and he had acquiesced. And just as Selena had expected, she found her jewels and gold sovereigns embedded in the roughly crafted phallus itself, where Yolanda had concealed them. Selena had guessed the nature of the hiding place that night aboard the *Liberté*, gazing up at the star-flecked sky, seeing in it the glittering gems of God ablaze in blackness. It was almost as if Royce had sent her a hint from heaven; the communion between them, in many ways, would never end.

The jewels—the meaning of which Selena still did not understand—were now sewn inside the lining of a greatcoat made for her by the Hidden Harbor seamstress. Weather in France could be quite intemperate, she was informed, and a greatcoat was just the thing.

After Yolanda's demise, those in the Hidden Harbor household could not have been more gracious or grateful toward Selena. Yolanda had long held most of them in thrall with the mere threat of the powers she possessed. But only Selena had finally come to the conclusion that the Haitian girl's use of symbols, such as Martha Marguerite's ring and Erasmus Ward's cross, was not a ploy to guard herself against the perceived powers of others, but rather, by assuming their symbols, to rob them of the power and identity they might have had. That was why Yolanda had been so startled to see the cross concealed in cloth. She had been divested, she believed, of her hold over Selena.

How many of these things were real, were true, Selena herself did not know. But Yolanda Fee had *believed* in black magic, and her belief alone had armed her in *hubris,* with the gall to wreak terrible acts.

During the months that followed the discovery of Royce's sandy grave, Selena grieved, and sometimes took the sloop over to La Tortue, there to stand on the windy beach and look down at the cross that seemed so out of place, dreaming of things that might have been.

Things that now would never be.

But while it had at first seemed inconceivable that a man such as Royce, so vibrant, so full of life, should ever die, gradually the mysterious healing forces that salve and balm the human heart began to do their work. Selena went less and less frequently to La Tortue.

Then Jean Beaumain, who had wisely and lovingly left her alone in grief, came forward. He was neither tentative nor cautious—these traits were not prominent in his nature—but he was gentle and considerate. He did not wish to press her too hard too soon, lest by mischance or excessive ardor he drive her back into herself.

He was thoughtful: making sure that her room was filled with fresh flowers, seeing to it that her favorite dishes—lobster stew, poached marlin, pickled pigeon eggs—were served often. And when he returned to Hidden Harbor from one of his trading forays to Mexico or the Bahamas, he always brought her something—a necklace, a vase, a rare artifact—to wear or to enhance the rose room.

Finally, one night after returning from a trip to Florida, he came almost shyly, as if he might be rebuffed, to her room. Without speaking, he held before her eyes a broad gold ring in which a cluster of rubies gleamed scarlet in the light.

"This is for you," he said.

Selena took it, held it, turned and admired it.

"Put it on," he said.

She did, on the third finger of her right hand.

"Right finger, wrong hand," he said.

That was how it began, or how it began again.

He had chosen precisely the right time, when Selena's heart was well on its way to healing, and when she had begun again to turn outward toward life, driven by the instinctively spirited forces of her nature. They made love slowly and reverently that night, but afterwards, as they grew more comfortable, more natural with one another, the hindrance of customary inhibitions fell away completely. Sensuality, now fierce, often wild but never wicked, opened for them its casket of myriad treasures, and each thrill, each variation of love, was keener than the last, leaving them soaring and shaken in the splendor of its grace.

Selena used upon him delights she had learned in India, intricate caresses and movements and touches that enhanced and prolonged his ecstasy, so that when she finally brought him lingeringly to the heights, he would pass for long moments into dreamy unconsciousness from the effects of pleasure alone.

And she taught him how to do the same for her, with the added benefit that, given the female nature, she would go on and on and on before dropping free from the top of the world. All the variations of the *Kama Sutra* became familiar to them, and she rejoiced at his shape inside her.

But most of all she grew to love most the comfort of his presence beside her in the night.

Then one night at the dinner table, Martha Marguerite, who approved of Selena as strongly as she had once deplored Yolanda, held an open letter before them and began to read.

> Dear Mme. LaRouche (for that was her surname):
>
> It is my fond wish that this missive finds you in good health. It is my fonder wish, indeed my fervent hope, that you will immediately board ship for Paris as events suddenly threaten to engulf and submerge the fate and welfare of properties that it has taken your esteemed family generations to attain. I must regretfully report to you that peasants in the province of Côte d'Or have, in a shockingly bold uprising of heinous consequences, seized your lands and burned your château to the foundations. Given the situation here in Paris, I think that I am perhaps erring on the side of sanguinity when I tell you that a similar fate might well befall your family home on the right bank of the Seine, along with all of the great houses in that *arrondisement*. As the people, more and more, gather and conspire to de-

nounce privilege, it becomes difficult for me to protect the estate of an owner who is absent therefrom. Do favor me, madame, with a letter at first opportunity and with your presence here as soon as possible.

> Your servant,
> Vergil Longchamps
> Counselor-at-law

Martha Marguerite folded the letter. She didn't say anything. She didn't have to.

"Well," decided Jean Beaumain, lifting a glass of rosé to the light, "if we sail now, we ought to be able to reach France by early July. Mind you, I shall not set foot upon her soil. I have not yet had done with Chamorro, though I curse him wherever he may be. But I can take you as far as Le Havre, at the mouth of the Seine.

"Or perhaps we might sail in late summer," he went on, thinking over the possibilities. "Could you wait that long?"

"I don't think so," Martha replied. "Monsieur Longchamps is nothing if not urgent. Our poor château! Oh, the happy summers I spent there as a girl! What kinds of devils have those peasants become?"

"*We* had best sail as soon as possible, darling," Selena spoke up, meeting his eyes, her voice soft.

"Oh?" he said. "You have a reason?"

"I think so," she replied, smiling now. "For a woman in my condition, it is inadvisable to travel too late in the term."

"Well, yes, I guess that's right," Jean allowed casually, thinking perhaps of the preparations that would have to be made. "You've got a point there. . . ."

Then he realized what she'd said, her words coming back to him now, and he leaped up so suddenly that his chair overturned.

"Selena!" he cried. *"Selena?"*

Selena just smiled.

Selena knew from the start that Jean Beaumain would make a wonderful father, and for that reason, as well as for her own joy at having conceived, she exulted in her pregnancy. According to her calculations, she would be about five months gone by the time they reached France—showing a bit by then—so other matters involving parenthood needed to be discussed. Marriage, for one.

That was no problem. In one way or another, Jean had been asking to marry her almost since they'd met. Now aboard the *Liberté*, bound for the Canary Islands and thence to France, he asked again, and she accepted.

They kissed to seal the bargain. Then he said, "I mark that look in your eyes, Selena. Your mind sees a little cloud somewhere in the sky. What is it?"

"Jean," she said, holding him, looking up at him, "exactly when will we be married? And where?"

He grinned. "You don't think I'm planning to weasel out, do you? After I spent so much time winning you in the first place?"

"Yes, how you suffered in our bed all those nights!" she shot back in jest. "It must have been terribly hard." Then she turned serious again. "Darling, you've already agreed that our son should be born in Europe"—they both *knew* the child would be a boy—"where the midwives and doctors are well-trained. So why can't we be married in Paris as well? France is your homeland, and without a homeland there is something missing. You know how much I long to return to Coldstream one day. Surely now, with our son coming and a new life already upon us, you can set aside your quest for revenge against Chamorro. Rise above it. Forget it—"

"Would you forget your dream of Coldstream?" he replied.

"That's different."

"Oh, is it?"

"I simply want what is rightfully mine."

"Well, perhaps evening things with Chamorro is rightfully *mine.*"

"It will come to no good."

"Who is to say?"

"But think about it. And let us wed as soon as we reach Paris."

Jean did not say yes, but neither did he say no. He promised to think about it. That, Selena felt, was a good sign.

When the Canary Islands came in sight, the port city on the north coast of Tenerife, Selena was up on deck. The *Liberté* would stop there for several days to take aboard water and provisions for the final leg of the journey to France. Sometimes she thought she felt the child moving within her, but it might also have been the motion of the ship. The trip thus far had been swift and peaceful, but a glimpse of the islands upon the horizon stirred old memories.

It had been just north of there, years ago, that Royce Campbell, feverish with buboes and expecting death, had put her off his plague-ridden *Highlander*. Alone, she'd floated into shore aboard a dinghy, to be befriended by a woman on Tenerife called Senora Celeste.

Selena remembered her thoughts that day as she'd drifted toward shore, watching Royce's ship, manned but by terror and disease, sail out of sight. She'd accepted the fact of his approaching death and hoped that, in some eternal port, he would find the ghost of the wolf that lived in his dream-haunted past, a meeting of mates in a mythical Highlands beyond misery and time. And recalling these things now, Selena knew why the cross on La Tortue had seemed so incongruous. Royce would never have chosen to be buried beneath a cross. It was not *him* at all, nor was it the way of his riotous Campbell kin.

She sighed. His well-meaning crew had erred.

But the cross gave comfort too, and so it had to be all right.

Just not . . . just not *fitting*.

Anyway, too late now.

Tenerife had not changed much since Selena had been there before. The streets were still narrow and dirty, the buildings along the waterfront and in the town crowded together and somewhat dilapidated. Except for Senora Celeste's hotel in the center of the village, which itself was unprepossessing, there was nothing of distinction.

Jean, however, suggested that they spend the night on *terra firma*, and in a regular bed. Selena was not opposed to the general idea, but she balked. Jean wondered why.

"When I was here before," she explained, "the woman who runs the hotel pretended to be my friend. But she drugged me with wine. I awoke aboard a ship called the *Massachusetts*. I had been abducted by Captain Jack Randolph who was in league with Senora Celeste. He took me to India and sold me in concubinage to a maharajah."

"Well, that is certainly not going to happen this time, darling. Come, let's go to the hotel and get a room for the night."

"I don't . . . I don't know if I could see her again without . . . without doing something drastic."

"Selena, I recall your lecture a very short time ago about forgetting the evils of the past. You mean to tell me—"

"All right, let's go," she said. After all, how could she counsel him against vengeance in one breath and admit to a craving for it in the next? This was her opportunity to give Jean Beaumain an object lesson in letting bygones be bygones. Senora Celeste might be dead by now.

But she wasn't.

The woman who had deceived Selena years ago lounged in a wicker rocking chair in the lobby of her establishment. She was much heavier than she'd been, and looked a lot older. One of her eyes was afflicted with cataracts and the other was rheumy and unfocused, although this was quite possibly due to the effects of an empty rum bottle on the wicker table beside her.

"Yes?" she inquired in Spanish, as Selena entered the hotel with Jean and Martha Marguerite. "What do you want?"

Martha had a bit of Spanish, Selena less, so Jean asked for rooms. "One night, perhaps two," he said.

"It shall be done," declared Celeste, drawing a cane from beneath the folds of her skirt and banging it on the floor.

"I have a little trouble with my old bones these days," she explained gruffly, as a young man in a soiled white jacket appeared in answer to her crude summons. "It's not as easy to get around as it used to be. Pablo," she commanded the clerk, "take care of these people. Nothing but the finest now, understand?"

This was clearly a fatuous remark, idly made and meaningless, given the state of the hotel, but the pretension in Senora Celeste's tone irritated Selena. She dropped to the floor in front of the old woman's rocking chair and stared into her good eye.

"Do you still serve that fine wine here?" she asked pointedly. "The kind that makes sleep come so readily?"

Senora Celeste looked back with a baffled expression. "If you wish . . ." she said vaguely.

There was a long, uncomfortable silence. Selena continued to stare at the woman. "Don't you remember me?" she asked finally, unable to stop herself.

Celeste blinked a number of times, trying to focus clearly upon

Selena. "Do I know you?" she asked finally. "Have you been here before?"

Martha Marguerite stood by, mystified. "Selena," said Jean, a kind of warning.

But Selena took no heed. The old, bad blood of outrage and betrayal rose up again. She recalled how Celeste had seemed to rescue her from Captain Jack's amatory proposals in the barroom, then had seen to it that Selena was ensconced safely in her room, away from Jack, alone in her quarters—with a drugged bottle of wine!

"Are you sure you've never seen me before?" Selena demanded. "Do you remember a Captain Jack Randolph?"

Senora Celeste was searching her memory. She was genuinely confused. And embarrassed.

"I'm sorry, honey," she said. "You look a dear child to me, but if you've been here before, I can't recall. And there've been so many sea captains who've stopped here over the years. No, I'm sorry, I just don't know. . . ."

Selena gave it up, angry at herself for being angry, yet satisfied in a way that Jean had been there to witness the exchange. Surely he would see now, with their son coming, with a new life already gifted to them, how disastrous it would be to persist in his obsession with Chamorro.

Jean admitted as much that night in bed.

"Don't you see, Selena," he asked, holding her after they'd made love—gently and with Selena on top because of the child— "don't you see? Celeste didn't even remember you."

"Yes. Let us put our pasts away forever. Nothing matters now but the future."

In the night, however, Jean turned in his sleep, rolling away from her. Lying there in a state of semiwakefulness, a bit uncomfortable with her swelling belly and trying to adjust to the unfamiliar bed, Selena saw upon Jean's back the evil, branded letters of Chamorro's name.

How could a man—how could anyone—forget something like that?

Yet he had promised that he would.

A real man. A true man. She slid across the sheets, pressing her body to his, the two of them like nested spoons that last night in the bed on Tenerife.

Next morning, Selena and Jean had a breakfast of oranges, eggs, fried fish, and coffee in their room, after which Jean went down to the pier to oversee the provisioning of the *Liberté*. Selena washed and dressed, then lounged about for a time, simply enjoying the sensation of a place, a room, a floor that did not rock or sway, dip or plunge. Presently, the room began to grow uncomfortable—the day promised to be hot—and she decided to go out and walk down to the harbor. All waterfronts excited her with the sight of ships arriving and departing, loading and unloading, for they spoke of the great wide world of which she had seen much but not enough.

She was at the door, ready to open it, when a thunder of footsteps came up the hotel stairs and across the hall outside. The door crashed in upon her, into her, and she fell, twisting, trying to gain her balance, onto the hard floor.

Jean Beaumain stood over her. He did not seem to think it odd that she was lying there.

"Selena!" he cried, his face flushed with dark passion. "Selena!" He pulled out his fat black wallet and showered her with bills and notes of every nation, a fortune in money. "Selena, you and Martha Marguerite are taking the *Lancia* to Le Havre. It is in the harbor now and leaves for France on the morrow. A Portuguese vessel. I have made the arrangements. Your luggage is already aboard her."

Having said that, he turned to race away.

"Jean," she gasped, trying to regain the wind that had been knocked from her by the fall. "Jean, wait . . . what—"

"Chamorro!" he shouted, already pounding down the stairs. "He has been sighted in the Azores. I have him this time for sure. . . ."

And so he was gone.

Selena and Martha Marguerite, as instructed, boarded the *Lancia* and sailed for France next day. She was a good ship with an expert crew and a captain, Raoul Telémas, who was kind.

He aided Martha Marguerite in caring for Selena when her pains began, almost as soon as the *Lancia* departed Tenerife.

And he wept along with the two women when Selena gave herself up of a perfectly formed male infant, so startling, so tiny.

So dead.

11   Two Worlds in One

Not since her flight from Scotland aboard a rat-infested freighter had Selena made as sad a trip. The sight of her child disappearing beneath the waves of the Atlantic, wrapped in a Portuguese flag provided by Captain Telémas, was as hard a thing as she had ever had to bear. Not only did she feel anguish for her own loss: how devastated Jean would feel when he learned what had happened! Perhaps to spare him, she would refrain from mentioning that his carelessness in knocking her onto the hotel floor had probably contributed to the miscarriage.

Revenge. Chamorro. Human passion. Why had things happened as they had? The world had many answers, always. Davi the Dravidian would have told her that her actions in a previous life had surely led to the loss of the child. But if that were true, what could she have done? How terrible a person could she have been to be forced to bear this agony now? And wasn't that explanation incomplete anyway? Jean Beaumain, too, would have had to have been evil. Or considering the tragedy from another angle, from the perspective of Yolanda Fee, for instance, perhaps Senora Celeste's hotel was truly evil and the aura of the place itself led to disaster for those who dwelt therein. A Christian would have said that Jean's sudden appearance at the door was God's will, as was the miscarriage that followed. But Selena had no interest in a god who would allow such a thing to happen. Maybe fate alone—vast, random, impersonal fate—was the culprit. Yet the very vagueness of that explanation was difficult for grief-stricken Selena to comprehend, and robbed the child's death of any meaning. A chaplain on board the *Lancia,* Pere Giroux, a kindly little old man, came to Selena's cabin and spoke movingly, tearfully, of the web of life, which would not be understood until the end of time.

The end of time? Selena reflected.

That was too damn late.

So she suffered, knowing that she would always suffer.

By night, she cried herself to sleep. By day, drawing upon those reserves of strength, which were still, incredibly, present within her and which had never failed her before, she began working with Martha Marguerite in an attempt at improving her French. The effort distracted her from sorrow, at least temporarily, and her mental acuity was a source of satisfaction.

If the baby died for a reason, she found herself thinking, *then there is a reason for my wits, my life, as well.* Out of such knowledge grew a conviction that a future still beckoned her onward and, when Selena realized this, she began to recover. By the time the *Lancia* entered the English Channel, homing on Le Havre, Selena's spirits had improved to the extent that she slept more, and cried less, in her cabin at night.

Indeed, the green haze of England, lying in the mist to port, roused both her emotions and her blood. What had the poet written of that isle? "A green jewel set upon the sea"?

"Aye!" murmured Selena, standing on the tossing deck. "Aye, and well enou' t' say such a thing." It was as if the mere proximity of Britain, which had so long and so cruelly held Scotland in thrall, evoked her fiery Scots emotions and loosed her Scots tongue. "Well enou'," she said, "but England, ye've na seen t' end o' Selena MacPherson yet. Because ye've got Coldstream Castle, an' I mean t' 'ave 'er back!"

Brave words. Cruel world. Wide ocean. Small ship.

"I will!" she declared, smacking the ship's railing with the butt of her fist. After all, if life was a web, if there was indeed a plan that underlay all events, she had not traversed the great globe of earth for nothing! There was a purpose in her nearness to England now.

"There has to be," she said.

"I hope you have not begun to talk to yourself," said Martha Marguerite, approaching Selena with a smile that did not conceal a measure of concern.

"Don't worry. I enjoy the conversation," Selena shot back, and Martha smiled because she knew the younger woman would, in spite of her burdens, be healthy in her mind and in her heart.

"Have you ever been to England?" Selena asked, as the mists cleared for a moment, showing the coastline inviolate since William the Conqueror's invasion in 1066.

"No. Nor do I wish to. I am French," pronounced Martha with a sniff of her nose and a lift of her chin. With each day at sea, as her homeland had drawn nearer, the older woman had grown prouder of her ancestry and more prideful in bearing. *"La belle France,"* she repeated, over and over, as if it were a land of milk and honey—or at least wine and cheese—superior to all others.

"When I return to England," Selena said, still gazing at the coastline, "it will be in glory."

"Well, indeed you are of the nobility." The older woman shrugged. "And thank the Lord for that. Because in France, we of high birth know how to keep the lower orders in their places."

Selena sighed. For all of Martha's numerous good qualities, she had never known what it was like to be penniless and hunted and alone. Perhaps the truly unbridgeable gulf between peoples was the one separating those who had never visited the abyss of impotence and poverty from those who had.

"When we are in Paris, my dear," Martha Marguerite went on, "I shall see that you live like a queen until Jean's return. I have friends at the highest level, you see, including Marc and Zoé Moline, who design all the clothing for Marie Antoinette and the women of her court. And Jeanne, the Comtesse de la Motte, was a childhood friend of mine. She is now a favorite of the queen's."

"You haven't been home in years," wondered Selena. "How do you know these things? And your château has been burned to the ground—"

"Trifles, my dear," Martha sniffed. "The *canaille* will soon learn who is in command. First, I shall stiffen the spine of Monsieur Longchamps, my family's lawyer. Then in consort with the clergy and the nobles of Côte d'Or, I shall tax the peasants until they have coughed up enough money to rebuild our country home. As my dear father used to say, God rest his soul, 'If you flog a dog long enough, he will whimper at the sight of you.'"

Selena, who had very narrowly escaped a brutal whipping in Oakley's Room of Doom, looked away and said nothing, having attributed Martha's arrogant pronouncements to high emotions attendant upon homecoming. She knew, based upon her reading of history and her more recent experience in America, that one land, one country, could not indefinitely sustain its internal peace, let alone its position in the affairs of the world, when it was disastrously divided within.

Alas, however. When Captain Telémas sailed into Le Havre and tied up at the swarming pier, Martha appeared on deck dressed as if she were to be carried straightaway to an audience with King Louis XVI himself. A diamond-studded tiara rested atop her careful coiffure. She wore a silken gown complete with train, which in spite of the fact that it was years out of date, conveyed wealth and breeding. The heat of July had not dissuaded her from draping an ermine stole about her shoulders, a piece of fur that did nothing to conceal the strands of pearls at her neck, nor the bejeweled golden bracelets at her wrists. Selena, who was worried enough about her own mysterious cache of treasure—still in the greatcoat's lining, the coat in a battered portmanteau—gasped in alarm.

"We must still journey all the way up the Seine to Paris," she told Martha. "Surely you don't mean to wear those valuables on the river boat?"

"This is France!" declared Martha Marguerite. "I am safe here."

"If I might be so bold," interjected Captain Telémas, stepping toward the two women, "the young lady is correct. France has changed, I am afraid, since you last were here. Look." He gestured down at the docks upon which stevedores labored and all manner of men and women scurried hither and thither.

Martha complied, scoffingly at first, and so did Selena. Her misgivings and the captain's outright warning were neither idle nor misplaced. Even as the three of them stood on the *Lancia*'s polished deck, hundreds of eyes, hungry or hard or hate-filled, glared up at the handsome woman wearing the jewels and fur.

Martha Marguerite shrank back. Selena, dressed simply in dark-colored cotton, almost did so as well.

She had suffered enough acquaintance with danger to know it when she saw it.

"I told you," the captain repeated, a bit sadly. "France has changed."

He was right. Selena scanned the crowd and saw in a moment at least five different people who looked prepared to kill, if only for a piece of bread. There was the gaunt, knife-thin young man leaning against the wooden wheels of a tumbrel. He looked close to starvation, although not for lack of food alone. Hatred, too, consumed his bones; his fury weighed more than his body did. Or the slattern lounging in a warehouse gateway with a prospective customer. She and the man both eyed Martha's white throat, not only for the pearls thereon but for the blood therein. An old woman, bent and stooped, wielded a tin cup, begging for alms and calling, "Save yourselves while you can. Save yourselves before the deluge comes." Even a little boy, scarcely six years old, unwittingly revealed an implacable and remorseless fury at the sight of Martha's ostentation. He was just sitting on the dock and kicking his feet. But there was power in each kick, and murderous meaning.

Selena saw this and more. Suddenly she imagined a France in which all the poor, the outcast, the lowly and dispossessed were huddled on the howling threshold of flashpoint. Martha and her kind lived in one world, they in another. And they had borne enough. The time to turn tables was imminent. The smell of revolution rode the very air, obliterating the rich, multifarious odors of the harbor and the docks, of oil and grain and leather, even fish. Indeed, Selena did not sense here even a jot of the forces that had driven the American uprising, in which a strong draught of rationalism had seasoned martial fervor. No, this was different; this was malice promised in return for malice performed.

This was biblical. This was an eye for an eye.

Martha Marguerite finally saw it as well. "I shall go below and change," she said huffily.

The riverboat journey up the Seine was uneventful, save for Selena's enjoyment of the ordered beauty of the French countryside. Yet here too she saw the stark contrasts. Great châteaux and noble cathedrals rose above grimy, stinking peasant villages and towns. The nobility rode fine horses, better fed and cared for than the men and women, and children too, who tilled the nobles' lands from dawn to dusk. Fat clerics, drawn in gleaming carriages, waved desultory blessings from closed cabs, as if a languid sign of the cross would put bread in a man's mouth. The miracle of the loaves and fishes was not to happen here. A smoldering fury, ready to leap into flames, was evident behind the hedgerows and across the jade-green fields.

"*La belle* France," murmured Martha Marguerite, somewhat sadly.

But if Martha sensed the changes at work during her absence, the changes building to a crescendo now, that insight deserted her as soon as the riverboat reached Paris.

"Look at it!" she exulted.

And Selena did. She was thrilled from the start, but a little disconcerted. Compared to this gleaming, light-filled city spread out before her eyes, Edinburgh was a small town, Bombay a plain of hovels, New York a backwoods village. She had been taken by her father to London once, but she'd been too young to appreciate it. For her, for now, Paris could not but be the most wonderful place she had ever been.

She had been a toddler in London, a Scottish princess in Edinburgh, a slave in Bombay, and a spy in New York.

All she could do was wait and see what Paris might make of her now.

"It will be very simple," explained Martha, as the two women walked up the gangplank and left the riverboat. "I'll hire a cab to take us to my family's home, we'll settle in, and tomorrow I'll begin sending invitations. Oh, we'll have a grand time, we will.

"You there, boy!" she called, hailing a loutish young fellow in threadbare shirt and battered cap. He was busy currying a swaybacked horse hitched to a sagging buggy. In the buggy, asleep on the seat, was another young man of the same age, equally unimpressive in his attire. "You there! See to our bags here on the street. I wish to hire you."

Selena saw at a glance that Martha had erred again, not by her apparel this time—she was dressed sedately, if well—but by the lofty presumption of her tone.

"Oh, and is that right?" the lout responded, continuing to brush the beast. He seemed lackadaisical on the surface, good-natured enough, but with a hint of something like meanness in his eyes. He glanced contemptuously at the pile of luggage on the street. "Well, you may want to *hire* me, as you say, so I'll try to make up my mind while you and that pretty little piece with you trundle your junk over here and put it in the buggy."

Martha Marguerite was aghast. She'd never been spoken to that way in all her life. "How dare you address me in that manner!" she sputtered.

"You're lucky I'm talkin' to you at all," the fellow drawled, grinning at Selena.

She understood. However this young man's father or grandfather might have rushed to please a rich woman, he would not do so unless he chose.

"I'll have you . . . I'll have you beaten soundly for your impertinence!" vowed Martha.

The man laughed. "Sebastian! Sebastian!" he called.

His partner in the buggy awoke and sat up. "What is it, Hugo?"

"We've got us a rich woman here who's going to have us beaten if we don't jump right smart."

Hugo and Sebastian laughed in unison. Martha was on the verge of apoplexy. "I'll have you arrested!" she shrieked. "Gendarme! Gendarme!"

Hugo and Sebastian thought that this too was wildly funny.

"Madame," said Hugo, when he had stopped laughing, "all the police are in the center of the city, trying to contain a demonstration. Now why don't you calm down and find yourself another hack? As you can see, we're busy."

He returned to currying his horse. Sebastian pulled his cap over his eyes and leaned back against the buggy seat. He was still chortling to himself.

While this exchange had been taking place, riverboat passengers had hired the rest of the waiting buggies. This was the only one left. Stepping forward, Selena decided to see what she could do.

"Monsieur Hugo," she implored, hearing the Scots accent clearly in her new French, "I'm afraid my companion doesn't quite understand what is happening in France these days. She's of the old school, if you know what I mean."

"She'd better learn the coming ways right quick," Hugo growled. But he looked her up and down with interest. "You look like a *comtesse* all right," he said in appraisal, "but you seem fairly human. How'd you get stuck with that old cow?"

He pointed rudely toward Martha, who was close to dancing with outrage.

"Please. She's all right really. Could you take us in your buggy? You'll be well-paid."

Shouldn't have said that! she realized. *Now we might be robbed.*

"Oh? How well?" asked Hugo, his eyes narrowing.

"We don't . . . that is, we don't have any money with us. But when we reach our destination—"

"Which is?" he snapped.

Martha Marguerite, with great dignity, gave the Right Bank address.

"Hey! Maybe we ought to hold 'em for ransom then?" commented Sebastian, from his seat in the buggy.

Hugo laughed, not entirely pleasantly, but Selena decided, before things got further out of hand, to give him the full benefit of her violet eyes.

"Please?" she asked, so kittenishly she might have meowed as well. "Si'l vous plait? My companion does not mean what she says."

"Ah!" commented Sebastian sarcastically, heat of anger in his voice now. "And the Archbishop of Rouen did not mean it when he had my grandfather's hands lopped off for failing to tithe. Nor did the chief magistrate of St.-Cloud mean it when he hanged my sister for stealing a loaf of bread to feed her starving children."

"When the Third Estate takes its rightful place in affairs," added Hugo grimly, "the tyrants will receive their just due."

Third Estate? wondered Selena. She did not know exactly what the men were talking about, but their meaning was clear enough. They were outraged at the order of things.

All she wanted to do now was to reach Martha Marguerite's home in safety. Selena and the older woman lugged their bags over to the carriage where Hugo changed his mind and deigned to help them lift the luggage into the vehicle. It was large enough to seat six, with a canopied top but open sides. She helped Martha inside, the men swung up into the driver's seat behind the horse, and the buggy moved off.

"What is the Third Estate?" Selena asked Martha in a whisper.

"Oh, nobodies. The workers and the peasants. They have no power and mean nothing. They have always been poor and will always be poor. It is the order of things. Philip the Fair said it best: the duty of the Third Estate is 'to hear, receive, approve and perform what should be commanded of them by the king.'"

"I don't think Hugo and Sebastian quite share that view."

"They will when I get through with them. As soon as we reach home, I shall have our family servants seize these obstreperous brigands and take them to the magistrate. Then we shall see how things are!"

Martha was so agitated, so furious, that Selena decided not to discuss the matter further. Perhaps when Martha reached the safety of her house, she would look more charitably upon the young men who had brought her there.

The carriage passed first through a haphazard neighborhood of narrow, winding streets. Tall houses of gray stone were jammed together here, houses with steep, slate-shingled roofs and grimy brick chimneys. Many people walked about, apparently idle, most of them ill-clothed. They glanced sullenly at the buggy, inspecting its occupants with something barely short of malice. Then Hugo guided the horse out onto a wide street that ran along the Seine. Selena had heard of Notre Dame and now she saw it for the first time in all its hoary, historic magnificence. She held two thoughts simultaneously: how grand it was, and how many poor people had gone hungry in order that it might be built and maintained.

On the roadway and all around the great church a vast crowd of people blocked the buggy's progress. Hugo reined the horse to a halt.

"Go on!" commanded Martha. "What is the matter?"

Sebastian glanced over his shoulder. "We'll move along, madame," he said sharply, "when we're able. Or would you have us run down these people in our path?"

"What's happening?" asked Selena. She could hear someone shouting in the distance. Welling roars of approval followed each spate of shouting.

"It is someone giving a speech," said Hugo. "And I intend to listen."

Selena stood up in the carriage. She saw, perhaps fifty yards away, a man speaking from some sort of wooden platform. He was half-hidden from her by the crowd. Hugo and Sebastian were standing up in the driver's seat for a better view, so she crawled up on top of the canopy for a look as well. She could hear the speech more clearly now.

"—and so we demand these things," cried a young firebrand, dressed in a cheap, black suit and flailing the air with his fist. "The inequalities of feudal times must be ended! Serfdom must be abolished throughout France. Taxation must be applied equally on nobles, clergy, and peasants alike. Officials ought no longer be allowed to buy the positions they hold. And the *lettres de cachet,* by which our citizens can be imprisoned at whim, without trial, must be abolished as well!"

The great crowd roared its approval. Selena saw the speaker smile. He was quite young, no more than thirty, she thought, still with a young man's leanness. His thick, chestnut-brown hair looped down over his forehead, and he brushed it back with a gesture that was at once graceful and self-assured. She who had known many men, and politicians among them, was immediately struck by the casual air of command he showed, whether speaking or simply standing there in front of the throng. It was a gift of natural leadership, a characteristic to which she had always been attracted.

"And so," the man continued, when the shouting had died down again, "tomorrow, July fourteenth, we shall—all of us, every one of us—march as a body to the fortress of Bastille on the east end of Paris, in the past a prison for so many of our unfortunate citizens, and seize it in the name of our cause!"

The roar that followed this announcement was overwhelming. Selena pressed her hands to her ears. In the buggy seat, Martha Marguerite had turned pale.

"Why is such talk permitted?" she complained with incredulous outrage.

Hugo and Sebastian were cheering along with everyone else.

"Oh, my France! What has become of you?" Martha mourned.

"Maybe you want to go back where you came from?" said Hugo sassily.

From her perch atop the buggy, Selena saw a phalanx of plumed and uniformed horsemen riding toward the crowd, their glittering swords upraised. People scattered, shrieking, and began to run.

"The Royal Guard! The Royal Guard!" someone screamed in warning and alarm. "Flee for your lives!"

"Well, thank heavens!" Martha said.

It was sickening, and Selena saw it all. The guardsmen, at a gallop, rode directly into the crowd, their horses plunging and rearing. People fell, trampled, to the stones in front of Notre Dame, wailing in agony, slashed and mauled by iron-shod hoofs. The fiery speaker had leaped down from his platform, which was overturned in the melee, and Selena caught a glimpse of his glossy, flying hair as he fled the horsemen and came toward the buggy! She saw too that, with the confused and swirling mob blocking his way, he would never be able to reach the safety of distant alleys.

Instinctively, not merely for his words but because of his plight, her sympathies were with him. She herself had been hunted by authority that possessed vast power but little mercy, and she could imagine what his fate would be if he were to be seized. Royal Guard or no, men who would trample children and slash out willy-nilly with great swords were not those with whom she would ever ally herself.

So when the speaker came near the carriage, she waved her arms, caught his eye, and beckoned him.

He looked puzzled at first—she almost thought there was a flicker of amusement in his eyes, seeing her there atop the canopy—but he turned in her direction and pushed his way through the crowd.

Twenty yards away, two guardsmen had halted their mounts, turning this way and that, scanning the crowd in eager search of their quarry.

Selena jumped down from the top of the buggy, grabbed the speaker by the hand—which was, to her astonishment, dry and cool—and pulled him up with her into the carriage itself.

"Move along!" she shouted to Hugo and Sebastian, who were grinning with surprise and delight. "Get down on the floor!" she commanded the speaker. He looked younger than he had at a distance, and more handsome. But his hard, clever brown eyes left no doubt that he was someone fearless in principle, decisive, perhaps even ruthless in action.

"Selena, have you gone mad!" shrieked Martha Marguerite. "We could be arrested for harboring—"

"Yes, and we will be too, if you give any sign that something's amiss."

The buggy was moving now, rolling slowly through the thinning crowd.

The young firebrand was crouched down on the floor of the vehicle. Selena arranged her skirt and that of Martha, spreading them out and fluffing them to conceal their new passenger. She could feel him hunching down, shifting around, against her legs. Then she felt his hand on her ankle for a moment, patting her as if to say, Thanks, thanks, I'm fine down here.

The coach was stopped by a mounted guardsman who held up

a gloved hand and looked at the drivers and their passengers with cruel, hostile eyes.

"Where are you going?" he demanded, scanning every inch of the buggy.

Martha Marguerite had taken all she could, and here at last was a man sworn to serve the interests of her family, her king, her class.

"I am of the family LaRouche," she informed him coldly, proudly. "I have just returned to Paris after a long absence and I have had to endure this . . . this distressing *monstrousness!* This sort of thing would never have happened in the old days, nor frankly today, if you and your men were performing your duties correctly. Now stand aside and let me pass. I want to go home."

Chastened and chagrined, the guardsman moved aside and let them proceed.

"Thank you, Madame LaRouche," said the speaker from his hiding place beneath the skirts. "Perhaps what I have said about the nobility is not true in every instance."

"That was damn clever of you, old lady," added Hugo, more prosaically.

Martha sputtered helplessly. Old lady indeed!

Selena looked around carefully. They had left the plaza and the crowd behind and had entered an area of elegant, imposing homes with courtyards and gardens and great walls.

"It's safe to come up now," she said, and the young man complied, cocky and grinning.

"I want to say in my own behalf, ladies, that I do not make it a habit to hide behind women's skirts."

"Who are you?" demanded Martha Marguerite, shrinking away from the man who had said all those alarming things and who had, moreover, urged the mob to storm the Bastille fortress.

He ignored her question. "So you are a LaRouche, are you?" he said. "If memory serves, your grandfather made his fortune in tenement rentals. Eduard was his name. 'Eviction Eduard,' he was called. And wasn't your château burned to the ground by peasants awhile ago? I think you had an uncle, Pierre LaRouche, dead now. Instead of taking half the harvest from his subjects, which, though standard, is outrageous enough, he raised the levy to eighty percent. I'm afraid there was retribution."

Martha Marguerite went white and said nothing.

Selena, who had been watching the young man's face as he denounced Martha, decided that she'd been all too correct in her initial estimate of his unyielding nature. She then saw his eyes swing appreciatively, gratefully, toward her.

Suddenly his expression changed. His mouth twisted in surprise and his eyes widened in . . . disbelief. He was looking not at her face but at the cross she wore around her neck.

"Where did you get that?" he demanded. "Who are you?"

"I think I see a guardsman up ahead!" warned Hugo.

"All right," said the firebrand. He gave Selena a last look of appraisal, then jumped from the moving buggy, vaulted over a stone wall, and was gone.

There was a momentary silence in the buggy. Selena fingered the cross at her throat.

"Hugo," she asked, "do you know who that man is?"

"Of course I do," the lout replied, grinning with the pleasure of familiarity. "He's a radical leader, a comrade of Monsieur Mirabeau. You've just made acquaintance with Pierre Sorbante."

12   Troubled Hearth

"We are getting close now," said Martha Marguerite excitedly, leaning forward in the carriage and looking at the fine old houses along this grand street. "Almost home."

Selena was much impressed. The LaRouche residence must be in one of the most exclusive *arrondisements* of Paris. Huge old elms lined the streets, and in the gardens beyond the walls, she glimpsed fountains and statuary, beds of exquisite flowers laid out in geometric designs, circles and octagons and crosses.

Which of course reminded her of Erasmus Ward's cross on the chain around her neck.

Sorbontay.

Pierre Sorbante?

Why would exceedingly different men, LaValle and Ward, speak his name at the very moments of their deaths? She recalled how Ward, lying on the planks in the Battery fortress, had flailed at his neck while dying. Had he known that the cross was gone? That Penrod had taken it? Certainly he could not have known that Gilbertus Penrod had given it to Selena. And she recalled too the significant glance that had passed between Penrod and Royce regarding the fact that Selena was wearing the cross. *"It's all right, Gil,"* Royce had said. *"The cross is in good hands. . . ."*

In good hands?

Safe?

Then there must be some important purpose attached to it, but Selena hadn't the slightest idea what that purpose was. Ward had been a spy, however, and LaValle something of a smuggler, so Selena could not help but reason that the little talisman represented or conveyed or presaged a meaning of dangerous import.

"Everything has meaning," Davi the Dravidian had taught her, *"and often it is the opposite of what it seems to be."*

That wisdom, however, did not help Selena at all just then. She was very much at sea in the matter of the cross.

"Turn in at the next gate," Martha ordered Hugo, who obediently did so.

Great tears appeared immediately in the woman's eyes when she beheld her family home, but they were not tears of joy at returning after so long. Selena stifled a gasp of surprise. Hugo and Sebastian hooted derisively. Vergil Longchamps, the lawyer, had understated his letters woefully with regard to conditions prevailing in affairs LaRouche.

"You better pay us, and that's a fact," warned Sebastian. "We didn't take you here to be made fools of."

"There must be some explanation . . ." faltered Martha.

The old horse clopped through the iron gate, which was thickly rusted and stood wide open to the street.

"We *always* had a servant in livery at the gate," Martha Marguerite said apologetically.

Cobblestones were loose or missing on the drive. The lawns and gardens were untended and unkempt. The branches of trees, unpruned, hung down to the earth, and a fishpool, stagnant and filled with leaves, sent a fetid odor into the air. The big gray house was imposing only in its size. There was a look of decay about it, like a proud old dowager gone to seed.

"Oh, my!" mourned Martha.

The carriage stopped in front of the house. Selena got out.

"No funny business now," warned Hugo, getting down from the driver's seat. "We mean to be paid, I tell you."

"And you will be," Selena snapped. She had the money Jean had given her, not to mention the sovereigns and jewels. "Get the luggage down, will you, please?"

The two men reluctantly went about that task, as Martha and Selena climbed the wide stone steps and knocked on the massive bronze door of the house. They waited for what seemed a long time, then finally heard footsteps inside. The door swung open slowly, with a great elongated *creak,* and two little old ladies, nearly identical and bearing some resemblance to Martha, stood there blinking rheumily in the July sunlight.

"Martha? Is that you?" bleated one of the women.

Then with great sobs and heartrending exclamations, they embraced Martha, she embraced them, and all three of them cried at once.

"Oh, Martha, you're finally back! We were so worried. . . ."

Pulling herself together, Martha Marguerite introduced her sisters, Charlotte and Colette, to Selena. They were twins, somewhat older than she, and upon them had fallen the burden of the family after the death of Uncle Pierre at the hands of the Côte d'Or peasants. Obviously, the burden had been too heavy.

"What in God's name has happened here?" wailed Martha, drawing Selena and her sisters into the house so that Hugo and Sebastian, busy with the luggage, could not overhear family business. "Where are the servants? Why haven't the grounds been tended?"

Charlotte patted her thinning gray bun of hair in woeful nervousness. "Somehow there is no more money."

"What? Father was a millionaire many times over!"

"But there is no more money. You must see Monsieur Longchamps at first opportunity. We could not pay the servants. They ran off, taking with them what they could carry of our furnishings and jewelry. The gendarmes can do nothing. The lower orders are in the grip of a political fever. Oh, Martha, we don't understand what is happening. We can't understand what Monsieur Longchamps tries to tell us."

"It is true," Colette corroborated. She wore her hair exactly like her sister. Selena thought they resembled two frail ghosts out of some *ancien regime,* baffled by a new world, vulnerable and wandering around beyond their time. "It is true, we don't understand. Only old Stella, the cook, has remained with us. And she is nearly blind now."

At the sound of her name, a heavyset old woman in a faded yellow frock appeared at a distant doorway and peered owlishly toward the rueful conversants.

"Oh, Stella!" wailed Martha Marguerite, rushing over to the cook and embracing her warmly. "Loyal Stella, one out of all of them."

Stella, Selena noted, did not look especially happy to see Martha. Another mouth to feed. Perhaps she had stayed on here only because of her physical disability.

"How can we run a house without staff?" cried Martha. "We

must, at the very least, maintain a front until such time as I speak with Longchamps and our fortunes are restored!"

Selena was doubtful, in the present condition of the house, that any servants could be attracted.

"Hey, there!" called Hugo, clearing his throat loudly and scraping his boots in the foyer. "We got to run along now. You going to settle up with us, or what?"

He looked more than a little worried that he would not get paid, and threatening as well.

"Oh, Lord . . ." said Martha, unconcerned with the problems of mere commoners, looking at the walls of the house, where the outlines of stolen paintings were visible.

"I'll take care of you," said Selena. She walked to the door and down the steps onto the ruined drive. Hugo followed her. Sebastian joined them.

"Look," said Selena, "this place is obviously in a bad way . . ."

"That don't mean nothing to me," Sebastian growled. "We want our money."

"And you shall have it," replied Selena, drawing a couple of hundred-franc notes from her bodice.

The two young men gaped at the sight of such wealth. Selena gave them one of the notes.

"Now," she continued, waving the other before their acquisitive eyes, "I want to make a proposal. We need help around here. I want to hire the two of you, and your horse and buggy, for . . . oh, let's say a month. You may, I think, stay in the carriage house"—she saw this structure off to one side of the mansion—"and do all manner of jobs. At the end of the period, I shall give *each* of you five hundred francs, and you may remain in my employ after that, if you so choose. Fair enough?"

"We won't take to being bossed about, though," warned Hugo. "We're citizens of France now, you see, and bound servants of no one."

"Understood," agreed Selena. "Just deal with me. The ladies inside may find it difficult to change their ways, but leave them alone. Do we have an agreement?"

They did. And when Selena informed Martha Marguerite, the woman was too dispirited at the scope of her problems to demur.

That night at dinner, however, she regained a small measure of her *élan*, especially when Selena insisted upon contributing whatever was required for the maintenance of the household. She was, after all, in fact if not in law, the wife of Jean Beaumain, a wealthy man. And had Jean been here—which he should have been, damn the Chamorro obsession—he would have offered no less.

Hugo and Sebastian, using Selena's money, had managed to procure two piglets, which old Stella roasted to a crisp, crackling turn, and several dusty old bottles of excellent Burgundy were brought up from the long-neglected wine cellar. Thieving servants had stripped the dining room of silver, china, paintings, sideboards, and assorted valuables, but the heavy Louis XIV table and chairs remained. So with a few candles, common tableware, and cracked glasses for the wine, the women made the best of things.

"First thing tomorrow," Martha declared, slicing her portion of roast piglet, "Selena and I will call on Monsieur Longchamps and get to the bottom of this lack of money. I swear, I do hope for his own sake that Longchamps has not been deceiving us. I don't like the look of things one bit."

"An evil man," said Charlotte. "He told us a terrible lie about Uncle Pierre cheating his serfs."

Martha and Selena let that pass. It was one "lie" that seemed to be true.

"And after I've confronted the counsellor," Martha went on, "I shall see Marc and Zoé Moline, the couturiers. It is my duty as a titled woman to call upon their majesties at court, and I wish to wear the latest fashions. I am a LaRouche, after all. Appearances must be maintained, even during this difficult time.

"I shall engage gardeners and artisans forthwith, and then begin sending out invitations. This house shall ring again with the sound of music and laughter. . . ."

Martha Marguerite's eyes were already far away, entranced by a glorious future that would be exactly like the glorious past.

"Remember how it was when father and mother gave those grand masques? Such fun! The dauphin came once dressed in the costume of a frog, and all of us kissed him. In the end, he pulled off his headpiece and became the prince that he was. Oh, it was priceless!" exuded Colette.

"You *never* kissed the prince," Charlotte disagreed. "You were much too shy, and hid all night in the pantry."

"That is not so," whined Colette.

"Is!"

"Is not!"

"It doesn't matter," interrupted Martha, shushing them. "The important thing is to restore things to their former beauty. And we are fortunate in having Selena to help us."

The old twins regarded Selena with polite curiosity. She was just a passing stranger, no more a part of their world than serfs were, or starving laborers or radical political firebrands were. They would not realize, not even at that last shred of a second as the guillotine blade hissed downward toward their necks, that the world had changed forever.

For dessert, old Stella had outdone herself, using fruit from the overgrown trees in the garden. But her eyes failed as she carried her masterpiece to the table, and the whole dish fell in a mess upon the floor. The LaRouche women wailed in disappointment, but Selena didn't really mind.

It had been a plum pudding.

The night was windless and very hot. Selena had been given a room on the third floor, obviously long unused and recommended mainly by the fact that bed and bedclothes had not been stolen by former servants. The room overlooked the front of the house, the street, the Seine, and that part of the city that lay beyond the river. After lying in bed for a time, trying to sleep and trying not to perspire, Selena gave it up. Tossing her sweat-soaked chemise onto a chair, she stepped to the window. She was naked, shadowed by towering elms, looking out toward the city and lusting for the faintest breath of cool air.

Which did not come.

There are nights, too, when sleep will never come, and this was one. Selena herself contributed to her own unease. She was worrying about Jean. What if, instead of seizing Chamorro, the monster captured Jean? It would be death for sure, and Jean Beaumain would be as lost to her, as gone from this world, as Royce Campbell was!

Then Jean would die without knowing that he'd fathered a son. But the child was dead, so maybe it was better that he not know.

Nothing was ever clear.

Not even the Paris that Selena looked out upon, lying there hot and silent and dark along the river, beneath the sky. Selena, whose instincts had been made keen by struggle and triumph, anguish and defeat and flight, sensed not peace in the city, but rather a wary, waiting stillness, a chilling, resolute unrest like that of a panther on the branch of a tree, who lulls his prey to carelessness by the appearance of sleep.

The citizens of Paris were that panther.

Outside the city, only twelve miles distant, stood the palace of Versailles. And in it slept a well-meaning, slightly overweight, graceless heir to the fading glory of the Bourbon dynasty, Louis XVI.

He was the panther's prey.

Oh, he knew it—he had been so advised—but what did it matter? The panther could be killed or de-fanged or put in a cage and tamed. The panther might even die or go away, who could tell?

Louis XVI *knew* he was the panther's prey, but he did not *believe* it.

Greater than the difference between the sick and the well, much greater than that between the rich and the poor, more final than any gulf except that which divides the living from the dead is the chasm between knowledge and belief into which King Louis had already fallen.

Although he did not yet know that either.

But Selena sensed it, knew it, believed it, *felt* it out there in the uneasy, sweltering city. Far away she heard the watchmen calling, "All's well, all's well." They meant, "No fire! No thieves! No storm!" Poor watchmen, they were already, without knowing it, relics of a vanished age like Charlotte and Colette. They did not know what it was that they must guard against, nor hear the snarl, the drooling smack of chops, nor see the red eyes of the revolutionary beast that stalked them in the hungry night.

Selena, who'd been leaning upon the window sill, engaged in troubled reverie, fighting the heat, jerked suddenly upright as the realization came to her.

Pierre Sorbante was the prowling beast.

And somehow, because of Erasmus Ward's cross, she was a part of him.

13   Longchamps and the Molines

The law offices of Vergil Longchamps possessed a fading splendor alongside a comfortable workaday clutter of papers and books. The building he occupied was old now, adjacent to a gritty, beleaguered marketplace and a district of working class apartments, but its wrought-iron balustrades, its marble floors, its rococo facade: these bespoke past grandeur. Longchamps' own chamber, fittingly, revealed an occupant who clung, not always successfully, to lingering habits of order in the face of mounting harassment.

"What a great honor, madame!" exclaimed the lawyer gallantly, as he greeted Martha Marguerite at his door. Then, catching sight of Selena, "Ah! How charming, mademoiselle, to make *your* acquaintance!"

Selena appreciated his manners; it was his appearance that, at first, put her off a little. *This* was the man to whom the LaRouche affairs had been entrusted? Perhaps that was why they had proceeded so badly.

Longchamps bade the two women be seated, then settled uneasily into a straight-backed chair behind his jumble of a desk. "Bad back," he said apologetically. "Thus the chair. Old age. Bad bones. Bad dreams.

"Bad times," he added gloomily.

Vergil Longchamps, Selena guessed, was over sixty years of age, and in a day and time when most people were lucky to live to be forty, his waning but still obvious vitality was admirable. He ought to have added "bad teeth" to his list of woes, however, because intermittent black gaps marked the places where incisors and molars had once been. Missing teeth gave the lower part of his face a sunken, wasted look; his presence in a court of law, while perhaps intellectually formidable, would not have been physically striking.

Longchamps impressed her, though, by coming straight to the point and mincing no words.

"Martha, my friend," he said, sympathetically but frankly, "I'm afraid that all I can report to you is bad news. With the exception of your house, you're broke."

"But—" replied Martha Marguerite.

Longchamps lifted his hand. "Hear me out. The situation regarding your family affairs is as tenuous as the state of the country, and they are intertwined in cause and effect. I shall let others regale you with the gossip and scandals of the court."

Martha seemed disappointed and Selena had to admit that her appetite for licentious news was not entirely dormant either.

"Suffice it to say," the lawyer continued, "that France is broke as well. The country is like a machine running out of control. His majesty does not take charge of anything. Two finance ministers, Turgot and Necker, have failed to set things aright, primarily because the king cannot muster the nerve to act upon their recommendations."

"But what has this to do with our being . . . insolvent?" Martha wondered. "Father was rich—"

"That he was. But in your absence—my condolences, by the way, on the death of your husband, Hugo. . . . Haiti, what a place to die—your uncle Pierre made several mistakes. He overruled my counsel, I am sorry to say. First of all, in order to pay his gambling debts, he sold the block of apartments by which your estate received its main monies. Secondly, hoping to earn enough to keep things going, he raised the levy against your peasants in Côte d'Or. And he got himself killed in the bargain."

"But why don't the provincial authorities press charges then?" asked Martha.

"Because they don't know what is going to happen. They do not know who may be in power tomorrow, or next week. France is at a standstill because of turmoil in the Estates General."

Martha knew nothing of this, nor did Selena. Longchamps explained. "For centuries," he said, "the three estates, clergy and nobles and peasants, have voted as classes, each estate having one vote. Since the interests of the nobles and the clergy were similar if not identical—they wished to protect their privileges—the

Third Estate was always outvoted two to one. But of late, the leaders of the Third Estate, Mirabeau and Sorbante, have been demanding a vote by head, that is, one vote for each man present in the Estates General. If this comes to pass, as I believe it will very soon, the numbers of the Third Estate mean that the balance of power in France will swing immediately in favor of the lower classes. In addition to that, there are nobles and some clergy who are disgusted with unfairness and corruption and who are siding openly with the Third Estate."

"But the king—?" said Martha.

Vergil Longchamps shook his head, took a little silver box full of snuff from a desk drawer, placed a pinch in his left nostril, and inhaled with noisy satisfaction. "His majesty is a fool. If he were to decide right now to accommodate the reformers, he might be able to save the monarchy, but he believes it is his holy duty to resist change. He is doomed. Everyone out there in the street knows that today a mob will attempt to storm the Bastille, symbol of Bourbon tyranny. If it falls, and I suspect it may, the king will have compromise forced upon him. Whereas, had he compromised earlier, he could have retained at least a measure of authority. No, Madame LaRouche, his situation is more than desperate."

Selena, with her antipathy toward hereditary monarchs, particularly if they were blind, bullheaded and ineffectual, was not at all unhappy to hear this news.

"Surely we must have *some* funds in various accounts," Martha said hopefully.

"No," said the lawyer. "Your sisters, Charlotte and Colette, lived exceedingly well during your absence. You will forgive me for saying this, madame, but they were never trained in even the rudiments of financial responsibility. Nor, I am sorry to say, was the king. Do you know, even now, how he spends his time? He plays at making locks in a workshop at Versailles. And he hunts. Oh, yes, he hunts! He shoots tame deer from a palace window. That, ladies, is the current state of our leadership, and it is no match for a man like Sorbante, who is not afraid to go out among the people, to stir them up, to strike at the paper tiger that is our government. Even the queen, that Austrian interloper, Marie Antoinette, arouses the fury of the people. She is, first of all, a foreigner, and there have been the various scandals. . . ."

Longchamps let his voice trail off. He did not intend to get into such matters.

"So what is Martha to do?" Selena asked, quite worried for her friend.

The lawyer shrugged and took a pinch of snuff into his right nostril, inhaling greedily.

"She must wait," he said. "It is too late for me to offer any other advice. If Louis XVI finds the wisdom to join the tide of reform, all may yet be well. Order may yet be restored, both in Paris and in the provinces. When land is redistributed, the peasants in Côte d'Or are surely going to be given some of it, but there may be enough left over for the family LaRouche to live a comfortable life."

Martha Marguerite sagged in her chair. The reality of Longchamps' words had not really sunk in yet, not all the way, but she had grasped enough to know that things were very bad.

"What if the monarchy is actually overthrown?" asked Selena.

Longchamps paused for a moment. "Our previous king," he said, "Louis XV, is reported to have said: *'Apres moi, le deluge.'* After me, the deluge. You see, he knew. He knew that a great flood was coming. Feudal times and manners are gone. The millions of starving workers and peasants will no longer be satisfied to believe the clergy's promises of a reward in heaven. They want something *now!* Nor will a Third Estate, able to read and to understand the message of human freedom and independence, be content to follow the orders of a corrupt, lazy, often depraved nobility."

"To which Estate do you belong?" asked Selena.

"My father was a carpenter, when he could find work. I rose on my own. If you wish to know, my sympathies are with the Third Estate, although I fear they will be misled. Dangerous times are imminent. When power is the prize, men stop at nothing. Power is far more deadly than money or love."

Martha Marguerite was on her feet, livid and shaking. "You?" she cried. "You, whom I believed to be my friend, favor the rabble? No wonder your words here have made no sense. You are wrong, you are a fool —"

"Please, Martha!" Selena said.

With a loose gesture of his hand, Longchamps told her to save her words. They would be of no use. His message had been too stark, too certain, too indisputably true. Martha Marguerite could not accept it because to do so would be to admit that the world she had loved, of which she'd dreamed during her exile, was no more.

And that meant her place in the world was gone.

It was as hard a blow as any other, and a lot more savage than most.

"Now I see why our affairs are in such horrendous disarray!" Martha stormed, heading for the door. "Come, Selena. There is a stench here. Sir," she said to the lawyer, "I shall sue you at first opportunity. And you need not expect me to pay any fees you may think I owe you!"

Longchamps held out his hands, palms upward, glancing at Selena as if to say: *You see how it is; there is nothing I can do.*

Selena thanked the man with a nod, and left with her friend.

Hugo and Sebastian were waiting at curbside. They had acquired a glossy new horse and polished the carriage thoroughly, quite delighted, apparently, to be working regularly for real money. They wanted to make a good impression.

"Take us to Moline, couturier, Rue de la Cardinal Le Moine," ordered Martha.

"Hah!" she said to Selena, as the carriage moved away. "What rubbish that awful man spoke. He is a doomsayer, that is all. Everything will turn out splendidly, and I am going to proceed upon that belief. Why, I have jewelry. I have my furs. . . ."

This was, indeed, true. Martha had insisted on wearing her fur piece today, in spite of the heat, and against Selena's advice, sported large gold bracelets on each wrist and several glittering rings on various fingers. Selena herself was dressed in a simple dark-gray dress with decorative but inexpensive brass buttons down the front. Even so, she kept a wary eye on the many people swarming in the streets today, men and women and even children who gazed with hostile, sullen avarice at Martha Marguerite's finery.

The panther was awake and prowling the streets.

On the drive toward the couturiers, where Madame LaRouche intended to refurbish her wardrobe, Selena saw first a column of armed horsemen cantering in the opposite direction.

"National Guard," commented Sebastian. "Not half so bad as the Royal Guard or, God forbid, the constabulary."

The column was led by a handsome man riding a white horse. Selena looked, looked again, and gave a start of recognition. He was General Lafayette, who had aided Washington in America and whom she had met once, briefly, in Gilbertus Penrod's New York home.

His presence here brought back all the memories of America and a realization of the time that had passed. America was truly free! And the French people, many of whom had fought in the New World, could not but have returned here bearing the seeds of independence and revolutionary fervor. Because after all, if the British monarch, George III, had been bested by men desiring freedom, why could not the same fate overtake Louis XVI?

Then, turning onto the Rue de la Cardinal Le Moine, Selena received another unexpected—and very different—jolt. An officious policeman, shouting and waving his arms, stepped directly in the path of Hugo's new horse, causing it to rear and whinny in fright.

In a minute, after the initial tumult, Selena realized that the officer was holding them up to allow passage on the main thoroughfare of a glittering, high-wheeled coach drawn by six sleek Arabian geldings. This was a coach of imperial class, and she at first thought a member of the French royal family might be riding in it. Then she saw the immediately identifiable red-coated uniform worn by the driver, and similar attire on the four armed men serving as escorts to the coach. British.

The carriage passed directly in front of Hugo's nickering horse, affording Selena a perfect, if fleeting, view of its occupants. One of them was a youthful, lordly looking man with gentle, intelligent features. His face was turned toward her, but he did not look her way because he was laughing and conversing with the second occupant of the majestic coach. A young girl just on the verge of womanhood, her long, blond, shining hair held in place by silver barrettes.

Lord Sean Bloodwell, diplomat, Selena's former husband. And Davina, almost grown now, Selena's adopted daughter.

A whirling admixture of profound emotions came down upon Selena then, to see so close to her two who had shared a part of her life. What had Sean told the girl about Selena? What was the girl's life like now? Did she remember her mother at all? And if so, what memories did she hold?

It was all Selena could do to keep from calling out, but then the carriage was gone down the broad avenue, perhaps to a state breakfast or some grand reception.

God bless you both, she thought.

The policeman stepped aside and, with an arrogant gesture, permitted Hugo to proceed.

"The situation here cannot be as bad as Longchamps claims," Martha Marguerite decided hopefully, "if foreign dignitaries can ride about."

Selena did not mention the armed escort.

The sign outside the dressmaker's salon read:

MOLINE

Couturiers to the Royalty

Selena accompanied Martha into the building, which had an impressive facade of Italian marble and, inside, an equally striking, high-ceilinged foyer. Marc Moline's clientele could wait for their fittings on couches of plush velvet, watching the sparkle of three small but exquisite chandeliers, or partaking of wine, coffee, and sweets proffered constantly by a squad of cool, tight-lipped stewards. Sketches of the latest Moline creations, bound together in book form, were available for perusal while one waited. And after Martha Marguerite had given her name to a steward, Selena pored through one such book, looking for a wedding gown. She had not found one—although she noted several garments designed to leave one breast exposed—when, together, a man and a woman rushed out from the inner rooms of the salon as if in a competition to embrace Martha first.

The woman won.

Zoé Moline had a lush, big-hipped, big-breasted body. She moved decisively like a man. With her strong jawline and bold, commanding eyes, it was clear that she did not normally expend a great deal of time on trivialities.

"Martha, you've come home!" she cried in a deep, throaty voice. "Oh, let me have a look at you!"

Zoé stepped back a pace to take this look, and Marc Moline

found his opportunity to embrace Martha as well. *"Dar*ling, *dar-ling,"* he said.

Monsieur Moline was quite thin, handsome in a pale sort of way, vaguely dashing in silk cravat and satin cape. In England, he would have been called a fop. He placed an unexpected stress on certain syllables when he spoke and only shrewd, mercenary eyes belied the pleasantly irresolute, comfort-loving man he otherwise seemed to be.

"Mar*tha!* You are *here*. I *hope* you have come for a *com*plete wardrobe. Let us go *back* into my working *cham*bers and I will show you de*signs* that will make you *swoon.*"

This was the sort of reception that Martha Marguerite had been waiting for, which flattered her presumed status even as it salved her vanity. In her ecstasy, she almost forgot to introduce Selena, but did so as the four of them entered Moline's designing and fitting parlors.

Zoé, who had first assumed that Selena was perhaps a companion or even a maidservant, now made a closer inspection. It was very thorough and not at all discreet.

"With the right clothes," she said, "I think you might turn more than a few heads at court, young lady. Are you married?"

"No, but I—"

"Oh, *very* good." She turned to Martha. "You *are* going to pay your respects at Versailles?"

"Of course."

Martha studied Selena some more, as if a plan were forming in her mind. "Hmm," she mused, but that was all at the time.

Marc proceeded to show Martha and Selena sketches of his most recent work, which Selena had to admit was exquisite.

"I'll take two of each," said Martha. "No, three. You choose the colors, monsieur. I trust your taste implicitly. And do the same for my friend, Selena. She needs a trousseau."

"Oh, is that right?" asked Zoé. "Who is the man?"

"Jean Beaumain."

"I'm afraid I . . . that I do not know of him."

"He's a fine man. For Selena," said Martha, somewhat apologetically.

"A *comte?*" asked Zoé.

"No," replied Selena.

"A *vicomte* then?"

"No, he's—" Selena did not care for this kind of ranking with its air of privilege and class. She was just about to say, "Jean Beaumain is an outlaw and a privateer," but Martha, thinking of her own reputation more than of Selena's comfiture, stepped into the breech.

"Monsieur Beaumain is a tremendously wealthy entrepreneur, don't you know?"

Zoé didn't know, but she accepted wealth as a sufficient criterion for a prospective bridegroom. Things might have been worse. Nevertheless, as Marc brought out his tape and began to measure Martha and Selena, Zoé persisted in her questioning, as if a plan she seemed to have involved Selena quite directly.

"Your French is raw; I know that," Zoé said bluntly. "There is an accent behind it. What?"

"Scots," answered Selena. Monsieur Marc was lingering over her bust measurement. He winked at her conspiratorially.

"Indeed," nodded Zoé. "Scots indeed. I have met several of your countrymen at court over the years. In fact—I'm not certain of this; it is only a rumor—Marie Antoinette has recently taken a Scot or an Irish or a Brit—beg pardon, Selena, but they're all the same to me—as her newest lover."

"Oh, please!" implored Martha, standing there in her corset and awaiting Monsieur Marc's sure fingers, "Please tell me the news at court. I have been dying to know. The rest of the country is in a shambles, but how fine the court must be still!"

By news, of course, Martha meant gossip. Zoé was full of it, and Selena did not denounce herself too harshly for the attention with which she listened.

"Well, of course you'll recall," Madame Moline began, "that the King, upon his marriage to the Austrian woman, proved quite incapable of being a man to her. Thus, in the early years of their marriage, she took her pleasures with others."

"Some of the men at court are *very* depraved," commented Marc happily.

"Naturally," Zoé continued, "the news got out among the public. Marie Antoinette was disliked anyway, being a foreigner, and the financial excesses at Versailles, combined with her illicit loves, left her with an unsavory reputation she has not been able to shake until this day!

"Surgeons, however, were able to correct His Majesty's . . .

ah . . . inability. They had a son, Louis, born in . . . what was it?"

"Seventeen eighty-one," said Marc, still ignoring Martha but doing a very careful job on his measurement of Selena's waist and hips. "But he died last year."

"There is a second son and a daughter, though," said Zoé. "The children seem to have calmed the Queen somewhat, but naturally it is *de rigeur* to have at least a few lovers."

Here she gave Selena a searching look again, and this time, given her previous conversation, its meaning was more obvious. Zoé saw a certain advantage for herself in Selena's beauty, and it had something to do with life at court.

". . . at least a few lovers," Zoé laughed, "so affairs proceed apace. Martha, do you recall the Comtesse de la Motte?"

"Jeanne? Why of course I do. She is the Queen's best friend."

"She was. There has been a terrible scandal. More than anything else, it has fired the people with fury over excesses at Versailles. You see, there exists a fabulous diamond necklace, worth one million, six hundred thousand livres. The *comtesse* wanted it for herself, but she did not have the money. She knew, though, that a certain Cardinal Rohan was out of favor at court and wished to be readmitted to the royal circle. She approached him, telling him that Marie Antoinette wanted the necklace for herself, and that if only he, Rohan, procured it for her, he would once again be accepted.

"Now the cardinal did not have that kind of money, but he was desperate—to be out of favor is almost to be dead—so he approached the jewelers with a promise to buy. He never actually took possession of the necklace, but he reneged on the first payment, which angered the jeweler, who went with his complaint to the Queen, who of course didn't know anything about it."

Zoé was laughing now; she thought it all very funny.

"What happened?" asked Selena.

Zoé was choking with glee so Marc, who had finally begun to measure Martha, finished the tale.

"The cardinal," he said, "was disgraced and sent to a monastery to live out the rest of his days. Comtesse de la Motte was sentenced to flogging, branding, and life imprisonment, but she managed to escape to England, where she has published memoirs very unflattering to the Queen. Marie Antoinette herself, although innocent in this particular affair, has succeeded in further discrediting the monarchy, thus throwing more faggots on the revolutionary fires."

"What do you think will happen in France now?" Selena asked.

"Nothing." Marc shrugged. Finished with Martha, he draped the tape around his thin neck. "Things will go on as always."

Martha cast Selena a look that said, *I told you so!*

But Selena knew these three—Marc and Zoé and Martha—were whistling in the wind. She knew what it was like to want and not to have, to feel the fury of desperation and gut-hungry need, to be scorned and hunted by those who presumed to be the aristocrats of earth.

She knew that things would not "go on as always" because she had seen the eyes of Pierre Sorbante.

After a long morning's work, the Molines provided their customers with a fine, gay lunch of champagne and lobster salad. They were all friends. Money was not mentioned once.

"Our seamstresses will begin work immediately," Zoé declared expansively. "You two will be the new Queens at court. And," she added, glancing at Selena, "perhaps the King may look favorably upon a new delight."

"He has always been pleased with your choices before," said Marc proudly.

This woman procures for the King! Selena realized.

Martha looked mightily pleased, as if a child of hers had just been admitted to study at the Sorbonne.

Selena said nothing. She did not intend to whore for anyone, King or no, but she had an embryonic scheme of her own. Zoé had mentioned a Scot at court. It was chancy and tenuous of course, but perhaps—just perhaps—he might give her news of events in her homeland.

He might be a first step in her dream of reacquiring Coldstream Castle

"By the way, Selena," oozed Monsieur Marc, as he helped her up into Hugo's buggy, "that little cross is a canny piece of work."

Selena thought that he meant the craftsmanship and thanked him for the compliment.

"No, you mistake my meaning," he protested. "I refer to the words thereon. *Liberté, egalité, fraternité.* That is the revolutionary motto. It may well be that your little cross will serve as protection.

"And," he added in a whisper, "watch out for our friend, Martha Marguerite. She is dangerously overadorned. The people are starving and mad. One of her rings alone would feed a family for a year. So just you be careful, eh?"

14   Bastille

"You may now convey us homeward," decreed Martha Marguerite, settling into the buggyseat. Hugo and Sebastian glanced at her with narrowed eyes—they did not like her tone—but shrugged and did as they were told. Selena, after all, was paying them good money.

As the coach moved through the city, Martha chattered away happily, exclaiming again and again over the fine clothes she had just selected. She also, now and then, made disparaging references to Vergil Longchamps, but the visit to the Molines had quite effectively restored her sense of personage, and she was oblivious to the streets through which the buggy passed, and to the people in those streets.

Selena was not. With each minute there were more people about, as if a crowd were forming and moving toward the center of some forthcoming human storm. Selena herself sensed too late that the street down which they drove had become an angry maelstrom.

"I think we're in trouble," said Hugo, over his shoulder as, turning a corner, he found their way blocked. They were in the Rue St. Stephen, a narrow old avenue of stores and little shops. Normally, it would have been crowded with people seeking whatever goods were available—and not many goods were in these hard times—but today it was jammed. For a split second, half-standing in the coach, Selena thought provisions had finally reached the city, and that citizens were here to buy, but then when she heard the crash and tinkle of breaking glass, the real meaning of this mob became apparent. A riot had begun and hundreds of Parisians, out of control, were crashing into shops to loot and plunder. Such fury, once unleashed, is well-nigh unstoppable; it does not wane until excess spends itself, the level of violence mounting higher and higher until the very emotions which fuel the outbreak are exhausted.

"Back out of here!" she cried to Hugo. "Fast!"

Martha, yapping away gaily about going to Versailles, looked around, stunned. "What—?"

"There's a rich noble bitch!" someone yelled.

"I can't back up," shouted Hugo, over the rising din in the avenue. "Our way is blocked."

"Look at her furs and jewels! Get her!" shouted a hideous, one-armed beggar. "Pull her bloody eyeballs out!"

"They're . . . they mean *me!*" wailed Martha, hunching down in the buggyseat.

Down the street came the sounds of glass shattering, people cursing and screaming, and the wrenching shrieks of doors being ripped from their hinges. Furious, maddened faces, twisted and terrible, appeared all around the buggy.

"You take the old woman and her finery," yelled a bearded young ruffian, shirtless in the heat, his chest hair glistening with sweat, "I want the young one with the yellow hair. . . ."

Me! Selena knew.

A thick arm reached inside the buggy and closed around Martha's wrist. In an instant, one of her gold bracelets was gone. She didn't even have time to cry out before another rioter seized her hand, scratching and clawing, trying to get the rings off her fingers. She kicked out helplessly at her assailant, and the beautiful eye-shaped ring was gone, lost forever in a human tide of want and greed. Selena thought, in a flashing second, of the jewels and sovereigns in her greatcoat at Martha's house, and wondered how long it would be before mobs like this invaded the homes of the wealthy. Then a hand closed around her ankle. Someone was trying to drag her from the buggy. She fought, catching a glimpse of a long, red, lantern-jawed male face, mouth open in a grimace of yellow, protruding teeth. She kicked out with her free foot. Broken teeth and blood hung in the air, and the grip on her leg was loosed. She stood up in the carriage. Sebastian was out in front of the horse, which the mob had decided to steal, and Hugo was striking every which way with his whip. The melee around the buggy was as great as that in the looted shops along the street. Selena did not know how so many people could occupy such a small space, nor how so many could be so maddened.

For a moment, just for a moment, the tide seemed to turn. Martha's fur piece was gone, true, and she had scratches on her arms and hands where the rings had been pulled from her. But Sebastian had the horse under control, and Hugo's whip drew hellish cries of agony from those who felt its hiss and fire. The mob surrounding the buggy drew back for a moment.

But after gathering new resolve, incensed by the resistance, the assailants came forward again, this time with incomparable frenzy. Men seized the wheels of the buggy, pressing forward in unison, snarling, shouting, lifting the little vehicle right off the cobblestones. It felt to Selena as if she had been transported suddenly to the deck of a pitching sloop. Buildings along the street swayed and tilted dizzily in her field of vision. The buggy was turning over onto its side and she was falling.

The very mob that seemed intent upon tearing Martha and Selena limb from limb saved them, although not deliberately. Had there been only a few thugs engaged in upsetting the carriage, the two women would have been slammed down onto the paving stones. Instead, they were tossed through the air upon the heads and shoulders of the massed crowd. Selena tumbled and ricocheted above a sea of people, who pressed toward the overturned buggy, apparently in the belief that great treasures must be concealed therein. Hands tore at her dress, somebody scratched her face, but she was no longer the object of the crowd's wrath. She slid down between the shoulders of rioters and came to her feet, gasping, pressed against the wall of a ruined breadshop. She could not see Martha Marguerite, but Hugo and Sebastian were mounted on the horse, trying to fight their way through the mob.

Hugo saw her. "Selena!" he cried. "Over here!"

"I can't. I'll be all right. Save yourselves."

The buggy collapsed like a child's toy beneath the stomping frenzy of the mob.

Then in the distance, everyone heard the thunder of iron-shod hoofs upon stone.

"Gendarmes! Gendarmes are coming!" someone yelled. And the rioters, seeking to save themselves, poured down Rue St. Stephen, carrying Selena along with them onto a broader avenue she did not know, joining another great throng of people moving eastward through Paris. Flags of red, white, and blue fluttered above their heads. Many of them wore the cockade, symbol of the revolution, a small button with three circles of color, also red, white, and blue. Red and blue were the colors of Paris, white the color of the Bourbons, but Selena recalled another country with a flag of similar hues.

The only thing to do is to pretend I'm one of them, Selena decided. She'd lost sight of Hugo and Sebastian as well as Martha Marguerite. She would have to survive on her own, and they as well. Fortunately, with her torn dress and the blood on her face, she looked at least as disreputable as anyone in the mob. Pausing for a second, she ripped a piece of cloth from her skirt and bound it around her head.

"To the Bastille!" people were chanting. "Down with the monarchy."

A decrepit, shambling giant of a man grabbed Selena around the shoulders and stared into her eyes. He was a frightful sight. Selena was certain that he was mad as a loon.

"Gold!" he cried, spying her cross, shaking his huge, long-haired head in triumph. "What have we here, a poseur?" But then he read the words on the cross and drew back a bit. "Ah!" he said. "You stay with me and all will be well."

With his great arm around her, Selena had no choice but to rush on.

"Down with the Bourbon tyrants! To the Bastille!"

She noted that, even in this mob, people around her and the giant gave way a little to make room for them.

"Citizen, you are bleeding," said the man, not unkindly. "Pray, are you all right?"

"It's only a scratch."

"Good. You stay with me. I think we've been expecting you."

Marc Moline must have been right about the motto on this cross, Selena thought. But if it were protection to be in the grip of this gigantic, lunatic-looking creature, she thought that the word *protection* must surely have different meanings for different people.

At length, with the sun burning hot overhead, the mob came out of the avenue and swarmed about a squat, ugly, brooding fortress. Here was the Bastille, once a prison for political opponents of the monarchy and still a symbol of tyranny, guarded by a small garrison of royal troops and a contingent of Swiss mercenaries. Some of the officers, arms at the ready, stood before the fortress; the troops were inside.

198 *Vanessa Royall*

To her surprise, because she and the giant who held her captive were far back in the mob, Selena saw the crowd suddenly part before them, and the huge man, still holding her tightly around the waist, strode forward like a lord toward the fortress gate.

"Mirabeau! It's Mirabeau!" the people cried, and sent forth a great, bloodthirsty cheer.

Mirabeau, Selena thought. Vergil Longchamps had said that this man was in league with Pierre Sorbante. Mirabeau's father, a marquis, had had his son jailed time and again in an effort to save him from his own excesses, but the only result had been a greater hatred of all authority.

Obviously, this revolution had many actors. She made a tentative attempt to twist away from her lumbering captor, but he tightened his grip on her. They reached the front of the mob, where Pierre Sorbante stood facing the officer in charge of the fortress.

"Pierre!" chortled Mirabeau. "Look what I have found!"

Selena felt herself caught and held by Sorbante's ruthless, triumphant eyes.

"So we meet again, mademoiselle," he said. "But wait. We will confer later. I have business to attend to now."

He made an abrupt, peremptory gesture. Two young warriors wearing headbands bearing the cockade stepped forward. One of them grabbed Selena's right arm, the other her left.

"You just stay with us, *cherie,*" ordered the man at her right.

Mirabeau and Sorbante turned to face the Bastille's governor-general, who was attempting, unsuccessfully, to control his mounting terror. The great crowd howled and cursed.

Mirabeau turned to glare at them. Sorbante raised his arms. A wave swept through the mob like wind in wheat. Silence fell.

"In the name of the people of France," Sorbante began, his fine, resonant voice rising on the air, "in the name of the Paris commune and of the National Assembly, formerly the benighted Estates General, we are here to liberate this accursed fortress!"

The crowd howled, then became silent. Selena felt the iron grip of hands around her wrists. But her own tension was as nothing compared to that of the mob, nor that which existed between Sorbante and the governor-general. *The poor man has been left alone to deal with this,* she realized. *He is defending the monarchy with a handful of men, but the king whose interests he serves is lounging at Versailles, or perhaps crouching behind a windowsill waiting for a deer to stroll by.*

"*Liberté! Egalité! Fraternité!*" bellowed Mirabeau, and again the crowd howled and fell silent. The very air crackled with bloodlust and mayhem held barely in check, awaiting only a word to be unleashed.

And the word was given.

If the governor-general expected demands, negotiations, any of the give-and-take of bargaining, he was wrong.

"*Onward!*" cried Mirabeau, and of an instant the mob, as one, surged forward. Centuries of French history and culture, of society and manners, of order and struggle and gain, poised once and forever on a delicate precipice of time, and plummeted. No one on earth knew what would happen.

The governor-general did not live to find out. He was run through by a pitchfork as soon as the wild crowd moved forward, and decapitated by a peasant's scythe a few seconds later. Soldiers within the garrison began firing on the crowd. The tumult and din, the small white puffs of smoke from the weapons, the flash of scythes and hoes and forks: these rendered strange and surrealistic all that was happening. Within minutes, the vanguard of the mob had broken down the Bastille gates. Blood-stopping cries of agony from the Swiss mercenaries filled the air. Millennia turned upon one hour; rent flesh and spilled blood sounded the death knell. Oh, Louis XVI was still king. He was safe at Versailles. But his days were numbered now.

Pierre Sorbante had gone into the fortress with his followers, but Mirabeau remained outside, giving orders, exhorting the mob. Presently, he turned to the men who held Selena.

"Take her to the place," he snapped. "We'll be along when this is finished."

Before she had a chance to question, much less to protest, Selena found herself led away from the whirling chaos in front of the fortress, back among the alleys of Paris, and suddenly through a gate, down a long stone stairway, and into abrupt darkness. She heard the sound of dripping water, smelled musk and mold. It reminded her of the prison in New York Harbor.

"Where are you taking me?" she asked, when the men stopped for a moment.

"Don't worry," said one. "You're safe. We're to take good care of you."

The other found a torch that stank of oil and lighted it, revealing before them what appeared to be an ancient tunnel, which led into another and then another until Selena could see no farther. She heard the scraping skitter of claws upon stone as rats fled the flickering light of the torch.

"The sewers of Paris," said one of the men. "But out of these sewers will come power. Let's go."

Walking single file, with Selena between her captors, the three moved along a stone walkway alongside a channel of water and murky sludge. She tried to remember how far they proceeded, what turns they made, but very soon she'd lost her bearings completely. Finally, when she thought they would never stop, the man with the torch turned into a cavernous room and slid the torch into a sconce embedded in the stone. He then lit candles and she saw a subterranean meeting place—how far beneath the city she did not know—with a table, some benches, and even a few cots. There were several nearly empty wine bottles on the table. A rat, chewing on a crust of bread in one corner, glared malevolently at the interruption, then fled, red-eyed and squeaking in outrage.

"Make yourself comfortable," said one of Selena's captors casually, checking the wine bottles and finding one that had not yet been drained. He hoisted it and helped himself to a swig, then passed the bottle to his comrade.

The man, just about to drink, looked over at Selena, who had taken a seat on a bench.

"Wine?" he asked.

She shook her head. In the gloom, they seemed older and more experienced than she'd thought, hard-muscled, tense men who looked as if they hadn't eaten properly in a long while.

"Who are you?" she asked hesitantly, as they settled down beside her on the bench, passing the bottle back and forth. It did not appear as if they intended her any harm, and this fact emboldened her somewhat.

"I am called Citizen Marat," said one.

"Edmund Danton," replied his mate.

"What do you want of me?"

Danton looked her up and down. "Surely you know!" he scoffed. "You wear the cross of Erasmus Ward."

So the cross is a symbol or a signal of some kind, thought Selena.

"I don't know what you mean," she said. "It is Ward's cross, I admit that, but—"

"Come now," said Marat. "We certainly did not expect that you would be the courier, but all the same, you are. Now before we are joined by Mirabeau and Sorbante, why don't you just tell us where our treasure is?"

Treasure? The jewels and sovereigns? She imagined her great-coat hanging inconspicuously in the back of the closet in her room at Martha Marguerite's house. Marat had referred possessively to the "treasure." *But how could he know of it?* Somewhere in the great, obscure series of events that had begun with Royce Campbell's mysterious leather pouch and that had led to this Parisian sewer, there were conduits and consequences she could not fathom. But one thing she did know: she had no intention of admitting anything to these shadowy men. At the rate Martha was spending the money Jean Beaumain had given Selena, and with France in such an unsettled condition, the jewels might well become her only ticket to safety.

If, in fact, she ever managed to get out of this underground lair.

"I'm sorry," she said. "I know nothing of any treasure. I do have—not with me, but I do have—paper money. French, British, Spanish. Even American. Just permit me to leave and you can have all of it."

"She's lying," Danton said to Marat, without heat.

"We'll wait and let Sorbante deal with her. He knows more about the situation than we do."

It was just an idle remark, but Selena gave it some consideration. Either Royce had known from the start that the jewels had a special significance or he had somehow acquired—legally or illegally, by accident or design—a fortune mysterious and fraught with ambiguous importance. And if the pouch was indeed the "treasure" to which these men referred, what connection might it have to the little cross? Perhaps it was all like a great puzzle in which each of the players—Royce, LaValle, Sorbante, even she—played a limited role, held but a single piece in the grand design.

But who held the master piece? Who knew the parameters of that overriding plan?

If, indeed, there was one.

I'm stumped, she concluded. *But I'm not about to blabber away*

before I have a clearer understanding of what I'm dealing with.
Then another thought came to her: she *knew* that her possession of the jewels was due completely to mischance, her ownership of the little cross scarcely less so. Royce would *never* have placed her deliberately in danger. He would have explained things to her first.

But they had become separated unexpectedly, fleeing Lieutenant Clay Oakley in New York. And then Royce had been killed by the cannon of HMS *Prince William*.

So Selena *had* to be, unwittingly and unknowingly, a piece in a dangerous puzzle.

She knew nothing about the nature of that puzzle.

Except that perhaps when she had given up the jewels, willingly or by coercion, she would have served her purpose.

And her physical existence, not to mention her knowledge of the puzzle, *would no longer be required!*

I am getting out of here right now! she decided.

There was about a half an inch of wine left in the bottom of the bottle. Danton offered it to her. "Go ahead, *cherie*. It'll ward off the chill. Did you know that rheumatism has ended more revolutionary careers than the guillotine has? We have to hide and even sleep in places that are no good for the bones. Here, for example."

Selena murmured her sympathies, but declined the wine. Danton finished it off.

"Have you ever heard of Lieutenant Clay Oakley?" she asked the two men.

They looked at each other grimly. "It's Captain Clay Oakley now," Marat said. "He's the new chief of secret intelligence in London. I have never heard of a man to whom monarchy is so sacred. You would think that every little prince was Jesus Christ. He captured, last week, one of our men who was in Britain, seeking to gain editorial support for our cause. Oakley had him beaten to death. Why, do you know the monster?"

"Yes," Selena said. She told her story about interrogation in Oakley's cork-lined room of paintings, of her surprise at the coexistent ugliness and beauty within him.

"His parts are too disparate," Danton decided. "They will never fuse. He will come to an evil end, and I hope to have a part in it."

"As do I," said Selena.

The conversation, their agreement about Oakley, their isolation here beneath the streets of Paris: these softened the tension among them.

"Where in the devil's name is Sorbante?" Marat wondered, getting up and pacing about. "We had the Bastille in our hands even before we came here."

"He is probably giving another speech," snickered Danton. And for the first time, Selena sensed in these men the hint of a belief that they could outshine the luminous firebrand, perhaps even surpass him. If given the opportunity. And she recalled something that her father had told her long ago, while he was tutoring her in the history he loved so much and understood so well. *"Selena,"* he'd said, *"war is fairly simple. It kills everyone in its path. But a revolution eats its young, like a tomcat or a boar hog who does not recognize his own."*

The swish of the blade.

Marat paced. Danton fretted and looked about. Selena began to fidget. Then she began to fidget more.

"Something wrong with you?" asked Marat.

Selena cast her eyes downward. "I'm sorry, but . . . but I must . . . relieve myself soon. . . ."

The two men laughed. "Well, you are certainly in the right place for that!" Danton said.

It was agreed forthwith that Selena should go just outside the cavernous room and do her business on the stones alongside the sludge-filled channel.

"Here," said Danton, "take a candle with you. We may be radicals, but we are Frenchmen first. No woman should slip into the muck."

They laughed again. Selena, taking the candle, tried to look as embarrassed as possible. "Please don't look, will you?" she pleaded.

"On our honor," chortled Marat.

Selena knew that she had only minutes, at most, to get a decent head start.

The candle, while inadequate, was better than nothing. Selena slid along the wall of the tunnel as fast as she could go, holding the candle before her. She could hear the voices of the men diminish behind her, and she barely heard her name when one of them called her. There were various crevices and nooks alongside the stinking channel, places in which she might hide for a time, but her larger problem was the trackless labyrinth of the sewers. First things first. When she heard one of the men shout, his voice echoing and re-echoing off the stones, she pressed herself into a cranny and blew out the light.

Then she waited.

Danton and Marat cursed energetically and seemed just about to come searching for her when other voices joined theirs. Mirabeau and Sorbante had arrived. There was more cursing then, as the men debated what to do. "If she wants to die down here, that's her affair," one of them said, "but I'm not about to."

She heard footsteps on the stones, uncertain whether they were coming her way or not. Finally, there was silence.

But now her plight was worse than it had been before. She was alone, and her candle was out. In her mind's eye, Selena pictured the whole vast spinning globe of earth, and all the people upon it, and all the cities and mountains and plains. Then she saw herself, all alone, huddled beneath one of those cities, in the bowels of the earth. There were three possibilities. She could make her way back to the room and wait for someone to come, which might take days. Or she could move on in the opposite direction.

Or she could die there and let her bones be found untold years from now.

This last possibility was unattractive. She dismissed it, and stepped from her hiding place. The channel of sludge gurgled a few feet away, moving on, moving toward . . . the Seine. Yes, it would lead to the river. In complete darkness, she got down on her hands and knees, began to feel her way along the stony chasm. The most oppressive part of this strategy was that she did not know how far she'd have to go, and soon her hands and knees were bruised and bleeding. When she was tired, she lay flat against the cool stones and waited until her energy returned. But then she moved on again. Several times, misjudging the way, she cracked her head on a rock, and once she almost slipped into the slimy sewage. But the foul channel, distasteful and stinking as it was, gave her a measure of cheer. Because judging by the sound of its flow, she knew she had to be heading toward the Seine.

And then, at last, the wet stones reflected a bit of faraway light, a dim, phantasmagoric ray of hope. She allowed herself a long rest to celebrate, and then moved on. The channel flowed into a culvert which emptied into the river. Pulling up her skirts, which were by now incredibly tattered and filth-ridden, she sloshed through the sewage-filled culvert, swung herself out over the water and onto the riverbank, panting as if her lungs would explode.

The sun was rising in the east. She'd been underground for almost eighteen hours. The day was already hot.

15 Invitation to Versailles

Stumbling toward the LaRouche mansion in the eerie haze of morning light, all too conscious of her matted hair, tattered dress, and still-bleeding cuts, Selena looked like an apparition from hell itself. She was glad that no people were in the streets, but just when she grew confident that she'd reach the house safely, a uniformed guard stepped through a gate in front of one of the neighboring homes and confronted her. The rich, terrified by yesterday's riot, had stepped up their defenses.

"Get out of here immediately, you filthy old hag!" he cried, unable to conceal his own disgust at her appearance.

He wore a pistol at his belt and carried a riding whip, which he lifted to strike her.

"Please!" she cried, raising her arms to ward off the blow. "I am a guest of Madame LaRouche's."

"Like hell you are."

"No, it is true. I was caught in the mob yesterday. I am a foreigner, unfamiliar with Paris, and only now have I managed to find my way back."

The guard lowered his whip. "You're Selena?" he asked doubtfully.

"Yes."

"Oh, my God. Come with me. I'm sorry. Madame has been beside herself with worry about your fate. She is at home now, under doctor's care. Which you ought to be as well."

He shrank from touching her, and in fact walked several paces ahead of her as he led her to Martha Marguerite's home. Selena did not blame him for his squeamishness; the awful stench of the sewers was upon her and she was unsure if it could ever be thoroughly washed away.

Hugo and Sebastian, half-awake, were sitting on the floor in the foyer, drinking coffee.

"Jesus, Selena!" they exclaimed, leaping to their feet when the guard brought her in. "We thought you were dead for sure."

"Maybe I am . . ." she managed to say, and collapsed onto the floor.

When she awoke, Selena was lying in bed, clean and cool. Old Stella and Martha were seated on chairs next to the bed.

"How do you feel, Selena?" asked Martha, who did not look any too well herself.

Selena tried to sit up. The effort was unsuccessful. But she was able to move her arms and legs. A good sign.

"The doctor washed you as well as he could, and dressed your cuts," said Martha. "His orders are that you rest completely in bed for several days at least."

"He will get no resistance from me," Selena groaned. "But I need a real bath right away. I want to soak for hours."

"Stella, get the hot water ready," Martha ordered.

The old cook, who had been blinking dully at Selena, protested. "That's not my work. I want an extra bit of money for all this additional work."

"You'll have it," Selena said. "Are Hugo and Sebastian still here? Have them help you. They'll be rewarded as well."

"I cannot say how grateful I am to you," confided Martha, after the cook had gone to see about the bath. "You know, of course, that I'll repay you for everything as soon as my affairs are in order."

The previous day's meeting with Longchamps, which seemed years in the past, had been dismissed completely by Martha. She had decided to think of herself as a rich woman, evidence to the contrary notwithstanding. Selena sighed.

"By the way, we received our first billing from Monsieur Marc," Martha went on casually. "If I could possibly trouble you for five thousand francs . . just temporarily, of course. And the decorators will be arriving later this morning. . . ."

Selena was too tired to protest. Later, when she regained her strength, she would attempt to explain to the older woman that their straits might soon be desperate, especially if Jean Beaumain did not arrive soon. Martha had chosen to live in a dream world, and it was obviously very pleasant there.

"Yes, I'll take care of things . . ." Selena said without spirit. There were always the jewels. . . .

After bathing in lilac-scented water, then changing the water and bathing again, Selena drank some pigeon broth and began to feel vaguely civilized. Hugo and Sebastian appeared to inquire about her welfare and to present to her a concern that weighed heavily on Martha's mind.

"As you know," Hugo said, shuffling his feet, "madame wishes to go to the palace as soon as her new wardrobe is completed. . . ."

"Yes?" prodded Selena, propped up on pillows in her bed. The sounds of hammers and saws drifted up from the lower floors of the house.

"Well," interjected Sebastian, "our buggy got wrecked in yesterday's brawl. We managed to rescue madame, and we would have you too if we could've—"

"But our buggy got wrecked," Hugo said. "We think we're owed a new one."

"One fine enough to take you to Versailles," commented Sebastian.

It doesn't pay to be rich, thought Selena. *There's no end to what people think you can afford.* But she herself wanted to go to the palace, if only to meet the Scot Zoé Moline had claimed was in residence there.

"All right," she said. "Step out of the room for a moment."

The two men, after glancing at each other, did so. Selena dragged her battered body out of the bed and made her way into the closet. Her greatcoat hung there, and a moment's inspection assured her that the jewels and sovereigns were still in the lining. She took a fistful of Jean's paper money from inside the lining of a traveling bag, counted out three thousand francs, called the men inside, and gave them the money. "Mind, choose a carriage carefully," she warned.

"Oh, I'll bet there's more where this came from." Hugo leered playfully, waving the bills like a sheaf of foolscap. "Isn't there?"

"Don't bet on it," replied Selena.

Eventually, as the summer wore on, the carriage, overly grand, was acquired, the refurbished house began to look almost normal, and after fittings and refittings, the magnificent clothing of Marc Moline filled whole closets.

But the summons to Versailles did not come.

Martha was at first puzzled, then exasperated, then hurt. "I sent word that I wished to call upon their majesties weeks ago!" she wailed. "Zoé promised me that everything would be arranged. What is happening, anyway? Am I perhaps out of favor? Why, I've done nothing to warrant being ignored in this manner."

"The King does have a few other matters on his mind," Selena replied dryly.

Indeed, if he were not too feckless to read the tide of events, his neck ought to have been on his mind. The fall of the Bastille had been a clear sign that the masses were behind the new National Assembly, rather than the King. It put real force behind the Assembly and substituted popularly elected officials for royal agents. The National Guard, commanded by Lafayette, who was sympathetic to the revolution, now numbered forty-eight thousand men. The King continued to command the army, but how the soldiers might behave if forced to choose between the monarchy and the revolution was anybody's guess.

The fall of the Bastille had been such a clear signal of danger that even Louis XVI did not fail to perceive its meaning. He visited Paris in person, sought outwardly to ease hostility toward himself by praising the revolution, and even made a point of putting on the cockade, as if he too were a champion of the new order. It was, given the King's characteristic maladroitness, a reasonably canny ploy. And for a time, it seemed to work in his favor.

Indeed, for a time during the late summer and early fall of 1789, it looked as if radical reform might proceed peacefully. The freedom of the Assembly had been affirmed. Paris had settled down once more into repose, if not placidity. Even the King had apparently decided that resisting the revolutionary tide was madness. His powers waned by the day; as for respect, he had little left. But the victory of the revolutionaries, Mirabeau, Sorbante, and the others, had been won so easily that they were emboldened. Once they determined that the tyrant had no teeth, they began to plan further mischief.

Another in France had also determined that Louis XVI lacked sufficient backbone. His wife, Marie Antoinette, was bitterly opposed to the reforming policies of the National Assembly and the diminution of her husband's authority. Besides, her clique of friends at court disliked the sudden decrease in the pensions and amusements to which they had long been accustomed. To the frivolous, nothing seems more essentially cruel than a sudden withdrawal of frivolity. Marie Antoinette and her corrupt, idle friends began to harass the King, to plead for an iron fist with which to smite the radicals, to *act!*

The result of this whining and harping was furious intrigue, and the result of the intrigue was an incendiary scheme to employ force against the deputies of the National Assembly and the people of Paris, who were still suffering grievously from a scarcity of food and provisions. The scheme involved bringing an entire garrison of troops from Flanders to the capital, troops still loyal to Louis. The officers of this contingent, upon arriving at Versailles, were guests at a fabulous banquet, at which no expense was spared. News of this feast, or "orgy" as it was called, spread like wildfire in hungry Paris.

Selena heard the news as she and Martha prepared to climb into Hugo's glistening new coach, an enclosed vehicle with real glass windows, thin, shimmering wheelspokes, and silver lamps mounted on either side of the driver's seat. The invitation from Versailles had finally arrived, and Martha Marguerite was so excited she fairly quivered in ecstasy.

"Seems we might have a bit of rough going on the drive to the palace," Hugo allowed.

"Why is that?" asked Selena.

"Look, Selena, my partner and I couldn't be more grateful for what you've done on our behalf. We think you're the salt of the earth. But there are thousands of furious people getting ready to march on Versailles. They figure if the King can afford a feast for officers called here to crush their revolution, he can also afford bread for women and children."

"Another mob? This one to march on the palace?"

"Let's get started right away. If we get spotted in this coach, they might mistake us for nobles."

She wanted to say, "You're the one who bought this ostentatious carriage to show off," but held her tongue. *What good would it do?* Louis XVI had managed, again by what seemed to be congenital insensitivity, to re-inflame a firestorm that had at least died down slightly. The situation here was far more dangerous than it had been in America. There, with the vast distances between battlefields, relative freedom from real want, and a tradition of parliamentary give and take, conditions had been quite different. Also, the tyrant, George III, had been in England, three thousand miles away. Here in France, however, hatred rode like a dragon in the very air, and the King was separated from the mob by only twelve miles of road leading to Versailles.

Even a hungry person could walk twelve miles, with rage in the belly for fuel.

Selena stood outside the coach for a moment. Hugo and Sebastian waited. *Should we go?* she wondered. It seemed inconceivable that a mob would storm the King's own residence, but a short time ago, it had also been unbelievable that the radicals, with very little difficulty, could occupy the Bastille.

"What's the matter, Selena?" asked Martha Marguerite from inside the coach. "Did you forget something?"

"Yes," said Selena, and rushed back into the house. If Versailles fell, not one of the gorgeous homes in this privileged *arrondisement* would be safe for a minute.

Rushing into her bedroom, she found that a vanguard of the revolution was already attacking. Old Stella had her greatcoat laid out upon the bed, and was preparing to slice its lining apart with a carving knife.

"Oh!" exclaimed the startled cook, looking up.

"Give me my coat," said Selena. "The nights are getting colder now that it's October, and I wouldn't want to catch a chill."

"I'll give your bones a chill, you rich young beauty," snarled the old woman, lunging toward Selena, blade flashing.

Only Stella's semi-blindness saved Selena. The slashing knife missed her by mere inches, and the cook was off balance. Selena darted around her, grabbed the greatcoat, and ducked back from a second attack. She headed for the door and pulled it shut behind her just as the cook struck again. Her blade pierced the door. Stella was still cursing as Selena ran down the stairs and out to the coach, climbing in hurriedly.

"Oh, how nice!" said Martha Marguerite. "Now you'll be safe if there's a fall of dew."

"I hope that's all we'll have to be concerned about," replied Selena. "Hugo, you may set out."

The coach began to move through this section of the city and toward the Versailles roadway. The drive, at first, was uneventful. But presently Selena heard what seemed to be a low hum in the distance, like a swarm of angry bees. It was the mob that Hugo had mentioned, and what a strange appearance it made, forming up there in the city. Hugo had to skirt the raggedy edges of the mass which, through the coach window, Selena determined was comprised of *women!* Poor and destitute Parisian women who had endured enough and were intent upon presenting evidence of their woes to the King at Versailles.

"Oh, my Lord, what is happening?" exclaimed Martha apprehensively. "They may ruin our stay at the palace, and I have so much looked forward to it."

Then, peering more closely, Selena noted that some of the women had very thick, very hairy arms, and particularly strong-jawed faces partly shadowed by sunbonnets. There were men in the crowd too.

In the distance, upon his white horse and surrounded by officers of the National Guard, sat Lafayette, viewing the scene dispassionately. He had apparently decided to make no effort to forestall this demonstration.

Once again, as she had before, Selena sensed the hungry presence of the panther, and its lusty yen. *"Bread! Bread! Bread!"* chanted the mob, as if warming up collective vocal chords of rage. *"Bread! Bread! Bread!"* But what the panther of revolution really wanted was blood.

The passage of the gleaming new carriage created something of a stir. There were sudden, angry cries: "Rich bastards! Get them." Hugo, on the driver's seat, snapped his whip. The coach lurched forward as the horse responded, and began to move faster. A rock flew through the air, striking the vehicle with a sharp *crack.*

"Get down!" said Selena, not a moment too soon. Another rock shattered the window glass, covering Selena and her companion with flying shards, followed by the malicious sound of triumphant laughter. Hugo was whipping the horse frantically now; more projectiles struck the carriage, but in a minute the immediate danger ended. They were out of range.

"Are you two all right?" asked Sebastian, leaning down from the driver's seat and looking in through the ruined window.

"I . . . I guess so," Selena replied, checking herself and Martha for cuts. None that she could find.

Madame LaRouche, however, was shaken to the quick by the attack. "Why on earth would they do something like that?" she wailed. "I've never done anything to hurt anyone."

She failed to see that, to the mob, anyone owning a coach as fine as this was automatically a despised symbol of privilege. The animosity was not a personal thing at all.

"They would have thrown rocks at St. Francis of Assisi," explained Selena, "were he riding today in this carriage. They have nothing against *you*."

"But they would have *killed* me," cried Martha, brushing away fragments of glass.

Quite true, thought Selena.

After that, the ride to Versailles, while uneventful, was ruined for Martha Marguerite. She crouched down in her seat, scarcely noticing the lovely countryside through which they passed. Peasants toiled as always in the fields along the road, and a few of them even paused in their labors, out of long habit, to lift hats or hands to the passing vehicle. At one point, a little boy ran alongside the horse, begging for food or money. Sebastian tried to shoo the little fellow away, and finally Selena tossed him a couple of coins.

"You oughtn't to have done that," Martha snapped. "Charity only discourages them from working as hard as they should."

Selena said nothing. If Martha Marguerite did not yet understand that exactly such an attitude had brought France to its current danger, it was unlikely that she ever would.

Martha brightened quickly, though, when the palace came into view, and Selena herself was captivated. She experienced a moment of chagrin, for in comparison to Versailles, Coldstream Castle was decidedly rude. But then she gave herself over to the order and splendor of the place. Over the center of the building, in which the royal residences were located, stood a bronze statue of Louis XV on horseback. Great wings stretched to the left and right, and gardens fell away from the palace on every side. There was a beautiful terrace adorned with ornamental basins, statuary, and bronze groups. Wide, tree-lined avenues ran along a vast green lawn.

"It is called the *tapis vert,*" instructed Martha. "This, my dear, is truly the center of the civilized world."

Selena sniffed the air, catching the ammoniac scent of urine. Gentlemen were in the habit of relieving themselves outside the palace walls. It was said that, in imitation of their monarch, owners of châteaux throughout France encouraged their guests—and even their peasants—to piss in shrubbery and flower beds, that their own homes should smell just like Versailles.

All around the palace today, troops of the regular army stood alongside men of the Royal Guard. News of the mob in Paris had reached Versailles, and every possible precaution was being taken. The carriage was halted, in fact, before being allowed to proceed to the palace, and a crisp, suspicious colonel of the Guard determined from a list of names he carried that Madame LaRouche and Mademoiselle MacPherson were expected.

At the entrance to the palace proper, the two women were met and welcomed by a captain of the household staff and turned over to maidservants who would show them to their separate quarters. Hugo and Sebastian, blinking at the unfamiliar magnificence surrounding them—and thinking their new coach quite pedestrian compared to the colossal, gilded vehicles lining the drive—were directed to the stables.

Selena and Martha were led quickly through the opulent interior—they would have time to be fully awed by it in due course—to suites set aside for them during their stay, which was expected to last for a week. Selena's suite of rooms, on the second floor of the palace, overlooking a section of the gardens, took her breath away by its luxury and size. Had the suite been cleared of canopied bed and tapestries, of divans, tables, chairs, and statuary, she might almost have played games inside it.

Selena's maid was a shy, dark-haired slip of a girl named Chloé who, after inquiring whether mademoiselle wished refreshments, informed her that Monsieur and Madame Moline would be waiting for her shortly in the garden. Then after helping Selena unpack her things, including the heavy greatcoat, Chloé withdrew.

Selena changed from her navy-blue traveling outfit into a pale lavender frock with matching jacket—for there was a chill in the October air—and left her rooms to have a look about. Servants moved constantly through the corridors, up and down stairs, some barely noticing her, others nodding politely, none of them challenging her passage in any way. When she saw two sword-bearing Royal Guardsmen standing sentry before a great bronze double door, however, she realized that she'd strayed near the royal residence, and retreated. A dinner and a ball had been planned for the evening; she would meet and satisfy her curiosity about the monarchs then.

At length, after admiring a few of the countless portraits and paintings with which the walls were hung—Clay Oakley would have admired them as well—Selena left the palace and walked out onto the spectacular terrace overlooking the gardens. She did not see the Molines, who had arrived here on the previous day, nor was Martha Marguerite about, but in the distance, standing beside and gazing down desultorily at a bed of white roses, was a woman alone. By the slimness of her figure, Selena judged her to be quite young. She was just about to call out in greeting when she noticed a telltale tremor about the woman's shoulders. And although she stood with her back to Selena, it was obvious that she was weeping quietly.

Stirred by pity, Selena was also undecided about whether she ought to intrude. Perhaps the woman wanted privacy. But she seemed so young and vulnerable, her hands pressed to her eyes, her shoulders shaking, that Selena's choice was swift.

"Is something wrong?" she asked gently, walking over.

The girl—for at close distance she seemed no more than fifteen or sixteen—turned to face Selena in embarrassed surprise. She had wonderful ash-blond hair, a small, sensitive mouth, and a round, pretty face. Her slightly slanted blue eyes were reddened by tears, however, and tears had splotched the front of her demure, ivory-colored outdoor frock, against which her young breasts pressed as she sobbed.

"Enschuldigung," she said, hiding her face with her hands. *"Enschuldigung sie, bitte."*

It seemed to be some sort of an apology, in a language Selena did not know.

"I'm sorry for intruding upon you," said Selena in English. "Are you all right?"

The girl stopped crying, and regarded Selena with interest.

"You're English?" she asked.

"No. Scots. My name is Selena. I couldn't help but wonder what is troubling you so."

"I have not seen you here before," said the girl, still in English but with a heavy trace of guttural accent.

"I've just arrived. I'll be a guest for a short time."

The girl showed signs of starting to cry again. Whatever troubled her seemed monumental indeed.

"Come, sit down with me," said Selena, taking her hand. They walked over to a nearby bench and took seats in the warm sun. The girl was rubbing her eyes, looking miserable. Selena asked the obvious question: "What causes a lovely child like you such woe?"

She feared that perhaps someone the girl knew had died, in which case there was little but words she could offer, or that an episode of early love had suddenly turned sour. That would be a lot easier to treat. A little time, a new beau . . .

"Thank you for being so kind to me," the girl said, in French now. She dried her eyes on her sleeve. "It is just that I learned a bit of awful news this morning from the Queen. You see, I am Francesca of Austria, niece of Marie Antoinette."

Now Selena understood. The tongue in which Francesca had initially spoken was German. She debated whether or not a curtsy of obeisance was in order, and decided it would be a bit ridiculous since she and the princess were already conversing. Moreover, the girl was preoccupied with something far more important than protocol.

"Yesterday the world was bright," said Francesca, with the somber portentousness of youth, "but today it is as black as a pit."

"And tomorrow it may be bright again," observed Selena.

"Oh, no! You see, I was on my way from Austria to England for my betrothal to Prince William, one of the King's sons. The best one! But now I must stop here for God knows how long. Aunt Marie informed me that the situation is too dangerous for further travel. She said I might be kidnapped. But I miss William so, and if I do not reach London, he may change his mind. He may decide upon someone else. . . ."

She began to cry again.

Selena, regretting that she did not have a handkerchief, pondered the princess's words. She had been chosen to *marry* Prince William of England, for whom the warship that had killed Royce Campbell had been named. The world was not only small, but webbed with mysterious filaments of time and chance. Her heart went out to the girl, however, separated as she was from the one she loved. Selena herself had suffered enough such separations to know full well the bleak aloneness, the feeling of pointlessness and impotence such trauma engendered.

"Nothing lasts forever," she said feebly.

It was the wrong thing to say. "That's what I'm afraid of," replied Francesca, crying harder.

"Oh, dear," thought Selena. "What I meant is that this political travail must end sometime."

"But what if that's too late?"

The victims of woe have an answer for everything, and each answer contributes to their misery.

"Are you unsure of William?" asked Selena, trying another tack. "Because if that's true—"

"No. Oh, no. We love each other more than any two people have loved each other from the beginning of time."

"Of course," agreed Selena.

"I've loved him ever since I met him last month in Salzburg—"

"Last month," said Selena.

"—and I simply *must* get to London for our betrothal. But Aunt Marie and Uncle Louis will not permit me to go just now."

"They are thinking of your welfare."

"No. If they were then they'd find a way to get me to England." She managed to stop crying. "So I've made a plan," she said conspiratorially.

"May I ask what it is?"

"You won't give me away?"

"I swear it."

Francesca glanced over her shoulder to see if anyone was around. So did Selena. She saw the Molines and Martha Marguerite coming out of the palace and onto the terrace, but they were still quite a distance away.

"I'm going to go on my own," the princess confided. "I'm going to disguise myself as a commoner, perhaps as a peasant or some such, and make my way to England."

Selena, who knew something of what the world was like, and who knew too the incendiary situation in Paris, was aghast. For all her spirit and resolve, Francesca was an innocent young girl, cosseted and protected since birth by the vast embracing comforts of privilege. The world outside Versailles would chew her to pieces, and if anyone found out that she belonged to the royal family, she would be doomed.

Yet Selena also had the shrewdness to judge that the princess was strong-willed enough to carry through with her disastrous scheme. *If I try to convince her that she'll fail,* Selena reasoned, *I'll only augment the stubbornness of her intent.*

"May I make a suggestion?" she asked carefully.

There wasn't much time, for the Molines and Martha were coming toward them.

"What is it?" asked the girl.

"I may be able to help you," said Selena, quietly and quickly. "Can you wait until dinner this evening before you set about your plan to leave?"

"Why should I?"

"Just until I can consult with a few people—"

"But you promised not to tell!"

"And I won't. But I may be able to acquire information that will make things easier for you."

Selena had no idea what this information might be, nor whom to consult. But the ploy sounded plausible, and she wanted to protect the princess from herself.

Francesca thought it over. Perhaps in a lucid, rational part of her mind, she was aware of the danger in the plan she'd proposed.

"All right," she agreed. "I guess I can wait until this evening. Traveling at night will be safer anyway."

Good lord, Selena thought. *Safer at* night?

Martha and the Molines reached them then, the eyes of the couturiers opening wide as they recognized Francesca.

"Your Highness!" exclaimed Marc, dropping to one knee.

The imposing Zoé curtsied nervously, like a girl.

Martha Marguerite followed suit. She did not know who Francesca was, but the presence of royalty demanded its due.

After some brief chatter, the princess departed with a cool, impressive display of *hauteur.* One could not have guessed that, only moments earlier, she'd been crying her eyes out.

"Do you know who that *was?*" Zoé asked Selena, looking after the departing Francesca in awe. "She may very well be the Queen of England one day!"

"And I designed that frock of hers," said Marc happily. "It becomes her, don't you think?"

Martha, by now aware of the girl's identity, stared at Selena respectfully. "Whatever did you talk about?" she asked.

"Oh, not a great deal. This and that."

"My dear, one does not speak of 'this and that' with a princess of the blood."

"Nevertheless, that is what we did."

Not entirely convinced of this, the three joined Selena in a walk through the stunning gardens.

"If we could stop time now," Martha said whimsically, "if we could just stop it now and never go on another moment, I vow I'd be absolutely content."

The Molines agreed. But Selena said nothing. Across the countryside, between the spires of little churches and over the roofs of peasant huts, she heard the measured, implacable chant of the approaching mob, not pleading but demanding, *"Bread! Bread! Bread!"*

Presently, as the foursome strolled, Zoé took Selena's arm and guided her away from Marc and Martha Marguerite.

"My dear," she said, "are you ready?"

"Ready for what?"

"It is all arranged," whispered Zoé excitedly. "This evening we will first dine, and then the ball will commence. The banquet will be intimate, just ourselves and the monarchs and a few others. But at the beginning of the ball, to which a great number have been invited, certain honored guests will be announced."

"Yes. So?"

"After these people have been presented and just as the dancing begins, you will retire from the ballroom for your assignation with the King."

"My assignation with . . ." exclaimed a startled Selena. Zoé had alluded to something like this back in Paris, but Selena had heard nothing more about it, and was glad that she hadn't. "What on earth gives you the idea that—?"

Madame Moline looked hurt at first, then angry.

"Don't tell me that you are going to be difficult, you silly goose! After all the trouble I went through. Why, if you play your cards right, His Majesty may actually follow through on his promise."

"What promise?"

"Selena, I had thought that you were canny. I hope to God I have not been mistaken. You see, Martha has told me of your desire to return to Scotland. You have a home there, or some sort of castle, to which you want to repair. But, as I gather, this is impossible because you are considered *persona non grata* by George III—"

"All of that is true," said Selena, exasperated. She had no idea why her problems should be of interest to Zoé Moline.

"Well," said Zoé, "I have mentioned this to the King. If he likes you, if you *please* him, he told me that he might be inclined to offer a word in your favor."

"And that 'word' will mend my fences with England and win me the return of Coldstream Castle? To whom will he make these felicitous remarks about me?"

"The British diplomat, Lord Sean Bloodwell!" exclaimed Zoé triumphantly. "It is said that Lord Bloodwell has great influence with the English monarch."

Dressing for dinner that evening, Selena was vexed and distracted. Although she had informed Zoé that she had no intention of going to bed with the King, Madame Moline had brushed aside the declaration as if it were a puerile quibble which Selena would soon reconsider.

What would Sean think of me, Selena asked herself, *if he learns that I have attempted to sleep my way back to Coldstream Castle?* The very idea was preposterous! *If I must be with His Majesty,* she decided, trying to select an appropriate gown for the occasion, *I will simply have to level with him and tell him that a great mistake has been made.*

Which is unlikely to make him happy, she realized bleakly.

Marc Moline had made so many garments for her that choosing just one proved impossible, especially in her current mood of perplexity and unease. So she closed her eyes, reached out, and grabbed the first dress, on its hanger in the wardrobe, that touched her fingertips. It was just the thing to suit her state: a striking but rather somber jet-black gown. "Ah, you should see the way it sets off your hair and coloring!" Marc had exulted. It was bare at the shoulders and back, beaded at the bodice, and with a skirt sufficiently voluminous to dance in, should anyone ask her.

At this moment, she did not care if anyone did or didn't.

She put on the gown, applied makeup, a touch of rouge, and then brushed her hair. It was difficult to concentrate. The mob of women and men dressed as women had arrived at Versailles, swarming all around the palace walls, held back by the army and the Royal Guard. Their numbers and the dull menace of their ceaseless cry for bread upset her with their implied suggestion of imminent violence. She stepped toward the window and looked out into the twilight. There were thousands of demonstrators amassed along the walls, shouting and shaking their fists in promise of mayhem. Selena could not believe that the King and Queen were actually going forward with their plan for a dinner and a dance. It seemed an added affront to those desperate people outside. Perhaps the monarchs thought, if only they proceeded as though things were as always, the crowd would go away. Perhaps they thought, in some dim recess of the autocratic brain, that the mob deserved only the contempt of casual arrogance.

Or perhaps—just perhaps—Louis XVI and Marie Antoinette were simply not thinking at all.

Watching the increasingly more troubling scene, Selena saw how the Guard officers rode their horses up and down the line of demonstrators, exhorting their troops who were trying mightily—and thus far successfully—to keep order. Then a woman suddenly slipped between two soldiers and ran toward the palace wall. She was caught and wrestled to the ground, then returned to her frantic companions.

One woman. But she *had* reached the wall.

Selena felt the ghost of a premonition awaken and stir far back in the corners of her mind.

But no. This was Versailles. It was impregnable.

Wasn't it?

Beyond the mob, in the distance, sat General Lafayette on his white stallion, and behind him, at rest, waited the troops of the National Guard he commanded. They were making no effort whatever to aid the army.

Selena knew enough about politics and political authority to conclude that Lafayette was very sure of his ground. He was waiting for something. Her premonition grew stronger. Fate was out there in the gathering darkness, waiting too upon this October night.

There was a knock on her door. Selena, thinking it was Chloé come to summon her to dinner, pinched her cheeks, bit her lips, and gave her shining hair a final brushstroke. "Come in," she said.

Zoé Moline entered, all bubbly and gay. Her face fell when she saw the dress Selena had chosen. "That?" she mourned. "After my husband outdid himself to make you so many dresses much better suited to this occasion?"

"This is the one I have decided upon," snapped Selena, in a tone that brooked no disagreement.

"Well, all right. But wait a moment before we go down to the banquet. I wish to tell you certain things that will aid you in giving pleasure to His Majesty."

She'd decided that Selena had come to her senses, and would offer no protest when Louis XVI sent for her.

"As you know," Zoé babbled, "His Majesty was impotent until he had surgery. But since that time he has been, shall we say, making up for earlier deprivation. He enjoys pleasure in all ways, sometimes, I do declare, in the Greek fashion. Do you know what I mean?"

Selena did, but the fashion did not appeal to her at all.

"Well, a woman with your looks surely knows the ways," Madame Moline rattled on. "Just do whatever he wishes. And mind, he likes a jolly bedmate. He likes to laugh."

"Then perhaps I shall tell him some jokes," said Selena dryly, moving toward the door. "For example, what do they call a king who has lost his head?"

"Why, I don't know," replied Martha, somewhat uncertainly. If this were a joke, Selena seemed quite grim about it. "What *do* they call a king who has lost his head?"

"Dead," said Selena.

Outside, the women chanted.

"Bread! Bread! Bread!"

16 Walpurgisnacht

On the way to one of the more intimate dining rooms at Versailles, so vastly different from the stupendous halls designed for banquets of state, Zoé Moline was in a stew. Did not her protege, this straight-eyed, straight-talking Scots exile *appreciate* the honor that was being bestowed upon her? Oh, it was true that in a pleasure-loving court such as this of Louis and Marie Antoinette, just as with the English Stuarts and the Russian Romanovs, barriers of blood and rank were frequently honored in the breach. Even if possessed by mere commoners, a great artistic talent, a cardinal's hat, a ready wit, or a pretty face and a provocative behind, were more than sufficient for admission. *But*—fumed Zoé as Selena walked along beside her—*this lofty, violet-eyed Scotswoman would not even be here were it not for Marc and me, were it not for Madame LaRouche's lineage!*

Well, when she got into the bed with His Majesty, she had just better roll whichever way he wished, and do what she was born for!

It occurred to Zoé, briefly, that perhaps Selena was truly in a state of romantic love vis-à-vis her absent fiancé, Monsieur Beaumain, a condition which might make it difficult for her to consider bedding another man. But the King was not simply another man, and anyway no intelligent woman of the modern age would pause to think twice about such a tedious scruple.

Zoé hoped His Majesty would want Selena in the Greek way. It would be a good experience for the girl.

And—thinking of something else—why didn't His Majesty confront and disperse that awful horde of rabble shrieking their fool heads off outside the palace? The whole situation was disgusting, that was what it was!

All that yowling could ruin the whole evening.

Upon reaching the dining room, Selena and Madame Moline

were shown in and seated at a rather small round table, on which gold plate and crystal shimmered like the chandeliers overhead. Save for their royal majesties, the other guests were already present: Monsieur Marc, Martha Marguerite, the Princess Francesca looking anxious and wan, and a beak-nosed, dull-eyed naval officer with a duelling scar down his left cheek. He was introduced to Selena as Captain Jacques Pinot-Noir. She was seated between Captain Jacques and the princess. Captain Pinot-Noir eyed the new arrival concupiscently; Francesca tugged at Selena's sleeve.

"Have you learned anything that will help me get out of here?" she whispered.

Selena was just about to fabricate a reply when a splendid steward appeared at the door to announce: "Ladies and gentlemen, His Royal Majesty, King Louis, and Queen Marie Antoinette!"

Everyone stood.

Selena had read the ancient legends. Her idea of a true monarch was King Arthur. And except for the unfortunate fact that she'd been British, Elizabeth Tudor seemed the paragon of a queen. Oh, Marie Antoinette was attractive enough, fair as to coloring and features, with a high forehead and good hands, but she had a vapid, inconsequential air about her that was unappealing. It was true that she'd had to enter this marriage as a pawn in the greater political schemes of Europe, and it was true that, as a foreigner, she was unpopular. But a queen, thought Selena, could at least carry herself as such.

Louis XVI was even more unprepossessing. It was not that he did not look manly, in spite of his considerable girth. It was more that he seemed without particular character or personality. His attempt at projecting a gregarious air was unsuccessful; he seemed harried and bewildered.

Selena knew one thing for certain: she could not imagine herself in bed with the man, or even kissing him, for that matter. Then she saw Zoé Moline studying her, and realized that her reaction to His Majesty was all too readable.

Be careful, she thought, veiling her expression.

"Did you find out anything?" Francesca hissed again, as the King and Queen took seats at the table.

"Hush," said Selena. "Later."

The princess smiled in relief, eager to believe that her prayer of joining William in England was soon to be answered.

Fires of Delight 225

This dining room was located deeply within the interior of the royal residence, and only an intermittent, faraway rumble reminded hosts and guests of that hungry, unwelcome host outside the walls. Marie Antoinette chattered away about whatever came into her head, as if to block out the distant mutter of dissent. But Louis seemed unable to keep from listening to it, although he attempted, time and again, to rouse himself by interjecting some new topic for conversation.

"Ah, my good friend Marc, what wonders you have wrought for these fair ladies!" he exclaimed over the sorrel soup.

"Ah, Francesca, why the long face?" he inquired over the poached sea bass. "Never you fear. Nothing untoward will befall the Bourbon dynasty. I have it on good authority from the British diplomat, Lord Bloodwell, that England will send an army to protect us if the rabble resort to violence."

Zoé sent Selena a fierce glance: *You had best prepare to do what's expected of you, young lady!*

Selena was somewhat puzzled, not by Zoé, but by the King. For a man who planned to have her later, he seemed barely to notice her. Well, maybe that was his way.

If so, it was fine with her. Perhaps it would continue.

"Ah," said Louis, over Burgundy and beef bordelaise, "pray tell us, Captaine Pinot-Noir, of your recent adventure."

Captaine Jacques, who had thus far manifested little to reveal his personality except for rather loutish table manners—he tended to chomp and drool—cleared his throat noisily and became loquacious and wildly animated. Selena was afraid he would overturn wineglasses, perhaps even hurl away his fork, as he related the great sea battle of which he'd been a part.

"We were sailing north from the Azores," he declared, scattering morsels of partially chewed beef into the air above the table, "when what should befall but we see in the distance the ship that has been hunting us for years. I swear and vow, my lord, there is nothing comparable to being stalked by an enemy you know not who, for a reason you know not why. But on all of the seven seas he has come after us, and always we have fled."

"Why not turn and fight, my man?" asked Marc Moline, fierce dressmaker.

"It is not only that the demon ship is well-armed," Pinot-Noir went on. "It is rather something terrible and remorseless in its pursuit of us, almost as if there were nothing we could do against it anyway. And most curious, even horrifying, is its flag, the likes of which I have never seen before. Why, that foul banner bears the images of camel, snake, and elephant! Has ever the like been heard?"

Captaine Jacques banged on the table for emphasis.

"Witchcraft, I'm sure," said the Queen, interested.

Selena and Martha Marquerite managed not to look at each other. They knew now that Jean Beaumain had finally gotten close to his quarry, knew too that they could not mention Jean's name here, since Zoé Moline had been informed that he was Selena's betrothed.

Things were complicated further when the King sighed, "Ah! Hubert Chamorro. My good, kind friend. And how was the matter resolved, Captain?"

Pinot-Noir rinsed out his mouth with Cabernet Sauvignon and continued. "The evil ship had us outrun and outgunned," he said. "I shrink to tell you this, but we ran up the white flag. Not to surrender, mind you, but as a trick. Chamorro had decided to let the villains come aboard where we would slaughter them, as they so richly deserved, at close quarters."

He fell silent.

"And they came aboard?" prodded Marie Antoinette.

"Oh, yes. It was terrible. Never have I seen men fight like that. We had no chance. They battled without thought for their lives. I wish I knew what drove them, but whatever it was could not be resisted. A dozen of our men were killed in the first moments. They lost not one, due to the passionate frenzy of their assault."

"Had I been there, I would have aided you," said the King.

"I have heard that you are a great hunter," commented Selena innocently.

Louis scowled her way, knowing she'd heard of his deer-shooting from the palace window.

"The strangest thing of all," Pinot-Noir went on, "is that after our crew was subdued, the attackers took Chamorro away. Only our leader, no one else. And we have not heard from him to this day."

"Ah! Poor Hubert," said the King. "Could you recognize the bandits?"

"Alas, no. But the name of their ship was the *Liberté*."

"Drat," declared the King. "That foul word again."

Selena noticed that Princess Francesca was staring at the little gold cross, which was, as always, around her neck.

"I will send forth word to the fleet," promised the King. "The *Liberté* is to be sunk on sight!"

Selena took a contemplative sip of wine. She was, in a sense, pleased that Jean Beaumain had at last closed with and captured his death enemy. She was already sure that Chamorro lived no more, and that his death had not been easy. But the great irony was that Chamorro hadn't even *remembered* Jean Beaumain, or what he'd done to him. She recalled that old Senora Celeste hadn't remembered what she'd done to Selena either. Of what consequence was revenge when one's enemy had no recollection of the wrong that was being redressed? It was all rather tedious and sad.

"Let us toast Hubert Chamorro," said Pinot-Noir, standing up and swaying drunkenly, glass in hand. "We shall not see his like again!"

Everyone stood and drank, although Selena merely touched the rim of the glass to her lips.

From outside the palace, into this secure little dining chamber, intruded the echo of a wild, raging cry. There was something terrifying about it, and the diners quieted, looking at the ceiling and the walls as if knowing that neither stone nor plaster nor wood could offer protection from an enemy that was more spirit than flesh.

"Have you decided what to do about the mob?" Selena heard Marie Antoinette ask the King. "My God, what do those fiends *want?*" she asked of no one in particular.

"They have no bread," said Francesca.

"Then," replied the Queen, smiling nervously, "let them eat cake."

Pinot-Noir burst into laughter and the Molines tittered appreciatively. No one else reacted.

The King stared gloomily at his bulging belly.

"Let us repair to the ballroom," he said, as if honoring an invitation to his own funeral.

Princess Francesca sidled up to Selena and walked alongside her to the ballroom. The shouts of the mob outside were quite audible now, and everyone was nervous. "I could not help but notice the motto that is inscribed upon the cross you're wearing," she said. "Pray tell, what does it mean?"

Selena looked at the girl. She truly did not know; her question was not facetious in the least.

"It is what some in your uncle's kingdom desire."

Francesca was mystified. "Why, they have liberty, equality, and brotherhood *already*. Can't they see that? Perhaps we—you and I—should go out and explain things to them. Then they will go away and we can have fun at the ball!"

"I don't think that would be wise."

"Perhaps you are right. Men are better at that sort of thing. But tell me, what have you learned to aid me in my plan to reach England?"

This was the question Selena had been expecting. She decided to buy more time. "I'd advise you to wait *at least* until the morrow," she said.

That was not what the princess wanted to hear.

"No," she said, lifting her chin.

"Please. You may place yourself in some harm."

"But I must reach William and be at his side. Uncle Louis has been saying that this revolution, or whatever it's called, will burn itself out of its own accord."

"I hope, for your sake, that he is right. But I doubt it."

"Well, I don't care. My mind is made up. There is nothing stronger, did you know, than a Hapsburg who has decided upon something."

Nor anyone more stubborn, thought Selena.

"I am going to flee tonight, just after the dance," Francesca whispered.

"Why don't you leave now?"

"I don't want to miss the dance."

"I see," sighed Selena. Now she would have to watch out for this young girl, who was so obviously smitten by love, so clearly untutored in the ways of the world that she would risk great harm on a course of action sure to tempt disaster.

Captaine Pinot-Noir came up then and offered one arm to Selena and the other to the princess. Thus escorted, they followed the monarchs into the ballroom. Marc Moline, likewise, accompanied Zoé and Martha Marguerite.

Selena had been informed that the ball was to take place in something called the Hall of Mirrors. She'd been looking forward to seeing it, particularly in the light of Martha's constant, awe-filled comments regarding the wonder of the place. But even so, she was stunned by its breathtaking, magnificent immensity. This spacious grandeur, like Versailles itself, or Notre Dame, was a monument to genius and beauty. The other side of this wondrous coin, however, was the starving mob outside. The best of all possible worlds, she thought, would be one in which splendor was not created at the expense of humanity.

A large, festive crowd had already assembled in the hall, men and women alike garbed in clothing the cost of which would have sustained a peasant family for ten years. Selena had never seen such a display of personal ostentation. Louis XVI and his Queen passed through the bowing men and curtsying women, and mounted twin thrones at one end of the hall. A steward stepped discreetly in front of Captain Pinot-Noir, halting his rather lurching progress, and Selena released his arm. She found herself standing in a small group of noblewomen, who were smiling and hissing to one another.

"I have heard that the Queen's new lover is here tonight!" tittered one. "Has anyone seen him?"

"No," answered one of her companions, "but I managed to catch a bit of chatter between my maidservant and the girl who attends Madame de Golier. The King has a new lover too."

This announcement interested everyone in the little clique, and they leaned toward the speaker for further news.

"Yes, she is a Scots girl, quite beautiful."

"Probably quite common," sniffed one of the women.

Selena touched her shoulder and smiled at the woman when she turned.

"Aye, I've 'eard she's common enou'," Selena said sweetly, "but 'tis known there be none t' compare wi' 'er in mastery o' men."

The little gaggle of gossipers, with their powdered faces and high-piled hair, stared at Selena for an instant, then turned away in angry embarrassment.

"Pray, tell me when ye see the Scot," added Selena in the thickest brogue she could muster, "I want t' 'ave a look m'self."

A steward stepped up next to Selena just as the King and Queen were getting settled on their thrones.

"Mademoiselle Selena," he whispered, with a kind of pleasant confidentiality, "His Majesty must first receive several dignitaries, but he will join you in his residence thereafter. I shall escort you. Meet me in perhaps ten minutes at the far entrance to the hall."

Selena nodded, and he went away.

Then the King clapped his hands. A liveried majordomo swung open mighty doors at the main entrance and proclaimed in a booming voice:

"My lords and ladies, the Duke and Duchess of Westphalia!"

Two rather small people entered the Hall of Mirrors, crossed to the twin thrones and made their obeisances.

"The King wishes to shore up his relationships with European nobility," a bewigged, middle-aged bystander whispered sarcastically, "so that if he must go into exile, one country or another will harbor him."

Exile? thought Selena. So Louis *was*, deep down, aware of the current danger.

Princess Francesca joined Selena then. "Maybe I should leave right now?" she whispered. "No one will notice."

The girl appeared quite ready to make the attempt. Selena thought fast. "Listen," she said, "go to my chamber and wait for me there. No one will suspect a thing."

"How excellent!" Francesca cried. "It will be completely unexpected." She hurried off.

That will protect her for the time being, Selena thought.

"The Count and Countess of Venice!" intoned the majordomo.

"The Marquis and Marchessa of Alsace!

"The Duke and Duchess of Devonshire!

"Lord Sean Bloodwell of the British Foreign Office!"

Selena's heart jumped to her throat as her former husband, blond as ever, erect, in ruddy good health and smiling slightly, crossed the hall and bowed to their majesties. He was quite popular here, Selena realized, because a spontaneous, good-hearted ripple of applause welcomed him. *Of course,* she thought. *I should have expected him to be here.* Had not the King mentioned that Sean Bloodwell had assured him of English protection in the event of full-scale revolution?

Sean exchanged a few pleasantries with King and Queen, then

Fires of Delight **231**

stepped away from the thrones. Selena attempted to catch his eye —she wanted, at the very least, to say hello to him. Of all the people in the world, he would be pleased to know that she was safe. And perhaps—just perhaps—he would arrange for her to meet with Davina at least once. Oh, certainly he would.

But he did not look her way, nor even sense her presence. Selena recalled, once more, the mystic pronouncements of Davi the Dravidian regarding the voices of the heart, the secret means of communication by which lovers speak, by which they sense each other's presences. Such a communion no longer existed between Sean Bloodwell and her. True, theirs had not been a union founded on passionate attachment, but it made Selena sad anyway to think that a gulf lay between them.

Still, she *would* speak to him, and she began to move through the assemblage in his direction.

"Ladies and gentlemen!" cried the majordomo.

"Ah, here comes Marie Antoinette's latest favorite," a woman whispered smirkingly.

"The Vicomte Royce Campbell!"

Selena was moving toward Sean Bloodwell, preparing words of greeting. She *heard* Royce's name announced, but for a moment it did not truly register in her mind. She kept on walking toward Sean for a few more paces. Then the reality of the announcement, of the name, gathered force and came crashing into her consciousness. Royce Campbell, who was dead and buried beneath a wooden cross on the isle of La Tortue half a world away, had just been introduced into the Hall of Mirrors.

She was not breathing, her heart was not beating. Every cell in her body burned as she spun dreamlike, in slow motion, for a thousand years toward the entrance. As she turned, there in a thin, poised pirouette of time, his name reverberated in her ears.

Royce!
Royce!
Royce!

And reflected in those multiple mirrors of wonder on the walls, image upon image upon image, striding like a king reborn, like a brilliant dark god come to earth for a night, was

Royce!
Royce!
Royce!

And then it happened, that mystical flicker of the heart that Davi had told of. There in the great hall, where fully three hundred people were watching him approach the monarchs, Royce Campbell's eyes narrowed slightly. He made a quick, reflexive movement, lifting his head slightly, like the keenest of animals noting a minute change in the wind, aware without knowing how or why of a tremor in the heart of time.

And instantly, his eyes found Selena in the crowd.

During that instant, when their eyes met and touched and held, the earth ceased to spin, the moon to glow, the wind to move about Versailles. Paris was gone from the face of the earth, and London too, and Prague. France was gone, England lost, America no more. There were no millions dreaming in the night or awaiting the dawn. There was no mob at the gates of this palace, no king, no queen, no courtiers within. There was only a memory of Coldstream Castle, and of the Highlands. The dream-haunted ghost of a wolf shimmered suddenly in the air, too fleet for the mirrors to catch him, and disappeared.

In that instant, there were only Royce Campbell and Selena MacPherson.

No others.

In order to reach the thrones, Royce had to pass within the reach of Selena's hand. She wanted—she actually tried—to reach out and touch him, but between her brain's command and her body's response intervened a barrier as impervious as iron. He was alive, that was certain, which meant that her understanding and acceptance of the past had to be discarded. *All right, I'll discard it.* But it wasn't that simple. No mere act of will could temper the shocking realization that he *was* alive, so she stood there, stunned and motionless.

He passed so close to her that she could feel the heat of his body, the movement of his breath in the air.

But after that first instinctive, preternatural meeting of their eyes, he did not look her way again.

Even worse, he did not seem to want to!

Selena was too numb just yet even to be miserable about it. That would come later. Misery has plenty of time. It waits around forever, choosing propitious moments of depression and chagrin to make its full force more damaging.

Besides, the tide of life and activity had begun again. People turned to watch in salacious curiosity as Royce Campbell approached the monarchs and bowed. They wanted to see how much aplomb he could maintain while confronting his lover and the man he was, apparently, cuckolding. It was not every day that any man put the cuckold's horns upon a king after all, and the court, which was at least as much a theater as it was real life, savored a delicious scene.

Selena had, of course, read Shakespeare. But until this moment, the concept of the world-as-a stage had held merely symbolic meaning for her. This time the meaning was heartbreakingly direct. It was no mere actress, but the Queen of France who offered Royce her hand for the kissing. It was no thespian, either, but a Bourbon dynast whose hand also accepted Royce's kiss of fealty.

It was just this obeisant ritual that roused Selena from her daze and brought her back to reality.

What on earth was Royce doing? What had *happened* to him?

Had all of her efforts availed nothing? Had all of her influence gone for naught?

When she'd met him, he'd been an opportunistic adventurer. But their relationship had deepened both of them, and he had taken from her the spirit and fire of her essentially individualistic nature, which was also his, and added to his personality her concern for the downtrodden and disadvantaged. Selena's heart truly went out to the exiled and the dispossessed, because she had been both. And she had come to believe, by Royce's energetic participation in American revolutionary espionage, that his essential heart had begun to beat as one with hers.

But now she remembered the jewels and sovereigns in the lining of her greatcoat right here in Versailles.

(She also recalled that Francesca had gone to her suite.)

And Selena recollected the curious tale of Royce's having dealt with the smuggler, LaValle, in Haiti.

Not to mention that Royce was now the King's friend, the Queen's lover, *and* a *vicomte*. There were only two ways to become a *vicomte*. A man might be born one; that is, he might inherit the title. Or he might—and this was very rare—be given a title by a monarch in return for some great deed. That would hardly include bedding the monarch's queen, would it? Unless the

French court was even more depraved than Mirabeau and Sorbante believed it to be.

Selena also recalled a story, probably apocryphal, about the Englishwoman who importuned the king in her scoundrel son's behalf: "Please, milord, make him a gentleman," she'd begged.

"I regret that I cannot make your fool of a son a gentleman," the king had responded. "But I *can* make him a lord if it pleases you."

Royce Campbell was no fool. He had a French title.

The question was: how had he won it?

Or earned it?

Although the realization caught at her heart, Selena could not entirely discredit the possibility that Royce had gone back to his old opportunistic, self-aggrandizing ways.

Royce stepped back from the thrones, careful not to turn away from King and Queen. He was immediately surrounded by a herd of frothy females. Louis XVI clapped his hands. The orchestra, which had been awaiting his pleasure, began to tune up for the dancing that would follow. A platoon of stewards bearing trays laden with champagne began to circulate among the crowd. Selena remembered that it was time for her to leave for her assignation with the King. But she could see that he was still seated on his throne, conversing earnestly with a Royal Guard officer. Absentmindedly, she took a glass of wine from a floating tray and just stood there, moving now a little left, now a little right, trying to keep her eyes on Royce's face.

He was laughing and chatting with the admiring women.

He did not look her way, or even seem to remember that he'd seen her.

Selena, who'd always tried to be honest with herself, came to this conclusion: *He doesn't want to know you at all!*

So much for Davi the Dravidian and his theories about the mysterious communications of lovers.

The delirious whirl she'd experienced upon seeing him again had been entirely personal. *His* reaction, into which she'd read so much, had been mere surprise. She was just one woman out of his past, a woman he hadn't expected to see again, a woman he obviously did not wish to see now. Why take up one's time with a quite-often-difficult Scots exile, however beautiful, when one could have for the taking a much more complaisant queen?

In the mind of an opportunistic adventurer, there wouldn't even be the trouble of a choice.

Still, Selena could not but remember, all too realistically, the sweet frenzy of their thousand and one intertwined comminglings, the incomparable feeling of possession when she had him inside her, the bucking surge of flesh upon flesh, and the ultimate moment when he became still upon her but throbbed inside her with tide after tide of his juice.

Oh God, she thought, bereft.

He was laughing with the women.

The King was being helped down from his throne.

Soon it would be time for Selena's next act upon this world's stage.

"Hello, Selena," said Sean Bloodwell, appearing before her. He touched his glass to hers. "My surprise at seeing you here—I noticed you right away, of course—is outweighed only by my joy."

She tried to tear her eyes away from Royce Campbell and succeeded, but not before Sean saw both the glance and the cost of her effort. His smile was sad but understanding.

"I see, of course, that you still love him."

Selena didn't even have the strength to nod. *She* saw that Sean still loved *her*, but that he was not again going to risk getting hurt. She remembered their days together in India, their wedding on the deck of the *Blue Foray*, and those wonderful years in America before she'd learned that Royce had not died of the plague, before she'd become a spy for George Washington. Until those things had happened, they'd led a fine, quiet life in their large, comfortable house in New York. She remembered how he'd liked most to make love upon awakening in the mornings, when their bodies were rested, their senses keener, their climaxes excruciatingly intense.

"I'm sorry, Selena," said Sean now, as he watched her trying to keep her eyes off Royce Campbell. "He's reverted to type, I'm afraid. All France knows how the Queen wants him, and how he has served the cause of the monarchy against the revolution. I am not in favor of revolution, either, but at least I have been consistent. Perhaps it was my predictability that tired you of me. In any event"—he touched her glass again and sipped—"I have often regretted that I let you go so easily."

Naturally, he would bring *that* up too. She remembered their last time together, in a rat trap tavern in Brooklyn. Gilbertus Penrod had passed a warning that Clay Oakley was looking for Royce and her. She and Royce had met at the tavern and were just about to flee across Long Island to the *Selena*. But Sean Bloodwell had also learned of their plans and he came into the tavern just as they were about to leave.

Sean had faced Royce. The two men looked at each other.

"I do love Selena," Royce said.

"I know that. So do I. And she loves both of us. But she loves you more, in a way that is more natural to her, just as it will prove to be more dangerous for her."

"I have told her that."

"I expect you have. It is something that would be hard to ignore, but it is something from which Selena has never been dissuaded."

Then he'd turned to face her. "You have made your choice, haven't you? Your presence here with Royce is proof of that."

"Yes," she replied.

"Selena, I shall always treasure what we had. But it is not there anymore. Perhaps we both destroyed it. We had different loyalties. Things happened. We changed. . . ."

Sean fell silent. Royce waited. He had no wish to intrude upon the conversation, and he respected Sean Bloodwell as a man.

Sean seemed about to speak again, then changed his mind. Instead, he leaned forward. He did not kiss Selena, but pressed his cheek against hers and then withdrew. It happened so quickly that she had no chance to respond. His skin upon hers was as evanescent as the touch of a butterfly's wing.

"Good-bye, Selena," he'd said softly. "Ride fast, ride far, farewell."

"I've ridden awfully fast at times," she said to him now, in the Hall of Mirrors at Versailles, "but I guess I haven't gone all that far."

Sean understood at once. He pressed his fingertips to her cheek. She felt like crying.

He saw it. "Davina asks after you all the time," he said, trying to cheer her. "She'd—we'd both—love to have you visit, but we're leaving for London on the morrow. I've been summoned back home for consultations due to the conditions here. Ah"—he paused—"just what is your situation here at court?"

"Nothing to speak of. I guess you might say I'm a lesser guest. . . ." She didn't want to discuss the details of her current life with him. That would mean bringing up Jean Beaumain, a subject that had grown complicated enough, emotionally and otherwise, with the reappearance of Royce. "Sean . . ." she began.

"Yes?"

"If I were to be allowed back into Scotland—"

He shook his head sadly. "Not at this time, Selena. Perhaps not ever. You see, royalty has a long memory, and you were a spy. Perhaps you still—"

"No."

"Well, there are such things as amnesty and pardon. If the British had won the war, a petition for pardon on your part might be considered. But England lost in America. Feelings are still running high."

"I see," she said.

"Now, if you were to do what Royce Campbell is doing—"

"What's that?"

"Why, he's become a veritable monarchist. I've heard there is no one more loyal to King Louis. You will forgive me if I reserve the right to doubt his sincerity, but he has already gotten Louis to send George III a request that Campbell's transgressions against the Empire be forgiven . . ."

Selena turned to see Royce still chatting and laughing with the group of adoring young women. A turncoat?

"And if the King considers this request and approves it," Sean concluded, "Campbell may go back to the Highlands free as a bird."

Or as a wolf, thought Selena. It did not seem possible. Royce might end his days in Scotland while she would ever be roaming the world, looking for a home.

"Do you know an officer named Clay Oakley?" Selena asked.

"Colonel Oakley? Oh, yes. He is in charge of all our intelligence operations. Indeed, if Britain must intervene on behalf of Louis XVI, Oakley will be in control of strategy. Why do you ask?"

"No particular reason," Selena said glumly.

"I shall be back here in a fortnight," Sean was saying. "If the situation is not too dangerous, I'll bring Davina with me. We can meet then."

"I'd love it."

"So would she. So would *I.*" He touched his lips to her forehead. She looked up at him. They did not embrace, but at that moment they were as close as they had ever been in their marriage bed. "I'm leaving now," he said. "Make sure you stay inside the palace tonight. No one knows how wild the mob outside will become." He took her hand and squeezed it affectionately. "It has made me happy to see you again."

"You have my love," she said, "and so does Davina."

"Au revoir."

Sean departed. Selena stood alone for a moment. The orchestra was ready to commence; the dancing would soon begin. At the far entrance, the steward was waving to Selena. *Come. Now. What is the matter with you?*

But the King was standing near his throne, Marie Antoinette beside him, chatting with the Duke and Duchess of Devonshire.

Selena decided, then and there, to walk over and confront Royce. Her initial burst of joy at seeing him alive was mitigated in a troubling way by a gnawing disappointment she did not want to face. He simply could *not* have gone back to his old opportunism. Yet how could she doubt that he had? The evidence was overwhelming. One part of her wanted to rush to him and lose herself in his arms; the other part wanted to get the jewels and sovereigns from her greatcoat and fling them at his feet.

"There!" she would say. *"It's Judas money. Take it."*

From outside the palace, a mighty roar arose, followed by gunfire. Everyone in the Hall of Mirrors fell silent. Before anyone could act, however, an officer of the Guard rushed in and approached His Majesty. The officer was too agitated for discretion, and his message to the King was easy to overhear.

"Majesty, the mob has charged the gates!" he cried, which set off a flurry of alarm in the hall.

Louis was no less affected. He stood there, sputtering, befuddled and, yes, frightened. The Queen took his arm.

"What are your orders, my lord?" the officer asked.

"Perhaps," said the King, "the Guard and the army should cease firing?"

"No!" declared Marie. "That is what the rabble want. There will be no hope for us then."

"But we wish to avoid bloodshed. . . ."

"Have them fire!" ordered the Queen.

The officer had no idea what to do, nor whose command to obey.

"If you will permit me a suggestion," said Royce Campbell then, stepping forward authoritatively, "I think I have a solution that might calm the mob somewhat."

"Pray, what is it?" asked the King, relieved.

Royce took the monarch and the officer aside, but Selena made haste to be as near them as possible, and she overheard enough of Royce's plan to catch both its shrewdness and its meaning.

". . . army and Royal Guard . . ." he was saying. ". . . people hate both. . . . only chance is to withdraw them, replace them overnight with Lafayette's National Guardsmen. . . . crowd knows he is sympathetic to their cause . . . but he is a reliable man . . . has seen war . . . will avert bloodshed. . . . I will go to him now and ask his help. . . ."

Louis was undecided, as always. "But what of the morrow?" he asked.

"Get all of your officers and ministers assembled," Royce said. "When I return from my meeting with Lafayette, it will be necessary to make some hard decisions."

Royce and the officer hurried away. Selena was torn. She had been completely ignored by Royce, but that was understandable under the critical circumstances, wasn't it? The howling of the mob grew louder and louder outside the palace. Moreover, although she could not help but be thrilled by the way he had taken command of the situation, his efforts and loyalties had certainly been marshalled in the monarchy's behalf. *I guess nobody really changes very much,* she thought ruefully.

At least she would not have to rendezvous with the King. He left immediately with a gaggle of courtiers and guards. The members of the orchestra began packing their instruments. Guests drifted away and very soon the Hall of Mirrors was vacant, save for a crew of servants scurrying about, straightening up, like attendants after a wake.

Selena left the hall alone, uncertain what to do or where to go. She thought of Francesca, but the girl would be safe enough. *I'll have a look at the situation outside,* she decided. Several long corridors brought her to the front of the palace, and a couple of elegant staircases led to a window overlooking the outside wall. Here the din of the ceaseless chant, *"Bread! Bread! Bread!"* was overwhelming, and in the torchlit swarm beneath her, Selena got a clear look at the beast. In vast, undulating surges, tides of flesh and blood, the mob pressed forward at points along the palace wall to be driven back momentarily by soldiers, only to regroup and press forward again. Rage was thick in the air, palpable as a hurled rock.

In the distance, beyond the mob, Selena saw Royce Campbell. He was standing on the ground next to Lafayette, who leaned down from his white charger, listening. Some kind of arrangement was made, some bargain struck, for as Selena watched, the general wheeled his horse and began to ride down the line of his waiting National Guardsmen. They took up their weapons and began to move toward the palace, slowly but surely threading their way through the mob, relieving and replacing the hated army personnel, who retreated gratefully but gracelessly as the mob cheered.

The situation had been controlled for the time being, but it was not defused. There were too many emotions, too many factions, for the revolution to be tamed by a mere change of tactics. One part of the mob was satisfied just to stand screaming at the palace. Another segment would not be content until they managed to breach the palace defenses. Still another would be disappointed unless Louis XVI himself were dragged out on the terrace and pulled limb from limb. Perhaps there were even some out there who would not consider the night a success until they ate and digested a tatter of his fat, raw flesh.

Royce's ploy and Lafayette's action had succeeded only in buying time.

The mob continued to howl for bread.

Then Selena saw Royce exchange a final word with the general and re-enter the palace.

"I'll go to him now!" she said aloud. If she hurried, she could intercept him before he retired to plan strategy with the King and his ministers. Racing down the staircases, she miscalculated her location inside the palace and made a wrong turn down an unfamiliar corridor. Heart pounding, blood racing, thinking of the precious minutes flying by, she retraced her steps and finally reached the main level.

Only to see Royce Campbell, escorted by two armed guardsmen, disappearing into an official chamber.

But he knows I'm here, she thought, hoping for the best. *He'll come for me when he has the chance.*

So, with nothing else to do, Selena returned to her suite.

A chambermaid was there, busily putting an assortment of unfamiliar dresses on hangers. They had been thrown onto the floor, over the backs of chairs, even on Selena's bed.

"What are you doing?" Selena demanded. "Whose garments are these?"

"Why, they belong to my mistress, ma'am. She didn't want to take them with her."

"Your mistress? Take them with her where?"

"The Princess Francesca," answered the girl nervously. "She bade me bring her clothes here and then selected some of them for her trip. She's leaving for England, you know."

"She is? When?"

"Tonight," replied the servant. "She just left a moment ago."

17 Sign on Satin

The little idiot! thought Selena, racing from the room in search of Francesca. *She'll get herself killed!* Although Selena understood full well how mad love could make one—certainly it had made her so in her time—there had to be *some* limits. If she'd had it in her power to see Francesca safely into the arms of Prince William, she'd have done so without a second's hesitation. Indeed, she had promised to help do exactly that. The princess had believed her. Selena had to accept responsibility for her part in the mess, but running aimlessly down palace corridors, she did not want to think about the guilt she would suffer if a tragedy were to befall.

It was past midnight now, and the palace, so glittering during the day, was as mysterious and gloomy as any other vast, unfamiliar place. No one was about, no one at all. Selena halted, gathered her breath, and decided to think with her head instead of her feet.

It was quite likely that there were secret passageways underground that led out of Versailles. If so, Selena didn't know them. *But,* she guessed, *neither does Francesca. She is as much a stranger here as I am, this being her first visit.*

And she is certainly smart enough to stay away from the front of the palace, where the main part of the mob is centered.

Where would the crowd be thinnest?

Selena pictured the sprawling grounds of Versailles. She recalled that Hugo and Sebastian had been directed toward the stables which lay some distance from the west wing. There too were the barracks of the Royal Guard, a busy area now that the Royals had been withdrawn in favor of Lafayette's National Guard.

If I wanted to get away from here, that would be the direction I'd take, Selena calculated, *and I might even acquire myself a horse in the bargain.*

She turned toward the west wing, walking, trotting, running.

No one challenged or impeded her. Palace staff were much too preoccupied with the tumult outside to patrol the inner corridors. At length, Selena reached the gigantic twin doors that led, here as at other entrances, onto the terrace overlooking the gardens.

No sooner had she stepped outside than a guardsman seized her arm. He was rather young, and either drunk or scared halfway out of his wits, his eyes wide and strange in the torchlit semi-darkness.

"Who are you?" he demanded shrilly, clamping down on her wrist.

"Let go! You're hurting me. Did you see a young girl pass this way?"

"And what business is that of yours?"

He was not going to be cooperative. Selena had wanted to keep this whole episode under wraps, to spare Francesca later grief, but there was no choice now.

"The Princess Francesca may have come out here accidentally," she said, twisting her arm away from the guard, "but in any event, I believe she came out this way. You must help me find her!"

The man gaped at her, then laughed scornfully.

"Princess indeed!" he sneered. "Ain't nobody come out this way on my watch but a little scullery maid. An' I got a kiss off her too. So how's that? Ain't no royal princess going to kiss the likes of me, I expect."

Francesca is more clever than I surmised, thought Selena. "What did this 'scullery maid' look like?" she demanded.

"Well, I couldn't see too clear. Not as tall as you. Had a nice, sweet little round face. Gave a good kiss too. . . ."

"That's the princess, you dolt!" snapped Selena. "Come help me find her before we're both in hot water."

She started to move away, but he grabbed her around the waist. "You ain't goin' nowhere. I got orders not to let no one pass."

"Fool! You've already let a princess pass."

"No, just a maid. But that's all right. It's the likes of you I got to risk my life protecting."

Selena saw no other way but to struggle. Every passing second was a crucial second lost. She had just decided to apply her elbow to the guard's solar plexus, when from far out in the garden came a strangled cry, "... Helll ..." which ended in an ominous silence.

"There, you see?" said Selena.

The man, startled by the cry, released her. She ran across the terrace and down into the darkened, dew-wet gardens. She could hear him following.

"Francesca!" she called. "Francesca!"

There was no sound at first, but then Selena thought she heard flesh on flesh, a slap, then a moan.

"This way!" she commanded the guard, who had by this time caught up with her. "Follow me!"

Another sound, an attenuated cry for aid, led Selena in the direction of an oval-shaped goldfish pool, surrounded by granite figures. One of the figures moved, however, attempting to flee, and another lay upon the ground. It was Francesca, shaken but unharmed. Her assailant, lumbering heavily in the unfamiliar skirts he wore, was tackled by the young guardsman.

Francesca's bag, with her clothing strewn about, lay by the goldfish pool. A frilly little chemise floated on the surface of the pool.

"Do you know what you've *done?*" accused the guard, straddling his quarry and striking him in the face.

The man cried out. "Have pity! Have pity, sir! I'm just a poor man looking for bread."

Selena helped the princess to her feet. "Are you all right?"

"I ... I think so. I should have listened to you. Why is that man wearing a dress? He tried to do something ... unspeakable to me. I've heard such tales, but ... but ... Selena, you were right. I made a great mistake."

"Come. Let us go back to my quarters. You have no business being out on a night like this. No one does."

She helped the princess gather up her things while the guard, after determining that Selena was not going to report him for negligence, escorted his captive to the Guard's barracks.

"Nothing like this ever happened to me in Austria," Francesca sniffled.

"Your homeland is not in the middle of a revolution."

"But I have to ... I just *must* get to England."

"And you shall. I know you shall. But not tonight. Let us see what the morning brings."

Fires of Delight **245**

The two women went back inside the palace and managed to reach Selena's suite without being challenged. The situation outside the walls seemed to have calmed somewhat, due to the influence of Lafayette, but there was still plenty of shouting. It was to continue all night.

Safely inside her room, Selena looked about with a sudden sixth sense that something was wrong, out of place. In a moment, she saw what it was. Her greatcoat, which had been hanging in the wardrobe, was laid neatly upon a divan. Had Francesca's maidservant mistaken it as one of her young mistress's possessions, and planned to pack it? Selena walked over and picked it up, examining the garment carefully.

It was still heavy with its own weight and the added weight of the treasure concealed in its lining.

But wait. At one place, just along the hem, there was a neat slit, made by a knife perhaps. Someone had made an inspection of the garment. Perhaps a diamond was missing, or a ruby. There was no way to tell for sure.

Odd. If someone had found the jewels, would not he—or she—have taken all of them? And the greatcoat too?

Francesca, recovering from what had almost befallen her in the garden, had lain down upon the bed, one arm thrown up to cover her eyes. She was paying no attention to Selena whatever.

"Had you planned to pack this coat?" Selena asked, as casually as she could.

The princess looked up. "What?" she asked. "What? Oh, no. That's not mine. I've never seen it before. . . ."

Then Selena noticed something on the pillow next to Francesca's head. She walked over for a closer look. There, on the satin pillow cover, was a scrap of Campbell plaid.

Royce had been here!

He had been *here!*

That meant he still loved her and he would come again!

Scarcely able to contain her excitement and joy, Selena managed to persuade the princess to return to her own quarters. A maidservant and two stewards were summoned to accompany the girl and ensure her safety.

"I will see you first thing in the morning," Selena promised the princess, over and over. Francesca, much taken by the fact that

Selena had saved her from ignominy and violation, was reluctant to leave her new friend, but at length she did so.

Then Selena, clutching the piece of plaid in her hand, ordered that a bath be drawn, and that food and wine be brought. When the servants had done these things and withdrawn, Selena lowered herself into the hot, soapy water and soaked long and thoroughly, preparing her body for Royce. It was difficult to concentrate, because the anticipation of ecstasy brought every fiber of her being to a state of enchanted excitement. She felt that she had only to touch herself in order for bliss to come burning. She knew that, if Royce were to touch her, she would immediately be consumed in flames. So filled was sweet flesh with need of pleasure that only a kiss, a caress, would rouse the smoldering sparks of ecstasy into raging fires of delight.

Her bath over, Selena selected her best chemise, filmy, transparent, and low about her breasts. She drank a glass of wine and extinguished all the candles but one on a table next to the bed.

Then she lay down, burning, to wait.

But Royce Campbell did not come.

18 Tuileries

Morning came cold. Selena, awakening from a restless sleep, perceived first that the mob was no longer chanting outside. Next, she became aware of great turmoil and confusion in the palace, as if everyone was rushing madly about. She heard calls and cries, and even a muted sobbing. Getting out of bed and pulling a robe over her little chemise—she felt a bit downcast and humiliated, thinking of last night's anticipatory excesses—she walked to the window. The mob was still there, but silent now, and waiting.

Strange.

And at the entrance to the palace, waiting too, was the great, lumbering, gilded royal coach, with six nervous horses hitched to it.

She caught her breath then, catching sight of Lafayette and Royce Campbell, both on white stallions. They were close to the carriage, engaged in earnest conversation.

Selena was just about to summon a servant in order to find out what was going on, when Princess Francesca burst into the chamber.

"Oh, Selena!" she cried, her eyes red from weeping, her sweet face darkened by fear. "It is the end of the world."

Selena glanced again outside the window. The weather seemed crisp and clear. The sky was blue. There were no hosts of angels mounted on the wind, no celestial trumpets of righteousness and doom.

"There may be a little time left," she said dryly, "to tell me why you think Judgment Day is here."

Francesca crossed the room and stood beside Selena at the window, looking out.

"Those people! Those awful, hideous people!" the girl mourned. "*They* are the messengers of death!"

A few more minutes, and her whole, shocking story had come

tumbling out. The night had been frightful. Lafayette and the National Guard had worked desperately to hold the mob in check, but even so a number of demonstrators had invaded the palace and killed several of the Queen's bodyguard. More people were on their way from Paris, and the general had informed His Majesty that the situation was hopeless. Louis XVI would have to act, in order to save not only the monarchy, but his life and the lives of the royal family. So a decision had been made: the King and Queen, along with all of their household, would accompany the mob back to Paris, there to be installed in the Tuileries palace under virtual house arrest.

"Uncle Louis feels it is the only way," Francesca sniffed woefully, "the only way to *save our lives!* Can you *imagine?* How could he—how could anyone—have done things so awful they would merit such a fate?"

Selena did not mention corruption, unfair taxation, the arrogance of privilege, or starvation. Francesca would not have understood. In her young mind, all monarchs were wise and just, all peasants docile, obedient, and happy.

"I must be shut up in the Tuileries too!" cried Francesca. "I do not know for how long. Please, will you come to see me there? You are my only friend. May I ride with you to Paris? Do you have a coach?"

"Yes," answered Selena, thinking of Hugo and Sebastian, and hoping they were still around. "But shouldn't you travel with your aunt and uncle?"

"No, that is also a part of what has been decided." She began to cry quietly. "You see, there is fear that the royal coach may be set upon by the mob. The King, the Queen, and the dauphin must ride together, in order that the crowd see them. But the rest of us have been advised to take other carriages. I will have guards, however."

Selena gave it some thought. Martha Marguerite would be next to apoplexy at the contretemps, and she herself, having witnessed the behavior of the mob, was more than a little uneasy at the thought of what might befall them. Having an armed escort was not a bad idea.

"If it is indeed all right with your guardians," she said, "it would be my pleasure to have your company. I will send a servant posthaste and order my drivers to have our carriage at the gate."

"Oh, thank you, Selena. Thank you so much. I shall see that Uncle Louis rewards you handsomely for this kindness on your part!"

Selena expressed her gratitude at this offer, not without wondering how the princess believed Louis could bestow rewards of any kind when France was bankrupt and he himself was the prisoner of his own people.

Francesca departed. Selena dressed and left her chambers. Guards and maids were dashing hither and thither, up and down corridors, in and out of rooms, carrying luggage, stacks of clothing, painting, items of great value and items of no worth whatsoever. The entire scene was one of disorganization, chaos, and panic.

The turmoil continued all morning long, growing more frenzied as time went on. Selena sent word to Hugo and Sebastian. They had, thank God, remained at the stables overnight, and would be waiting at the palace gates when the time came to leave. Chloe, the servant, had disappeared, so Selena packed her own things, brought here just yesterday in hopes of a fine holiday at Versailles. She thought of Royce Campbell as she worked, her feelings mixed and unsettled. What would have happened had she been there when he'd come last night? Would he have explained everything, told her to have no fear, no qualms, that his heart and hers continued to beat as one? Would he have made love to her in their old wild way, which was like being swept up in splendor, savage and sweet and pierced to the depths of the flesh? Would he have loved away her doubts, kissed away her cares?

Yes, yes, he would have! And today would have been wonderful, not . . .

. . . not like this.

But . . .

But would she have told him of Jean Beaumain?

That was something to think about.

However, if Royce no longer cared for her, no longer wanted her in the old way, then what would now transpire?

The only thing to do was to wait, which, for someone in love, is the hardest thing of all.

Finally, after orders given and countermanded, given and altered, given again, Selena was in the coach with Martha Marguerite and Francesca. Selena wore her greatcoat, both to ward off the chill and to protect the treasure within. The princess, according to plan, was dressed as a maidservant, and even Martha, too terrified even to look out upon the mob, had finally learned a lesson. She had on her oldest, drabbest coat, and wore about her head a sorry-looking scarf that would have seemed fitting on the head of any Parisian fishwife.

Hugo and Sebastian, in contrast to their passengers, were in fine spirits. Their heads were high, their chests puffed with pride at the great success of the people. In the new manner of the day, they addressed each other and everyone else as "citizen." There was to be no more rank, no more titles in this new France.

"Let me help you into the coach, Citizen LaRouche," said Sebastian to Martha, and since they did not know Francesca's name or true identity—they thought she was a servant too—Hugo addressed her now as "citizen mademoiselle" then as "citizen *cherie.*"

Even the two mounted guards who took up positions on either side of the carriage—the presence of the guards also adding to Hugo and Sebastian's sense of self-importance—did not escape the ritual of this new order. "Citizen yeomen," Hugo called them.

Even the king, riding three coaches ahead of Selena in this fateful procession, was being called "Citizen Capet." As the horses and carriages at last began to move toward Paris, a hoarse, rowdy cry arose from the ugly, triumphant mob: "We have the baker and the baker's wife and the little cook-boy. Now we shall have bread!"

Martha slunk down in her seat; Francesca stared gloomily out at the trudging mob, her hand in Selena's. But Selena herself could not see enough of the spectacle. All along the roadway, in the ditches and the fields and the villages through which the procession rolled, she saw overwhelming evidence that things were no longer as they had been just yesterday. There was no respectful lifting of hats on the part of the peasants, no calls of greeting, but only jeers and obscene gestures as the royal coach passed by. In spite of all he had done, by omission or commission, to bring this fate upon himself, Selena could not help but feel a certain pity for Louis XVI. When history itself turns against one, there is no refuge. She thought of what it must have been like to have been the last of the knights, the Middle Ages gone, feudalism dying, chivalry dead. In the new age, a knight would have been as out of place as a toad on a dinner table. She thought of this last knight riding into a village somewhere, his armor glistening, his sword and lance polished to a luster, only to be made fun of by the townspeople and called a fool by louts on the village green.

Even the evil have hearts that are capable of breaking, and Louis XVI was not an evil man. His fault—and she had a feeling it would cost him his head—was that he was ineffectual and indecisive in a time when the Bourbon dynasty demanded a leader capable of reading conditions and changing to meet them.

That huge carriage in which he rode *was* rather toadlike in the midst of this sea of jeering people.

"We have the baker and the baker's wife . . ."

"It is the end of the world," said Francesca again. "I shall never see my William in this life."

"Hush," replied Selena, passing on the advice that had sustained her in so many a dark hour: "The sky begins here. You are never defeated unless you believe it."

"What if the mob has invaded my home?" fretted Martha. "All things are possible now."

Presently, Selena grew warm in the coach and removed her greatcoat, laying it on the seat beside her. It was only twelve miles to Paris, but progress was slow because of the milling throng, which would grow enormously once they reached the city. She leaned out the window and saw that the royal vehicle was reasonably well-protected. Lafayette rode beside it on one side, and Royce on the other.

Royce Campbell, guarding a tyrant! Selena had never dreamed that she would witness such a thing. Well, it was his life, wasn't it? If he had changed so greatly that he would do such a thing—or rather, if he had not changed at all—so be it.

No, she decided, in the next moment, *I can't accept that, I just can't.*

He turned then, swiveling in the saddle, and saw her watching him. Before she could withdraw back inside the coach, he had slowed his horse and was dropping back. When his horse came abreast of Selena's carriage, he gave her a friendly, if casual, smile of greeting. It was as if they had never meant anything to each other at all!

"Selena," he said, peering into the coach at Francesca and Martha Marguerite, "I presume you're safe?"

"That I am," she replied. She wanted at least to thank him for the piece of plaid he'd left on her pillow, but the presence of the other two women made her cautious. As it was, both Francesca and Madame LaRouche were staring admiringly at Royce. He looked just as splendid as always—perhaps more so in a white uniform and a blue jacket, with a white-plumed hat to which he had affixed, hypocritically, the cockade—and he seemed not to have aged a day since she'd last seen him in New York.

"When we reach the Tuileries," he told her, "leave your coach and come with me."

Beside her, Selena felt the princess grow tense.

"She is to remain with me," Francesca told Royce. "It is all planned."

"Your Highness," said Royce, civilly but emphatically, "the mademoiselle and I have much to discuss."

Selena was somewhat astonished that Royce knew Francesca—the girl had spoken to him quite objectively, superior to subordinate—but no doubt his position in the royal entourage made him privy to a lot of things.

"I *would* appreciate the opportunity to speak with you, sir," she replied coldly, "but not today."

He laughed. "Come now, Selena. I feel that you may be confused about certain things."

"Perhaps I am. But my friend has asked that I remain with her during this unpleasantness, and I have agreed."

"Who is that?" whispered Martha Marguerite suspiciously.

"I know what is troubling you, Selena," said Royce then, in his direct way, his eyes locked on hers. "You feel that I am on the, well, the wrong side of things, don't you?"

"That, sir, is your affair."

"Sir? *Sir?* Are matters that bad between us?"

After thinking and worrying about him all night, after those suspicions about him which had begun when she'd found the pouch of jewels in the cabinet in their New York hideaway, Selena could not restrain herself. Neither Francesca's nor Martha's presence was sufficient to stop her tongue. "Once," she declared, "you seemed to have a place in your heart for the downtrodden and suffering of the world—"

"I did—" he started to interrupt.

"—but that is gone now, I can see full well. Look at them," she added, pointing at the dozens of poor men and women who had come near the coach to witness this exchange between lofty cavalier and fine lady. "See how they hunger! See the poor clothes they wear, even in this chill."

Royce shrugged. "Walking will warm them," he said.

"Hah! And they shall eat cake too."

"It seems to me, Selena, that your current situation is not unduly bereft of comfort. A coach of your own, horsemen—"

"Who is that man?" hissed Martha Marguerite. "I say, he is rather splendid."

Francesca may have agreed, but she did not want to lose her friend to Royce.

"Look, Selena," said Royce, laughing again, "I think you must prove your concern by making a sacrifice for the good of the citizenry. . . ."

Before she could stop him—before she had fully realized just what he was up to—Royce leaned down from his horse, reached in through the open window of the coach, and grabbed her greatcoat.

"Wait!" she cried, trying to snatch it back.

But he held it in the air, inspecting it. "Fine workmanship," he declared. "It would keep a chill from the bones too."

Then he looked around, scanning the faces of the poor who trudged alongside his horse. "Here, citizen!" he cried expansively.

And tossed the coat down to a woman marching along there!

No, it was not a woman. The recipient of this largesse was another of those men in disguise, who had fomented and executed the march upon Versailles. Selena saw his arms go up to grab the coat, caught a glimpse of an intense, captivating, *familiar* face, and saw the man move off and melt into the crowd.

Pierre Sorbante!

"Good Lord, what have you done!" Selena cried.

Royce looked perplexed. "You spoke of suffering," he said. "You spoke of chill and hunger and the heart. Don't you feel better for having donated something of yours to the cause of human comfort?"

Was he mocking her or not? She couldn't be sure. Angry words came to her lips, but she called them back, smiling instead. *All right, so be it. His* secret treasure was gone now, and good riddance. The irony, in fact, was just too good not to savor. His own ill-gotten plunder, unbeknownst to him, had gone to the unfortunate of the world after all.

"I hope you know what you've done," she said, still smiling. "I look forward to telling you sometime."

"Ah! That means you will come away with me when we reach the Tuileries."

"No, it does not."

"We shall see." He touched the upswept brim of his plumed hat, touched his spurs lightly to the stallion's flanks, and rejoined Lafayette at the royal carriage.

"Who was that?" asked Francesca and Martha Marguerite in unison.

"A man named Royce Campbell. I used to know him."

Royce's departure, not to mention their somewhat contentious exchange, had left a sudden, empty feeling in her breast, as if some subtle but sinister power had hollowed her out and gone away.

"Campbell?" wondered Martha Marguerite. Too late, Selena remembered that Madame LaRouche knew of the lost love, the one who was supposed to lie buried beneath the sands of La Tortue. "The same Campbell? My God, yes! He was at the ball last night!"

Selena saw in the older woman's face, not curiosity that Royce should have turned up here in Paris very much alive, but a fear that her favorite, Jean Beaumain, Selena's betrothed, might be betrayed.

"Is that Monsieur Campbell something special to you?" Francesca was asking.

Before Selena was able to explain, Martha spilled the beans. "It seems that they were lovers once," she sniffed, patting the young girl's hand, as if this portentous information must be imparted maternally. "But Selena has now promised to marry someone else."

The princess's eyes sparkled dramatically as she regarded Selena with new respect. "Oh, my goodness, two suitors!" she exclaimed. "How marvelous!"

"Yes, isn't it?" replied Selena.

All Paris went wild at the arrival of the captive King. Oh, there were cogent, even plausible reasons advanced by Louis XVI to explain his return from Versailles to the Tuileries. He was, he claimed, a "part of the revolution now, at one with the people." From now on, his minions proclaimed, he would "put the cause of the people first." Reforms would be made. The decisions of the National Assembly would become the law of the land. Things would "get better."

That was what the royal ministers said. In truth, the King was in desperate straits and everyone knew it, from the most eminent crowned heads of Europe to the raggedy waifs in Parisian alleys. News that Louis was a veritable prisoner in the Tuileries swept like wildfire through the courts of Europe, and conservatives of the monarchistic persuasion immediately began schemes to aid or rescue him.

When the King's procession finally threaded through the mobs of Paris and pulled into the courtyard in front of the palace, no one believed—save, for a time, the King himself—that he might, somehow, take control of events.

Selena climbed down from her carriage, aided by Hugo. He and Sebastian were acting almost lordly now, having spent the night at one royal residence and been escorted onto the grounds of another. Princess Francesca took Selena by the hand and led her to the royal coach, from which the King, Marie Antoinette, and their children were descending. The entire scene was a human maelstrom, skittish, fretful horses, anguished functionaries, cold, dispassionate politicians, nervous guardsmen, and the howling, numberless mob outside the gates.

"Aunt Marie," said Francesca, unceremoniously presenting Selena, "this is my friend. I want her to stay here with us."

"Oh, no, Your Majesty, I couldn't," said Selena.

The Queen did not seem to hear either of them, but hurried into the palace with the dauphin and his sister.

Louis paid no attention to the two young women, either. With one terrified glance at the mob, some of whose members were screaming for his blood, he also hastened into the sanctuary of the Tuileries.

"What am I to do?" wailed Martha Marguerite.

"Hugo and Sebastian will take us home," said Selena. "Francesca, you stay here. You'll be safe. I'll come and see you tomorrow, I promise."

"No—"

"Do as she says, Your Highness!"

It was Royce on horseback. He looked down at them for a moment, then leaned from his saddle and put his arm around Selena's waist. She saw a glint of white teeth as he smiled, felt his long, strong fingers close about her ribcage. Then she was whirling in the air, coming to rest behind him on the horse.

"Where are you taking her?" Martha Marguerite demanded fearfully.

"To my apartments," he replied, wheeling the stallion expertly in the crowded quarters. "Sixty-nine Rue St. Denis. She'll be safe. Your Highness, I'll have her here for you to see tomorrow. Madame LaRouche, don't be concerned."

Martha emitted something like a wail of woe and consternation, but to no avail. Royce Campbell, with Selena on the horse with him, was gone from the courtyard, off through the gates, and free in the city of Paris.

Free too, that day, of the burden of vengeance that he had borne so long, Jean Beaumain docked the *Liberté* at Le Havre. Leaving Rafael in charge of his ship, he immediately booked passage on a riverboat up the Seine to Paris. With him he carried a heavy wooden box, but it was no weight at all. It was lighter than air. All the world was light for him this day, and filled with promise. News had it that the accursed monarchy was in its last gasps. He had a sweet journey to make, a son to see for the first time, and a woman to marry and hold, once again, in his arms.

19   69 Rue St. Denis

Charging on horseback through the streets of the city, clinging to Royce, Selena rehearsed everything that she would say when they were alone. She would keep her distance. She would be cool. She would demand—no, she would ask—for explanations. Why had he concealed the jewels in New York? Why had he consorted with the smuggler, LaValle? Why had he left a false grave? Why had he reverted to his previous, ignoble behavior and beliefs? Why—?

But for a long, long time, she asked no questions at all.

His apartments were on the second floor of an old but elegant building overlooking the Seine. Dismounting hurriedly, as if there were little time left in life, Royce put his hands around her waist and swung her down from the stallion. He did not set her down on the cobblestones, however, but swept her into his arms and carried her, two steps at a time, to his lodgings. He did not set her down there either, but kicked the door shut behind them and transported her through a series of airy rooms to his bedchamber. It was, then and in retrospect, the greatest journey of her life.

He put her down upon the bed, not ungently, and for a moment she lay there stunned, her senses dazzled by what she knew was going to happen, by what she wanted with all her heart to happen. Already he was pulling off his boots, tearing off his uniform, gazing down at her with stark, sharp longing in his eyes.

"Can we talk?" she heard herself asking.

"Yes, but not with words," he said, and stripped her bare.

She was too dazed, as he hovered momentarily over her, to appreciate fully all that lay in store, knowing only that she wanted him. Nothing mattered but that, not jewels nor graves nor worlds. They cried out together as he entered her and she took him unto herself. The familiar, unforgotten shape of him inside her roused Selena instantly to primitive, atavistic frenzy. She drew up her slender legs on either side of him, so as to have him even more deeply, closed herself around him and began to rock her body in time with him. The first pale patterns of rose-colored heat stirred in her then, and as she gave herself, slowly, religiously, cunningly, the heat spread throughout her body. With each of his powerful, deliberate strokes, currents of insidious voluptuousness ran up into her belly, down along her tender, living thighs. They knew each other so thoroughly, so well, that thrust and clutch of flesh, expertly given and just as expertly received, blotted out all the world save that of sensation. He knew just how to stroke her, and she to grasp him, release, and grasp him again. Currents of ecstasy lanced down her legs to her toes, up her body, into her arms, and to her hands which he had pinioned with his own upon the pillows. Then Selena sensed herself approaching the great brink, that which in French is called "the little death," and she was coming up, coming up to the precipice, which cannot be accurately designated because one is either on this side of the gulf or on the other. But she was there, and suddenly the heat, which was of themselves and which had spread throughout her body, came flashing back to its source, up her legs and down her arms, through her breasts and belly, down, and then it was there, there, *there*, and they pulsed gorgeously together as of old.

"I thought you were dead," she gasped, a long time afterwards, lying beside him, each caressing the other in the savory, lingering enchantment of afterglow.

"I thought you were."

She braced herself on an elbow and looked into his eyes. "You *did?*"

"Of course. Or I would have come for you. I tried. I scoured the Caribbean for word of you. Finally, one of my men came back from Port-de-Paix with word that you had been killed in a fire there. The same fire that ended a man I knew. His name was LaValle."

"Ah, your friend the *smuggler*," she said disapprovingly.

Royce grinned. "He had his uses to me."

"Doesn't everyone? And I thought you were gone forever." She told him of the graves on the island of La Tortue, and of the cross with its swath of plaid and the name Campbell scratched on the wood. She told him of the ancient village woman who'd described him so well.

"Yes, I was there," he said. "I buried my men there, after our sea battle with the HMS *Prince William*. But whyever did you think that a pagan like me would be content to lie beneath a cross?"

Now Selena knew why she'd thought something had been wrong, out of place, about that cross.

"Yet your *name* was on it," she said. "I saw it with my own eyes."

"How did you come to search La Tortue? How did you get there?"

Selena was silent for a moment. The answers to those questions would require mention of Jean Beaumain. So bedazed was she by Royce's nearness to her, so utterly shaken by the pleasure of the love they'd just made, that she had not the will to tell him of Jean just yet.

"All I know," she said, "is that when I saw that grave, the world went black for a long time."

"And for me as well, when I heard about the fire."

"I guess it is best not to give too much credit to the tales of Haitians," said Selena, only half in jest.

She bent to kiss his smooth, bronze breast, and then looked up into his eyes. She saw renewed desire in them, both his and her own reflected need. Wordlessly, she turned in the bed and lay on her side next to him, their bodies reversed on the rumpled sheets and blankets. With one hand, she cupped the taut, finely veined, essence-making gourd of him, and with the other stroked and squeezed his long, thick staff. It trembled beneath her ministrations, and she trembled at its sweet and powerful perfection. Only minutes before, she had called forth from it, evoked in it, all the pleasure it could bear, and now, without thinking, she took it into her kiss, running her tongue again and again around its smooth, majestic circumference. It was then, too, that she felt him parting her legs, felt his lips and tongue upon her fevered thighs, and after a delicious pause as long as time, felt his kiss upon that part of her, sorcerered to ecstasy by his magic again.

The only sadness was that, finally, it had to end when flesh could bear no more.

But they ended it together, and there was great joy in that.

"My God, darling," sighed Selena, when she was again in his arms, kissing him, his taste on her lips, hers on his. "My God, think of the time we've lost."

"But what we've just shared makes up for it."

"No, it doesn't. Not really. There is all the joy we might have had."

"But will have now."

"But will have now," she agreed, "and always."

The word *always* brought her partway back to her senses. Jean Beaumain. The revolutionary tumult of Paris. An uncertain future.

Well, now was as good a time as any. "Darling," she said softly.

"Hmmm?" His eyes were closed, but he was not asleep.

"Darling, how did you come to be so much favored by their majesties?"

His eyes snapped open. He was alert, if not on guard. "What do you mean?"

"It puzzles me, that's all. In America, you were at the forefront of those who fought for independence against George III. You and Erasmus Ward—"

"Yes, and I see that you still wear his cross."

"As I will always. But in America, you stood with Ward and Gilbertus Penrod and Washington himself. And now you seem to be in league with the most corrupt elements of the monarchy and the nobility. And it is said"—her tone sharpened—"that you were Marie Antoinette's lover?"

"Is that what they say?" he asked, laughing lazily, almost with pleasure at the thought. "My, my."

"Royce, this is serious!"

"My dear, I believe you're jealous."

"Is it true?"

"A gentleman would never answer that question, whatever the answer."

"You're playing with me. I have to know."

"Why?"

"Because"—*go ahead,* she thought—"because I have to know if you're still the man I used to know."

He looked at her with a playful, half-mocking expression, then got slowly out of bed and strode naked to a huge mirror hung upon the wardrobe door. He examined his reflection carefully for a time, turning this way and that. Then he came back and joined her in bed again.

"Yes, I believe I'm the same man," he said. "Perhaps a tad older, but—"

"That's *not* what I mean!"

"Selena," he laughed, "what on earth *do* you mean? Of course I'm the same man."

"I don't think so. No one who would risk his life for one revolution founded upon the human spirit would play turnabout and, in another such revolution, support the causes of repression."

"Why not?" asked Royce, still in that easy, teasing way. "In both cases, I saw my opportunities and I took them."

"What?" she cried, scarcely able to believe the underlying cynicism that marked his response.

"So did you," he added. "How much did you get for that pouch of jewels and sovereigns I left with you in New York?"

Her stunned look was his answer.

"I assume you sold or bartered them. No poor girl gets invited to Versailles in the company of the nobility you claim to deplore. Did you buy yourself a position? Or perhaps you still *have* the pouch?"

Cleverly, he had turned the issue against her.

"I became friends with Madame LaRouche in Haiti," said Selena in her own defense. "The question is, how did *you* come by those stones? They were obviously taken from rings and brooches—"

"Is that right?"

He was patronizing her! "All right," she told him, anger flashing, "I'll tell you what happened. I kept the jewels safe all the time. I sewed them into the lining of a coat. Which *you,* on the way here from Versailles, *gave away* to a radical named Pierre Sorbante, who was disguised as one of those women demonstrators!"

He looked at her for a long time, his eyes unreadable. "Well," he said finally, "easy come, easy go. There's more where those came from, I guess."

"Is that all you have to say!"

"For the time being, love. Lie down quietly now. I want to have you again."

And she did, and he did, and for a while it was wonderful again.

But their secret garden had a thorn in it.

Across the river, at the exact moment Royce and Selena brought each other once again to those heights they always scaled so effortlessly, Jean Beaumain, still lugging his wooden box, knocked on the door of the LaRouche mansion. He could see that refurbishment had been going on, but had apparently been broken off, since no workmen were about.

A young man in faded livery—it was Hugo—answered the door.

"Madame LaRouche, please?"

"Who shall I say is calling?"

"Jean Beaumain."

"Do you know her?"

"Very well, my man. Just go summon her, please."

Hugo complied, and in a minute Martha Marguerite came to the door. "Oh, Jean, Jean." Their embrace was energetic and heartfelt. "Jean, come in. Things are at a terrible point. . . ."

"Selena? Is Selena here?"

Her eyes told him that something was wrong, and he had barely the courage to face whatever it was. *Nothing* could have happened to his darling! It would be the end of the world if she had died, especially now that he had achieved his dream and evened the score with Chamorro.

But what Martha had to tell him, about the miscarriage and about Royce Campbell, was almost worse than if she had indeed told him that Selena was dead.

He listened. He had neither words nor tears. His face grew dark, and a light in his eyes went out forever.

"Where is she now?" he asked dully. "Where did the rogue take her?"

Martha did not remember what address Royce had given, only that it had been someplace in Paris. She summoned Hugo and Sebastian.

"I don't remember the house number," Sebastian said. "Somewhere in the Rue St. Denis, as I recall."

Hugo nodded in corroboration.

"I shall rest for the night," Jean Beaumain decided, "although

I do not think that I will be able to sleep." He sat wearily down upon the wooden box he carried. "In days to come, I shall search the Rue St. Denis from one end to the other, building by building, cellar by cellar, house by house."

A new burden of vengeance rested unwanted upon his broad shoulders, a malevolent bird that pecked into his flesh, sought and found the sweet meat of his beating heart.

20 Night and Day

Never before had Selena lost herself so utterly in the tumult of passion. All that afternoon and into amber-tinted twilight she held Royce to herself, within herself, drifting from pleasure to pleasure, until their flesh could no longer rise to satisfy the appetite for pleasure. Yet when he finally withdrew from her, she cried out with regret at the sudden emptiness.

He got out of bed and began to dress.

"Where are you going?"

"Where are *we* going. Come along. To eat, to drink. I have no servants here. It has been a bit . . . dangerous for me. There are those who know the King made me *vicomte*, and those with titles are rather *persona non grata* in most parts of the city."

She looked alarmed.

"Don't worry," he said. "Just dress. I will find a place that is safe."

They left his residence. First, he took the stallion to a stable and gave a handful of coins to the proprietor, a choleric, one-eyed humpback who ogled Selena shamelessly.

"Feed and water the animal," Royce ordered. "Give him a rubdown. Perhaps I'll return tomorrow. Perhaps not. You can handle it?"

"Hay I have," muttered the troglodyte insolently, running the coins through his dirty, stubby fingers, "but money none."

Royce reached into his pocket and added a franc note to the coins. "Now you do," he said. "Mind, see carefully to the beast."

Then he and Selena set out down the street in gathering darkness. Walking with her arm in his, Selena could not help but remember that, on just such a night as this, they had been parted in New York. That would not happen tonight. She also realized how hungry she was.

"I have heard there is no food in Paris," she worried.

"There is, though. One must know where to find it, and have the money to buy it."

"And you do not care that others are starving?"

He was silent for a long time. She could not see his expression. When he spoke, his voice was as nonchalant as it had been earlier, when he'd learned that he'd given away his jewels to a rebel. "Life is unfair, and I guess I can't do much about it."

You could, she thought, with an ache in her heart. But she was *with* him, and for the time being she permitted her love to override the nature of the differences between them.

They must have walked for at least a mile, avoiding groups of ragged citizens that moved through the city in surly directionlessness, shouting threats and slogans and oaths.

"They haven't gotten the bread they were led to believe was forthcoming," said Royce. "And I doubt that they will. All France is at a standstill. Commerce and industry lie dormant. No one knows what will happen. Farmers are not selling their grain today, because the price might go up tomorrow. The King can do nothing, and meanwhile people here in the city grow more desperate."

"What *will* happen? Something must."

"I think the revolution here in the city will grow ever more feverish. We should attempt to leave at first opportunity."

"Where would we go?"

"Scotland, of course," he said.

Selena felt sad. "Yes, of course. But sooner or later, we'd be found out. I have no home to go to. Coldstream is in the hands of the King."

"Oh, I should think a cave in the Highlands would do us just as well. . . ."

Suddenly, he grabbed her around the shoulders and pulled her into and along a dim passageway, through an opening in a wall, and down a long flight of stone stairs. For a moment, Selena thought they were descending into the sewers, but then she heard the muted sound of voices somewhere ahead, saw a tiny light flickering behind drawn curtains.

"We are going to the Tavern Richelieu," Royce told her. "All manner of people come here. Talk flows like wine. Perhaps we may learn the exact nature of the present situation. I should not like to try and flee Paris if the roads are blocked. We'd be taken as Royalist fugitives and imprisoned, or worse."

"I've had enough of prisons for the rest of my life," said Selena.

The Tavern Richelieu surprised her. Royce had been correct. There were still places in Paris where one could eat and eat well, if one had the money.

Royce had eschewed his splendid uniform and wore a common pair of breeches and an old shirt. Selena still wore the nondescript dress she'd chosen at Versailles that morning. They might have been notable in physical appearance, the svelte, blond beauty and her tall, saturnine escort, but they were inconspicuous as to attire when they entered the tavern and found seats at a table toward the back. It was dark there, and Royce did not light the candle on the table. All around them, people were eating and drinking and talking. So much talk, and argument, and debate.

"Language is the fuel of revolution," Royce said, ordering a pot of rabbit stew, potato biscuits, and a bottle of red wine.

Selena looked at him, seated there with her at the little table, thinking of all that had happened to them in life thus far, and wondering what would yet befall. How darkly, how gloriously intertwined were their lives, but what was the resolution to which they sped? What was the *meaning?* Her love was so great that she trembled as she lifted the glass of wine to her lips. Yet in spite of such joy, she was troubled by the insouciance with which he assumed and discarded ideas and beliefs as if they were suits of clothing, or horses, or . . . women?

I'll tell him about Jean now, she thought, when the rabbit stew had arrived and they'd begun to eat. *I have to do it anyway, and after all, he was pretty damn casual about his association with Marie Antoinette!*

"Darling," she said, her spoon midway between bowl and mouth, "there's something—"

"Just a second," he replied, lifting his hand. "I want to hear this."

Two men at an adjacent table, who had been speaking quietly with their heads together, now raised their voices in disagreement.

"The King must be executed forthwith as an enemy of the people," said one. "We *know* he is planning to bring foreign troops into the country in order to end the revolution. We *know* he has a treasure chest with which he has been attempting to bribe the members of the National Assembly. We *know* he is only pretending to support the reforms that have been wrought. I tell you, he must die!"

Selena made the mistake of turning toward the speaker, even as Royce touched her arm to discourage her from so doing. She turned quickly back to her own table, but not before she had seen —and been seen by—a fiery-eyed, foppishly dressed, yet oddly pedantic looking young man. He looked out of place in silk stockings and powdered hair, particularly in this tavern, but his words left no doubt of his extreme revolutionary intensity.

His interlocutor, who sat with his back to Selena, responded with equal heat, although his words seemed more reasonable.

"Don't you understand?" he asked. "Don't you understand that if Louis XVI is executed, the British *will* invade, the Dutch *will* invade, the Germans *will* invade? By killing the King, you will be accomplishing exactly what you most fear. Besides, the National Assembly has been successful on all fronts. Serfdom has been abolished. Tithes and all sorts of ecclesiastical privileges have been renounced. Offices must no longer be sold. Land in the provinces has been given to peasants. And His Majesty has agreed to all these things!"

"Yes, but he cannot be trusted. When the foreigners come and destroy you and me and our compatriots, how long do you think Louis will keep his word? Hah! How long? And as for the peasants, land given is land easily taken back by the nobles."

"You're wrong, my friend."

There was a crash and clatter as the firebrand stood up, knocking over his chair.

"You are not my friend, sir!" he declared, and stormed out of the tavern, but not before giving Royce and Selena a penetrating look of hatred.

"What was that all about?" Selena asked cautiously, when things had quieted down a bit.

"That is the fate toward which the revolution is tending," answered Royce, refilling their glasses with wine. "Things, unchecked, will proceed from the inevitable, such as the King's departure from Versailles, to the pragmatic, such as the recent decrees of the National Assembly, to the self-destructive. That young man was Maximilien Robespierre. Mirabeau and Sorbante are reactionaries compared to him. He will not be satisfied until the King is dead, and thousands of others, I'm afraid."

"Darling," she said, a bit worried, "he saw us. I think . . . I may have been mistaken, but it seemed as if he *knew* you."

"Unfortunately, he does. I think it would be best if we left now."

Selena, who had not even begun to sate her hunger, looked up in alarm. Royce was cool and self-controlled. Only the haste with which he drained his wineglass betrayed tension.

"I wanted to find out what was going on," he told her, smiling slightly. "Things have been changing too fast. Even a week ago, men like Robespierre would not have spoken so freely, even here."

"Exactly who is this Robespierre?" Selena asked, as they climbed back up toward the street.

"The worst sort of man for politics," Royce answered, halting at the corner of the building and peering up and down the street. "He is an idealist and a dreamer. Such men misjudge human nature. First, they feel that people are more noble than is really the case. Then, when they become disillusioned, they turn against the very humanity in which they originally placed such great hopes."

It was now quite late and the streets, while not deserted, seemed less threatening than they had earlier. Royce and Selena, hand in hand, began their walk back to his home. The thought of being alone with him again re-ignited physical need, and she forgot the other, lesser hunger of her stomach. But they had not gone more than halfway to his apartments when he squeezed her hand and whispered, "Don't turn around, but I think we're being followed."

"By whom?"

"Robespierre. You were right. He did recognize me. I cannot let him find out where I am staying. It would be the end of us both."

"What will we do?"

"Do you think you can find the way back by yourself?"

"Oh, darling, no. We can't become separated again—"

"It's the only way. I'll lead him on a chase and lose him."

"What if you don't?"

"I shall."

"I'm not sure I can find the way back."

They continued to walk for a short while more.

"Selena, we have to do something," he said. "We'll leave Paris as soon as possible, but we have to keep Robespierre from learning where we're staying. Trust me when I say that. It's very important."

"All right. What do you want me to do?"

"We are coming to a hotel that I know," he said. "We'll both go inside. You go straight through and exit in the back. Wait in the alley there. I'll have a glass of wine at the bar. If he comes in, he may assume we're staying there, and that you're in our room. I don't know if he'll wait or be content to have found our lodgings and leave until another time. I'll join you as soon as I can."

She agreed, with some trepidation, to this plan.

They turned off the street and entered the dingy, lamplit lobby of a down-at-the-heels establishment. A small taproom was at one side of the lobby, where a handful of men and several apparent prostitutes were drinking. An old concierge dozed behind a desk near the door, her thinning hair wrapped in a bandana to which the cockade had been attached. She reminded Selena of Senora Celeste.

"Yes? Yes?" she asked, peering at them as if trying to establish the precise degree of their carnal intent. "You want a room for the night?"

"No, just wine," said Royce. He led Selena toward the taproom, then released her hand and said, "Go!"

She obeyed, noting that the concierge was nodding back into sleep, walked hurriedly through the lobby, down a greasy, closet-lined hallway, and out the back door. It was dark in the alley, and cold. She smelled garbage. Above her, in the narrow space between two buildings, she could see the stars.

After standing there for a few moments, it occurred to her that Robespierre—if, indeed, he'd been the one following them—might well have the wit to inspect this alley himself. She felt her way along the side of a building, walking slowly into the darkness. A cat hissed in protest; she'd disturbed its nighttime hunt. Then she pressed herself against the wall, and waited.

A long time passed, and although she tried to fight it, her tension mounted. Finally, Royce appeared in the doorway. She could see him outlined dimly in the faraway lobby light. The words *here, darling* rose to her lips, but at the last instant she choked them off. The man was not Royce, but Robespierre himself. He stood there for a minute, looking about, and took several steps toward her. The cat hissed again. He stopped. Selena held her breath. If he came nearer, should she fight? What?

But he turned and went back inside the hotel.

Breathing a sigh of relief, she relaxed slightly and continued to wait.

Finally, Royce came. "Selena?" His whisper was low and hoarse.

She raced to him and put her arms around him. He smelled of wine, and handed her half a loaf of bread.

"That was him?" she asked.

"Yes."

"What happened?"

"He watched me for a while. I pretended not to know him, and played up to one of the girls. This disgusted him, apparently. He went away. But he thinks we're staying here. Let's go now. I'm sure he'll be back to try to have me arrested in the morning."

She chewed on the bread as they walked, and by the time they reached his residence, one of her hungers had been satisfied.

Royce soon satisfied the other, but after he was asleep beside her, Selena got up and walked to the window. She pondered her own happiness, knowing that in spite of its magnitude she would not be wholly content until she could convince her lover to relinquish his—*face it, Selena, his* selfish—ways. She thought of Francesca too, whom she must go and see on the morrow. The poor girl, one lone person craving only her lover, while it seemed the whole earth was falling down about her ears.

Then, looking out upon Paris, she shuddered, sensing in the shadows there the frightening presence of this man, Robespierre, ruthless, fanatical, totally dedicated to a cause that he considered as pure as the grail.

Selena was reminded straightaway of her old nemesis, Clay Oakley.

When she awoke in the morning, Royce was up, dressed, and brewing a pot of tea. He poured her a cup and brought it over to the bed, sitting down beside her as he handed her the tea. She sat up, leaning against the pillows, and sipped as he fondled her bare breasts. There was sugar in the tea.

"Sweet," she said, appreciatively.

"Which?" he smiled.

"Both. Come back to bed."

"I can't. I have much to do today. If we plan to leave the city, I must see someone. There are arrangements that have to be made."

Selena admitted to herself that this was true, but she had a sneaking suspicion that perhaps he would try to see the Queen one last time, or that he had some sort of a shady scheme in progress that required completion.

"Well, I hope you are able to turn a profit," she said, just a bit sourly.

"Always the main thing in my mind," he shot back, grinning.

"I'll bet."

"And you are determined to go to the Tuileries?"

"I promised Francesca. She's expecting me. Also, I must go back to Madame LaRouche's to collect my things, and I should leave a message for Jean."

"Forget about that. If you go out at all, you must dress as if you were the poorest of the poor. Please, why don't you just stay here? It will be much safer, and I'll be sure of where you are. Look, I'll bring some suitable garments back with—"

"No, I can't. I'm worried about the princess. She's so young, and with what's been happening—"

"My dear, the princess will be perfectly all right."

"*You* don't have any sympathy for people who are sick and yearning with love. *You* were always a Campbell, calculating everything like so many numbers on a bill of lading, even *emotions*."

She wasn't truly angry, just complaining a little, and he took it in that light. "I should think that after yesterday and last night, you'd feel somewhat differently about my emotionlessness."

He leaned toward her and kissed her on the mouth. The teacup trembled in her hands. A little of the hot liquid spilled onto her breasts, but it was as nothing to the flash of heat that shot through her body.

"Come back to bed," she pleaded, clinging to him, wanting him again.

"Sorry," he replied, laughing. "I am just as you say. Calculating. Business before pleasure. I must leave now." He stood up. She saw by hard outline against cloth that he was fully aroused.

"Oh, yes! I note precisely how much your mind is upon business just now. . . ." She reached out, closed her hand around him, and drew him gently back toward her and down upon the bed. He did not undress but undid his breeches only, and had her fast and forcefully. It did not matter. It was as good as it had ever been, the urgency only serving to enhance the piercing delight.

After Royce had left, Selena washed, brushed her hair, smoothed the wrinkles from her dress as best she could, then went out into the street and made her way to the Tuileries palace, which was almost two miles away. Several passersby glared at her, and one of them snarled threateningly for no reason she could fathom. But then a sympathetic adolescent, who'd witnessed this abuse, handed her a cockade, telling her to put it on and keep it on.

" 'Tis like a passport," he advised.

Selena pinned it to the collar of her dress and made her way to the palace without incident.

It was surrounded by a great crowd, as it had been yesterday, but the mood was more subdued, less unruly, than it had been. She kept her head down, avoided speaking to anyone, and pressed slowly but relentlessly toward the gate. Royal Guards were on duty there, attempting without too much success to appear fearless and in command. They knew what had happened at the Bastille; they'd been present during the bread riot at Versailles; they were very aware of just how vulnerable the Tuileries was. Given even half an excuse, the suggestion of a reason, this sullen, smoldering mob could tear the place apart, and the Guard along with it.

Selena presented herself at the gate, and gave her name to a sergeant on duty there. She was a bit tentative, truth to tell. It was one thing for Princess Francesca to invite her here; it was quite another to be shown inside.

To her relief, however, the sergeant had been given his orders. He recognized her name immediately, and turned her over to a pale, lisping steward, who escorted her into the palace even as many in the crowd sent angry hisses after them.

"The Princeth Francethca has been waiting for you thince early morn," he said. "My God, thoth awful people outthide!"

The Tuileries, while scarcely as magnificent as Versailles, was nevertheless sufficiently grand to impress Selena all over again. To think of this incredible wealth and grandeur! Any member of the mob outside the gates would have been driven to a frenzy of regicide at the sight of the artwork alone.

Francesca received her friend in her bedchamber, a room so large and elegant that the young girl looked almost like a child or a doll in it. Selena noted that she'd been crying again and had attempted with powder to conceal the fact. She was seated on a couch of crushed velvet, magenta in color, and the pages of a letter she'd been reading fell to the floor when she stood to welcome Selena.

"Come, sit down beside me," she said, beckoning Selena toward the couch. "Do you wish tea? Food? Anything?"

Selena, who'd had no breakfast, eagerly accepted this offer, and within minutes two huge silver trays were brought in, piled with eggs and sausages and fruit, breads, cakes, butter, various preserves, and enough tea to serve ten people.

In spite of this bounty, however, which Selena attacked with zest, Francesca merely nibbled at an orange, reading and re-reading the pages in her hand.

"This is a letter from William," she said at length, when Selena had finished her meal. Tears pearled at the ends of her exquisitely mascaraed lashes. "Please read it and tell me what you think."

Selena wiped her lips on a glossy white napkin and took the missive. Written in English, in a clear, bold hand that yet betrayed traces of shakiness, it read,

> My Dearest,
>
> Divine Providence alone knows if this message will reach you. Day after day, more tales of horror arrive upon our shores, and with each new chronicle of mayhem, I wonder and I suffer about your safety. Pray this letter reaches you! Pray you are well and safe and thinking of me—of us—if it does.
>
> I cannot believe there is a God so cruel as to end our dream of happiness before it has fully begun.

I cannot contemplate, nor accept, the thought of a future without you.

While I know it is folly to write of these things, be assured that if worst comes to worst, if the rabble rise up and threaten your illustrious uncle's domain, England shall retaliate. I was allowed to attend a conference yesterday, at which our ambassador, Lord Bloodwell, and a certain officer named Oakley assured my father that everything would be done to guarantee the safety of you and your relations.

You must know that I am thinking of you with greatest love in this time of trial and separation, that I shall cherish forever our moments alone during the holidays in Salzburg, and that no matter what happens, no matter what becomes of us, I will always love you.

Yours undyingly,
William

Selena finished reading the letter and looked at the princess, who had been watching intently.

"It's a lovely letter," Selena said.

To her surprise, Francesca began to bawl. "He doesn't love me anymore," she wailed. "He's telling me good-bye."

Selena put her arm around the girl, while scanning the letter a second time. "Why do you say that?" she asked. "I see nothing at all to indicate, or even to suggest, such a negative reading."

"You don't understand! You don't *understand!*"

"All right. Explain it to me."

Francesca grabbed the letter, her teardrops falling upon it and smudging some of the words. "Look what he writes," she said. " 'I cannot contemplate . . . the thought of a future without you. . . . no matter what happens . . . I will always love you.' "

"So?" asked Selena, puzzled.

"That is his gentle way of telling me good-bye!" the princess wailed. "He will not wait for me. He thinks I will never reach England, as it was arranged!"

"I beg your pardon, but you are upset. To me, the letter is filled with nothing *but* love. William is wise to recognize the present difficulty, but he has not given up at all. The words of the letter are eloquent, and fairly glowing with his love for you."

The princess stopped crying and thought this over. She even read the letter again. "Do you really think so?"

"Oh, yes. There is no doubt. I have been apart from those I loved, and one is prone to misunderstand at such times."

Francesca snuffed and sniffled. "You wouldn't lie to me?"

"Never, but least of all over something like this."

"Well . . ." said the princess, brightening at this new interpretation of things.

"How did you come to receive this letter?" Selena asked. "I had thought that, with the National Assembly in control, diplomatic messages would be difficult to come by."

"A private traveler brought it here at great risk. William paid him handsomely."

"So there you have it! Why would he have done such a thing if he did not love you anymore?"

"I . . . I guess you're right," the girl agreed. "Little good that it will do."

"What do you mean?"

"Because we are all leaving very soon. Uncle Louis has decided to flee toward the eastern frontier and seek safety in Germany."

Instantly, Selena realized the nature of the secret to which she was now, unwantedly, privy. It meant that the King *had* been false in his statements of support for the revolution. It meant, further, that the maniac Robespierre had been correct in his suspicions. Safe outside the borders of France, Louis XVI could legitimately hope to rally and direct foreign armies in the destruction of revolution and reform.

She tried not to show her surprise that Francesca would have blurted such a thing, but the girl was too innocent of politics—and too concerned with her lover—to notice or to care what she'd said.

"It means," the princess continued, "that I may be trapped in Germany for years. If there were only some way that I could reach England. . . ."

"When is His Majesty planning to flee?" asked Selena, as casually as she could.

"As soon as everything can be arranged. We will all travel as peasants."

"That seems to be the vogue these days," Selena said wryly. Momentarily, she considered whether somehow Francesca might leave Paris with Royce and her, but that was impossible. The two of them alone could expect to encounter problems enough. In short, except for sympathy and encouragement, there was little more that she could do for the girl.

"I'm speaking from experience," Selena said. "Whatever happens, never give up hope."

"Oh, I shan't, I shan't," Francesca replied. "Would you like to come with us to Germany? I think I might be able to arrange it."

Selena considered the suggestion quickly. It *did* make sense. Royce was a favorite of the royal family's, or at least of its Queen. He and she might escape the conflagration in France, reach safety, and be on their own to Scotland in due course. She would mention it to Royce.

"May I return and see you again tomorrow?" she asked. "Perhaps I might be able to give you an answer then."

"Oh, do. Please do!" the princess said.

21 The Worst of All Possible Worlds

Selena was advised to depart from the palace via a rear entrance, but even so her exit was not without incident. "Traitoress!" people screamed when they saw her come out. "Villainess! Reactionary bitch!" Even worse, she saw—or thought she saw—Maximilien Robespierre amongst the crowd, and took great care to make sure he was not following her as she sped back to Royce's residence.

There she waited alone, in growing concern, for his return.

When he finally came back, sweating and smelling faintly of the sewers, she told him what had happened.

He could not believe it. "The King is preparing to flee!" he cried. She had never seen him so . . . not exactly agitated, not that, but . . . genuinely alarmed. "Are you certain?"

"That is what Francesca told me. We might be able to accompany them. Why, is something wrong?"

"Is something *wrong?* He will never make it. All France is expecting just such a foolhardy ploy on his part." He put on his hat and grabbed a coat.

"Where are you going? You've only just returned."

"Selena, there are things you don't know. Let me put it this way. If Louis flees, whether he is successful in flight or not, he will be playing into the hands of the extremists, Robespierre and his ilk, and the revolution will become like a bloodthirsty animal. The only way to maintain a measure of peace, and insure that the reforms already enacted remain intact, is to keep Sorbante in control. . . ."

"What?" she asked, mystified. She understood the political implications of what he'd said all right, but why was he so suddenly concerned about the welfare of the revolution? He was a monarchist.

Royce was striding toward the door. "You stay here," he ordered. "I must go at once to Pierre Sorbante and tell him—"

The door flew open with a crash. Royce stopped in his tracks. Selena started in astonishment and cried out.

Jean Beaumain, sword in hand, death in his eyes, stood there in the doorway. "Aha, my darling!" he said, looking at Selena. "I have found the love nest to which you fled."

In spite of his rage, there were tears in his eyes.

"Oh, Jean," said Selena.

Royce was unarmed. He backed slowly away from Jean as the sailor entered the room and shut the door behind him.

"I gather you two know each other," Royce said dryly.

"I meant to tell you—" Selena began.

"I'll just bet you did," snapped Jean. "Well, now's your chance." He brandished the sword. "Both of you," he commanded. "Get over there to the bed. I'm sure it's a fitting place to die. Go on! Get over there and sit down."

Selena stood riveted to the floor. Royce turned toward her, his dark eyes grim. "Do as he says, Selena. We're in no position to resist, and I want to find out what this is all about."

Royce and Selena sat down on the edge of the bed. She could feel him tensed to spring. Yet when he spoke, his voice was calm.

"All right, sir," he said, addressing Jean Beaumain, who stood over them, sword at the ready, "I assume you have an explanation for this intrusion?"

"I'll explain," said Selena, looking at Jean. In his eyes was that wild-eyed, drugged look he'd always had when he spoke of Chamorro. His body trembled, but the blade was steady in his hand. It was keen as a razor's edge. She imagined her severed head upon the floor, and Royce's beside it.

"No, I'll do the talking," Jean declared. "You may not know it, Campbell, you charlatan, but you are with *my* betrothed."

Royce's eyes widened slightly. He looked inquiringly at Selena. She nodded. "It's true. I meant to tell you, but I . . . I couldn't. I gave my word to marry Jean, but only after I thought you were dead. You see, when I saw your grave—"

"Ah, Campbell," interrupted Jean Beaumain. "See how faithful she is!"

"Please, Jean—" Selena began.

"You be quiet!" he snapped, tears running down his tanned

cheeks. "I spoke to Martha Marguerite. She told me. She told me with what haste you forgot me and joined this skirt-chasing rogue!"

"There is no need, even now, to be uncivil," Royce said coolly. "Sir, I know nothing of what you speak. I assure you—"

"And you be quiet as well! You will have ample opportunity to vent your thoughts before you die."

Selena knew that he meant it. Jean intended to kill them both.

"Jean," she implored, meeting his eyes, her heart overcome by the pain she saw in them, by knowledge that she had caused that pain. "Jean, Royce is telling the truth. He didn't . . . he doesn't . . . know anything about us."

"As soon as I leave you alone," he accused her, "just as soon as you are out of my sight—"

In spite of the circumstances, Selena's anger flared. "Yes, that's right," she shot back. "Yes, it is my fault, isn't it? You go off to sea with your evil dream of revenge, and leave me alone with child—"

"There are quite a few things I don't know," Royce said, looking at Selena.

"It's true," she said. She told him about the baby, the miscarriage, and about Chamorro.

"I killed him too," said Jean bitterly. "I cured his head and nose and ears and private parts in brine, and brought them back here to Paris, just as I said I would. I meant to throw them at the palace gate, so the King might know what befalls the scum who revere him. But one cannot even get near the palace these days, so I dropped them into the Seine instead. Perhaps I shall do the same with both of you."

"Jean," said Selena, trying again, "if it is revenge that you must have, then kill me. Royce is innocent of this—"

"No," cried Jean Beaumain, gripping the weapon. "You shall first watch *him* die! Then you may know how it feels to lose a—" He broke off, choking back sobs. "Oh, God, Selena, I loved you so much. . . ."

"And I did love you, Jean. Truly I did—"

"Shut up!"

She saw him brace and steady himself. She thought the sword would flash now.

"Just one moment," said Royce, obviously thinking too that the moment to strike had arrived. "You said I'd have a chance to speak."

Jean glared at him. "What have you got to say?"

"There is one thing that puzzles me. It is not that Selena did not tell me about your . . . relationship with her. That, while unwise, is explainable by the nature of emotions. And it is not that she loved you, which I am sure is true. She is not one to deceive about such a thing. No, my question is: *How did my name come to be on that grave marker?* I was there myself when we buried my men on La Tortue. We carved only the initials of the men's names on those crosses, so as not to provide any curious British with surnames. A man like Clay Oakley, for example, would have gone back to England and begun hounding families with those names. . . ."

Jean was staring at the two of them, his eyes going from Royce to Selena and back to Royce again. Selena, who'd known him intimately, saw in his expression, in spite of his barely contained rage, a flicker of shame and chagrin.

"Selena believed I was dead because she saw my name on a cross," Royce continued logically, "and . . . ,"

"And because an island woman told me she had seen you dead . . ." Selena added.

". . . therefore . . ." said Royce.

Jean Beaumain cut them both off. "All right!" he cried. "Stop talking. I can't stand to hear it. *I* carved your name on that cross! *I* bribed the woman to tell Selena her tale! You see, I knew she'd never let herself love me if she thought you were still alive—"

He was looking at Royce, as if imploring him to understand.

"—and I had to have you because I loved you so much. . . ."

He turned toward Selena, beseeching her to understand.

Royce Campbell made his move. While Jean was speaking to Selena, he sprang from the bed and crashed headlong into the troubled sailor, grappling for the sword. Jean, knocked off balance by the assault, managed to get one arm around Royce's neck. They fell to the floor, kicking and writhing. Jean still held the blade.

"Selena," gritted Royce. "The wardrobe. My pistol."

Selena ran to the clothes cabinet and looked frantically about. *Pistol? Where? In the pocket of one of his coats?* She began to search, her hands shaking like leaves in high wind. One coat. Another. Nothing. . . .

Jean, fighting like the wounded, desperate man he was, unconcerned about death and with nothing to lose, gathered his strength and threw Royce off him. The two men scrambled to their feet.

"In the boot, Selena . . ." gasped Royce.

Jean Beaumain slashed at him with the glittering sword. Royce dodged, tripped, and fell again. Jean lifted the blade.

Selena bent to a pair of boots on the wardrobe floor. She reached inside one of them and her fingers closed around a piece of cold steel.

Using both hands, Jean Beaumain drove the sword downward, through Royce's left hand, which he'd raised in a futile attempt to ward off the thrust, and into his abdomen.

Selena pulled the pistol from the boot and turned.

Royce lay curled and bloody on the floor. He tried to rise, to stop Jean, who now charged toward Selena. He tried to rise, but fell back, gasping in agony as the full pain hit him.

Jean was charging at Selena, drawing back the sword, death in his eyes, tears on his face.

For the shred of a second, Selena froze. Her heart felt as dead as Jean's eyes looked. It was like seeing a once-familiar friend gone completely mad.

He started to swing the blade. She heard the sound of it cutting the air.

She raised the pistol, and fired.

A small, red crater erupted in the center of Jean's forehead. His momentum carried him forward, past her, then he fell heavily onto the wardrobe's floor. The sword clattered down beside him.

She knew that he was dead.

The report of the pistol reverberated all about the room like a miniature thunderclap. It seemed impossible that such a small weapon could produce a sound so shattering. The ensuing silence was broken by the clatter of footsteps on the stairs, coming up toward the door. Royce lay helpless on the floor, his shirt and breeches soaked with blood. His eyes were dazed. He was passing into shock.

Then came a banging at the door. "You all right in there?" A male voice. "I say, are you all right?"

Royce managed to nod, instructing her to speak.

"Oh, yes," she called sweetly. "Thank you. Everything's fine. I just . . . I just managed to knock over a . . . a chair. Silly me."

A doubting silence was evident on the other side of the door. "You *sure* you're all right?"

"Oh, yes. Completely. Thank you."

Another pause, and she heard the footfalls going down the stairs. The outer door swung shut at street level. That particular problem was over, for the time being, but it was the least of the burdens Selena faced now.

Jean Beaumain was dead, his body lying there in the wardrobe. She could not even take the time to mourn him.

Royce Campbell seemed to be bleeding to death on the floor. He'd lost shocking amounts of blood, and it continued to seep slowly from his wounds, onto his clothing, and thence upon the floor.

She rushed over and knelt beside him, stripping away the shirt and breeches. The wound in his hand was bad enough; it was the wide, angry slit in his lower abdomen that really troubled her. Jean's blade had plunged deeply, and if it had sliced into a section of Royce's intestines, irreversible poisoning would already have commenced. The only thing she could do now was to try to bind the wound, stop the flow of blood.

Incredibly, Royce was still conscious. "Selena," he said, his lips dry and his breathing heavy, "elevate my feet. Don't try to move me. Get some towels and press down on the wound."

She did these things, trying not to hurt him further. Blood soaked into the towels.

"It's not every day," he said, "that a woman loses two lovers."

"Hush. You just be quiet."

"No. What happens will happen. You must leave me now."

"Leave you? Are you out of your mind?"

"No, Selena. There are things more important than you and I. And because I cannot see to them, you must."

"Would you just *stop talking!*" The flow of blood seemed to be slowing a little, and she began to nurse a tiny fragment of hope.

"Darling, you must go and find Pierre Sorbante. Tell him the

King is planning to flee. Tell him to try to get word to His Majesty that flight would be folly."

"Darling, I know how you must feel about the King who made you a *vicomte,* but—"

"Selena, you don't understand. I am in favor of the revolution. I always have been. I posed as a Royalist only to learn what the King and his minions were up to. I am a spy."

Selena looked at him in absolute bewilderment.

"You know those jewels, Selena? They were given by women in America to support Sorbante and his revolutionaries. Erasmus Ward was to have taken them to France. The cross around your neck was to be the sign by which Sorbante recognized the person carrying the treasure. After Ward was killed, it was I who was chosen to make the journey. . . ."

Suddenly, everything was clear, all the pieces of the great puzzle fell into place.

"Oh, darling," she said, "if I'd only known—"

"I couldn't tell you. Things didn't go as planned. We were separated. . . ."

He seemed to fall momentarily into a faint, then roused himself. "You must go to Sorbante now, Selena. He must be informed that the King is going to attempt foreign exile."

"I can't *leave* you here."

"You won't be leaving me alone. Not really. Where you go, I am. It will always be thus. The cause for which we struggle, human freedom, is far more important than you or I."

Now Selena knew how terribly mistaken she had been. Not only had Royce remained true to their shared ideals, at great danger to himself, he had moreover sought to protect her by keeping her innocent of his activities.

"God, I'm so *thirsty,*" he panted. "Perhaps a bit of water . . ."

But Selena knew, as did he, that in the case of abdominal wounds, all ingestion was proscribed. If his bowels had indeed been cut by the blade, leakage of fluid would already be enough to cause peritonitis. The only hope for his life was that, somehow, Jean's sword had missed his vitals. The bleeding seemed to be under control now, and she ripped apart lengths of sheeting to bandage his torso and also his hand. He had been weakened tremendously by loss of blood, and he passed out as she finished wrapping his wounds.

"Oh, Lord, oh, Lord . . ." she prayed. "I must find Sorbante. He will know what to do. He will help me with Royce, and somehow we must get Jean's body out of here."

The only thing she could think of was to cover Jean with a blanket, touching his cheek in gentle farewell as she did so. If only he'd not come here like this, if only they'd been able to talk . . .

Too late now. Once again, she was on her own, the servant of a cause greater than she. If Royce was correct about the bloodlust of Robespierre, only Pierre Sorbante could keep the revolution on an even keel. So many wonderful reforms had been enacted. It would be disastrous—it would be sinful—to have everything ruined now.

Before leaving, she went over and knelt beside Royce again, making sure that he was thoroughly bundled and tucked. His eyes flickered open. At first, she did not know if this was merely a reflex or if he was actually conscious.

"Darling," she said. "Darling! How do I find Sorbante?"

Royce stared at her, as if he were a long way from her, and she an apparition out of a dream. "Perhaps . . . perhaps in the palace crowd . . ." he whispered through cracked lips.

It was all Selena had to go on, so she left his apartment, walking as calmly as she could. A couple of men standing on the street corner stared at her.

"Sounded like a gunshot up there," one of them said, eyeing her suspiciously.

"No, no," Selena smiled, "just a chair. I'm rather clumsy sometimes."

"Never guess it judging from the rhythm of the bedsprings that I keep hearing," the fellow observed *sotto voce* to his mates as Selena walked away from them.

Please, God, don't let them go up and look around, she prayed.

It was almost noon by the time Selena reached the palace. The crowd outside the gate was sparser today, as if the novelty of holding a King captive had begun to pall for everyone. She walked all around the great building, searching faces for a glimpse of Sorbante, without success. *If he is not here himself, he must have compatriots present, though, mustn't he?* They would be watching for any sign that Louis XVI might try to flee.

What if she could not locate Sorbante? Not only would he

remain uninformed about the monarch's scheme, he also could not be called upon to help her with the mess back at Royce's apartment. *I should have ignored Royce's instructions and gone for a doctor instead,* she thought. *I'll do it now.*

But she took a final swing right past the main gate, looking for the political leader. It was a fateful decision on her part. The sergeant of the Guard, who had admitted her yesterday, recognized Selena immediately and grabbed her arm, pulling her inside the gate.

"So here you are again, *citizen,*" he said sarcastically.

"Let me go!" she cried. "I've done nothing. Let me go!"

The onlookers, many of whom recognized her too, were unsympathetic. "There's the bitch who went in yesterday!" someone said. "What's the matter, *cherie?* Tired of hobnobbing with the swells?"

Laughter.

"Serves you right," another called, as the guard propelled Selena into the palace. "Turncoats are always found out."

"What is the meaning of this?" Selena demanded, but the sergeant paid her no mind. His hand was tight on her arm as he rushed her down one corridor, then another, and pushed her into what appeared to be a small office. Startled, she recognized the King and Princess Francesca. Both of them looked strained and weary.

"Oh, Selena! Thank God!" the girl cried.

"Here she be, Your Majesty," said the guard, withdrawing.

Louis looked at her and sighed. He did not seem much a monarch at all this day, just a harried, overweight man approaching middle age.

"This is the one?" he asked Francesca. He did not appear to recognize her as his dinner guest such a short while ago.

"Yes," said the princess. "Selena, I'm sorry—"

"Too late for that," shrugged the King. "Sit down, mademoiselle."

Selena obeyed, wondering what was happening.

"You tell her," the King ordered his niece.

Francesca faltered at first, embarrassed and apologetic. "Selena, my friend, it seems I've gotten you into a terrible mess. I shouldn't have told you that our family is going to flee to Germany. I was so concerned about William . . . I didn't think—"

"Have *you* told anyone?" the King demanded of Selena.

"What? About what?" she asked, trying to appear innocent and bewildered.

"Don't lie," replied the King wearily. "It does not become you. I have already admonished my niece regarding her loose tongue which, I am afraid, will make it necessary for you to remain here today, and accompany us when we leave after nightfall."

"I cannot do that!" protested Selena. "I have responsibilities. . . ." She thought of poor Royce, wounded and perhaps dying. It occurred to her that she might tell His Majesty that Vicomte Campbell needed aid. But what if the King had already learned of Royce's complicity in the revolution? There was no way of determining how fast things were happening and what information the King had at his disposal. No, it would not be wise to connect herself with Royce. She would have to fashion a plan to get out of here and go for a doctor.

"We all have responsibilities," said Louis. "Mine is to the survival of royalist France, and to my family. That is why we must flee. You, who know of our plan, might jeopardize everything—"

"I wouldn't say a word. I promise!"

Louis laughed. "Too late," he said.

Francesca sat there looking helpless and mournful. "I'm sorry," she bleated.

"I can't go with you," Selena tried. "Just hold me here. Imprison me, if you must. But please, release me—order me released, that is—after you've reached safety."

"What if the rabble learn of our departure?" countered His Majesty. "What if they learn of it before we reach safety in Germany? They might break into the Tuileries and learn from you the direction and destination of our flight. It is a long way to the border, you know. No, you are coming with us. You are too dangerous to leave behind."

Further protests were useless. The King clapped his hands. Two guards appeared and escorted Selena and Francesca to the princess's bedchamber, where they were to spend the afternoon.

"I'm so sorry," Francesca said, over and over. "This is all terribly sad."

"You don't know how much so," replied Selena. Then she had an idea.

"Your Highness," Selena said, as they tried on peasant disguises that had been brought for them to wear during the flight. "I must ask a great favor of you."

"Yes, what is it?"

"It must be done secretly, however."

"If you tell me what it is, I may then judge."

Selena knew the princess was, like most young girls, a romantic, in love with love. "My man," she said, "my lover, lies ill at his lodgings in the Rue St. Denis." She did not say how "ill" Royce was. "He requires the care of a good physician. Now, I do not wish to jeopardize the safety of you and your kin by revealing the fact that I am with you, or that I shall not be able to return to him tonight, but do you think that you might arrange for a doctor to go to him? That is all I ask."

The princess, instantly intrigued by the situation, agreed. She left the bedchamber and at length returned.

"I have seen to it," she said.

22 A Fateful Lunch

The plan was set in motion just after dark.

The Tuileries, like all the royal palaces, was staffed with hundreds of servants. God forbid that one of royal blood should lift a finger in his or her own behalf. Members of the permanent household staff resided in the palace itself, but many more worked only during the day and returned at night to their own lodgings. This state of affairs made possible the departure of the royal fugitives—Selena among them—from the palace.

Dressed in old clothes, escorted by a Guardsman who was similarly attired, Selena and the princess left the Tuileries and proceeded perhaps a quarter of a mile. Here they entered a respectable but unprepossessing house that, judging from its expensive but ponderous furnishings, seemed to be that of a prosperous but unimaginative merchant. The King, the Queen, and their two children were already there, as were several retainers. Everyone was tense, and the young dauphin fussed and fretted.

To Selena's surprise, however, the members of the royal family had changed from the peasant garb worn to sneak out of the palace, and now wore clothing of the middle class, dark in color, well-made, but not ostentatious. She and Francesca were instructed to change into similar attire. The second phase of the plan went into effect: the King would flee by coach, posing as a merchant.

Jammed together in a large coach pulled by four bays, the party left quietly in the darkness. It was two hundred miles to the German border. Even with frequent changes of horses, the trip would take several days. The most dangerous portion of the trek, naturally, would be in the vicinity of Paris. Out in the provinces, it was unlikely that many people had ever laid eyes upon either Louis or Marie Antoinette. If the secret of the royal flight could be kept from members of the National Assembly, chances of reaching foreign sanctuary were excellent.

By dawn, the fugitives were far from Paris, and a lighthearted mood, almost of giddiness, took hold. A merchant traveling with his family was a not unfamiliar sight, and Selena noted that few paid much attention to the King when the coach stopped in one town or another to acquire fresh horses. Day passed into night and then into day again, and on they sped.

Conversation inside the carriage was sparse and inconsequential. The Queen seemed devoted to her children, and did her best to keep them calm and amused. The King brooded. Princess Francesca worried about William, in spite of the reassurances of everyone—Selena included—that everything would eventually turn out for the best.

Selena herself was not so certain that this was true, and she grew almost sick with anxiety about Royce's fate. Without care, his condition was bound to deteriorate, and not to mention the suffering, lack of food and water would also take their toll.

The King was concerned about his own stomach, and as the trip wore on and the German border neared, he became increasingly vociferous about his hunger. The quick, furtive meals they were able to snatch at way stations did not suffice to sate an appetite cultivated during years of rich foods and fine wines.

"Now we are coming to Varennes," he declared, "and the border lies just beyond. We shall stop, rest, and partake of a fine meal."

"Do you think that is wise?" asked Marie Antoinette, with a worried look.

Selena was hungry herself, but she would have recommended against such a pause, had anyone asked her. While Francesca seemed to take some comfort in her presence, to the monarchs Selena was merely a nuisance to be gotten rid of at first opportunity. They seemed hardly to notice her existence, and it was quite likely that they did not. The Queen had not spoken a word to her during the entire trip.

The coach rolled into Varennes, a quiet, peaceable frontier town, on a warm June afternoon. Citizens went placidly about their business. Farmers and peddlers attended their stalls in the market square which, characteristically, faced the local church with its Gothic spire, the livery, and the town hotel and brasserie.

290 *Vanessa Royall*

A fair-sized crowd filled the square. Many buggies and coaches and carriages were lined up on the street in front of the livery, as the horses of traveling parties were hitched and unhitched.

The King ordered one of his footmen to go inside the hotel and inquire about whether a meal might be served immediately, brushing aside the objections of the Queen. The driver went to see about an exchange of horses.

"Hah!" cried Louis then, with a glance in the direction of the market. "Look at those stalls, laden with fresh fruits and vegetables. And they say that our nation is starving! Come, Francesca, let us go over and have a look."

Selena, left to her own devices, climbed down from the coach and strolled up and down in front of the hotel. *I could get away right now,* she realized, debating whether or not to do it. *I could melt right into the crowd and . . .*

Then she saw a familiar figure browsing near a row of market stands. It was Zoé Moline, examining the workmanship on a pile of peasant-sewn quilts offered for sale. Selena walked over. The presence of the famed couturier's wife here in remote eastern France was more than a little surprising.

So was the other woman's reaction when Selena greeted her. Zoé almost jumped back in alarm.

"You!" she cried. "My God!"

"I'm sorry to have startled you. What on earth is wrong?"

"Don't play the innocent with me, my dear!" said Madame Moline in haughty accusation. "You . . . you murderess!"

"Murderess? What—"

"Yes. Don't lie. I heard all about it from Martha Marguerite. How much the poor woman suffers from the pain you have caused her! And after all she did for you too!"

"I don't understand. . . ."

The older woman marshalled her full supply of righteous sanctimony, which was considerable, and stated her case. "You needn't pretend with *me,* my dear. When you did not return, Madame LaRouche sent those two louts who work for her in search of you. They found the apartment in the Rue St. Denis, in which you apparently nested with a lover. And there they also found a man named Beaumain, who was supposed to have been your betrothed, dead of a gunshot wound. Ah, my dear, I know why you are here! You are on the run! They are hunting for you in Paris. . . ."

Selena, in spite of her horror, noted that Zoé had said nothing about Royce being in the apartment. She did not know what that portended, but she was not about to stand here and let Madame Moline run roughshod over her.

"Well, if you think I am a murderess, why don't you just go fetch up the local authorities and turn me over to them?"

Zoé's expression became cunning and just a little sheepish. "Oh, you'd like that, wouldn't you? What satisfaction you would derive if the King's couturier were to be captured by the rabble and sent back to Paris."

"Marc is here as well?"

"He is at the hotel, settling our bill. I would like nothing better, my dear, than to turn you over to the gendarmes, but we must make haste to Germany and safety."

"You? Why?"

"Because that is where their majesties have gone, and all those who loved and served them are seeking exile as well."

"The King has fled?" asked Selena. If Zoé Moline knew this dangerous bit of information, then how many others did too?

"All Paris knows!" the woman declared. "The National Assembly has issued a decree calling for His Majesty's arrest. But that has not happened yet, so we believe that he is safe in foreign sanctuary, God bless him. Ah, there is my husband. Our carriage is about to leave. I hope you get your just deserts.

"And you needn't bother to tell me *au revoir,*" she added, before huffing away.

Selena watched their carriage move off toward the border, then hastened back to the royal party. The footman had judged the hotel dining room to be too crowded, and had instead ordered a huge picnic lunch, which he was lifting into the coach as Selena approached. The King was standing on the ground next to the coach, looking somewhat irritated that his plans for a real meal had been thwarted.

"Better get inside," he told her coldly. The Queen, Francesca, and the children were already waiting in the vehicle.

Selena obeyed, but as she was settling herself in the seat, she glanced toward the hotel. There, on top of the steps, she saw a man. She did not know him, nor did he look her way. He was looking—staring—at King Louis XVI.

Selena knew right away: The King had been recognized. Even as she watched, the man turned decisively and moved off, as if going in search of aid.

"Your Majesty," Selena said, "I fear that your identity is no longer a secret here."

Louis looked startled. He climbed quickly into the coach. A brief order, and the party was on its way again.

"Why do you think I was recognized?" he demanded of Selena.

She told him about the man on the hotel stairs.

"He could have been anyone," hoped Louis. "Thank you for your concern, but there is no need to alarm my family."

Marie Antoinette was listening, aghast.

But Selena felt she had a responsibility in this situation, so leaving out that it had been Zoé Moline who'd given the news, she also mentioned having heard in the marketplace the fact that all Paris had learned of the King's flight.

Marie Antoinette gasped. Louis himself grew pale.

His fright did not last long, however, for as the coach left Varennes behind and approached the border, the royal stomach renewed its demand for sustenance.

"We must stop!" ordered the King, calling out to his driver. "Stop. I can wait no longer. Look, there is a fine place to picnic, right here along the roadside. . . ."

His wife protested, but the monarch was not to be gainsaid. Had he not traversed half of France in complete safety . . . and constant hunger? Was not the German border just up there ahead?

What could happen now, alarmists like Selena notwithstanding? She was not only a commoner, but a foreigner. Had he not been so kindhearted, he would have had her killed. His father would almost certainly have done so, and with his grandfather it would have been *ipso facto*.

The coach was halted, the food and wine spread about beneath gentle trees. Ah, a picnic in the countryside, just the thing for a fine June day.

The peasants and townspeople who crept up and surrounded this little band in the glade were resolute, but courteous and even deferential, as if reluctant to spoil the royal repast.

But they did.
The man from the hotel steps in Varennes was among them.
How fate and chance must laugh at the deliberate schemes of man.

23 Into the Fire

So the royal fugitives were turned back to Paris, which became a prison rather than a capital for them. Although the King swore to uphold the constitution passed by the National Assembly, news of his attempted escape destroyed whatever remnants of personal popularity he had managed to retain. Marie Antoinette who, it was discovered, had been in correspondence with foreign governments, was more detested than ever.

Just as dangerous to stability as the King's weakness was the growing power of the radical Robespierre. Not content with the reforms that had already been achieved, and driven on by the fecklessness and cowardice of Louis XVI, he sought more and more concessions, made ever more outrageous demands.

The Paris to which Selena returned was a far more dangerous city than the one she had left only days earlier. To say nothing of the fact that she was apparently being sought for the murder of Jean Beaumain.

If the flight to Varennes had been uncomfortable, the journey back to the capital was sheer psychological torture. The children were terrified by the people who gathered around the coach at every way station and peered insolently within. Louis mustered what dignity he could, but it was obvious that he was a beaten man. The Queen took refuge in a remote, icy reserve, which fell away only when darkness came.

"I want to thank you," she said to Selena, at one such moment, "for thinking so quickly when we were . . . when we were . . ." She could not bring herself to say "seized" or "arrested" and instead said ". . . required to change our itinerary."

Selena, mindful that her name might well be known to the Paris police, had identified herself as Yolanda Fee, maidservant. And while Princess Francesca had faltered in fear before her captors, Selena had given her name as Colette, also a maid.

Then they were again at the Tuileries, with the mob screaming and the torches blazing and the revolutionary banners waving and all the rest of it.

"I will be leaving now," Selena informed His Majesty, as they disembarked from the dusty coach and stood in the cobblestoned courtyard.

"Oh, please don't go," Francesca cried. "I feel so alone. Pray, remain here with me."

"No, I cannot."

She had to find Royce. They had to get out of Paris at once.

Then a steward approached the King. Selena overheard the message he conveyed. "Sire, your ministers await with Citizen Sorbante of the National Assembly. What is your pleasure?"

At that moment, Louis XVI was only a human being, fatigued beyond endurance, humiliated, beaten in spirit, reduced even in the eyes of his loved ones. "My pleasure is never to see any of them again!" he flared. "Get away, you jackass, and don't trouble me again."

But an instant later, he pulled himself together. He had to. "It's not your fault," he said to the shaken, crestfallen steward. "Tell them that I will join them within the hour. Why is Sorbante among them, I wonder?"

Selena, whose heart went out to the King at this time of travail, wondered the same thing.

And she decided that she had to reach Sorbante as well. He was, insofar as she knew, her only link to Royce Campbell.

"Your Highness," she said to Francesca, "I fear my mind is not with me. I spoke too hastily. If you will still have me, of course I shall be delighted to remain with you."

Francesca agreed gratefully, even soberly. She was still a very young and inexperienced girl, but the abortive trip to Varennes had begun a process of change and maturation. She had begun not only to grasp the nature of the political turmoil in France, she also understood that, if events grew more dangerous, life and death did indeed hang in the balance. The possibility of never seeing Prince William again had, only a short time ago, been fraught mainly with romantic pathos. Now it had become merely one eventuality, however important, in a commingled whirl of time and blood and duty.

The princess was growing up.

"Come with me to my bedchamber, Selena," she said. "Perhaps we can think of something . . ."

"You go along. There is something I must do. I shall join you presently."

Selena, still in her drab traveling clothes, entered the palace and made her way to the stateroom in which Louis was meeting with his ministers. Outside the closed bronze doors, awaiting a summons inside, stood Pierre Sorbante. For a man whose dream of revolution and power had come to pass, he seemed weary and rather dejected. The fact that he was here at all attested to his success, but it did not seem to cheer him much. He glanced at Selena, but did not recognize her until she spoke.

"It is you!" he exclaimed, breaking into a smile. Then he lowered his voice and glanced around, making certain that no one was eavesdropping. "There are many who would like to find you."

"I know. I have heard that I am being sought by the authorities."

"True, but that is not my meaning. The Vicomte Campbell has been worried about your welfare."

Selena's heart skipped a beat. Royce was alive!

"Where is he?" she asked. "How did you—?"

Sorbante lifted a hand. "He is safe. That is all I am going to tell you. It would be folly for you to attempt to go to him now."

"But I must!"

"In due time. In due time. He is a very lucky man."

"He was badly wounded . . ."

"Yes. But he is recovering. He was supposed to have met with me on the evening of the . . . of the incident in his apartment. When he did not appear, I sent one of my lieutenants to find out what had gone wrong. That is the only thing that saved him. We were able to get him to a doctor in time."

"And Jean Beaumain? The other man?"

"Buried. Some rich woman from the Right Bank arranged it all. But as I believe you know, she also gave your description— and her suspicions—to the police. May I ask what you're doing *here*?"

She told him, briefly but thoroughly, all that had transpired. "Royce and I had made plans to leave Paris," she concluded. "And I think we must follow through, or risk arrest."

"Or risk death," he corrected. "The shadow of death is all around us now. That is why I have sought an audience with His Majesty, and I hope he will listen to what I must tell him. Robespierre and the radicals are in control of the revolution now. There are demands for the heads of the King and the Queen, particularly after his ill-advised attempt at flight. Oh, I tell you, hundreds of heads will roll. Perhaps thousands. I see no hope of stopping it, unless the monarch abdicates."

"Do you think he will do that?"

"No."

"And what will happen then?"

"He and his entire family will be executed."

"My God, do you really think so?"

"I know so. Have you ever looked into the eyes of Maximilien Robespierre?"

Selena had, and she'd been reminded of Clay Oakley.

"I believe you," she said. "All the more reason for you to tell me where Royce is, so that we may flee immediately. He is still *vicomte*. We might be able to reach England."

Sorbante shook his head. "No, my dear. Campbell's title has been withdrawn. His espionage was discovered. I am protected now as a delegate to the National Assembly, but he is without shield. And let me further advise you, the people are watching those who leave Paris most carefully. In Brittany last week, a mob of villagers set upon a family of nobles who were attempting to escape to England and tore them apart. It was a frenzy of bloodlust. That is only one example out of many. Flight will be most difficult; everyone will be suspected. Moreover, Campbell is very weak. He should not travel at all. Riding a horse for any distance would open his wound and kill him."

Selena had listened and understood all these things with their attendant problems and difficulties. Yet in spite of hindrances, obstacles, barriers, there was always one way to prevail, wasn't there? If a person could only think clearly enough

That was difficult to do in a time of crisis, but she made the effort, reducing the problem to its simplest components.

She and Royce were both being sought in Paris.

To be safe, they ought to flee France.

But if they were caught during flight, they would be accused of trying to reach foreign shores in order to subvert the revolution therefrom.

And Royce was not fit enough for hard travel.

Down a corridor in the glittering Tuileries, just lounging casually against a wall, Selena saw death. He grinned at her, and winked. Death on a prison block in Paris? Or death in some unnamed village in the green countryside?

Did it matter which?

"We're going to try," she told Pierre Sorbante. "Can you arrange things so that Royce is brought down to the Seine, where the riverboats are?"

"Yes, I think so, but—"

"Please do it. And disguise him as an old man. As a very old man."

Sorbante regarded her quizzically. "I don't know if he'll like that. He *is* rather vain, you know."

Selena smiled. "You just tell him to do as I say, and I'll reward him well when I have the chance."

For the first time since they'd begun speaking, the revolutionary displayed a glimmer of genuine amusement. "I suspect that might convince him to obey," he said. "You will flee tonight, of course?"

"No. Tomorrow at mid-morning, when everyone is about. We shall hide in plain sight."

"Where have you been?" asked Princess Francesca, somewhat suspiciously, when Selena appeared in her quarters.

"I . . . I needed some time alone. To collect myself. But I am all right now."

The readiness with which the younger woman believed this deceit shot a stab of guilt through Selena's conscience. If what Sorbante had told her was true—and she had no reason to doubt him—Francesca's neck, as well as those of her aunt and uncle, were destined for the guillotine's caress.

There is nothing I can do, she told herself. *Royce and I must survive.*

But what of Francesca and William? her conscience demanded. Is their love any less precious than your own?

No, but what can I do about it?

You think you are so clever, contriving your own plan of escape! You might at least try and fashion a ploy for her.

It is out of my hands.

Francesca was called to dine with her family. Selena, of course, remained behind, eating from a huge tray of cold meats, cheeses, and vegetables that had been brought to her. There was even a bottle of Rhine wine. This largesse, too, made her feel guilty. Francesca was taking care of her, but she was prepared to abandon her young friend.

Fend for yourself, cherie. *The world is cruel.*

Sipping the wine, sitting near the window and watching darkness fall upon Paris, Selena remembered all those who had helped her in life.

Will Teviot, who had saved her from Darius McGrover in the Highlands long ago.

The common seaman, Slyde, who'd smuggled her aboard a ship in Liverpool. True, he hadn't done it so much out of charity as lust, but it had cost him his life.

Dick Weddington, the American spy.

Sean Bloodwell.

Royce.

Even Martha Marguerite, and Rafael, Jean Beaumain's friend.

So many had helped her during times of trouble and need, perhaps Davi the Dravidian most of all. He was long dead, but the remembered power of his beliefs stirred again, and she felt him alive and moving within the borders of her soul, dark and deft and wise.

"Do you feel the cross at your neck, Selena?" he asked her gently.

Yes.

"Take it off and read the words."

Selena did.

"There you have your answer," said Davi, departing.

Liberté. Egalité. Fraternité.

There is a lot of room for friendship in three words.

"I'll try to think of something," Selena said aloud.

Francesca returned from dinner, her face white as the tearstained linen handkerchief she held. Selena got up and rushed over to her. "What is it? What has happened?"

It took quite a while to bring the story out. A man—Sorbante—had informed Uncle Louis that very afternoon that the safety of the royal family could no longer be guaranteed. Riots had broken out in Paris and throughout the provinces—riots fomented by the radicals and Robespierre. Convents and monasteries were being sacked, priests and nuns mocked, tormented, and slaughtered like so many pigs. Men and women were copulating on the altars of cathedrals. Châteaux were afire, their owners hanged from trees. The pavingstones of Paris had been torn up for use as barricades, behind which mobs of workers stoned the authorities.

"And," concluded Francesca, "Uncle Louis has been advised that he might begin to give some thought to his own death."

So it had come to that. "Francesca," said Selena, "please take me to the Queen."

"But she has retired to her bed. She is distraught."

"Just take me to her."

"Why? There is nothing you can—"

"There is nothing I can do for her, true. But I can try to save *your* life, and that is what I am about to do."

Pomp and panoply are the most fickle, the least loyal of fair-weather friends, and the bedchamber of Marie Antoinette, Queen of France, was a contrast between grandeur and despair. The glory was all silk and softness, gilt and silver and bronze; frailty belonged to flesh alone.

The Queen lay face down on her extravagantly canopied bed. Her pillow was wet, but she had cried herself out for the present. A gaggle of ladies-in-waiting surrounded her, looking impotent and uncomfortable.

"Her Majesty does not wish to be disturbed," said one of them to Francesca.

"You just leave," replied the princess, showing a steel that Selena admired. "This is a private family matter."

The women did so uncomplainingly, with relief in fact. There are few things less pleasant than to attend the suffering of another and be able to do nothing about it. Moreover, each of those ladies, who had led a grand, privileged life at court, had begun to wonder if the price they might have to pay—death—made such a life worthwhile. They withdrew readily, if not gladly.

"Aunt Marie," said Francesca, "my friend wishes to speak with you."

In spite of her predicament, the Queen turned and looked at Selena with a touch of curiosity. "You again? What was your name? I have forgotten."

"Selena MacPherson." She rolled it on her tongue, proudly, as always. It was not her name itself, but the history of the name, the family, that made her pronounce it so.

"Another Scot," said the Queen, somewhat vexed. "The last Scot I befriended turned traitor on us."

She was obviously referring to Royce Campbell, and once again Selena wondered about the degree of intimacy that had existed between Royce and Marie Antoinette. But this was certainly not the time to inquire about it.

"My lady," Selena began, probing for the words she had spun out in her mind, "I have learned of the conditions now besetting France, and the danger they pose to you and yours."

"So?" interrupted the monarch, sitting up on the edge of the bed. "I do not want your sympathy. Go away. If I must die, let it be with honor, not pity. His Majesty and I both feel that way."

This meeting was getting off on the wrong track. Now it was Selena's turn to interrupt.

"My lady, I can arrange for your niece to be transported safely to England. There is no need for her to perish, if in fact, anyone must perish at all."

Marie Antoinette regarded Selena for a long moment, then gave a scornful little laugh.

"A nameless young thing like you?" she doubted. "What could you do? With your looks, what might you *ever* have done, seduction or attempted seduction excepted?" She made a loose gesture with her hand, as if dismissing Selena. "Child," she addressed the princess, "do not trouble me with this feeble prattle now. You are not going anywhere."

There was a long moment of silence. Selena tried to fashion a rebuttal. She did not have to, for suddenly the princess declared, without heat but with absolute conviction: "Aunt, I am going. I trust this woman, who is my friend."

The Queen looked shocked, then horrified.

"No, hear me out," Francesca went on. "When I was stumbling over my tongue in Varennes, it was she who gave our captors an alias. My presence here in France is not generally known. And Selena is aware of how matters work in England—"

Yes, indeed, thought Selena wryly. *I was thrown out for such knowledge.*

"—and knows her way about. I shall go with her."

"My lady," Selena pressed on, "I may look to you like one who is used to comfort and ease, and I confess that at times this was the case with me. But more often than not, I have had to deal with burdens that would have confounded many a man. And here I am alive to tell the tale."

"In any event, I am going with her," Francesca declared. "Of what use is it if we all perish? If I reach England, I shall marry William as planned, and perhaps one day our son will be a King. Is that not worth a risk, I ask you?"

Marie Antoinette, pressed thus to a facet of logic she understood very well, acquiesced. "Let it be done then," she said. There were fresh tears in her eyes when she embraced her niece this final time.

"Tell my story truly in days to come," she said. "I was a woman. I was as weak as any man. But if I must die, it will be as a Queen, not some vagabond emigré growing old in alien lands, dreaming of what has been lost.

"Go, both of you," she said. "May God be with you."

24 Sanctuary Deferred

Gendarmes swarmed about the river piers. Where once they had gladly obeyed the King and protected the nobles, their bread was now buttered on the other side. They swore fealty to the revolution, wore the cockade, and were on the watch for any nobles foolish enough to try to escape Paris by boat.

Selena knew that she would have to deceive them somehow.

The regular boat down the Seine to Le Havre was preparing to leave. Passengers were boarding, but the captain and an officer of the police stood at the base of the gangplank, questioning all prospective passengers. There were few travelers this day, which troubled Selena, who had counted on a crowd to hide amongst. Moreover, although she checked the dock carefully, she could see no sign either of Royce or Pierre Sorbante.

Selena and Francesca, dressed respectably but simply in togs of the *petit bourgeois* and carrying small bags, stood waiting near the gangplank. The captain, it appeared, was eager to be off. A portly, choleric man, he strutted nervously about. The police officer, however, was taciturn and observant.

"You there," he challenged the women. "What is your business? Do you wish to board or no?"

"Yes," said Selena, giving him the benefit of her smile and her eyes, "but we are waiting for our *grandpère*. He is to meet us here."

The officer squinted and examined Selena carefully, then Francesca. "Is that right?" he asked. "What are your names? Where are you bound? You wouldn't be members of the nobility, would you?"

"I resent the latter question, sir!" Selena said.

It had been decided that she would do the talking, since Francesca's Austrian-accented French was more noticeable than the remnants of her own Scots lilt. The officer spotted it nonetheless.

"You're a foreigner, are you not?"

"I do resent that as well, citizen gendarme. My parents sent me to study for a time in England, years ago. I am Yolanda Fee of Provence, and this is my sister, Colette."

The princess nodded emphatically.

"We go to take our *grandpère* to the coast. He is quite ill and requires the sea air."

Selena met his eyes all the while and contrived to look as innocent as possible, and just resentful enough of his questions to seem injured by them. If the man began interrogating Francesca, however, the game would become much more difficult.

"And where is this illustrious grandfather of yours?" asked the officer suspiciously, looking about. "Or perhaps he is a figment of your imagination?"

"Ready to leave in a few minutes," advised the boat's captain, ordering his crew to make ready for casting off.

"You would be surprised," the officer continued pointedly, "how many complicated stories I hear from people who are trying to leave the city. I admit, though, that a sick grandfather is a new one."

Royce, where are you? thought Selena. She had a momentary and extremely disquieting concern that perhaps she'd been gulled by Pierre Sorbante. What if this were all some monstrous treachery, with her as the victim? What if Sorbante, the revolutionary, had learned about Francesca and sought to have her captured? What if he'd been lying, and had known nothing of Royce's whereabouts?

What if Royce was dead?

A desperate political situation in which numerous groups with conflicting ideas battled one another led inevitably to virtually trackless patterns of betrayal and intrigue.

"You ladies boarding or not?" the irritated captain called out. "We're leaving."

"Please wait just one more minute," Selena pleaded.

"You don't say much, do you?" the officer asked, turning toward Francesca. "I don't like the smell of this at all. Perhaps the two of you ought to come with me to the barracks. I suspect a long chat might produce some facts."

"Hold up there! Hold up, if you will!"

It was Pierre Sorbante, moving slowly across the dock. Behind him, moving even more slowly on crutches, was a tall, bent figure in a cheap suit and a floppy shapeless hat that concealed his hair and a good portion of his face. Several days' growth of scraggly whiskers, powdered to look lighter, obscured a strong jawline that no grandfather, however healthy, would have retained. It was Royce.

"Grandpère!" cried Selena excitedly, so that both Royce and Sorbante would understand the ploy she had chosen. "Oh, *Grandpère,* I knew you'd arrive in time."

She rushed over to him and put her arms around him gently.

"Grandfather?" whispered Royce. "I hope you are enjoying this, Selena."

"Shhh."

Taking her cue, Francesca also approached Royce and gave him a daughterly peck on his stubbled cheek. He gave her a sharp look; he had no idea who she was.

Pierre Sorbante did, however, and for a long moment, as the revolutionary leader stood looking at the princess, Selena believed that her entire plan was about to fail.

"Citizen Sorbante," said the police officer, saluting smartly. "You know these people?"

Another long, long moment, then: "Yes, I do. You may permit them to board."

Royce, with Francesca's help, hobbled up the gangplank. Selena remained behind for a minute, and held out her hand.

"Thank you," she said.

"Now it is you who are in danger. I understand the feeling. Soon I will be in your shoes. Good fortune, whatever the future brings."

He released her hand and smiled.

"And you as well," she said.

Selena moved toward the boat, then turned. Sorbante had already begun to walk away.

"Citizen, before I leave . . ." she called after him.

He stopped and looked back at her. "Yes?"

"Let me give you this," she said, unfastening the gold chain and the cross from her neck. "It was meant for you, and it is a bit overdue, but I think Erasmus Ward would sleep more peacefully if he knew you had it."

"No, you keep it," the man protested. "It has served its purpose, and you have worn it faithfully and well."

"I insist," she said, walking toward him and pressing it into his hand. The moment was rich with meaning for them both, and tender.

"It is not considered gallant to refuse the request of a lady," said Sorbante, accepting the cross. "But," he added enigmatically, "when I have no more need of it, I shall see that it is returned to you."

"All aboard!" the captain shouted.

"See to your man," said Sorbante. "He is still very weak."

"I shall," Selena promised. "Love has a way of making people strong."

Then they parted. Selena walked onto the boat, where "grandfather," crutches at his side, had already been helped into a deck chair by Francesca. Ropes were loosened, knots unbound, and the boat drifted slowly away from the riverbank and out upon the waters of the Seine.

Later she would shed her tears for Jean Beaumain, and there were many. Later she would regret the turn of events that had set Martha Marguerite, once her friend, against her. Later she would appreciate, with a shudder or two, all that had happened to her in this city of lights, the maelstrom into which she had been drawn, and out of which she had emerged richer than before, in the mysterious process by which every event in life makes one richer.

Those things would come later.

But for now, joined again with Royce, Selena added Paris to the list of special places in her heart.

The journey to Le Havre took many days, since the boat stopped frequently along the way, either to take on passengers and goods or to off-load them. And at every stop, local revolutionaries would board to ascertain that enemies of the newly proclaimed Republic were not attempting to escape its authority. Royce had considerable money with him, should bribes be necessary—some things never change, no matter who is in power—but Selena kept him belowdecks when the boat was boarded. There, on a bunk in a dark cabin, out of the light, his beard growing longer and his face powdered white, he did indeed begin to resemble an older fellow.

"Mature and dignified," he proclaimed.

"Rickety and decrepit," laughed Selena.

But while the boat was on the water, he spent his time on deck, resting in the sun and growing stronger every day.

When they finally reached Le Havre, Royce was fit enough to move about without the crutches, albeit slowly. His abdominal wound was healing well, and his hand even more quickly, although a full measure of strength had not returned to it. He used a goodly share of his money to purchase a sluggish old one-sailer from a fisherman whose ears and nose had been cut off years before, and waited for a dark night and a good wind.

These came with July. Royce, Selena, and Princess Francesca got into the old scow, raised the sail, and moved slowly out into the English Channel. They struck a course northward toward Calais, thence westward. The boat was slow, the wind intermittent, but when, on the morning of the third day, Selena saw the first rays of sunlight playing upon the white cliffs of Dover, she let out a shout that must have carried all the way up the coast of England, to Scotland, must have echoed against the walls of Coldstream Castle itself.

"Almost home!" she cried. *"Almost home!"*

Those old stone walls of Coldstream seemed close enough to touch.

Elation proved to be transitory.

Royce eased the boat alongside the pier in Dover, and pulled down the patched old sail that had served so well. Francesca and Selena roped the vessel to the timbers of the dock, the princess looking eagerly, nervously, at this first manifestation of her new homeland. Initially, she'd thought the small but busy little port of Dover was London itself, and disappointment had darkened her features. Reassured by Royce and Selena, however, she was eager to set out for London, only sixty miles inland.

This she was able to do, in a stagecoach with Royce and Selena, but only after a fateful confrontation. Each of them ought to have foreseen it, in which case they would have put ashore not in Dover but somewhere along the coast. They should have foreseen it, but they did not, and the consequences of the confrontation itself did not seem particularly important at the time.

As they climbed up from the boat and onto the Dover docks,

the three fugitives, relieved to have made the journey safely, were approached and greeted by a blue-coated naval ensign. He was brisk, well-spoken, courteous, young. Even as he addressed them, his eyes went again and again toward Francesca.

"In light of the conflagration in France," he said, "I have been charged by military intelligence and the Foreign Office to make certain inquiries of those who arrive upon the shores of England."

"Go ahead," Royce said agreeably. His beard had grown in thickly; his color was good; his Scots accent proud and strong.

"Ah," exclaimed the officer, "none of you are French?"

"No," said Royce. "We managed to escape in the nick of time. All we want now is to go home."

"I congratulate you on your good fortune. May I ask your names?"

"Campbell," said Royce. Selena winced inwardly, even as she understood that Royce was incapable of giving any name but his own. Had he been before a firing squad, and told that he would be permitted to live if only he claimed to be someone other than he, he would not have done so. Pride in the name and pride in the man were one and the same.

"And I'm Mrs. Campbell," said Selena quickly, also in the accent of her land. She pointed toward Francesca. "And this is my sister, Colette."

The princess smiled at the guard, who blushed.

"Welcome to England," he said. "You may be on your way."

The three left the docks, found a hotel, ate a magnificent breakfast of ham, kipper, poached eggs, oven-toasted bread, butter, preserves, tea and brandy. Then they boarded the stage for London for a journey that would last all day.

Just before the coach pulled out, a messenger rushed up and handed the driver a thick, wax-sealed envelope. It had been sent by the naval officer on the Dover pier, and in it were several pages containing the names of all those who had entered the port during the preceding twenty-four hours. *Campbell, Mrs. Campbell, Colette (sister of Mrs. Campbell)* were the final entries on the last page.

The envelope was addressed to Colonel Clay Oakley, Military Intelligence, London.

There was not much opportunity for conversation in the coach, which the three travelers shared with a cigar-smoking tobacco merchant and two raucous, jubilant sailors on leave who ogled the women boldly until they noticed Royce staring at them. Francesca sighed deeply, repeatedly, as the journey progressed, her excitement mounting. By the time the stage reached London, shortly after dark, she was beside herself with excitement. Selena did not blame her one bit.

Once in London, Royce hired a horse-drawn hack.

"Buckingham Palace," he said authoritatively.

"I wonder if they shall permit me to enter," worried the princess. "What if they turn me away? I wonder if William is in residence there now?"

Selena patted her hand. Royce smiled. "Have no fear," he said. "We shall take you right to the front door."

"You shall enter with me!" Francesca decided.

Royce and Selena exchanged glances. "No, I think not," said Selena. "We have our own affairs to manage."

She and Royce needed to be alone and plan what to do next. They were, after all, both outlaws in the eyes of the crown; it was dangerous for them to be in England at all. His chances of achieving a pardon through the good offices of Louis XVI had vanished when his espionage activities in France had been uncovered; she was still considered a traitor to the throne and a spy to boot.

"But I simply cannot let you go off, not after what you have done for me," protested Francesca.

"Oh, I'm certain we shall meet again," Royce told her reassuringly. "You needn't go to any trouble on our account. In fact, you don't even have to mention us."

"Umgaublich!" cried the princess. "Unbelievable!"

"Truly, it would be for the best," Selena said, hoping she sounded casual and modest. "We have had enough excitement and attention. All we want now is to pursue our private lives."

"I don't think I understand," said the princess dubiously.

Selena herself did not feel that it was possible for Francesca *not* to mention those who had helped her flee France. She just hoped that she and Royce would be able to leave London before any connections were made, any inquiries pursued. Everything had gone so smoothly since the departure from Paris that she had almost begun to hope again. *Even plagues have to end sometime, don't they? Well, so do exile and bad luck.*

Then the palace loomed ahead of them, huge and broad and stolid, but looking somehow smaller than she remembered it as a child. There were torches evenly spaced atop the walls surrounding Buckingham, and soldiers on guard at the gate. Their boots and buttons gleamed even in the fiery light. The men themselves were impassive, incredibly dignified, cold as stone. Selena gave way to apprehension for a moment, then remembered how impressive her jailor, Corporal Phineas Bonwit, had looked in uniform, yet what a dull, common lout he really had been. These guards were men, that was all. She relaxed.

Francesca, however, did not. "Oh, I just hope William is here!" she fretted. "I have never met his family. It was all supposed to have happened so formally, so properly. Are you sure his letter, which you read in Paris, was not really just a gentle message of farewell?"

"I'm sure," said Selena.

"Any man who'd turn you down," added Royce, "would be a fool of the first order."

His words boosted her confidence instantly. She prepared to get out of the cab.

A high-hatted guard strolled insolently toward the vehicle. "Move along there," he admonished the hack driver. "It's not allowed to stop in front of the palace."

"But I have a passenger," the driver bleated cravenly.

"Bah! No one who comes here arrives in a flea-ridden junk like yours!"

Then Royce stepped down from the cab and addressed the guard. "Captain," he said, having noted the man's bars of rank, "how would you like a promotion?"

His manner of speaking, the deep voice and the authority in it, had an instantaneous effect.

"Sir?" asked the guard.

Francesca was getting down from the cab. (Selena thought it wise to remain inside, out of sight.)

"Here," said Royce, "is the Princess Francesca of Austria, betrothed of Prince William. She has just arrived from France, having managed to elude the revolutionary demon there. . . ."

The guard stared at Francesca, then bowed.

"You will take her inside immediately. Do I make myself clear?"

"Yes, sir. Yes, *sir!*"

His mission completed, Royce got quickly back into the hack. "Be off," he ordered the driver. He did not wish to remain there for the inevitable questions.

"The better part of valor," he said to Selena as the driver cracked his whip and the cab rolled away from the palace. Then he leaned over and kissed her on the mouth.

"We've done our part for love today," he said.

"Not yet. Not quite," Selena murmured.

Royce smiled. "Driver," he called. "Take us to a good hotel."

"You want something expensive?" the man asked over his shoulder.

"Just a nearby place with good food and good beds will be fine."

"Ah!" said the driver, urging the cab's horse into a hasty trot.

Princess Francesca's stunning appearance at Buckingham Palace produced a welcome that was as dramatic as anything she might have imagined in her wildest, happiest dreams. Prince William was there and he embraced her and embraced her again, unable to restrain his rapture. Every member of the huge royal family gathered to see her, to hear her tale. She had arrived, quite truly, as a heroine. Even the gouty old King, George III, roused himself from his bed and came down to have a look at her. Once, in celebration of her sixteenth name day, she'd drunk a glass of schnapps. The feeling she received in William's embrace was quite like that. No, it was better.

The only thing to mar her arrival—and it was just a silly little thing of no consequence—was the momentary appearance of an ugly, bald, hulking, monstrously muscled officer who wheezed disquietingly as, with the permission of George III, he drew her aside for a moment of conversation. He held a piece of paper in his hairless hand.

"Your Highness," he said respectfully, "when you entered at Dover, did you give your name as 'Colette'?"

"Yes."

She had never seen a smile, nor a mustache, quite like his.

"Thank you," he said. "That is all I need to know."

25 Tower

Selena pressed Royce's hand to her lips and kissed the small, scarred indentation left by Jean Beaumain's sword. She kissed all down the length of his arm, across his chest, down along his belly, and kissed also the healing scar at his lower abdomen. They were in bed, a good bed in a lamplit room in a good hotel in London.

"Does it pain you still?" she asked huskily.

"What are you talking about?" he gasped. "I cannot feel a thing."

"Ah, but you prevaricate, my darling," smiled Selena, "or do my eyes deceive me?"

She took him into her hands then, kneeling above him, one hand caressing slowly, remorselessly, up and down, up and down, the other circling and teasing and squeezing. He began to move beneath her, a powerful, involuntary, undulating rhythm. She inhaled audibly, closed her eyes, and threw her head back at the very thought of it.

"Lie down with me, Selena," he pleaded, bucking within the slip-slipping grasp of her flowing fingers. "I must have you."

"And you shall. If you promise not to move."

"What?"

"I have you again, after so long a time. I do not wish to be responsible for opening your wound. You must not move."

"How can I not? I—"

"Be still and I will show you."

In one sweet symphony of motion, Selena mounted and slid down upon him, crying out as his great shape pressed upward into her. She could feel everything, the swelling staff, the ridge of vein along its underside, the sudden, blunt rim of corona, the delicate cleft below the tip, which so often her tongue had teased.

"Oh, God. Selena—"

"Don't move," she commanded again. "I will do for both of us."

She began, with exquisite slowness, to rock back and forth upon him, back and forth and up and down, using her body as a velvet glove, pressing him ever more deeply into her, pressing herself against him, feeling his pleasure and her own. She was satisfied with this for a time, smiling as rapture darkened his face and dulled his eyes with ecstasy and love.

But there came a time when this was not enough, insufficient, when flesh began to beg for more. And although she had promised herself, vowed to herself, that she would ride slow as time across the highlands of delight, the demands of her body rose up to overthrow resolve and will. She did not know—and very soon she did not care—just when her own will had slipped out of her control, but she was leaping and twisting and plunging, her body, her head, her flashing golden hair, all.

Then he began to move, once, twice, thrice, all but casting her off.

He stopped.
She stopped.
They waited.
Then it came.

They were silent and still in commingled, closed-eyed wonder, but every cell in their melded, mesmerized bodies screamed in holy joy.

"I told you not to move," she scolded him later, lying in his arms. The lamp had gone out and the room was very dark.

"I'm sorry. Give me another chance."

"Soon," she sighed.

"How soon?"

"Quite."

"Before dawn?"

"I don't want dawn to come."

Thought of the morrow sobered them both a bit.

"I expect we had better leave London as soon as possible," he said. "We can go to the Highlands for a time. We will be safe with my clan. There we can determine if there is any chance of getting Coldstream back for you. If not, we may wish to return to America. We're welcome there. I have berthed the *Selena* in Bremerhaven."

It sounded as good a plan as any, besides which they would be together. "I'd like to try to see my adopted daughter, Davina, before we leave here though," Selena said.

"If you think Lord Bloodwell can be trusted not to turn us in."

"He won't. I spoke to him in Paris."

"All right," Royce said. "It is agreed. Our good times are just beginning."

"I'll remember today always," replied Selena.

The words touched a chord in her memory. Happy times. Good days. Those were the things that sustained one during times of darkness and distress. She heard her father's words again: *"Pick a special day. One that warmed you so much and in a manner so fine; the heat of it can reach across the years. . . ."*

Selena thought back across the years. She was about four or five, playing in the summer garden at Coldstream, building out of vines and sticks, grass and flowers, her own miniature castle. For hours she had worked away at that castle, the tiny girl she had once been, and then—she couldn't remember exactly—something had happened. The wonderful structure was torn down, destroyed, or perhaps it fell in upon itself. In response to her cries and tears, her father had rushed out into the garden, viewed the disaster, and pronounced it less than the ultimate tragedy it seemed. And for the rest of that lost, golden afternoon, he sat beside her in the warm grass, with the perfume of flowers in the air, and together they built a new castle, of love as well as grass, that reached up to where he said the sky began. *"Right here, Selena,"* he had said, touching the castle top. *"Can you touch it? This is where the sky begins."*

"Yes," she had answered.

"Remember this, and remember Coldstream. Think of it now. Not as it looks when you ride down toward it out of the Lammermuir hills, but the way it looks when you come up to it from the sea, with the clouds moving in the sky beyond, and Coldstream riding against the sky like a great ship. . . ."

"Darling, you're crying!" said Royce.

"Good tears, though. Pay them no mind and love me again."

"Put out the lamp first."

"Why?"

"Because I have something in mind for you."

"I think that sounds delicious," said Selena, slipping out of bed and blowing out the light. But when, in complete darkness, she returned to bed, Royce was not there.

"Darling?"

"Lie down," he commanded. "Lie down and don't move. It is my turn to tease you now."

"I don't want to be teased. I want to be—"

"And you shall. But only when I decide it is time. I must, however, add one proviso to sweeten the stakes. You may cry out if you wish, but you must not move, no matter what happens. Or else I shall stop."

"Stop? Stop what?"

"You'll see. Lie down."

Shuddering with anticipation, Selena did as she was bidden. She could feel Royce's presence there in the darkness, very near, but she was unprepared when he suddenly bent to her bare breasts, kissing one nipple and gently caressing the other. She gasped, barely suppressing an impulse to thrust herself upward, reach out her arms and hold him to her.

Suddenly, just when Selena thought she could bear no more, Royce withdrew, laughing softly in the darkness.

"Midnight, and all's well," he said.

"Come. Do it again. I cannot wait."

"Oh, I'll bet you can, if you want more. . . ."

Then he began again, this time kissing her belly, and it was all she could do to keep from moving, writhing. On and on, he pressed and retreated there in the lingering, lambent darkness, igniting tiny bonfires of delight all over her naked, burning body. Everywhere he kissed her, everywhere, until Selena felt a trembling in the pillars on which the earth was founded. The soft, knowing flick of his tongue, when it came, sent her entire body into unspeakable spasms of splendor, shattering her to such an extent that her senses became disoriented. Her lips were dry, her fingers numb. Velvet darkness hung like a veil over her eyes. Even the air hung heavy with the scent of a familiar perfume.

No, it was a cologne.

"Royce?" she gasped, trying to sit up.

The door to the room swung open. Light from lanterns carried by a gang of soldiers spilled into the room, illuminating Royce and Selena there upon the bed, their skin glowing red like fire.

"Oh, how splendid!" said Colonel Clay Oakley, chortling into his scented handkerchief. "Bind Campbell," he ordered his minions.

There were half a dozen of them, all armed. Royce had no chance to resist.

Oakley approached the bed. Selena had hastily covered herself with a sheet, but he ripped it away.

"My beauty! I have you now, at long last. How tawdry that lust was your undoing. Lust, and a chatty hack driver. Such a disappointment, isn't it?"

"You touch her—you even *breathe* on her—and I'll kill you!" promised Royce.

"Club him," Oakley said, with a shrug.

One of the soldiers brought the butt of his blunderbuss down on Royce's head. He sagged unconscious to the floor.

Selena's scream was cut off when Oakley wrapped a huge hand around her throat. "Save your breath," he leered. "Your time has come to pass, and you will die screaming on the morrow."

He flung her aside and stood over her, triumphant, implacable and icy cold.

"Take them to the Tower," he ordered. "Chain them in the lowest level, in the same room. They shall watch each other die."

The Tower, in which so many had perished, in which so many more had suffered and languished, was not a tower at all but a fortress. Originally built by William the Conqueror as a lookout point on the banks of the Thames, it had been expanded willy-nilly over the centuries, and had also, in due course, assumed the function of a prison.

"You should be honored by your incarceration in this monument to pain," Oakley told Selena, gasping and wheezing. His affliction seemed to have worsened considerably since she'd first met him in New York.

"I demand a hearing," Selena said, as she was hurried into the depths of the fortress. "I demand a trial."

Oakley laughed a hacking, coughing laugh. "You and your lover are traitors and spies. Your only right is to suffer."

Royce had to be carried into the cell, and regained consciousness only as he was being chained to the wall. Selena had already been manacled to the stones. They were both naked, completely vulnerable. Oakley affixed a smoldering torch to a sconce on the wall.

"Pleasant dreams," he said. "I shall see you in the morning."

When he had gone with his men, the lovers looked at each other.

"Are you all right?" Selena asked.

Royce rattled the heavy chains. There was no way to free himself. "Certainly," he grinned.

"Me too," said Selena.

"I ought to have been more careful. We should have left London immediately."

"Perhaps. But I would not have given up what we shared tonight for anything."

"Nor I," he said. "Anyway, you were obedient. You didn't move at all."

In spite of themselves, they laughed, which alerted a guard who soon peered in between the iron bars of the door.

"My man!" said Royce. "A thousand pounds sterling to you if you set us free."

The man was mystified. "Are you mad, sir? I'd be killed if I so much as brought you a drink of water."

"Wine will do then," said Royce. "Or cake. That's it. Cake. Cake-eating is quite the rage these days, I understand."

Selena laughed.

"Don't mock me," said the guard, simultaneously bewildered and humiliated, although he did not understand why.

"Well, Selena," Royce said, almost sadly, when the man had gone, "we have no say in the matter of where we are born, nor in where we die. But at least we'll be together. It will be very bad, though."

"I know," she nodded. "But we *will* be together."

26 A Favor Repaid

Selena's arms were bound to the stone wall at the wrists, which were higher than her head, so by morning the blood had run out of her fingers and she was numb. She was also very cold. She and Royce had comforted each other during the night, and the strange thing about it was that they did not even mention death. What good would that have done? There is a certain solace in the inevitable. Uncertainty produces far greater quantities of vexation.

Colonel Oakley appeared just before Selena's feet had turned completely blue from the cold. He seemed almost boyishly cheerful and eager, and carried two flat, black cases which he set down on the floor. After putting a fresh torch in the sconce, he stood back and regarded his victims.

"Dawn," he leered, the firelight flickering on his gleaming pate. "The moment of truth."

"You wouldn't know truth," Royce grinned at him, "if it walked right up to you and yanked off that silly hairpiece on your upper lip."

Oakley flared, but kept his anger in check, and took a long whiff of his silk handkerchief.

"You are a moronic grotesquerie," Royce added.

The colonel gave his unsettling smile in return, bent and opened one of his two cases. To Selena's astonishment, he pulled out a sketch pad and a piece of charcoal. "You will forgive me," he panted, as he began to sketch them hanging there on the wall, "but I like to keep a record of my work."

He studied them for a long moment, lost in contemplation, and then proceeded. His eye was good, his strokes quick and sure. Now and again, he paused to add an extra detail, smiling with pleasure as he did so.

"You are completely mad," said Selena.

"Those with a devotion to beauty generally are," he responded, unperturbed. "Turn your head slightly to the right, will you?"

Presently, Oakley was finished. He showed them his handiwork proudly. Everything was right: the gloom of the cell, the curves of Selena's body and the musculature of Royce's physique, even the ponderous, bleak weight of the chains could be seen in his sketch.

"When you are gone from this life," Oakley said, "I shall draw quite another picture. I shall gaze upon it often in years to come. It will remind me how much pain you have caused me over the years, yet how—in the end—the balance of nature was restored when I evened things with you."

"Stop your blithering, you faker," said Royce. "Your talent is as common as a barmaid's swill-rag."

For an instant, Selena wished that Royce had not spoken thus. His words could only fuel Oakley's rage. But when she saw the colonel's face turn red, saw him fight for breath, she realized what Royce intended. Somehow, he meant to use Oakley's physical affliction against him, to take away his concentration and his strength.

But the evil officer was clever too, and saw immediately what Royce sought to achieve. He breathed through silk again, then smiled.

"I do not provoke," he said. "No, do not try me. Death can be quick, or death can linger. I am not, as you may think, a monster. Justice is my goal, not simply retribution, although, of course, the two are linked."

"Certainly in your foul mind," said Selena.

The grimace of a smile. "Think what you like."

"I shall."

"Think what you like of me, for now it is time to settle."

Having said this, he bent and opened the second case, which contained several pliers, thumbscrews, daggers, and a small, supple whip.

He stared at the instruments intently, then looked up at his victims. "My, my, nothing I have here will produce a quick death. Pity, isn't it. Now, which of you shall I begin with?"

"Start with yourself," said Royce. "Put a clamp on your hind end and tighten it until your brains run out—"

Maddened, Oakley took up the whip and slashed out wildly, cutting Royce once, twice, thrice across the shoulders and chest.

Royce cried out.

Selena screamed.

Oakley turned to her. "Ah! It pains you to see your lover suffer, does it? I suspect it will pain him more to watch you in agony."

Selena thought, as she watched the colonel pick up a brace of thumbscrews, that she heard a scurrying, a kind of commotion somewhere in the prison, but it was only a momentary notion. Her attention turned fully to the ugly little device that Oakley slipped over the small toe on her left foot.

"So cold," he oozed, stroking her bare foot. "We shall warm it up. Did it ever occur to you?" he asked, deftly turning the screw. "Did it ever occur to you how a part of the body as small and inconsequential as this could cause so much"—he turned the screw once again—"pain?"

Selena screamed.

Royce struggled against his chains. "You bloody bastard—"

Then from the doorway of the cell, which was open, came a voice of cold and utter command.

"Colonel, on your feet! At attention! Now!"

Lord Sean Bloodwell stood there, with a cold, frightening fury Selena had never dreamed he possessed.

Oakley, in spite of his immense powers, was merely an officer. Sean Bloodwell was a lord of the realm. There was no question about who wielded the greater authority. A covey of officers appeared behind Sean then, and his orders were quick and sharp.

"Arrest the colonel and put him in chains. I shall deal with him later.

"Take that device from the lady's foot. Unchain her and the man.

"Bring them clothing. *Now*, do you hear me!

"And food and drink.

"Fetch a physician, and be quick about it."

But Oakley was loath to capitulate without protest.

"You are meddling in affairs of which you know nothing," he whined, squaring his muscular bulk to face Sean. "These two are, and have been for some time, sworn enemies of the Empire. I am fully within my rights here."

"Not anymore. Royce and Selena rescued the Princess Francesca from almost certain death in France. His Majesty has proclaimed a full pardon for both of them!"

That was how it happened. That was how Selena heard the news. Naked, and chained to a wall in the Tower, she was reborn in glory.

"I had a suspicion that something like this must have happened," Sean continued, as Oakley was seized and manacled, as Royce and Selena were set free and wrapped in blankets. "And when I learned that our fine colonel had spoken both to the princess and to the cab driver, I set out on the trail myself. Had I been more effective as a sleuth, I might have gotten here earlier."

"Sir, you arrived most propitiously," said Royce, "and henceforth you may call my debt to you in any way, at any time."

Selena saw the two men regarding one another. She had loved them both; both of them loved her. Had it not been for that tremendous and complicated bond, of which she herself was at the center, they might never have met. Certainly they would not have grown to appreciate in each other the presence of vast reserves of honor. Sean's great gift was that he understood both his own nature and the nature of love. And he also understood Selena. He knew that her love would seek its own high, wild level, on a plane at which Royce Campbell also dwelt. His own character, gentler and more contemplative, would have been altered or destroyed were he to have forced Selena to remain with him. Love that is forced is love already dead. Sean knew that too.

"Selena," he said, when they left the Tower and came out into glorious sunlight, "Francesca and Prince William are to be wed at Westminster a fortnight hence. You and Royce, of course, will be expected to attend. But I know that there is something else you desire, the return of Coldstream Castle. It depends entirely upon you. While the monarch can grant a pardon, he cannot, according to parliamentary laws, restore your family estate. You must make an appeal, in person, to the House of Lords. If you can convince those luminaries, of which I am one, that you have earned the right to get back your lands, they will so recommend to the King, and he will approve. But first you must convince the lords. How soon can you prepare yourself to do that?"

"I am ready right now," Selena said.

27 Glory

London began to change. News of the forthcoming royal wedding served as a tonic to the capital city, which had been taut and bleak with continued tales of revolutionary depredations in France. Robespierre, it was accurately reported, had consolidated his control over political events, and each day new accounts of arrests and beheadings made their way across the English Channel. What better way to blot out such tidings than a wedding! Flags and pennants began to appear in the city, until the entire roadway from Buckingham to Westminster became a bright flutter of pageantry and festive banners.

Royce and Selena, due to their efforts on behalf of Princess Francesca, were offered apartments in the palace until the wedding was over. They demurred, wanting to retain what privacy they could, a task difficult enough in the light of new notoriety. Selena had also to prepare her plea to the House of Lords. Sometimes the thought of addressing those remote, bewigged, berobed dignitaries almost frightened her out of her wits, but the thought of Coldstream urged her on. Sometimes she sat in bed with paper and quill, Royce asleep beside her, pondering words. Other times she walked down to the banks of the slow-flowing Thames, brooding on history, life and time. Days went by, and all she had composed was one sentence:

My Lords, I stand before you, a daughter of Scotland.

It seemed sufficient to her, sufficient to attain Coldstream, which was rightfully hers. Yet she understood that one sentence was unlikely to sway the most important men in the Empire, who remembered all too well the historic centuries-long animosity between England and Scotland.

But she could write no more.

"It is up to you," she prodded herself. "It is up to you alone. You *must* find the words."

She searched for them, but none were revealed to her.

Several days before the wedding, she and Royce received an invitation to the Bloodwell mansion in St. John's Wood. They dressed, a carriage called at their hotel, and they went. Expecting some form of pre-nuptial gathering, Selena wore a stunning, ivory-hued gown, with a simple strand of pearls at her throat. Royce was resplendent in breeches and silk stockings, velvet jacket and gleaming white shirt. Yet no matter how he dressed, no matter how civilized his attire, he always seemed, just beneath the surface, the feral, spirited, half-ironic, half-amused animal he was.

"Selena, I yearn for the Highlands," he moaned, as they drove along toward Sean's residence. "After the wedding, I shan't wear another cravat for the rest of my life."

"I don't know about that," she retorted, "but I know that you won't have much need of attire for a while."

"Oh? I believe I have heard something along those lines before."

"From whom? Marie Antoinette?"

"A lady would never ask, and a gentleman would never tell."

"Hah! You are no gentleman."

"And there are times, I confess with gratitude, when you are not a lady."

Sean's home came into view then, a stone-and-timber masterpiece beneath the towering trees of St. John's Wood.

"You might be living there now, Selena," said Royce, "if you'd played your cards differently."

Selena kissed him. "I played my cards the only way I knew, and I have won," she said.

Selena, who had been expecting a great crowd, saw with surprise that the circular drive was deserted. No one was present but an eager footman, who grasped the reins of the horses and bade the visitors to go inside. This they did, Royce banging boldly the heavy brass knocker on the door. It was opened immediately, neither by butler nor doorman, but by a young woman of exquisite beauty, whose sweet face was drawn up in tension. Selena knew her on sight.

"Davina!" she cried, opening her arms.

"Mother!"

Tears flowed freely for a long time, as well they might. The waif that Selena had rescued out of the depths of ancient India was grown now, but in spite of the years between then and now, no love had been lost. Sean Bloodwell had kept Selena's memory alive in this house and in Davina's heart, and he had done well. He came from inside the residence now to take Royce's hand and hat. "Perhaps, sir," he said, "it would be best if the two of us were to withdraw for a short time?"

Selena held her adopted daughter, remembering the last time they'd been close in America. It was on the fateful morning that she and Royce had been attempting to flee America. Oakley's men had captured her; Royce was disappearing over the horizon on the *Selena,* and she stood there in the Long Island surf. Then another ship, the HMS *Lucifer,* had sailed by. On board her, Selena knew, were Sean and Davina, returning to England and to glory. The ship was too far away from shore for Selena to have seen them, even if they'd been on deck, nor would they have been able to identify Selena, standing in the surf, surrounded by Oakley's menacing redcoats. But she had raised her arm to them anyway in a farewell salute. *Think of me kindly,* she had prayed, *for I shall never forget you.* She let her hand fall. The *Lucifer* rode proudly to the wind, bearing two whom Selena loved, homing on both the future and the past.

Now, again, past and future were united in embrace. "Oh, Mother!" the girl cried, struggling to control her joyous tears. "You're not going away again, are you? I can't bear it if you go away again."

"I'll never be farther from you than Coldstream Castle," Selena replied, putting her daughter's head upon her shoulder and stroking her soft golden hair.

Not if I can find the right words.

Those words did not come, and on the morning of the day that she was to appear in the House of Lords, Selena awoke from a fitful sleep into an even more disquieting distress. Her thoughts seemed to be flying all over, shooting out of her head like tracers trailing sparks.

"You have never given way before, Selena," said Royce soothingly, bringing her a cup of tea, "and you won't give way now. The thought of regaining Coldstream has sustained you during times far darker than these. You are only one step away from your goal."

"That is what bothers me," Selena worried. "When I was in India, ten thousand miles away, Coldstream was a dream. When I was three thousand miles away from it in America, the reality was still remote. But now I am only a few day's travel from hearth and home. And if I fail in my petition to the lords, all is lost. The closer I get, the higher becomes the risk. I don't even know what I am going to say!"

"Just tell them what is in your heart."

"There are too many things in my heart; that is the problem."

The scheduled appearance of a woman in Parliament, and a woman rumored to be beautiful at that, lent an air of episode and event to the normally ornate and stuffy chamber. With the wedding imminent, many of the lords were loath to don their wigs and robes and come here at all. What did it matter to them, after all, that a castle in far-off Scotland hung in the balance? Still, the woman in question *had* saved the prince's bride-to-be, and they could not very well refuse to hear her out without risking the lift of royal eyebrows.

They took to their benches insouciantly, some of them still half-asleep, and not a few of them already tipsy with wedding champagne.

"I say," rasped Lord Rittenham to his benchmate, Lord Pulvester, "is this MacPherson woman kin to old Seamus, who tried to make Scotland independent of the crown?"

"One and the same, sir."

"What a cheeky wench, I vow. Has she no propriety whatever?"

"It is my understanding," whispered Lord Brockett to Lord Spencer, as those two stalwarts waited for Selena to speak, "that the woman, even now, is playing whore to that cutthroat, Campbell, right here in London."

"And 'tis not the first time, if I hear correctly," nodded Spencer. "Many's the man who has tended her garden."

The two looked at each other and chortled.

The Duke of Sussex, languid and haughty as always, happened to overhear their ribaldry.

"Perhaps she might give us a flower or two for our favorable votes," he snickered.

In the antechamber, where she waited with Royce until she

should be summoned to speak, Selena fought to control her nerves. Her hands were wet and her lips dry. Countless times in the past she had used her mind and guile to persuade others to act in her behalf, but never before had she spoken to an assemblage. She tried not to feel intimidated, tried to remember with what ease, humor, and grace her father had addressed great throngs, always finding the right words and tone, no matter if his audience was comprised of peasants or nobles.

"I *will* do it," she murmured.

"What, darling?" asked Royce.

"Nothing."

The sergeant-at-arms appeared at the antechamber's doorway. "They are ready to hear you now, madame," he said. "Come with me, please."

Royce took her into his arms and kissed her gently on the lips. "Just let your heart speak," he said, looking deeply into her eyes. "And remember this: even if you do not convince them, we still have each other."

Yet I must convince them, she thought. *Royce and Coldstream are my life. God, give me the words!*

Taking a deep breath, she followed the sergeant-at-arms out of the antechamber and into the well of the House of Lords. There was a buzzing in her ears, which continued even as the buzz of conversation among the desultory lords subsided.

Selena stood before them, all alone.

"Hear ye! Hear ye!" called a bewigged speaker ceremoniously. "We are gathered at the request of one of our members, Lord Bloodwell"—Selena saw Sean smiling encouragement from his bench—"to entertain the petition of one Selena MacPherson." Ah, it was wonderful to hear the MacPherson name intoned here. "So pray give your attention, my lords."

Dead silence.

Every eye was on Selena.

Her tongue seemed frozen, her throat dry as sawdust. What had she planned to say? *My Lords, I stand before you . . .*

Yes, yes. Say it! Speak! Get it out, get started. . . .

Not so easy.

Some of the lords began to shift in their seats. A few of them grinned. What travesty was this? The wench couldn't even open her mouth, for God's sake!

But then, far back in Selena's mind, she heard the wise, sympathetic voice of Davi the Dravidian, her teacher. *"Selena, have you come all this way to be defeated? You don't believe that, not even for an instant. Trust your heart, for the words are in it. Trust your life, for it has made your heart sing and be strong. Do not* think! *Open yourself and let that which is within emerge."*

Go!

"My Lords," Selena began, lifting her chin, "I am Selena MacPherson, and it is as a daughter of Scotland that I stand before you."

Her voice, low and powerful, carried easily in the historic chamber. She had the attention of the assemblage. But what next?

Don't think, just speak.

"I stand before you as one who has been cast out, cast out by time and circumstance and fate, cast out, yes, by folly, but who amongst us has not tasted the bitterness of life?"

"Lord be praised," whispered Lord Spencer to Lord Brockett, "the wench is a bloody orator." He leaned forward to listen more closely.

"I would ask you," Selena continued, "to think now upon your homes and your lives. And upon England. Yes, think upon England too, for then, if your hearts hold mercy, you may understand my need, my torment, here this day."

"I thought she was a Scot," wondered Lord Pulvester, harumphing to himself.

"When I was still a young girl, my father fell upon bad times. I am not here to debate whether he erred, for it is not my right to judge him. He was good to me and kind to his subjects and acted according to the knowledge God had granted him. Because of his actions, he was dispossessed and later murdered. I love him still, no matter how men may gauge him, and I love my home as well.

"Who among you," she continued, "has not in some way, at some time, felt alone? Even in the comfort of your great halls, has there not been a moment at which life seemed to fall down upon you, in all its random complexity? I was abducted to India, and there I was very alone until befriended by Lord Bloodwell, who sits in honor among you. I was alone in America too, until I chanced to meet kindred spirits with whom my heart beat as one. Right or wrong in the eyes of the world, yet I was true to my heart as God had given me to know it.

"Yet always I have thought of home, of Coldstream Castle, and of this green, mighty isle of which it is, and ever shall be, a part. We, all of us, have that feeling inside us. We, all of us, would do most anything to find the path back to hearth and peace.

"If you can understand that, then you understand me as well.

"I wish you all safe havens, and sweet journeys thereto."

She stopped and looked around. Every eye was upon her, but she could not read, in the rapt faces of the lords, any reaction to what she had said. The chamber was completely silent.

I have failed, she thought.

The sergeant-at-arms led her out without comment.

"Oh, Royce!" Selena cried, throwing herself into his embrace. "It is all over. They listened, but they did not hear."

"I wouldn't be too certain of that. You were magnificent. I almost had tears in my eyes."

"Almost?"

"As you know, I am not easily given to tears. Neither, I think, are the lords."

Sean Bloodwell entered then, and kissed Selena on the cheek, taking her hands in his own. "It was beautiful, Selena," he said.

"But the lords did not react!"

"How could they? They could do nothing in the spell of your words."

"What is going to happen now?" she asked, a trifle anxiously.

"Well, they will take your plea under advisement, and make a decision in due course."

"In due course? You mean I must wait?"

"Selena, many of these men have not, in twenty years time, decided anything more complicated than which horse to ride on a hunt. But their word will be passed in due time, and I believe it will be to your liking."

"You only *believe* it?"

"All right, it will almost certainly be in your favor."

"*Almost?*"

Sean smiled. "Selena, all I am trying to tell you is that you did splendidly, and everyone who heard you knows it. These matters take time. You must, for once in your life, be patient."

"I shall go mad being patient."

"Well, then do something distracting to try to put the matter out of your mind. Why not join Davina and me for the wedding festivities? We will be in the line of march from the palace to Westminster." He turned to Royce. "You are welcome too, of course."

"You honor me, sir," said Royce, bowing. "And may I add that you are possessed of more courtesy and grace than I have found in any man?"

Yes, thought Selena. What Royce said was true. But would the rest of the lords prove to have even a portion of Lord Bloodwell's gifts?

Selena stood beside Royce and watched as Princess Francesca came out of the palace and walked, attended by the ladies of the court, to the carriage in which she would take her final ride as a maiden. She looked radiant, glowing, transported already by the wonder awaiting her. Trumpets heralded her appearance. She was a flower, a shining, white rose, and the ladies around her were as flowers too. The early morning had been gray, damp, foggy, but now the sun pierced through clouds. Always a good omen.

A sign of sanguine portent also were the tens of thousands of cheering citizens who flocked the route of the nuptial procession. Some of them had waited all night for a choice spot along the thoroughfare from which to glimpse the bride. Their numbers and their unrestrained enthusiasm meant that the princess would be accepted in England, in contrast to the animosity that her aunt had engendered amongst the people of France.

Adding to Francesca's luster was the news, which had been widely bruited, of her spectacular escape from France, and many cheers were directed toward the open coach in which Royce and Selena rode with the popular Lord Bloodwell and his daughter. They were hailed all along the way, and when the procession slowed at corners, men, women, and children jam-packed in front of pubs and shops lifted glasses of ale or gin to toast the saviors of the princess.

"Is it not passing fine," smiled Sean to Selena and her man, "to be a king and ride in triumph through Byzantium?"

Selena could not but agree that everything about the day was thrilling, and she would have enjoyed it more had the lords seen fit to hasten their decision. She noted, too, that Royce seemed a trifle reserved, he who always loved to cut a figure, to enjoy himself to the fullest. While they were disembarking from the coach and preparing to enter Westminster for the wedding ceremony, she inquired about the reason for his mood.

"You oughtn't to worry on my account," she said, taking his arm. "As you said, we'll be together no matter what befalls."

He smiled sardonically. "It is not that, Selena."

Something else? What? "You think they will deny my petition, don't you?"

"No."

She could see that he did not mean to speak further about whatever was on his mind, and she could not pursue it anyway because the time had come to enter Westminster. Among all the great churches of England, this was perhaps the most famous, yet it was nothing compared to the cathedral of love and devotion built between—and by—William and Francesca when they took their vows. *Royce and I will be married at Coldstream,* Selena decided as the ceremony ended. The very air shivered as the mighty organ blasted joyous chords, and a choir of two hundred voices sang in praise of love. Leaving the church down the main aisle, her arm upon her new husband's, Francesca's eyes met Selena. Momentarily, she eschewed protocol, stopped, and embraced Selena right there and then. It was something so natural, so moving, that people waiting and watching in the pews began to applaud, a tribute that increased in enthusiasm when the princess hugged Royce too.

"That cannot have hurt your cause with the lords," Royce said. Still, he seemed uncharacteristically subdued in the carriage on the return drive to the palace, where a great reception had been planned. Champagne did not alter his mood, and he barely partook of the feast: oysters, crabmeat pate, lobster, salmon, and roasts of beef, pork, lamb. Roasted chicken, coated with chocolate, proved a great favorite, and there were breads and fruits and vegetables of every kind.

Selena found herself feted by hundreds of people. She did not have a chance to ask Royce what was troubling him, and saw that he watched the proceedings warily. As the dancing was about to commence, she made an attempt to break through his reserve.

"What is the matter?" she asked directly.

"Selena, perhaps it would be best if we left now."

"Now? The fun is barely started. I—"

She was interrupted then by the Duke of Sussex, haughty and supercilious, who appeared before them out of the gay, swirling crowd. He had the reputation of an indefatigable—and successful—schemer in political matters, as well as a notorious and energetically earned record as a prodigious womanizer. He bowed formally and coldly to Royce, who returned the greeting in kind, and then stared into Selena's eyes.

"Pray grace me with the pleasure of your company in the minuet that is about to commence," he said smoothly, as if he were doing her a favor.

She had an impulse to refuse. His cold, thin, colorless face, while not unappealing in a primitive sort of way, possessed little human warmth. But he was one of the men who must vote on her petition—perhaps he wished to speak to her about it—and she could not afford to offend him.

"I am honored, sir," she said. Nodding to Royce in a plea for his understanding, she took the duke's proffered arm and walked with him out upon the dance floor. To her surprise, however, he kept on going, past the people who were taking up positions for the dance, through the drinking, laughing onlookers beyond, and into a sunlit alcove near a tall window. The window looked out upon intricate gardens, and the sun flooding through it showed the duke's cold face in all of its unsuccessfully veiled cruelty and ruthlessness.

"My Lord?" she asked. *They have turned down my plea for Coldstream. He wants to enjoy telling me.*

But no.

"You are a very lovely woman, Selena," he oozed, addressing her with casual—and calculated—familiarity.

A proposition. Dear Lord. "Thank you," she said.

His smile was as quick as the slash of a blade. "I want you to know that I shall do everything in my power to convince my peers—some of whom are quite reluctant—to bless your petition with favorable votes."

"I am so grateful, My Lord."

"But it will be difficult."

"I appreciate that fact."

He paused, staring at her. *Now he is going to ask me to go to bed with him*, she thought.

Wrong again. "I note that you are keeping company with the outlaw, Royce Campbell."

"Yes, that is true. We plan to wed. We are married, in point of fact, already."

"Yes, yes," he shrugged, unimpressed and uninterested.

"Nor is he an outlaw," Selena went on, trying to keep calm. "His Majesty has conferred a pardon—"

"I know all about that," interrupted the duke. "But the pardon is for acts of piracy and espionage only."

"What . . . what else is there?"

"Madame, I want you to tell me—and detail later in a written affidavit—everything you know of Campbell's revolutionary activities in France."

Selena was astonished and alarmed. She did not understand why the Duke of Sussex wanted to know these things, but she saw the glimmer of a nefarious reason behind his request. If some form of anti-monarchist charge could be brought against Royce, something having to do with his association involving Sorbante, the reactionary George III might be persuaded that Campbell was not so worthy after all.

"In return for such an affidavit, of course," the duke continued, "Coldstream shall be restored to your ownership with no strings attached."

"Why . . . why are you doing this?"

Sussex grinned malevolently. "Inquire of your lover when next you are in bed together."

"Sir, I tell you that I must refuse to comply with your request."

"Then you shall never see Coldstream Castle again, my dear."

The pain must have shown clearly on her face. He did nothing to diminish it when he added, "And you will not have Campbell, either, because I shall be forced to challenge him again."

"Again?"

"Yes. Ask him about that too. He ran away last time, but now I have him where I want him. . . ."

Selena saw the veins bulging in his neck, blood throbbing in the big vein at his temple. His fists were clenched in a fury barely suppressed.

"I am the best swordsman in Europe," he boasted. "That is why Campbell ran from me last time. So you see, my sweet, any way you look at it, your choice is between Coldstream and *noth-*

ing! Think about it. Get used to it. The rules of this encounter belong entirely to me!"

"How soon must I decide?" asked Selena, in an attempt to buy time.

But he did not afford her such luxury. "The two of us shall go and confront Campbell right now. I assure you that delay will serve no purpose whatever."

The minuet had commenced, so she and Sussex skirted the dance floor, moving slowly toward Royce, who was speaking earnestly to Sean Bloodwell. Selena's knees trembled as she walked, and her mouth was dry. Just when events seemed to have been moving toward a conclusion, this new threat had arisen. And it could not have been worse. In order to win Coldstream, she had either to renounce Royce or see him duel with the duke, whose confidence in his own prowess did not seem to be feigned.

The four faced one another. Selena took Royce's hand. Sean stared coldly at Sussex; there was no love lost between them. The duke was grinning.

"Tell him," he ordered Selena.

"Darling," she said, "I have been placed in a position whereby, in order to regain my estate, I must give an account of your activities in France."

Royce's eyes flew toward Sussex. But to Selena's surprise, he said nothing.

"You have outdone yourself this time, David," said Sean to the duke. "Even a vulture has better breeding than you."

"I am bred to honor," Sussex grinned cheerfully. "You were only elevated to it. A questionable decision on His Majesty's part, I think." Then he faced Royce. "If your whore does not comply with my wishes—" He leered. Royce and Sean stiffened at the insult; Selena was too numb to react. "—if she does not comply, I will repeat my challenge to you, and you must face me on the field outside Kingston tomorrow at dawn. You ran from me last time, as I recall."

Royce looked at Selena, and in his eyes she saw the unfamiliar look of tragedy.

"I did not run from you at all," he said to the duke, who laughed, "but if I accept this challenge and defeat you—"

"Defeat *me?* Never!"

"We shall see. But *if* I defeat you, which will mean your death of course, Selena will see her lands restored. Are you sure you want that?"

"The wench and her remote castle are but pawns in my game, Campbell. It is you I am after. I cannot bear to see a coward like you passing himself off as a warrior in this life. All that Highlands business about which you prate is so much malarkey, and I mean to prove it to the world. You are as common as a guttersnipe."

"Save your insults," Royce said. He turned to Sean Bloodwell. "Sir, would you be so kind as to serve as my second on the morrow?"

"It would be an honor," replied Sean, in a clipped, angry voice.

"Then it is decided," Royce said, turning on his heel as the Duke of Sussex chortled victoriously. "Come, Selena, let us go."

In the hotel that night, calm enough but burdened by a dark mood, Royce told Selena what had transpired in the past between him and Sussex.

"The man and I met once in Bermuda," he said, lying beside her in bed. "Eleven years ago. I was younger and more reckless than I am today. Or so I hope. And he was the same as he is now. We were in—I confess it—a house of unsavory repute, and happened to vie for the same woman at the same time."

Selena sighed. She would rather have been spared such specific knowledge of his past.

"The situation was inconsequential in and of itself," Royce continued, "and I proposed that we resolve the matter by a contest of knife-throwing. Whoever should hurl his dagger with greater accuracy at a small circle I drew upon the taproom wall would first enjoy the company of the woman in question."

"And you won?"

"Yes, I won. But he would not accept the defeat. He threw an actual tantrum, I swear, and challenged me to swords at dawn, exactly as he has chosen to do again. He has now—and had even then—a great reputation with the blade."

"Did you—"

"No. I did not fight. But I did not run from him either, as he claims. I sailed aboard the *Highlander* then, and that night a storm came up. We had to put out to sea, or else be washed up on shore by the wind. In the morning, I decided that prudence would keep us both alive, so I simply sailed away. He interprets my long-ago discretion as cowardice, which it was not. I let him live."

"But you said he was a great swordsman. Could you have defeated him?"

"I believe so."

She asked a question far more important: "Do you think you can defeat him now?"

"I suspect so." The room was dark. She could not see his face, nor could she read anything in his tone. She put her arms around him and clung to him as closely as she could. "Let us flee now," she pleaded. "The duel doesn't matter. Coldstream doesn't matter. If I lose you I lose everything."

"And if I flee, you lose Coldstream, which I will not permit."

"Death is not worth it."

"Neither is cowardice. That son of deceit must face the weight of his words, whatever befalls."

"Oh, darling, I'm afraid for us."

"Don't be, Selena. Things are not as grave as they appear. In his rancor and haste, Sussex made a fatal mistake."

"What is that?"

"When I return from the field at Kingston, I shall explain it to you."

"What? Return to tell me? No, I am going to be there with you."

"Selena, I forbid it."

"That is a power you may not claim over me."

There was a long silence, then he laughed softly.

"Even if I did claim it, the power would not work. You would come to Kingston anyway, wouldn't you? I might tie you to the bed, however."

"That you might, but not for long. Please, Royce. It may—God forbid—be our last time together." She imagined the thin, evil face of Sussex gloating in triumph, Royce's blood dripping from his blade. "Let us sleep now. Rest, and build your strength."

His hand brushed her nipples lightly. She felt the first waves of yielding heat. "Royce, no. I have heard that a man . . . that when a man has a great thing to do, it is best that he retain his essence."

This time he laughed outright, loud and long.

"Darling," he said, "there *is* something about men that you do not know."

Fog lay thick as coalsmoke above the streets and between the buildings of London. Royce and Selena, mounted on hired chestnut geldings, met Sean Bloodwell in the predawn haze. He sat on a nervous roan, and had strapped a long, leather case behind his saddle.

The sword, she thought, shuddering.

Wordlessly, they clattered out of London and into the rolling countryside. Selena bit her lower lip until she was afraid blood would come, but Royce seemed calm and quiet. Fate has two manifestations, one of which might be altered, the other not at all. He was about to confront the second form of fate, and there was nothing to be done about it.

They rode like ghosts through the fog, which thinned to wisps and whorls as the sun rose. By the time they reached Kingston field, drifting tendrils of mist shimmered like pieces of rainbow above the green and brilliant grass. Two black thoroughbreds were tethered beneath an oak at the far end of the field, where Sussex and his second were waiting. The second was to arm and prepare his man for battle, to congratulate him in victory, to see to his body in the event of wounding or death. Sussex, Selena noted, had no doubts about the outcome of today's confrontation. On a blanket beneath an oak was a bottle of brandy, a second bottle of wine, and a small basket of bread and cheese.

"Do you think it was wise to bring the woman, Campbell?" goaded Sussex as the trio dismounted.

Royce said nothing. Selena stood disconsolately beside her horse as the seconds conferred. Sussex unsheathed his long sword and slashed the air with it.

"This is death, Campbell," he grinned. "Have a look at it."

Selena turned away and looked out over the gorgeous, flower-filled field. She was overcome by the beauty of new day, and by the contradictory presence of strife and death.

Sean Bloodwell unstrapped the case from behind his mount's saddle.

"According to the rituals of dueling," he said softly, as the others watched him swing open the leather lid of the case, "the man who is challenged has choice of weapons."

Everyone looked. The cast contained two long-barreled blunderbusses. The duke's jaw fell. Royce grinned.

Too late, Sussex realized the error that his haste had caused him to make.

"This is unfair!" he protested weakly.

"Sir," said Royce, "you know that it is not. I give you the right to refuse this duel, and go your way. I shall think no less of you."

"I could *not* think less of you," he added mirthlessly.

Selena's heart jumped for joy. She had seen Royce shoot down a sparrow on the wing with a musket. The day turned even brighter than it was.

"Permit me to inspect the weapons," said the duke's second, a youngish man who seemed quite nervous, and more so now than he had been a moment ago.

Sean Bloodwell stepped away to allow the inspection. "I have powder and shot with me," he said. "You may, according to the rules, load your champion's weapon, or he may do so himself."

"Guns are uncivilized," cried Sussex. "Have you no honor?"

"As much as you, I think, sir. I offer again. Withdraw. Forfeit. And apologize to Selena for what you called her at the palace yesterday, of course."

The duke stiffened. "I shall not."

"Then load your weapon, sir," ordered Royce, his eyes cool slits of restrained fury.

Selena noted that Sussex's hands trembled as he measured out the gunpowder. Sean prepared Royce's weapon.

Royce came over to Selena and put his hands on her shoulders. "I hoped it would not come to this," he said, "but it has. I deliberately remained in the antechamber when you addressed the lords, so that sight of me would not provoke the duke. But he had his heart set on some form of showdown, it seems."

"Still, darling, be careful."

"You need not advise me about that."

Then the weapons were ready. Sean and the other second carried them out onto the green field. Royce and Sussex followed. Royce wore a black, simple suit, and stood bareheaded on the grass. The duke was garbed flamboyantly in pink breeches and a ruffled shirt of powder-blue silk.

"The combatants will stand back to back," Sean commanded. "I will call out twenty paces. On the count of twenty, turn and fire. In the event that both shots miss, the contest is a draw. The challenger, Duke of Sussex, has then the right to demand a second chance. Wounding or death, however, will satisfy the requirements of this contest."

Royce and Sussex took up their positions. The seconds withdrew to one side. Selena remained beneath the oak.

"One!" cried Sean. The combatants began to walk, pacing as the count mounted, inexorable as death. ". . . eighteen, nineteen, *twenty!*"

Selena's eyes were on Royce. She saw him turn quickly and raise the musket to his shoulder. She saw a look of amazement on his face, and turned toward the duke. Against all protocol, he had dropped to the grass and lay flat against the earth, taking aim.

"Unfair!" shouted Sean angrily.

Too late. Sussex's weapon jumped in his hands. A bellowing explosion rolled across the field. Royce seemed to shudder a little, but remained on his feet.

The lead ball had missed him.

Sussex lay helpless on the ground.

"Do you wish to stand like a man?" Royce asked. "It is against my principles to shoot a snake in the grass, much as I would like to."

Cowering, glowering impotently, the duke rose shakily to his feet, holding the musket as if he hoped it were a shield.

"In return for an apology and a vote in Selena's favor," said Royce, taking aim, "I offer you your life."

"No," replied Sussex, aware that his last shred of honor was at stake.

"Don't be a fool, man. Feel the sun. Smell the fragrant air. Imagine the taste of the brandy there in the bottle beneath the tree. That is yours, today and tomorrow and thereafter, just for an apology and a vote."

"No," said the duke.

"So be it," shrugged Royce, his finger on the trigger. Sussex braced for his doom, closing his eyes.

Explosion. Fire. Billowing smoke.

The duke opened his eyes.

Royce had fired deliberately into the air. "Let us end this foolishness now," he said, lowering his weapon.

But an expression of joy and resolve came over Sussex's face. He believed that Royce's shot had accidentally missed.

"Second chance! Second chance!" he crowed.

"Please reconsider, My Lord," pleaded his anxious second.

"God damn it, man, make haste and bring more powder and shot. I mean to win the day."

As the second hastened to comply, Royce motioned wearily to Sean Bloodwell, asking that he, too, bring a second charge of shot.

While Sean reloaded the weapon, Selena walked over to her lover. "Please get it over with this time," she said.

His expression was grim. "It seems I have no choice, doesn't it?"

Sussex's man was carefully measuring powder, but the duke, certain now that he would triumph and eager to get on with it, seized the materials and commenced his own reloading. "I note, Campbell, that you chose the wrong weapon. Fatal for you, I fear."

Royce did not reply.

Sussex used a thin ramrod to jam in the quantity of powder, then added the lead ball and tamped that in too, the movement of his arm jerky and pistonlike. He was in position for the second shot before Royce had readied his weapon.

Once more, Sean Bloodwell counted out the paces.

"One . . . seven . . . thirteen . . . eighteen . . . *twenty!*"

Sussex, delirious with anticipation, whirled on Royce with preternatural speed.

He took quick, sure aim.

Royce had only begun to lift the weapon to his shoulder.

Sussex fired.

The explosion of his blunderbuss was much louder than before, its force sweeping over the field, frightening the horses, shivering leaves on the trees.

A brief, pitiful howl of surprised agony followed the blast, then there was stillness.

Sussex lay dead on the ground, one arm blown away, his face ripped apart. He had loaded too hastily, with excessive gunpowder. His weapon had exploded in his hands. Forty paces from his opponent, Royce Campbell stood unharmed. He hadn't even fired.

"Coldstream awaits you, Selena," Sean Bloodwell said.

28 A Last Gambit

It was not quite that simple, however. Sean informed Royce and Selena, as they rode together back to London, that he would immediately begin to canvass the lords, which would require at least a day. He advised them to remain at their hotel, so he would be able to notify them as soon as he had word. Prospects for a favorable vote were excellent, though, since the Duke of Sussex had been Selena's primary—if not only—committed adversary.

"Few tears will be shed over his demise," Sean said.

And so Royce and Selena spent the day together, breaking the tension with long periods of lovemaking. When darkness fell, with yet no word from Sean, they hurried out to a pub for a rushed dinner of meat pies and ale. Selena forced herself to eat, for her appetite was scant.

When they returned to the hotel, a messenger awaited them, one of the young waifs of London who made a ha'pence here and a ha'pence there carrying letters and doing errands.

"My lord, my lady," he bleated shyly, "I bear you tidings from Lord Bloodwell of St. John's Wood. He requests the company of Sir Royce Campbell at his lodgings at once."

Royce and Selena exchanged glances. "Me only?" Royce asked the boy.

The youth nodded and withdrew.

"That is bad news," said Selena. "The vote has been against me, and Sean wishes to spare me the agony of having to hear the news directly from him."

"Do not give up hope yet," Royce said, squeezing her hand. "It may be another matter entirely. Perhaps there has been some new trouble in the wake of my duel with Sussex. Go to our room and wait for me. I shall return as soon as I can."

He hired a hack and departed for St. John's Wood. Selena went upstairs to the hotel room and sat there dispiritedly on the bed, trying to contain her tension. It did not seem fair, it did not seem right, after all she had endured, to suffer the loss of her great prize now. She poured herself a glass of brandy, thinking that it would make her feel better, but the effect was just the opposite. She began to brood.

"Steel yourself for bad news," she exhorted herself, many times. But strength did not come.

At last she heard slow, heavy footsteps on the stairs—not the tread of a man bearing glad tidings—and a gentle, almost hesitant rap on the door.

"Come in," said Selena, who was seated on a chair near the window, next to a small table on which an oil lamp burned dimly.

The door swung slowly open.

Light from the lamp was sufficient to glisten on Colonel Clay Oakley's hideous bald pate.

"Selena, my dear," he hissed, in all of his frightening, single-minded malevolence. "How beautiful you look, as always."

He held a dagger in his hand, as if it were a paint brush, prepared to alter her features according to his tastes.

She sprang to her feet, but he blocked the way to the door. The window was too high off the street; she could not jump without killing herself. Still, that was a better alternative than the blade.

"How did you—" she began.

"Escape from the Tower? It was not easy. It took a bit of time. But even a man like me has friends, after all the good I have done for England."

Selena fought to collect her wits. There was a murderous light in Oakley's eyes, as if he had passed far beyond the pale of faintest sanity. He meant to even things with her now, and she knew it.

"You have chosen an inopportune time to call on me, I'm afraid," she said, as calmly as possible. "Royce Campbell will be here momentarily."

Oakley's mustache lifted as he offered his eerie grin. "No, my dear. He won't. He has gone to St. John's Wood."

"How do you—"

"Because I sent him the message to go thither."

"You mean Lord Bloodwell didn't summon him?"

"No, my dear. I wanted to have these special, final moments with you alone, don't you see?" He took several heavy steps toward her; she took as many steps away from him.

Her back was to the window now. The blade of the dagger glinted in his huge hand.

Then he reached into a waistcoat pocket and withdrew something supple and glittering.

"Here's a message for you, though," he chortled spitefully, and threw the object on the floor at her feet.

It was Erasmus Ward's cross. Hastily, and confused, she picked it up and looked at him.

"What is the meaning of this? How did you—"

"Your friends seem to have the unfortunate habit of dying," he wheezed. In growing excitement now that his moment of revenge was so near, Oakley was forced to take out his scented handkerchief and inhale deeply. "That cross was intercepted at Dover today, when a mail pouch was inspected there."

Selena stared at the little cross in her hand, which she had carried through time, across a vast distance.

"Pierre Sorbante was beheaded today in Paris," Oakley smiled.

"When I have no more need of this cross," Sorbante had told Selena, *"I shall find a way to return it to you."*

"Louis the Sixteenth and Marie Antoinette were guillotined as well," said the colonel. "Maximilien Robespierre is in total control of the revolution . . . or will be until the beast he has created turns upon him. Which it will. Such is the tide of all revolutions, don't you agree?"

He took a few more paces toward her, and lifted the dagger. She felt the heat of his body; thick waves of his cologne spread out in the air.

He lunged.

His own great strength was his undoing. Had the movement of his arm been quick and deft, the dagger stroke would have been true. But he put too much power behind the stroke, losing his aim just enough for Selena to dart sideways and head for the door.

Safe! she thought ecstatically, rushing from the room and flying down the stairs, two at a time. She would race through the lobby and run out into the street. It was still relatively early, perhaps nine o'clock; there would be people . . .

A thuggish creature, obviously a man still loyal to the deposed colonel, stood sentry at the bottom of the stairs. His hand moved toward the pistol at his belt. Selena heard Oakley panting and lumbering along behind her. The way to the street was blocked.

She vaulted over the railing and landed on her feet in a dim passageway that led to the rear of the hotel. Gathering her strength and nerve, she raced into the darkness.

"Don't fire!" she heard the colonel gasp. "I want her for myself."

Two choices. Either the exit door, which opened into a narrow, twisting back street, or a door that led to some sort of cellar. *I'll be trapped down there,* she thought, reasoning with the perfervid instinct of a hunted animal.

She stepped out into a chilly, fog-shrouded alley.

Which way? Left or right? Where was the main street? It was impossible to tell.

She turned left and made her way along the building. She heard the door open and close.

"Selena, darling," Oakley gasped, "do not try to get away. It will not work. You and I were meant for one another. We must complete the circle of which we have been a part since first we met."

Even as slowly and carefully as she was moving, Selena's foot struck something, which overturned with a metallic clang and went rolling over the stones.

"Ah!" exclaimed the colonel in satisfaction. "Fate gives you away. . . ."

They both moved forward then, almost as in an exquisite, extemporaneous dance. She would feel her way a few more paces into the darkness; he would follow. The process went on for a long time, it seemed, and finally, with her heart pounding, Selena thought she saw the glow of dull light in the fog up ahead. Her hands found the corner of a building, and she turned into a wider street. Light came from a window far ahead. Pray let it be a pub or some gathering place, she hoped, remembering how, in America, she'd found refuge from him in the Nest of Feathers tavern.

She began to run.

She fell.

Before she had a chance to get to her feet, he was standing over her, gasping and wheezing, breathing into his handkerchief. The thick, coal-laden fog was afflicting his diseased lungs.

He lunged. She rolled to one side. He fell down on the cobblestones beside her, but caught hold of her ankle. She tried to rise, but he pulled her back down. The dagger hissed, missed, and struck stone. She heard the snap of the blade. He was choking for breath. Then his great weight was upon her. She felt his monstrous hands, so capable of creating beauty, close around her throat. Cologne filled her nostrils. Her ears buzzed. She could see nothing but his dark shape above her. The light in her brain faded, red, dull red, flickering red and black. His breath came in great, intermittent snorts, like that of a dying bull. . . .

And then his fingers loosened. His body shuddered, shuddered again, and then he lay still and silent on top of her.

Clay Oakley's lungs had drawn their last agonized gulp of air. The fog, the lovely, gorgeous fog, had killed him.

Great London itself had saved Selena.

She found the main street and entered through the front door of the hotel. The thug was still on guard at the bottom of the stairs. He seemed alarmed to see her.

"Your master is dead," she told him calmly. "I know he escaped from the Tower. Lord Bloodwell is my friend. I don't think I need tell you more."

The man swallowed once, twice, slipped through the rear exit and disappeared into the night.

Royce returned to find her naked in bed, sipping a tumbler of brandy.

"Strangest thing," he said, undressing. "Lord Bloodwell never sent for me."

"Oh?" she said. She saw that he was smiling.

"No," he said, slipping into bed beside her, removing the glass from her hand and taking a long swallow of the strong liquor. "No, he didn't, but he said he'd intended to do so in the morning. He was able to complete the canvass."

Selena scarcely dared to breathe. "And?" she managed. "And?"

"Selena, you will always have me," said Royce, taking her into his arms. He kissed her at the place where her shoulder met her neck, brushing away her long, golden hair. His fingers found the living pearl of all sensation.

"Oh, Royce!" she cried. If this were all there was, still it would be enough.

"You will always have me," he whispered huskily, "and now you have Coldstream too."

29 Home

They set out on horseback the next morning, just the two of them traveling alone. It was a journey of three hundred miles, but Selena had never made a happier nor an easier trek. Sometimes they managed twenty miles a day, sometimes less than ten, but it didn't matter because time no longer mattered. Each mile brought Selena nearer to the home she'd left so long ago, which she'd held close to her heart ever since, in good times and bad.

North through Hertford they rode, and Bedford and Hunt, lodging at night to make love in inns along the way. Pressing on through Lincoln and East Riding, North Riding and Durham, Selena could not but remember the thrilling returning journeys of her youth, when the people of Coldstream would welcome her father with great bonfires burning on the hills. Ah, that had been wonderful, but this was better still, to return with Royce.

And at last they were almost there, riding easily across the fields of Northumberland, hard by the sea. Darkness fell when they were perhaps ten miles from their goal.

"Shall we stop for the night?" Royce asked.

"No."

"That is what I thought you'd say."

There was a half-moon in the sky. Their way was well-lighted. Soon Selena recognized landmarks along the roadway, certain trees, the village of Wooler, and knew that the border was near.

She began to cry when they crossed into Scotland, and in her tears was a trace of every emotion she'd ever experienced, for her great journey was almost over, yet those souls who had been part of her life throughout her years of exile were not there to share the joy of homecoming.

Royce understood and said nothing. Selena was still weeping softly as they climbed the last rocky rise and saw it there in the distant hills: Coldstream, ancient, impregnable, eternal, and Scotland lying beyond, patient and mysterious and wise.

"I have come back!" she cried aloud.

And she was certain that, with her heart, she could hear her homeland whisper "Welcome" in reply.

And then in the distance, near and far, there rose a strangely familiar sound. The horses nickered and danced, pressing their ears back against their sleek heads.

Royce and Selena looked at each other.

"What is it?" he asked, alert for danger or surprise.

"I know," said Selena, as her heart remembered.

Torches flared upon the hills then, and faint fires blossomed like flowers in the night sky. Then the dry wood caught, and flames—six, seven, eight, nine of them—leapt crackling and roaring toward the heavens.

"Somehow they knew," Royce said softly. "Somehow they know."

"The hearth knows its own," replied Selena, through glorious tears. "Let us go."

She was home, but it was not until she rode beneath the great gate, with *Anno Domini 1152* engraved upon the stone, that she really was at home. The courtyard was filled with people, their voices lifted in an incessant, soul-stirring roar of greeting and joy. Royce dismounted and helped Selena down from her horse. They stood there in the courtyard, holding each other. The people cheered and cheered. They could not stop cheering.

"Everything is restored now, darling," said Royce, kissing her. "The past is laid to rest, is it not?"

She looked up into his eyes. "Except for one thing," she said.

"And what is that?"

She hesitated. The matter seemed silly, especially at a time like this, but something in her woman's heart wanted to set it to rest.

"Were you truly . . . were you truly Marie Antoinette's favorite?"

The question caught him off guard, but he recovered, smiling. "Darling, as I told you once before, a lady wouldn't ask such a question, and a gentleman wouldn't answer it."

"I see."

"But," he added, with a conspiratorial wink, "you're not and I'm not, so the answer is no."

Selena laughed and lifted her arms toward the towering, torch-lit walls of Coldstream.

"Home," she said, remembering the words of Jean Beaumain.

It was the best word in the world.

Next to love.

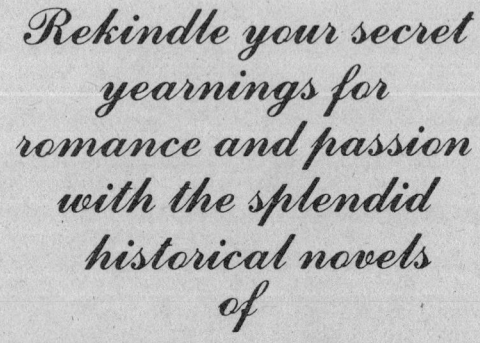

*Rekindle your secret
yearnings for
romance and passion
with the splendid
historical novels
of*

Vanessa Royall

___ FIRES OF DELIGHT 12538-3-15 $3.95
___ FLAMES OF DESIRE 14637-2-29 2.95
___ FIREBRAND'S WOMAN 12597-9-05 2.95
___ THE PASSIONATE AND THE PROUD . . 16814-7-11 3.50

At your local bookstore or use this handy coupon for ordering:

Dell   **DELL READERS SERVICE—DEPT. B1091A**
P.O. BOX 1000, PINE BROOK, N.J. 07058

Please send me the above title(s). I am enclosing $_____ (please add 75¢ per copy to cover postage and handling). Send check or money order—no cash or CODs. Please allow 3-4 weeks for shipment.
<u>CANADIAN ORDERS:</u> please submit in U.S. dollars.

Ms./Mrs./Mr._____

Address_____

City/State_____ Zip_____

A beautiful book for the special people who still believe in love...

RICHARD BACH'S

The Bridge Across Forever

10826-8-44 $3.95

By the same author who created <u>Jonathan Livingston Seagull</u>, <u>Illusions</u>, *and* <u>A Gift of Wings</u>.

At your local bookstore or use this handy coupon for ordering:

Dell — DELL READERS SERVICE—DEPT. B1091B
P.O. BOX 1000, PINE BROOK, N.J. 07058

Please send me the above title(s). I am enclosing $_____ (please add 75¢ per copy to cover postage and handling). Send check or money order—no cash or COD's. Please allow 3-4 weeks for shipment.
<u>CANADIAN ORDERS:</u> please submit in U.S. dollars.

Ms./Mrs./Mr._____

Address_____

City/State_____ Zip_____

Rebels and outcasts, they fled halfway across the earth to settle the harsh Australian wastelands. Decades later—ennobled by love and strengthened by tragedy—they had transformed a wilderness into fertile land. And themselves into

The Australians

WILLIAM STUART LONG

THE EXILES, #1	12374-7-12	$3.95
THE SETTLERS, #2	17929-7-45	$3.95
THE TRAITORS, #3	18131-3-21	$3.95
THE EXPLORERS, #4	12391-7-29	$3.95
THE ADVENTURERS, #5	10330-4-40	$3.95
THE COLONISTS, #6	11342-3-21	$3.95

At your local bookstore or use this handy coupon for ordering:

Dell DELL READERS SERVICE—DEPT. **B1091C**
P.O. BOX 1000, PINE BROOK, N.J. 07058

Please send me the above title(s). I am enclosing $_____ (please add 75¢ per copy to cover postage and handling). Send check or money order—no cash or COD's. Please allow 3-4 weeks for shipment.
CANADIAN ORDERS: please submit in U.S. dollars.

Ms./Mrs./Mr._____

Address_____

City/State_____ Zip_____

ROBERTA GELLIS

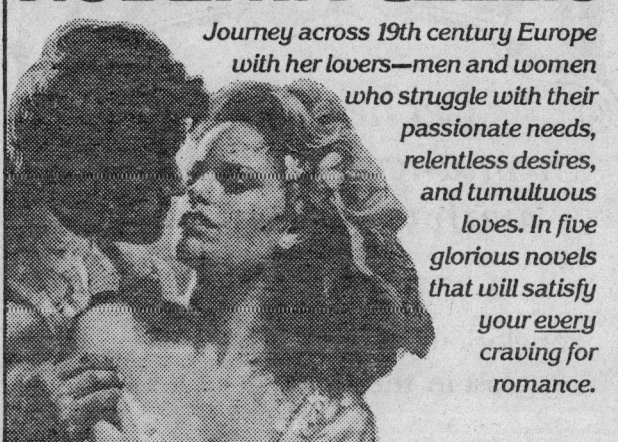

Journey across 19th century Europe with her lovers—men and women who struggle with their passionate needs, relentless desires, and tumultuous loves. In five glorious novels that will satisfy your every craving for romance.

____ **THE ENGLISH HEIRESS**	12141-8-14	**$2.50**
____ **THE KENT HEIRESS**	14537-6-12	**3.50**
____ **FORTUNE'S BRIDE**	12685-1-24	**3.50**
____ **A WOMAN'S ESTATE**	19749-X-23	**3.95**

At your local bookstore or use this handy coupon for ordering:

Dell DELL READERS SERVICE—DEPT. **B1091D**
P.O. BOX 1000, PINE BROOK, N.J. 07058

Please send me the above title(s). I am enclosing $_____ (please add 75¢ per copy to cover postage and handling). Send check or money order—no cash or COBs. Please allow 3-4 weeks for shipment. CANADIAN ORDERS: please submit in U.S. dollars.

Ms./Mrs./Mr._____

Address_____

City/State_____ Zip_____

LAURA LONDON

Let her magical romances enchant you with their tenderness.

For glorious storytelling at its very best, get lost in these Regency romances.

___ A HEART TOO PROUD	13498-6	$2.95
___ THE BAD BARON'S DAUGHTER	10735-0	2.95
___ THE GYPSY HEIRESS	12960-5	2.95
___ LOVE'S A STAGE	15387-5	2.95
___ MOONLIGHT MIST	15464-4	2.95

At your local bookstore or use this handy coupon for ordering:

Dell DELL READERS SERVICE—DEPT. B1091E
P.O. BOX 1000, PINE BROOK, N.J. 07058

Please send me the above title(s). I am enclosing $_____ (please add 75¢ per copy to cover postage and handling). Send check or money order—no cash or CODs. Please allow 3-4 weeks for shipment.
<u>CANADIAN ORDERS:</u> please submit in U.S. dollars.

Ms./Mrs./Mr._____

Address_____

City/State_____ Zip_____